Sheridan

Breaking Ground

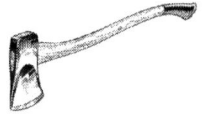

James Rogers

This book is a work of fiction. Names, characters, places and incidents are products of the author's imagination or are used fictitiously. Any resemblance to actual events or locales or persons, living or dead, is entirely coincidental.

ISBN-13: 9781540796752
ISBN-10: 1540796752

David:

Things aren't always as they
seem.

Jim Rog

For my grandmother, Edith Rogers, who touched so
many lives in Sheridan.

CONTENTS

ACKNOWLEDGMENTS

Thanks to my wife, Kerry, for her constant support.

Many thanks also to Linda Stirling at
ThePublishingAuthority.com
and to my fellow writers at
SW/WA Write to Publish.

Prologue

Tecomeoc dangled by his neck, kicking against the air. A rope stretched from a whiskey barrel lying beneath his feet to the leather-gloved hand of Lieutenant Phil Sheridan, seated on his stallion. Five other Indians, shackled hand and foot, stood in line, waiting their turns. The blood seeped into the whites of Tecomeoc's eyes as their blood vessels burst from the pressure. His jaw opened and closed like a salmon netted from the water.

Chenoweth, chief of the Cascade Indian tribe, stood behind Tsy, Captain Jo, Sim-Lasselas, Tumalth, Old Skein, Kenwake, and Four Finger Johnny. Three others already swung from ropes strung from a thick oak tree branch. Lieutenant Sheridan's horse grazed in the green grass growing in the shade of spring leaves. Sheridan's finger rested on the trigger of a Springfield rifle. Two militia members, eager to prove themselves, rolled a whiskey barrel beneath the next noose and set it on end. A third, tall and grim, the executioner, positioned a scaffold with steps beside the barrel. Each brave would climb the steps or be dragged to the barrel's top.

Tsy, a medicine man whose face resembled a dried prune, stood at the head of the line. A short, heavy-set militia man wearing thick glasses removed the Indian's shackles then reached cautiously to seize Tsy's wiry arm. Tsy shook off the hand and quickly climbed the steps and stood on top the wobbly barrel. He snatched the noose from the executioner, pulled it over his own head, and cinched the knot beside his ear. Sim-Lasselas and Tumalth shouted words of encouragement in their native tongue.

Sheridan asked Tsy if he wished to plead for mercy.

Tsy looked ahead, silent, as if already half-departed from this world.

Chief Chenoweth looked beyond Tsy to the forested hills blanketed with mist in the distance. He had sent word for his 500 warriors to prepare for battle in this sacred place. As he scanned the hills, he wondered if his army had heeded the call. Were they assembling in the tall grass and dense thickets of trees, awaiting his command?

Lieutenant Phil Sheridan had been sent to exact revenge for the Cascade Massacre that claimed the lives of fourteen civilians and three soldiers. Those facing the rope had been at the horse races on the banks of the Columbia River when he arrived with forty dragoons, a volunteer militia hungry for revenge. The Yakimas who carried out the attack had fled. The Cascades had obeyed Chief Chenoweth and surrendered peacefully. Each brave had given up his rifle and declared his innocence. Lieutenant Sheridan's questions had turned to accusations. When the braves refused to confess, his interrogations turned to torture. The truth had become clay in the soldier's hands, pressed into unfamiliar forms. Before the darkness had fallen, several had "confessed" to the murders and had named the others as conspirators. Though they were not citizens of the United States, Sheridan had found them all guilty of treason and sentenced them to hang.

"Do you wish reprieve?" Lieutenant Sheridan asked.

Tsy stood motionless and defiant.

Sheridan pulled hard on the rope fastened to the barrel beneath Tsy's feet. The barrel began to tip then the rope broke loose from the drain hole. The barrel rocked back, and the medicine man regained his balance.

Tsy smiled, let out a war cry, and leapt from the barrel. The noose jerked, and his neck snapped.

Four Finger Johnny laughed and let out a war cry of his own that mixed with Tsy's scream echoing off the distant hills.

Old Skein spat on the ground and cursed the small white soldier seated on his horse.

Sheridan dropped the limp rope and dismounted, rifle in hand. He stood before the brave, looking up into his solemn face. He drew back his rifle then thrust its bayonet toward the Indian's throat.

Old Skein did not blink.

Sheridan's steely-blue eyes glared at the Indian as he drove the butt of his rifle into his stomach. The Indian bent over, fell to his knees, and spat again.

The soldiers resumed the grim chore of rolling the barrel beneath the next noose and righting it again. The executioner dragged the scaffold to its place as Old Skein gasped for air.

Old Skein rose defiantly to his feet then spat in the face of the soldier unlocking the chains that bound his hands.

The soldier looked at him, saliva running down his

thick eyeglass lenses, then whipped the chains into Old Skein's face. Another soldier shoved the brave toward the scaffolding.

Blood streamed from Old Skein's mouth as the executioner tightened the noose around his neck. Old Skein stood shaking on bowed legs, his face swollen and bruised from the beating he'd suffered two days before. His swollen eyes looked over each of the remaining braves, and he encouraged them to be strong. They would meet again and retake their land. The ancestors would have their revenge.

The executioner tipped the barrel and held it as Old Skein's feet slid forward then shuffled backward on the slick lid. He gasped for air as the knot bit into his leathery skin.

Sheridan ordered the executioner to complete the act. The soldier kicked the barrel over, and Old Skein's feet searched for the barrel's surface as he slowly strangled.

Kenwake stood next in line, shaking, as soldiers rolled the barrel beneath the next noose.

Chief Chenoweth encouraged him to be strong. He spoke of the fertile land, the home of salmon, deer, elk, and bear, nourished by the cold rains of winter. He reminded Kenwake of the blood spilled there by braves in battle. Long ago the ancestors had spoken of fire and flood, punishment for men who acted dishonorably. Chief Chenoweth spoke of the spirits of their ancestors that still roamed the forests and would have their revenge.

As the soldiers unshackled Kenwake, Chief Chenoweth recalled how the white men had come in great numbers speaking of peace, but the terms of peace had always sent them far from their lands. Treaties had been made only to be broken. The white man's words could not be trusted. Many of their people had returned to their ancestral homes to find them occupied by the white man. The whites had seized control of the fishing places, slowly starving the Cascades into submission. The natives had risen up as the Yakima Indian Wars had swept through the Northwest. He had tried to make peace, but in the white man's world, peace could not be found with words. Peace was won with guns.

The soldiers dragged Kenwake up the steps and stood him on the barrel. They held his head while the executioner pulled the noose over his face. Kenwake bit the rope and tugged against it like a horse resisting the bridle. The executioner jerked violently downward and Kenwake's jaw popped, releasing the rope.

"Reprieve! I'll talk!" Kenwake yelled.

"You will tell us the names of those who conspired to commit this crime?" Lieutenant Sheridan said.

"Yes, Yes. Anything."

"Then tell me." He motioned to the bodies hanging beside him. "Are these men guilty of treason?"

Kenwake looked down. "Yes. Guilty."

"And these standing before you?"

His jaw moved silently. The executioner cinched the knot tighter against his neck.

"Guilty. Guilty!"

Sheridan waved, and the executioner removed the noose from Kenwake's neck. The executioner shoved him down the steps, sending Kenwake tumbling to the ground. They dragged him to the prisoner's wagon and chained him there.

"Lieutenant," Chief Chenoweth said.

Sheridan spurred his horse forward and looked down on the squat man.

"Is this justice?"

"What do you know of justice?"

"You killed Tall Jim, a friend of the white man. You raped and strangled his wife. You strangled his children."

"Orders I did not give."

"You chopped off their heads."

"We are not savages, I assure you." Sheridan leaned forward. "Tell me. What of the seventeen God-fearing souls your savages killed? In a civilized country, we don't allow the slaughter of innocent human beings."

"Seventeen we did not kill. We have lost thousands. Where is our justice?"

Sheridan leaned back in the saddle. "Justice? Another word you don't know the meaning of."

"Where is honor when the innocent hang."

"We believe in the rule of law. You've broken the law, and now you will pay."

"We broke no laws."

"That's not what the court says. Your own men have admitted guilt. Perhaps you weren't listening just now."

"Truth is lost on a coward's tongue. You beat me. Did I confess?"

"You stand condemned by the words of your own people and the smell of gunpowder on the rifles you carry. Like it or not, you are all subject to the laws of the United States and this territory. You break them at your own peril."

"This has been our land for a thousand generations and will be for many to come. You're a stranger. Not welcome."

"And you'll hang by the neck until dead." He turned the horse to witness the next hanging.

"One warning," Chief Chenoweth said.

Sheridan stiffened in the saddle.

"Let us go, you live. Or fall by my warriors."

Sheridan turned the horse to face him. "The chief's next."

A soldier grabbed the chain binding the chief's hands and dragged him to the scaffold. The executioner stood on the scaffold, holding the noose. They led Chief Chenoweth up the steps and turned him to face the lieutenant. He looked to the hills as the rough rope dug beneath his jaw.

Sheridan's hand swept toward the hills. "Where's your army now, Chief?"

The hills sleep. They have not come. "One day we will rid our land of you. Until then, your weapons will spill your own blood, your justice, strangle you like these ropes."

Lieutenant Sheridan shifted in the saddle, looking again to the hills. "Looks like your army got lost. Sorry, we can't wait any longer."

"Our blood is on your hands." Chief Chenoweth let out a war whoop. "I am not afraid to die!"

Lieutenant Sheridan nodded and the executioner kicked the barrel. The noose was poorly tied and the drop, too short. Chief Chenoweth dangled, the knot tightening only enough to force wheezing, coughing gasps.

The soldiers shouted insults as the chief thrashed amid the cheers of the remaining braves.

Sheridan pressed his rifle to his shoulder. "If your warriors won't save you, I will." He aimed at Chief Chenoweth's head and put a bullet between his eyes.

The braves were buried in hastily-dug graves by the banks of the South Yamhill River. The ropes used to hang the nine Indians were left to rot.

The natives all but vanished. Starving and diseased, the survivors were moved from the fertile land onto wastelands called reservations. Others sought refuge in the dark hollows of the big city.

More white men came to till the soil and raise cattle in the fertile plains west of the Cascade Mountains. A lumber mill consumed the forest. Where the hanging tree's branches once stretched, a farmhouse was built surrounded by fields of golden wheat. A Methodist Church, a store, a post office, and a saloon became the seeds from which Sheridan grew.

Philip Sheridan proved to be a capable military leader and astute politician who rapidly rose through the ranks to become General of the U S Army. During the Civil War, General Sheridan defeated Confederate forces in the Shenandoah Valley and was one of the first to use scorched-earth tactics, leaving the land burned in his wake. His thirst for war led him to further conquests in the Indian Wars of the Great Plains. Little Phil, as some called him, returned home a hero.

Some say his ghost still roams the town that bears his name.

Friday

Officer Terrence Washburn knelt on a mound of dusty rocks at the bottom of the South Yamhill River, seventeen feet below flood stage. His long fingers stirred the trickle of water, sending ripples through the reflection of his police cruiser parked in the gravel turnout above. Bronson, his ill-tempered German shepherd, stood guard in the backseat.

His thoughts drifted to the 1981 state basketball championship game five years ago. In the final seconds of the game, he'd jumped high, letting fly a half-court heave to beat the buzzer. He held his breath as the ball arced high then began its slow motion descent. The crowd rose to its feet, hoping for Sheridan High School's first state championship. The ball bounced off the rim once, twice, circled, and rolled off the side. He could still feel the wooden floor crumbling beneath him, his legs giving out, falling to his knees as if awaiting execution. His eyes drifted to the bleachers filled with Sheridan boosters looking down with judging eyes. Guilty. The buzzer grew louder in his mind and broke into two sharp pops as water splashed onto his face.

Gunshots.

Bronson snarled and barked above. Terrence froze, listening to the dog clawing at the steel bars that kept him from leaping out the car window.

He scrambled up the rocks and crumbling clay, drew his gun, and crouched behind a boulder. The rumble of a muffler's rattle and pop raced down the road. He peeked from behind the boulder as an RV towing a boat drove down the road, blocking his view. A cloud of blue smoke swirled behind. A Volkswagen van raced after the RV on a collision course, until its brake lights came on, and it slowed.

Terrence ran to his car and grabbed the police radio mic, staring through the spider web of cracks that ran across his windshield like crystalline bolts of lightning. Above the steering wheel, smoke and dust drifted through a hole the size of a quarter. Shimmering glass diamonds speckled the dashboard and seat. The hackles on Bronson's back stood up as he paced frantically.

Terrence fumbled with the ignition keys. Adrenalin made his fingers shaky and clumsy. Time seemed to slow as the cruiser's aging motor struggled to turn over. *Come on. Come on!* The car's engine coughed out a billow of smoke then raced to life.

Terrence's heart beat wildly, and his lungs heaved beneath his bulletproof vest. He flipped the emergency toggle switches, filling the air with the siren's wail. The red and blue overhead lights flashed off leaves and grass in the shadows. He cranked the wheel hard to the left as Bronson barked savagely. Terence's legs seemed charged with electricity as he pushed the Chevy Caprice's accelerator to the floor. The tires threw up a spray of gravel then dug in, whipping the car into a sharp U-turn. The power steering squealed, and the wheel shimmied beneath his hands. A truck stacked high with a load of hay honked and swerved. Terrence's tires dug into the warm asphalt, throwing him back in his seat.

"Shots fired! Shots fired!" he screamed into the mic.

"10-9? Unit, identify yourself," the dispatcher demanded.

He ordered Bronson to quiet, but the dog continued to let out stifled barks and high-pitched whines.

"Sheridan One. I'm in pursuit. We're southbound on River Road." He took deep breaths and forced his voice to lower. The van ahead pulled around the RV as they approached the first blind curve.

"Sheridan One," the dispatcher said, "license plate?"

"No plate. Still catching up. Standby."

The smoke ahead swirled, mixing with the dust the morning breeze skimmed from the dry fields.

Terrence pulled in behind the RV as it waddled along the twisting country road. He cursed as it slowed for the next blind corner. The boat weaved side to side, and its vinyl cover flapped like a white flag of surrender. Terrence's car straddled the center line as he looked for an opening in the parade of campers and trailers headed to the beach, fifty miles away. The blue trail of smoke continued to fade.

"Sheridan One, what's your twenty?" the dispatcher asked.

"Westbound on . . . standby." The world around Terrence slowly narrowed, tunnel vision they called it. Terrence feared it was more. He struggled to slow his breathing, to regain control, but the darkness was beginning to suffocate him. "No, God. Not now," he prayed.

His car drifted into the center of the road as the RV

edged further onto the right shoulder and slowed to a crawl. Its wheels sank into the dirt, and the RV began to pitch.

Terrence found a small opening before the next curve and pulled into the oncoming lane. He floored the accelerator, and the engine whined. Bronson barked louder and sprawled in the back seat as they shot around the RV into the blind curve. The car's tires screamed and began to break free. The sound of machine gun fire erupted beneath the car as the left wheel slid off the pavement, throwing gravel into the wheel well. His car continued its sideways slide as the grill of a log truck barreled toward him. He clenched the wheel and prayed the tires would find traction in time. The oncoming truck swerved hard around him, its horn blasting, then rocked back into its own lane. The cruiser's wheels bit the pavement and threw it into a fishtail. Terrence fought to straighten out as Bronson thumped against the door in back. The car steadied then shot forward. The blue smoke continued to fade from the roadway ahead as he pursued toward town.

"Sheridan One, location?" The dispatcher's tone grew more urgent.

Terrence grabbed the mic and stood on the brakes, slowing for the turn onto Washington Street. The smell of burnt oil and steam filled the cruiser's interior. "Still trying to catch up. Stand by."

He followed the blue trail toward the center of town where it faded to a wisp. "We're headed onto Bridge Street, southbound from Washington," he said with a shaking voice. His car seemed to be moving in slow motion.

"Southbound on Bridge Street from Washington," the dispatcher repeated.

He hit the brakes hard as the light turned red at Bridge Street. The driver of a pickup truck stopped mid-intersection, shook his head and pointed across the bridge. Terrence punched the gas and pursued after, grateful the streets were mostly deserted in the struggling four block business district. He accelerated as he passed Sheridan Grocery, Betty's Beauty Parlor, Sheridan Hardware and Feed, City Hall, and the Reservation Tavern.

The blue plume faded to a diffuse haze.

As Terrence slowed further, searching for the trail, the youngest Hewett boy sat on his bike, his head swiveling as if drawn by an invisible tractor beam. The Peterson twins pointed. George Simpson waved. Harriet Anderson scowled and pressed her palms to her ears. Terrence felt a tinge of shame as he passed Sheridan High School. In a few short blocks the downtown faded, and the cruiser began the climb toward the overpass that spanned Highway 18. The final trace of smoke was blown away in the dusty morning breeze, as Terrence crested the hill and rolled to a stop in the center of the span.

"Sheridan One, update?" The dispatcher said.

Terrence looked down at the cars passing east and west beneath him. "Sheridan One, terminating pursuit."

"License plate and description?"

"Negative."

"No description or license?"

"Negative!" He slammed the mic back into its clip on the dash and punched his fist against the steering wheel. Breathe, he told himself. Let it pass. He closed his eyes and listened to the rush of traffic beneath. Bronson poked his nose through the sliding steel mesh window in the screen that separated them and sniffed at

Terrence's ear. He reached back and stroked the dog's thick fur. As he watched the cars passing on the freeway beneath, his vision widened. He poked his finger into the hole in his windshield half expecting the glass to crumble into his lap. West on Highway 18, a Yamhill County cruiser's emergency lights flashed, snarling traffic in both directions, its wail growing louder as it approached. Terrence picked up the mic and shouted, "Pursuit terminated." The county car racing toward the overpass shut off its lights and siren and passed underneath.

A quarter mile up the road the dust was still settling along a long gravel driveway bounded by brown grass and a rusty barbwire fence. Behind an old farmhouse at the end of the drive, a Jeep Cherokee's idling muffler spewed blue smoke into the air. An ancient oak tree cast shadows across the Jeep and dropped brown leaves.

Hank Sherman sat behind the wheel, his heart pounding, feeling alive. He opened the driver's door, dragged his lame left leg out and stood. His mangled spine shot lightning bolts to his toes. He pulled the heavy sniper rifle from the back seat and smiled as he considered the police car stopped on the overpass.

Hank turned off the engine and leaned over the Jeep's hood, steadying the rifle on the warm metal. The weight of the rifle anchored him somewhere between the jungles of Vietnam and the wheat fields of Sheridan. He drew deep breaths, letting the whiskey-laden air flow from his lungs. Each breath grew longer and deeper as he peered through the scope, watching the target centered between the crosshairs bounce with each heartbeat. Slowly he emptied himself into the air, drifting into the stillness.

How many times had he done this? How many people had he killed in service to his country? Twenty? Thirty? He didn't want to know. He would have chosen to forget but for those above him who reduced war to tallies. In his dark moments, Hank could turn people into ciphers. Soldiers, civilians, mothers, or children became numbers, a body count, a quota. In darker moments still, the heat of battle called to him, its fire hypnotizing, fascinating, strangely peaceful. He'd dealt enough death to spend an eternity in flame.

The thumb and index finger on his left hand, the only fingers on that hand that survived the war, pinched the knobs that adjusted the scope for wind and distance. He grinned as the cracked windshield came into focus, and laughed as the big kid in uniform poked a finger into the bullet hole. After all I've done for you, Hank thought.

Six hundred yards to target. Hank had made longer shots a lifetime ago. The pad of Hank's index finger gently pressed the cold metal of the trigger. Tickling the trigger, he felt the urge to pull. His mind dissolved into fragments, yielding control to his many well-trained parts: his trigger finger pulling, eye focusing, arms steadying the heavy rifle, heartbeat slowing. He yielded, squeezing the trigger slowly back.

Terrence sat looking at the freeway below as Hank sharpened the rifle scope's focus on the thiner bones above his ear.

Hank recalled a past kill from his time in the jungle. The enemy's head had snapped back as if struck by an invisible fist. The bullet punched a small, bloodless entry hole into the bone as its heat cauterized blood vessels. He remembered blood spraying, bits of bone and brain splashing against the concrete wall of the command bunker when the bullet exited the skull with enough force to leave a small crater in the wall and spray shards of concrete across the room.

Hank let out a long, slow breath, imagining this bullet penetrating the flimsy glass of Terrence's windshield. He could see it burrowing through the thin, soft tissues of Terrence's head, spinning, deforming, the smooth bullet jacket expanding like a rose blooming, petals turning to jagged razor claws ripping nerves from their roots and severing delicate blood vessels. The bullet's shock wave would turn his gelatin-like brain to a pulpy mass, digging deeper, pushing before it a growing tumor of tissue, striking the bone again, splintering then exploding like a burst dam, sucking a baseball-sized mass through its jagged exit from Terrence's skull. He imagined the gore spraying through the wire mesh behind him onto his dog. Maybe I'll take out Bronson, too, he thought.

Hank's finger slowly squeezed, stretching out the time, prolonging the foreplay of death. The high peaked just before the trigger snapped. During the pull, he was God; he gave life or he took it.

A lifetime ago Hank's first kill left him shaken and confused before he learned to turn a person into a target. Targets were kills. Kills were numbers, marks of efficiency, easily added and subtracted. When he could not turn targets into numbers, he made them evil. Hank remembered how the enemy had cut down his friends, and he learned to hate them. But in time, he could no longer afford to hate. Hate drew the life out of a man, or worse, compromised the mission. A warrior filled with hate was like a machine gun with no safety. He'd seen hateful men, seized by rage, brutalize and slaughter. He'd learned it was better not to care. Apathy was the ideal warrior state. But apathy left a man empty, thirsty for feeling.

He'd tried to satisfy his thirst with the bottle, but found it could only be quenched by a kill. The taste of death became a craving, a drug that whispered in the shadows by day and haunted his dreams at night. Death was a release from the futility of a life without purpose. Hank was a soul discarded, used up, and sent to surplus. All his memories of ceremonies and medals couldn't numb the feeling of pointlessness that haunted him now.

His finger squeezed further, and he felt the rush like an addict squeezing a plunger, injecting the last drops of heroin into his vein.

The police cruiser's lights stopped flashing. Terrence grabbed the mic, hesitated, and spoke. He looked toward the farmhouse, seeming to see Hank for a moment, then turned to scratch Bronson in the back seat. The car lurched, pulled a U-turn, and started back toward town.

The rifle scope tracked the target smoothly through the final moment of decision. Hank considered putting a bullet through the rear window to match the hole in the front. No. Not today.

Hank's heart beat wildly from this fix of adrenalin and he let out a whoop.

"Who's there?" Edith Sherman called from the kitchen window.

Hank slipped the rifle back into its case and stuffed it under the back seat. "Just me, Ma."

Mayor Dickerson sat in his Cadillac waiting to turn onto Bridge Street. He thought he'd heard a siren's wail mixing with the low rumblings of a train and the steady hum of freeway traffic.

He scanned the hills. The drought had withered the fields and turned the trees to kindling. It seemed half the farms were shuttered, their barns leaning on rotting frames. Too many families rooted in the rich, brown earth for generations had been displaced, refugees of a war fought by greedy men who gave loans that promised to see farmers through hard times. Always there was next year and with it the hope of a bountiful harvest and a step toward freedom. But each year only found them with hands out again, exchanging more of their land for a little more delay.

With each failed season more foreclosure signs went up, more auctions practically gave away tractors, seeding equipment, harvesting machines, and homes falling into ruin. When the land refused to yield, strangers bought it for pennies on the dollar, erasing its history and future. Families were pulled from the land like weeds.

Their farms stolen and without a future, families blew in the breeze like seeds never finding a place to root and grow. Resented and unwelcome, they settled into low-wage factory jobs, toiling at work that never lifted them from poverty. They became interchangeable parts, easily replaced and discarded.

The light turned green as the air conditioning in Dickerson's Cadillac blew cool air into his face. The distant siren faded and he saw no smoke rising into the sky. The rumbling train had faded, but the steady hum of freeway traffic remained. As he crossed over the bridge, Dickerson glanced at the cottonwood trees lining the banks below, their roots lapping at the stream gurgling between rocks not seen for generations. The bridge's steel skeleton cast glancing shadows off his windshield and strobed through his sunglasses.

He drove through the quiet downtown, hoping Edith had remembered their appointment. Their visits had become more tense as the deadline drew nearer. Patience was a virtue he still struggled to master.

The town's police car approached. Terrence sat in the driver's seat staring vacantly ahead. Mayor Dickerson waved and saw the sun glance off a spider web of cracks in the car's windshield. Or was it the sun, or the shadows?

He's a good kid, Dickerson thought. Just the kind of example the young people of Sheridan need. They had too few. In hard times, it seemed the next generation, those who would take up the welfare of the town and make it their own, was draining like the park pool. The town was bleeding young people escaping to college, military service, or better paying jobs in Portland. They promised to return someday, but most visited only long enough to bury their parents or relocate them to human warehouses in the big city.

Sheridan needed an infusion of hope.

Terrence was one of the few who had chosen to stay. Dickerson had seen to that. He had persuaded Terrence with what men want most—respect—by offering Terrence a police uniform. In the minds of a young man, a uniform and respect are the same.

Dickerson smiled at the genius of it. Terrence was a promising young man who would serve as an example for others too willing to abandon their town. He was also a project to keep Chief Madison occupied, a Barney Fife for his Andy Griffith. He chuckled. Perhaps it was an illusion, but Terrence possessed that naive nature that trusts because it has yet to feel the pain of betrayal.

Young and eager to please, he was a much needed balance to the cynical police chief.

Dickerson drove up Bridge Street and swung into the police station looking for Chief Madison. He hoped to discuss their meeting later that night. The parking space reserved for the chief of police was empty. Beverly's Pontiac was parked in the volunteer spot, so he decided to pay her a brief visit. Perhaps she could tell him where the chief might be.

He walked through the door to find her seated behind the counter. "How is my favorite volunteer?" Dickerson asked.

Beverly looked around the room. "If you're referring to me, this volunteer is strictly code four."

At seventy-something, Beverly possessed the energy of half a dozen typical seniors. Her wits were equal to ten more. A widow of old money, she was also tight with a penny.

"I was wondering if you might know the whereabouts of one chief of the Sheridan Police Department?"

"Negative. This volunteer has not seen hide nor hair of said chief. Have you tried his other office?"

"Other office?"

"The one that sells copious amounts of liquor to the riffraff of this community, commonly referred to as the Reservation? I believe you are quite familiar with the location, being the proprietor."

Dickerson looked at the police department mail slots and found the chief's box overflowing onto the counter. He leafed through the chief's mail, noting postmarks from several weeks ago.

"When was he last in the office?"

Beverly snapped open the morning's edition of the *Sheridan Sun* and turned to the crossword puzzle. "I wouldn't know. Perhaps his employer could check with him for a full itinerary."

Dickerson opened the door to the mayor's office across the hallway. "I'll just be a minute."

"Flaccid," she said.

"Excuse me?"

"Limp, saggy, flabby. Twelve across. Seven letters."

Dickerson dialed the chief's number and waited for the chief's terse message to end before leaving his reminder. "Don't forget the meeting tonight, and be presentable for a change." He locked the door and bid Beverly goodbye.

"Feeble," she said. "Eight down. Six letters."

Dickerson looked up the street toward the Reservation Tavern as he pulled onto Bridge Street. The handicap spot frequently occupied by the chief's Suburban was empty. He crossed the freeway overpass, continued up the narrow country road, and took a right into Edith's long driveway. The faint odor of burnt motor oil filled the Cadillac's interior.

"Hank, is that you?" Edith Sherman, Hank's mother, stood behind the screen door, pruning shears in her gloved hand. Barney, her 160 pound English Mastiff stood beside her, the dark eyes in his enormous head staring.

Hank shut off the Jeep's engine. "Yeah, it's me."

Barney rumbled a deep growl and pawed at the door, ripping another long gash in the screen.

"What are you doing back there? Are you in trouble again? I told you last time, I don't need your shenanigans."

Barney stood on his hind legs, spreading his forepaws

against the door frame. Hank wondered if the dog was trying to get out or keep him from entering.

"Ya mind?" Hank said, nodding toward the dog.

Edith jerked hard at Barney's collar. "Down, boy. You behave." The muscles of Barney's thick neck flexed against the collar. His eyes remained fixed on Hank. His teeth bared, and slobber dripped from his jowls. "Stop that. Sit." She gave the leash another jerk, and Barney let out a low bark and sat beside her, wagging his stub of a tail.

Hank's dad brought the dog home eleven years ago. The runt of a litter, discarded along the roadway, he was about the closest thing to a friend Hank had. His mom and dad never understood him the way this big, stupid dog did. When Hank was dishonorably discharged from the service, it was Barney who stood by his side, but in his later years, Barney's disposition had soured toward Hank.

"Good boy," he said, scratching Barney roughly behind the ears.

"Hank, I asked you a question."

Hank walked into the kitchen, opened the refrigerator, and began rummaging inside. "Good to see you too, Mom." He picked out a bottle of milk, unscrewed the cap, and took a sniff. The sweet, sour smell confirmed his suspicions. He screwed the cap back on, slid it back in, and grabbed the last bottle of beer. "Is this left over from the last time? Oh, almost forgot. You don't . . . " He tipped the bottle, guzzled half, and began rummaging through the cupboards. Top Raman, SpaghettiOs, saltine crackers, and a toilet bowl brush. She's definitely getting worse, he thought.

He sat at the dirty kitchen table and looked her over. She's shrinking along with everything else, he thought.

More brittle, but still stubborn all out of proportion to her size. For a moment Hank felt something approaching sympathy. Barney plopped his paw on Hank's lap, and sniffed at his crotch.

Edith slammed the cabinet doors then slid a dirty skillet off the crusty stove burner. "Haven't seen you in six months. I don't figure this is a social visit." She dropped the pan in the sink, clanking against the week's dirty dishes. "What is it you want?"

Hank returned to the refrigerator and spied a piece of cherry pie. "Want? Maybe I just want to say hi to my dear old mom."

"Not likely. Money? You need more money?"

"Wouldn't hurt."

"Well, I don't have any. Sorry. Guess you'll just have to do something crazy like get a job."

Hank raised his two-fingered hand. "Maybe you forgot. Not a lot of folks wanting to hire cripples these days."

"Feeling sorry for yourself won't help."

"Yeah, I know." Hank turned and faced her. "I can do whatever I set my mind to. Potential and all that happy horse shit."

She fanned the air in front of her face. "Drunk again. I swear."

"Can't say I didn't learn nothing from the old man."

He pulled out a piece of pie and examined the blue-green fuzz clinging to the rubbery cherry filing. He surveyed the rest of the top shelf of Tupperware — moldy macaroni and cheese and a helping of meatloaf beneath a thick layer of green turf. "Got anything decent to eat? The smell — "

"There's vegetables in the garden. But I don't suppose you'd be interested in them since you prefer to drink your meals."

"Looks like you're growing a garden in here." He opened the freezer. It contained an empty popsicle box and another Tupperware container embedded in solid ice. If the fools at the fair who had pinned the blue ribbon on her cherry pie could see this. "Yep, just wanted to say hi."

"My ass."

"No, I don't want to say hi to your ass."

"Very funny."

Hank looked her up and down. "Don't you think it's about time?"

Edith grabbed a dish in the sink and turned on the faucet. A spray of rusty water belched, followed by a thin dribble of water. "Darn thing's clogged again. How am I supposed . . . " She began kneading a dirty dish towel.

Hank watched the woman he'd once respected and even feared frozen like a pillar of salt, searching for a missing puzzle piece. Soon he'd have to deal with her. Maybe sooner then he'd hoped.

Barney trotted over to Edith and pushed his muzzle into her side. She patted him on the head.

Her face knotted with some internal struggle. "Take your pie with you and get. I'm expecting company."

"Oh? Let me guess. Another visit from Dickie?"

"You mean Mayor Dickerson. He's a good man, something I can't say of present company."

"What's he want?"

"Wouldn't you like to know." She held open the back door to usher him out.

Hank poked a fork into the moldy pie, considering a bite. Barney sat at his feet watching as long strings of slobber slid down his jowls. "You're sweet on him. Shit yeah. I can see it on your face."

"Watch your mouth. He's a big step up from that pack of thugs you hang around with."

"If you weren't so senile, you'd remember that those 'thugs' were the only ones who stood by Dad." He raised his hand in mock salute. "Proud militia members who stand for freedom. Not a bunch of kiss-asses who suck up to the mayor as he ruins this town."

"Just go."

Hank took a bite of pie then spat it back onto the plate. "So what's he want?"

"None of your business."

Hank knew Dickerson had taken an interest in the farm ever since the feds named Sheridan a contender for the new federal correctional facility. Dickerson was cunning and determined, and his mom had no business talking with the likes of him about the farm's future. He had plans for the land and no sweet-talking politician was going to steal it. "What's the hurry? Old Shorty won't mind if I have a little visit with the two of you. Need to give my blessing before you two . . . you know."

"What are you talking about? He and Margaret are quite happy."

"Wouldn't be the first man who had a little something on the side."

"Don't be ridiculous."

"Just need to check out his intentions. That's all."

"Well maybe I'll call the police. You can check out Officer Washburn's intentions while you're at it."

Hank sat on the sofa, put his boots on the antique coffee table, and leaned back. "What? He's gonna arrest me for being in my own house?"

"No. For trespass."

"Trespass? This property's as much mine as yours.

Dad said so."

"Yeah, well, things change. Some people don't deserve a place like this. Besides, you'd just let it crumble to the ground."

"Looks like you already got a good start on that. It's up to me, I'd fix it up real nice. Put those extra bedrooms to good use. Maybe Junior could have a room of his own."

"Poor kid. He deserves better than the likes of you and that—."

"Careful now. Dickie might take offense at calling his daughter names."

"Well it's my house now, so unless you want to explain your concerns to the police, I suggest you leave the way you came."

Hank looked through the front window and saw a blue Cadillac churning a cloud of dust winding its way up the driveway.

"Well, well. Speaking of the devil."

Mayor Dickerson's Cadillac eased to a stop in front of Edith's porch. Dickerson shut off the engine and watched the dust settle onto the windshield. He suddenly felt weary and sank a little deeper into the leather seat, then straightened to look in the rearview mirror. His slender fingers twirled the ends of his graying, handlebar mustache. He frowned through bushy eyebrows and cursed a nonconforming hair. Old, you're looking old, my friend.

The front door opened, and the screen door swung out. Edith stood in the doorway, her leg bent out to the side, blocking Barney. Barney's big head peeked over her thigh, then he jumped over and lumbered out the door. He bounded down the porch steps to Dickerson's car and stood with his front paws propped against the window. His nails tapped and scraped as he sniffed the scent seeping from the car's cool interior.

Dickerson seethed as Barney's drooping eyes looked down on him. The dog's big nose smeared snotty streaks across the window. Dickerson smiled through clenched teeth and waved at Edith, resenting the indignities this unconsummated business had already inflicted on him. Enough was enough.

Edith waved as she walked to the car. "Down, Barney." Edith tugged at the thick leather collar swallowed in the folds of muscle and fir of the dog's neck. "I'm so sorry. He just won't listen." She gave him a sharp tug, and his paws slid down the door, digging scratches in the door's blue paint. "Still thinks he's a puppy. You know how they are."

Dickerson nodded and reluctantly opened the car door.

"Yes, they are a handful." He reached toward Barney. "Good boy."

The dog growled and snapped, sending slobber flying in ropes.

"Barney!" Edith said, pulling back on his leash. "Is that any way to treat a guest? Hold on, I'll put him inside." She tugged Barney onto the porch and coaxed him through the front door.

Dickerson ran his fingers over the fresh scars on the Cadillac's door.

Hank stood in the doorway. "Look what the dog drug in."

Dickerson pulled his handkerchief from his pocket and wiped a glob of slobber from his lapel.

"What brings the mayor of Sheridan out here on such

a fine morning?"

Dickerson started up the first step. "Just paying your mother a visit."

"Well ain't that nice."

"What have you been up to?"

Hank stepped out onto the porch, swirling a beer bottle in his hand. "Oh, you know. Looking after the place. Got big plans for it." He nodded toward the house and drew his dirty thumbnail across his throat. "When . . . you know."

The screen door creaked open, and Edith backed out juggling a tray with lemonade and cherry pie. "Hank was just leaving."

"Yeah, well," Hank said, "got things to do. You two don't do anything I wouldn't do." Hank tipped his beer bottle to Dickerson, drank the last of it, and set the empty on the porch railing. "You enjoy that pie. Just had a piece. It was blue ribbon." He stood at the top of the steps, giving Dickerson the stink eye.

Dickerson dabbed beads of sweat and grit from his forehead. "Mrs. Sherman, if this a bad time, I can—"

"Nonsense," Edith said. "It's a lovely day. Let's sit on the porch swing."

Hank draped his arm around Edith's shoulder and squeezed.

She pulled away, looking disgusted.

"See ya, Ma, Dickie. Got to get Junior. It's my weekend." The screen creaked and slapped as Hank went back inside the house.

From deeper inside, Dickerson heard another door slam shut. The sound of an engine belching to life rumbled from out back. Dickerson pulled out his handkerchief as the Jeep spun in the gravel, billowing a fresh cloud of dust and smoke as it bounced through the pitted gravel driveway toward the road.

Dickerson fanned his hat, warding off the drifting cloud. An itch crawled up his throat and seeped into his sinuses. He covered his mouth with the handkerchief and forced himself to breathe as he sat in the porch swing.

Edith poured two glasses of lemonade and cut the remaining slice of pie in half. She held out his slice.

"Thank you," Dickerson said, examining a patch of fuzz clinging to the filling. "How's that garden of yours doing?"

"Tomatoes are still coming in and some lettuce. Here, let me get you some—"

"No, I'm fine. Maybe later. You just sit with me and relax for a minute."

"Don't let me forget. My memory's not what it used to be." She stood beside the swing, petting the pitcher.

"Edith, why don't you have a seat?"

"Oh, yes. What was I thinking?" She put the pitcher on the floor then sat on the top step of the porch. "So what brings you all the way out here, Mayor?"

Dickerson sipped his lemonade that tasted more like dish soap. "Did you have a chance to sign the papers, the ones we went over last time I stopped by?"

Edith struggled to her feet, sloshing lemonade from her glass, then started pinching the shriveled blossoms off the fuchsia hanging above the porch railing. "Too dry. So hard to keep things alive in this heat. Poor thing's almost dead." She raised her glass in a toast to the plant then poured the lemonade into the basket. "There, that should help."

Dickerson added his glass to hers, hoping to save his stomach and not offend her in the process.

"What are you doing?"

"I thought . . . "

"Don't you like it?"

"It's fine. I just thought . . . it would help." The drifting dust scratched in his throat and turned to sand in his eyes. He sneezed, wiped his nose, and sneezed again. "The papers, Mrs. Sherman. Did you get a chance–"

"Ruined. It's ruined now." She lifted the basket from its hook and dropped it into the rose bushes below. "Ashes to ashes."

Dickerson returned to the swing and sat, his legs dangling above paint curling up like tiny scrolls from the maple floorboards. The house was slowly shedding its skin. Its arthritic bones broken and bent.

"Edith are you—"

She shook her head then stared at him. "Yes, I looked at the papers, not that any of it made sense. I signed them."

"Wonderful. Would you mind if I had a look? I can take care of the rest for you." He felt the growing pressure in his sinuses pushing against his eyes, making him dizzy. "I'm sorry, but I'm not feeling very well. Do you think I could take the papers . . . "

"Allergies?" She put both hands on his forehead like a faith healer preparing to send him swooning under the power of the spirit. "Don't feel any fever." She pulled her hands away, leaving his head feeling sticky.

"Could we—"

"Be right back. I've got just the thing."

"Mrs. Sherman . . . "

She hurried into the house as Dickerson glided back and forth, the energy suddenly wrung out of him.

Edith emerged and seemed to be walking on the rolling deck of a ship. "Here you go." She held out a cup with her left hand, and in her right, she held a rolled up manila envelope.

Dickerson looked at the envelope then took the cup. The warm, thick syrup inside smelled of whiskey and molasses. "I'm feeling better. Thanks, but I think I'll—"

"I swear you're just like my boys." She nudged the cup up to his lips. "Honestly. You need to drink it all down for it to do you any good. It may not taste like much, but you'll be glad you did."

He looked again at the manila envelope rolled in her hand. "Are those the papers?"

"Oh, yes." She held the tube up as if she might swat him with it.

He grabbed one end. Her grip tightened on the other.

"Now drink up."

Dickerson's lips parted, and the thick ooze began to slide across his tongue like a giant slug. His mouth filled, but his throat refused to open.

"You've got to swallow," she said, tilting his chin upward. Edith shook her head. "Just like my boys."

He swallowed and felt the sludge burn as it crawled down his throat.

"See, that wasn't so bad." She let go of the envelope and smiled. Now, if you don't mind, I have some wood to split. You might want to get home pretty soon. It has a powerful effect."

Dickerson snatched the envelope from her hand, fighting the urge to retch. He staggered to his car and leaned against the slobber-stained window, wishing the world would stop spinning. He opened the door and eased himself down onto the plush leather seat.

Edith stood on the porch, an axe leaning against her leg, pulling on her gardening gloves. She waved then hefted the axe over her shoulder and walked around the side of the house.

Dickerson opened the envelope and turned to the last page. His signature was written in flowing black letters. Signatures of other officials sat neatly inscribed above their lines. Edith's signature line remained vacant. He cursed and vomited on the seat.

The second and fourth Friday's of the month began with a kidnapping. This was the second.

"You getting ready?" Sharon asked over the cartoon noise of the television. "Hurry up, Junior. He'll be here any minute." She chose not to use Hank, Junior's first name, wishing its absence would somehow erase the existence of the man he'd been named after. She plucked some socks from the laundry basket as Junior stood behind her, struggling to pull up his jeans. He twisted one foot in, lost his balance, and leaned against the wall. "Careful now."

She dug his suitcase out of the bedroom closet. Burt and Ernie from Sesame Street were all smiles on the front. The Cookie monster gave a guilty, crumbly smile on the back. The knot tightened in her gut.

Sharon unzipped the suitcase and threw in his toothbrush and baggie of medicine. She opened his dresser drawer and stared at the G I Joe's in battle on the only pair of underwear in the drawer. Down the hall the bathroom door shut, and the lock clicked. The bathroom fan began to whir and rattle, mixing with the spray of the faucet. She lifted the GI Joe on Junior's desk and ran her thumb over its camouflaged face. Her thoughts drifted back to Junior's beginning.

Three weeks premature, Junior seemed to shrivel within the sterile white walls of the hospital. His puffy eyes drifted unfocused, and his tiny limbs jerked and flailed. His hands were perpetually clenched. He screamed the desperate, inconsolable cries of an addict who shared his mother's cravings for heroin.

Sharon remembered the condescending looks, the shame cast on her by the nurses and doctors who soiled their hands with her as little as possible. She deserved it. But when they handled Junior as if he bore some contagious disease, she finally understood how sin could get passed down from one generation to the next.

Two days after Junior's birth, Hank drove them home to their one-bedroom apartment. He busied himself clearing beer bottles and cigarette ash from the tables. He collected dirty dishes and even promised to wash a few. Sharon wondered if he was a changed man when he threw cotton balls, bent spoons with sooty undersides, and syringes into the garbage. He tossed empty baggies with their traces of residue. In their final days as a family, she'd regret he'd not cleaned the bedroom more carefully.

Back home, life continued to seep out of Junior. The shadow of Sharon's guilt blocked the light he needed to grow. Mother and child were entwined like vines, strangling each other in their struggle to survive.

Hank assured Sharon Junior would be fine, as if he could make it so by sheer force of will.

For a few months, Sharon and Hank were allies in Junior's struggle to live. The three of them were dug into a foxhole.

Three months later, Junior's fragile body began to grow. In his second year he took halting steps, spoke his first words, and cried less. He delighted in running his tiny fingers over Hank's scarred face. Sharon felt hopeful as she saw Hank beam with pride as he held

Junior in rare, sober moments. But as Junior grew, the responsibilities of parenthood fueled their fights anew. The tension between them built up like boiling black thunderheads around Junior, clouds with like charges, exploding unpredictably.

Sharon pretended not to notice when Junior's mind seemed to stall. Hank blamed her for pampering him. The doctor coldly declared that Junior suffered from fetal alcohol syndrome. A failure to thrive, he declared, a brain malformed, thanks to her alcohol and drug abuse during pregnancy. Junior would never know what it meant to be normal.

She blamed Hank for tempting her to drink and for bringing the needle into their home. Each time Hank shoved one into his arm, she felt the sweet sting in her own. He blamed her for being such an unfit mother. Blame made them cruel. Cruelty split Junior's world into unequal halves. Hank and Sharon forged a tenuous truce between enemies bent on mutual destruction.

When Junior was four, Hank came home drunk and smelling of perfume, and the truce suffered its final violation. He loaded his secret stash from his time in the service into the back of his Jeep and drove off. Junior waved, and Sharon cried.

The court ordered Sharon to hand over Junior twice a month for as long as they both lived or until Junior became eighteen. She knew which would come first.

The rumble of the engine echoed in the parking lot behind the apartment complex. "Don't forget your suitcase," Sharon said, as she quickly stuffed in his blanket and an extra pair of socks.

Junior sat in front of the television, his face aglow in the reflection of the TV. The Wiley Coyote stood scheming as an anvil dropped from the sky and the

Roadrunner watched. The anvil struck Coyote, embedding him in a small crater. The Roadrunner beeped twice, and Junior laughed.

"Turn it off. Your dad's here. Time to go."

More beeps came from the television followed by more giggles.

"Henry Joseph Sherman, don't make me say it again." Leaving his suitcase in the hall outside the bathroom, she hurried to the front door to see if Hank was climbing the stairs. She pulled back the sheet tacked over the window beside the door and looked through glass smeared with Junior's handprints. She slid open the drawer in the end table beneath the window and took out the heavy semi-automatic handgun. She pulled back the slide and peeked at the end of the brass bullet casing seated in the chamber. She stuffed the gun into her waistband and bloused her black work T-shirt over the rubber grip.

The television went silent. Junior grabbed her pant leg and tugged. "Mom."

She flinched and glared at him. "Get your pillow." She hoped if she could get junior out the door before Hank reached it, she might avoid a fight.

"I have to pee," Junior said.

She pulled back the sheet and looked down the stairwell. Hank stumbled up the first step, pinching the railing between the thumb and index finger of his mangled hand.

Junior held his crotch and danced as if he was standing barefoot on sizzling pavement. "I can't hold it any longer."

He squirmed as he struggled not to wet himself. The zipper always gave his clumsy hands trouble. She looked down the stairwell again. Hank steadied himself and took the second step.

Junior tugged again. "Mom!"

"All right! I'll be there in a minute."

Junior trotted to the bathroom and shut the door.

Sharon closed the sheet back over the window and felt the cold gun against her skin. Drunk son of a bitch, she thought. She watched through the stained cloth as his shadow climbed another step.

"Got it!" Junior yelled through the closed door.

Hank staggered upward, took the final step, and reached for the knob. He pulled his hand back, looked across the landing at the neighboring apartment, and twisted the doorknob.

"Lock the door," Sharon said. Her heart pounded as she curled her fingers around the pistol's grip. The door knob turned, and she wondered if the feeble links of the safety chain she'd installed after his last visit would hold. The knob continued to turn, and she wanted to grab it, to halt its rotation, but her arms wouldn't move. The latch scraped back and the door popped open, letting in a narrow ribbon of light. He's being careful, too careful. She took a step backward as Hank pushed the door inward, jerking against the chain. Through the crack in the door she saw the scars on his hand where three fingers had been removed, the bones bulging beneath puckered skin. The security chain rattled as he jammed the door back and forth. His fist pounded against the door.

"Sharon, open the door. I swear to God—"

"You're drunk."

Across the landing, her neighbor's voice scolded. "Why don't you just leave her be? Think about her son for a change."

Sharon's fingers tightened around the butt of her gun

as she peered through the crack in the door.

"Why don't you just mind your own business?" Hank said. "He's my son, too."

"Momma—"

"Junior, Shut the door!"

"I'm calling the cops. Sharon you hear me?" The neighbor's door slammed.

Hank cussed again then pressed his ear against the door. A bloodshot eye peered through the crack. His voice lowered. "Sharon, open the damn door."

"You're drunk. I told you last time, show up here drunk, no Junior."

"I ain't drunk." He hammered the door with his fist, then squeezed two fingers through the crack and wrapped them around the door's edge. "So help me, Sharon—"

Junior waddled out the bathroom with his pants around his ankles. "I did it!" He sat on the floor and struggled to pull his pants up.

"I'll send him out, but you have to stay outside. Got me?"

"Yeah, yeah, yeah." His fingers wiggled, withdrew, and his eye squinted in the opening. "Fine, just send the kid out."

"Wait there." She shouldered the door closed and locked it. Hank barked out a string of curses and her neighbor responded in kind. Something on the landing thumped and the neighbor's door slammed again.

Sharon pulled Junior to her and hugged him. She took a breath, unlocked the door and slid the chain free. The door swung open, and Hank stood swaying, reeking of whiskey. He began to kneel then fell against the wall. "Give Daddy a hug."

Junior looked at Sharon and threw his arms around

Hank's neck.

"Go on out to the car. I've got a surprise for you if you're good."

"A surprise! What?"

"Go down there and wait for me. You'll see. And don't mess with the key this time."

Sharon gave Junior a kiss and felt numb as she watched him scoot down the stairs on his bottom without his suitcase. She glared at Hank, his face blank, smelling of cigarette smoke and piss. "Wait here. I'll get his suitcase." He leaned against the wall and turned his face to the morning sun.

The hallway seemed to grow longer, darker as she went for the suitcase. She patted the butt of the pistol to make sure it was still there and curled her fingers around the plastic suitcase handle. As she began to lift, her scalp felt like it was being ripped from her skull. Her head twisted back as Hank threw her against the wall. She collapsed to the floor, and Hank climbed on top of her and straddled her chest. He raised his fist over her head and froze. "Want to call the cops?"

Her nails raked across his scarred face and her skull vibrated as she heard a distant echo. His fist swooped down, smashing into her cheek. The burn seared into her eye. Hank grabbed a fist full of hair and yanked her head back, teeing her face up for the next punch. She reached into her waistband for the pistol, but it was gone. As Hank yanked her head back again, she saw the butt of the pistol on the floor beneath Hank's foot.

I'm dead, she thought, and for a moment death seemed welcomed. Then she thought of Junior permanently delivered into the custody of this monster.

Rage ignited inside Sharon and she bucked her hips hard upward, throwing Hank over her head. She gripped the gun as Hank turned to swing at her again and smashed the barrel against his face. The metal edges crunched into his nose and split his lip. He sat, wiped the blood streaming down his face, and smiled. Free of his grip, she stood and jammed the gun into the base of his skull.

He looked up in his stunned, drunken stupor and laughed. "You ain't got the guts." He dabbed the blood dripping off his chin. "Go ahead. Call the cops now. They'd love to see this."

Sharon stepped back and pointed the gun at his face. Part of her wanted pull the trigger and for this nightmare to be over. Another part resisted, knowing that if she killed him, she'd never see Junior again. "Get out. Now!"

Hank leaned against the wall and raised his hands in surrender. He grabbed the suitcase and rose to his feet. "He's gonna need this."

"He stays here."

Hank spat on the floor and smeared his hands with the blood running from his nose. "I don't think so. He goes with me, or I call the cops." He wiped a long streak of blood on the wall. "I tell them you attacked me when I came for my court-ordered visit. That's a crime in case you forgot. I say you threatened me with a gun. Last time I checked, felons ain't supposed to have guns. He smeared more blood across his face. "Looks like I have lots of proof."

"Maybe I'll just put a bullet through your head."

"Go ahead." He smiled. "Might as well put one through Junior's, too. You'll never see him again. Least not till you get out of prison in thirty years."

Sharon's hand trembled as she lowered the gun.

Hank spat more blood on the floor. He lifted the

suitcase and staggered to the front door. He stopped, grabbed the security chain, and looked back at her. "You really think this'll keep me out?" He smiled and walked out the door.

Sharon slammed the door and peeked through the window for one last look at Junior sitting behind the steering wheel pretending to drive. Hank opened the Jeep door and shoved him hard across to the passenger's side.

Sharon leaned against the door as the Jeep's engine rumbled to life. She collapsed, clutching the gun in her hands, wondering if the trembling hands that held the gun really were her own.

The engine raced, and the tires chirped as it left the parking lot. Sharon sat rocking as the pistol slowly swung toward her face.

Saturday

The Jeep's over-sized tires churned through the loose gravel hugging the narrow road blasted into the walls of granite. Hank and Junior bounced and tipped past rusting mining machinery as they wound down into the abandoned rock quarry. The engine knocked and choked as Hank swerved to miss boulders fallen into the roadway from the decaying cliffs. A single-wide trailer was tucked against the rock face at the bottom of the pit some 200 feet below. Water drained from the rocks and left long, rusty trails to the lake that filled much of the quarry's bottom.

A haze of smoke and fog had settled into the quarry. The morning light penetrated diffusely from the rim above. Deep in the quarry, shadows clung to the rocks.

Hank had wiped most of the blood from his face. The scratches she'd dug into his cheek were a throbbing reminder that something needed to be done. Hank glanced at Junior staring ahead wide-eyed, then considered the rifles piled on the back seat. He lit another cigarette from the stub in his mouth and flicked the butt out the window into the brittle, brown scrub

41

that clung to the edge of the cliff. He popped the tab on a beer and hit the gas.

The ammo trunk filled the passenger's side floorboard. Forty boxes of bullets made it as heavy as two men. These bullets sliced the air a hundred times faster than an eye could blink, five times the speed of sound. So fast they'd hit you before the sound waves struck the ear drum. Shock was the first thing their target felt, followed by a daze as the brain groped to comprehend what had just happened.

Hank knew in a firefight you never had enough ammo. His team had gone through this heavy trunk's worth in a single operation as a member of the Tiger Force in Vietnam. There was nothing worse than the naked feeling of having to scrounge for ammo as enemy bullets struck around you.

The Jeep's wheels slid into a rut washed out during last winter's rain and slid toward the edge of the cliff. It pitched sideways, slamming him against the door, and launching Junior into his lap. Ash from his cigarette fluttered into Junior's hair, and beer sloshed against the windshield. He jerked the steering wheel back and hit the gas. The engine coughed a plume of smoke as gravel sprayed against the underside of the rusty Jeep. Hank cursed and shoved Junior back to the passenger's side.

Junior fumbled with the ends of his seatbelt and banged his knees against the ammo box as the Jeep lunged again.

"Hold on boy. Could get a little dicey." Hank reached beneath the seat and dug through the empties. He felt back further, blind to the winding road until his fingers wrapped around a paper sack he'd carefully stuffed into a hidden compartment. A hunger only the most desperate understood gripped him as he cradled the sack in his lap. He could almost smell the crystalline powder, feel it crawling through his lungs, setting hooks in his brain. He licked his lips then took a last drink of beer. The sack held enough to fix him and his boys up for a week.

The hillside had birthed a boulder the size of a calf and left it stillborn in the road ahead. Junior gasped and pointed. Hank snapped the wheel hard right, throwing the Jeep into a sideways slide. The hunched rock scraped along the Jeep's undercarriage, sounding like the moaning of some prehistoric beast. Hank let loose a string of profanity and snapped the wheel back and headed down the road.

Junior sat frozen, holding onto the ends of his seat belt. He's nothing like me, Hank thought. He dug out another cold one and peeled back the tab. The cool drink tickled his throat as he held it out to Junior.

"Take it," Hank said. "Come on, it won't kill ya'."

Junior scrunched up his face and grabbed the can with both hands, careful not to spill. He took a sip, winced, then swallowed. "That's good." He began to tip again.

"Leave some for me." Hank grabbed the can, sloshing some onto the seat. "Now look what you did."

"I'm sorry." Junior's eyes began to tear. "I didn't mean to."

"You got the targets wet. Quit being a baby and fix it."

Hank guzzled more beer as Junior crawled between the seats and began to wipe off the targets with his jacket sleeve.

"Effective combat training is as much mental as it is physical," Hank began. "Realism makes all the difference. Got to practice killing real people—or as close as you can get—that's the key. Then when you look in the eyes of the enemy, you're not as likely to

43

hesitate. Kill enough people, you get used to it. First one's the hardest."

Hank took a drink and considered the targets he'd made. They featured the presidents who'd presided over the Vietnam war—Kennedy, Johnson, Nixon, and Ford. Others bore the faces of the military commanders who'd ordered the Tiger Force into the jungles of Vietnam—the same commanders who were too cowardly to remember giving those orders when investigated for possible war crimes. General Westmoreland had his own target along with the rest of the bureaucrats who'd pushed the Tigers for higher body counts, and declared the hamlets of Vietnamese civilians free fire zones. *If it moved, it dies,* they'd said. The same ones who'd promised him medical treatment when his final mission left Hank crippled. The promise breakers who'd stamped the rest of his life Discharged. The locals weren't exempt. Two targets bore the likeness of the mayor and chief—politicians cut from the same cowardly cloth.

The tires splashed through muddy water as they reached the No Trespassing sign wired to the open gate. The trailer's windows were covered with cardboard and barred on the outside. Hank smiled at the fading Sheridan Militia sign screwed to the porch railing. The crest displayed a cross made of rifles with a crown of bullets.

The Jeep pulled in beside a jacked up 4x4 with its row of floodlights mounted on the roll bar. The quarry and clubhouse were his Carentan, his base of operations for a war marching his way. These boys were his brothers, his shock troops, the only real family he had left. Whether they would die for him, only time would tell.

The sun began to swell over the lip of the rock quarry, casting a brilliant orange glow onto the jagged rock walls above. Down here he felt safe, dug into a giant foxhole.

Hank stuffed the brown paper sack into his gear bag, grabbed his rifle from the back, and slung it over his shoulder. The weight of the strap felt reassuring, like a father's strong hand steadying him.

Laughter drifted from inside the trailer.

Junior peered out the Jeep's window, looking full of wonder, like they'd just landed on the moon. "Are we there yet?"

Hank looked at the trailer. "We're here."

The voices inside went silent.

Randy stepped out the front door and stretched. He looked puzzled and said, "What happened to you?"

Hank rubbed the long, seeping scratches on his face. "Sharon."

"Damn, man. She got you good this time."

Hank pulled up his T-shirt and wiped off some of the ooze. "Nothing a little time with the boys can't fix."

Junior opened the door and climbed out.

"Hey, Junior," Randy said. "How's it hanging?"

Junior shrugged and began to wander over the rocks that rose out of the puddles.

Randy said, "Saw Terrence this morning driving his police car past the Reservation. Seemed a little nervous about something."

They laughed.

"Junior," Hank said, "I got some stuff to do. You play out here." He dug in the back seat and pulled out a cooler. Here's some grub if you get hungry."

Junior held his crotch and started to hop. "I gotta' go."

Hank pointed to a boulder. "Over there if you need to. Stay away from the deep water. Got it?"

Junior nodded, the crotch of his jeans already wet.

"Pissed himself," Hank said, shaking his head. He grabbed his duty bag and scooped up the targets. "Get Jimmy to help with the ammo."

Junior peed swirls on a boulder as they walked inside.

"I'm the chief of police, for God's sake," Madison muttered as he approached the overpass to Highway 18. He turned up the air conditioning, reminding himself he'd agreed to visit the elderly and show a little charm if Dickerson required it.

He turned up the driveway, mentally rehearsing his spiel.

Mrs. Sherman, so nice to see you. My, what a lovely day. You're looking well today. Now if you could kindly hand over the paperwork so we can bulldoze your house and get on with building the prison, I'd much appreciate it.

Maybe he'd have to tone it down a little.

He pulled to a stop in front of the old farm house and waited for the dust to settle. The nose of her mutt, Barney, rooted aside the curtain in the front window, and his jowls flopped as he barked. He remembered the last visit when the dog nearly castrated him.

Madison hoped she'd remembered and waited for Edith to open the door. Barney propped his paws on the windowsill and barked again. When he could wait no longer, Madison walked into the dusty air and trudged up the porch steps. Barney's deep growl made his skin crawl.

The doorbell sounded a chime melody far too elegant for the old house, and still Edith failed to appear. He cupped his hands beside his eyes and peered inside. Barney's giant head rose up, and his black eyes stared into Madison's just before he barked a sling of drool onto the glass. Barney's forepaws danced against the glass, and Madison feared it would break.

Seeing no sign of life inside, Madison slipped a business card into the front door screen, satisfied there was no more to be done.

As he walked down the porch steps back to his Suburban, he noticed a beer bottle with a cigarette butt floating inside. Beside it, a fuchsia basket lay overturned in the bushes.

Hank's chair sat in the middle of a horseshoe of folding tables. President was written in felt pen on the back. The treasurer and sergeant at arms sat in labeled chairs on either side. The other militia members found their usual spots. Older members sat closest to Hank. Newbies sat at the far end, or stood. A picture of Paul Revere, musket in hand, hung on the wall above Hank. To the left, the Sheridan Militia's Creed hung in hand-written block letters. On the right was the target list. The names of the most reviled traitors to the cause of freedom, as judged by the group, were written there. The inspiration behind Hank's rifle targets came from this list. Representative Jordan Martinez, from the Fourth District, had been crossed out following his fatal accident.

Billy Marshall opened a case of Coors and tossed one to Hank. Tim Hirsch, who went by Tiny, wrapped his meaty paw around a bottle of Jim Beam and took two stale sandwiches to his seat.

Ashtrays littered the tables, each resembling a mini volcano of erupted cigarette butts surrounded by flows of ash. Their streams of smoke snaked and coiled around the room.

"Ten hut!" Randy shouted.

The nine regular members rose to their feet and saluted before settling back into their battered folding chairs. All eyes were fixed on the duty bag Hank plopped on the table before him.

"At ease." Hank surveyed those in attendance. Randy was a hangover shade of green, twitching worse than usual.

"How's everyone doing?"

They nodded, glancing around, shifting.

"Before we get to official business," Hank said, "I didn't forget." He unzipped his duty bag and gingerly removed a brown paper sack. The group sat at attention like dogs starved for the food about to spill into their dishes.

Hank slowly unrolled the crumpled sack like a stripper teasing an excited crowd then pulled out a clear plastic bag. The short-circuiting florescent tube above flickered, making the white powder sparkle. Hank held the bag of crystal meth in his hand for all to admire. More pure than crank and stronger than cocaine, six ounces was enough to keep them high for a week — unless someone got greedy.

Somebody always did.

"Here's how it's going to go down this time," Hank said, caressing the bag. "This time I divide it up, and we make it last." He looked each of them in the eye, stopping again at Randy. Satisfied that they were clear, he dug out some of the white powder and tapped it into his glass pipe. They watched silently as he sparked his butane lighter and the flame licked the bottom of the bowl. The white crystal melted into a brown liquid, and white vapor swirled inside.

"Me first," Hank said. He put the pipe to his mouth and sucked in. The vapor drew into the tube, and he felt it. From somewhere high above came an explosion of light, and a shower of pure energy vibrated through his skin. He was lightning. His eyes rolled back in pure ecstasy. "Shit. Shit. Shit. Jesus, Mary, and Joseph!" His eyes opened to see the others staring like a pack of ravenous wolves.

Hank passed the pipe and lighter to the sergeant at arms, who sucked in a deep breath. Next, the treasurer, a stranger to meth, but just as eager to satisfy his curiosity. The pipe passed from hand to hand. When the bowl reached Jimmy Anderson, the glass was black, and the vapor was gone. He complained there wasn't any left, and the pipe made its way back to Hank.

Hank filled it again and sucked in another cloud. His lungs tingled and his head burst as he began to drift in the haze. Should I tell them about the acid? he wondered. Nah, it's my special surprise. They'll figure it out soon enough. Meth and acid, a wild ride. Who'd complain?

He looked at the clock above the door, listening to the mechanical workings inside grind and click. Its hands smoothly circled, bent, and snaked on their spindles. Hank never knew what might happen when his senses broke loose from their anchors. The current could carry him anywhere, anytime.

This time he floated back to his final deployment in the dense jungles of Vietnam. The helicopter rotors beat the air with heavy thuds as rifle fire sparkled beneath them like stars fallen to Earth. Strings of light reached up into the night like octopus tentacles to snatch them from the sky. The helicopter rattled amid the whine of the engine, rocked by an invisible hand as lightning and thunder sent shards of metal ripping through the air. The Huey's skin rattled, then they dropped as if hit by a giant fly swatter. As the chopper plunged, Hank knew that was the day he'd die.

Eleven others were also dressed in tiger-striped fatigues, young men who eight months ago dreamed of glorious battle against the communists. These men were now old before their time. Gaunt with sunken cheeks and dark eyes, they resembled starved prisoners of war. In the flickering darkness below, he saw a montage of their atrocities—the eyes of villagers wide with terror as they ran, stumbled, and sprawled to the ground, bullets ripping through their tattered clothing and brown flesh. An old man kneeling, pleading, as a rifle barrel smashed into his face, and a bayonet pierced his back. He saw chips of bamboo spraying into the air as machine gun bullets shredded the walls of huts and ground up those huddled inside. He recalled the dark pits dug deep in the earth, places villagers hoped to hide from soldiers. He was there again, peering down into the black opening, holding a grenade, listening to their pleas for mercy. He felt the grenade in his hand as he pulled the pin and tossed it into the darkness. The flash was followed by another when the screams and moaning lingered. Count the bodies. How many were huddled in the pit? Count it twenty.

Then he was drifting on the ground. "Go, go, go," the captain yelled over the screaming engine. He grabbed his M16 and jumped into the dark, feeling the elephant grass clawing at his face. The helicopter's engines whined louder, and the Huey rose in a blast of wind as the last man jumped.

A hand pulled him to his feet, and he was running, stumbling through the muck of a rice field, then plunging into the tree line toward the village where the enemy was dug in.

The village perimeter had little protection beyond sharpened bamboo pikes tipped with human excrement. At least this time the target is military, he thought. If I'm going to die, it will be fighting the enemy.

The hamlet slept as they crawled toward the target's hut. The sentries who guarded the VC commander were just boys dressed in uniforms too large for their starved bodies. The Tigers crept up on the boys as they slept, and they never woke.

Hank's knife plunged into the side of the third sentry's neck and thrust outward, severing his trachea. When the guard tried to scream, air rushed out of the flapping hole. Hank sawed the knife, severing the nerves that gave life to his limbs. He dropped limp, eyes rolling as his jaw opened and closed silently.

The Tigers crawled toward the target under the half-moon's pale glow. A cool mist rose up from the jungle floor, enveloping the soldiers as they crept forward. Inside the hut, Hank heard the moaning of a man and whimpers of a child.

Hank motioned to two others, then they sprang from their crouches and charged into the hut, rifles raised, ready to kill.

The Vietcong commander held the naked girl, no more than ten, as a shield. The girl's tear-stained face had the vacant look of resignation he'd seen in the eyes of others kneeling before execution. Her eyes, empty of hope, gave silent consent to take her life, if they must, to kill the monster behind her.

The commander spewed a stream of incomprehensible syllables. Hank's partners yelled, their voices echoing from far away. He felt a hand pulling him back as he saw the girl's eyes roll upward, and a trickle of blood slide down from the corner of her mouth. In the timelessness, her head snapped right, then the commander's gun was smoking, flashing, bullet casings tumbling through the air. Then a blinding white light and the smell of burning flesh in the frozen moment.

A sizzle brought time rushing forward again. He felt the heat crawling up his back like a fuse burning up the nerves of his spine. As Hank was being sucked backward out of the hut, he aimed at the commander's head and squeezed the trigger of his M16. It didn't fire. Hank reached to clear the jam with his left hand and saw the bloody stumps where his fingers had been. Then the rebel commander's face erupted, white and black ooze splattering on the thatch wall behind.

"Medic, Medic!" someone was screaming. Another white flash and the air filled with black smoke and the smell of burnt flesh. A hand shoved his shoulder then a voice. "Come on man, show me some love."

Hank opened his eyes and saw Jimmy standing over him, reaching for the pipe. Hank sucked in another cloud of vapor, wrapping him in a cocoon of warm textures and colorful sounds, grateful to return from the butchering jungles of Vietnam.

The sun cast long shadows as the group worked their way through the water to the range. On the raised gravel road at the far side of the quarry, white stones marked distances from 100 to 300 yards. Old railroad ties stacked against rocks served as target backers. Each shooter picked a favorite target and hung it on a nail pounded into the wood. Confetti littered the rocks at the base of the ties, the paper remains of feeble-minded men who refused to rally to their cause.

Hank slung his rifle over his good shoulder, grabbed a target, and handed another to Randy.

Jimmy ran up to join them. "Man, what was in that?"

Hank shook his head and kept walking. "Wouldn't you like to know."

Junior threw a rock into the water and waved.

Randy shook his head.

Hank looked at Randy. "What?"

"Junior. I mean . . . "

Hank stopped. "What about him?"

"No. He's a great kid." Randy kicked a rock. "We all like him. But we're just wondering if it was a good idea to bring him here, the mayor's grandson and all? I mean what if he says something?"

Hank felt the pressure begin to throb behind his eyes. "Don't worry about that. The mayor gave up on him when he kicked Sharon out. Far as he's concerned, we're all dead."

"I'm just saying—"

"Hey, he's cool," Jimmy said. "We're not worried. I don't know what Randy's problem is."

Randy and Jimmy mean mugged each other.

"You got a problem with how I'm raising my kid, Randy?"

"No. No way. Forget it."

Hank glared at Jimmy. "What else has he been saying I should know about?"

"Nothing. Honest."

"You sure?"

"Yeah, I'm sure."

Randy stepped back a little too slowly as Hank pulled his K-bar, a seven inch bladed Bowie-type knife with a leather grip and rusty blade, from his ankle sheath and slashed upward. The blade sliced Randy's jeans and drew a thin red line on his thigh. The tip of the knife continued upward, stopping under his chin. Randy danced on his tip-toes.

"Anything else you want to say?"

Randy's jaw stretched up to avoid the knife's point. His wide eyes said he did not.

Hank lowered the knife and slid it back into the sheath. "Didn't think so. Next time, I take your nuts."

Sharon's Corolla pulled in behind the Reservation. Her hands were still shaking. She'd come so close to pulling the trigger yesterday. Everything that happened after Hank left was a blur. Maybe a concussion, she thought. Not her first.

Her jaw ached and the swelling on her cheek bulged up into an eye that struggled to focus. She tilted down the rearview mirror and pulled off her sunglasses. The swelling had darkened into a bruise. She carefully dabbed more foundation over the tender bump and slid the glasses back on. Through the open back door she saw the gloom inside, and for a moment, felt sick.

"Morning, Randy," Sharon said, walking through the back door into what felt like a putrid cave. "We ever going to get the air conditioning fixed?"

"Not likely. You know how cheap he is," Randy said.

She stepped around him as he worked on all fours, scrubbing at a wet puddle on the floor just outside the men's room.

"It's gonna be another hot one." She tucked her purse into the safe buried beneath two cases of Vodka in the back office and locked it. "What's that smell?"

"Tom got sick again last night. I swear we should have eighty-sixed him a long time ago."

She punched in on the time clock, and looked at the handwritten schedule on the clipboard hung on the thumb tack beside it. Another light week. "Who needs to eat?"

"What?"

"Nothing."

"Oh, got a group coming in tonight," Randy said. "Your dad and some folks from out of town. Six or seven, I think."

"Great. Let me guess who gets to clean out the back room."

"No. He wants us to fix up the banquet room, make an impression."

"Figures. He's always trying to impress someone." She walked to the bar and peered into the smoky film coating the mirror. She pulled her hair back, wincing as her fingers brushed the bruise on her cheek. In the dim light, her makeup covered the bruise well enough. The swelling was another matter. She knew some folks would be curious, but they would know better than to ask. "What time?"

"Four? No, five I think. There's a note on the desk."

Her scalp ached as she slid on her sunglasses. She took a final look in the mirror, searching for a faint resemblance to Jackie O. I wonder if Jack ever gave her a black eye, she thought. She began scraping away the dried nacho and beer crusted on top of the bar.

The toilet flushed, and Randy stepped from the men's room, stripping off pink rubber gloves. "Said he'd try to stop by to make sure things were getting set up right."

"He's coming here to show me how to do my job? Well he can put on an apron and serve them too, if he wants."

"I'd pay to see that, but I'm not sure he's tall enough to see over the bar."

"He's such a little—"

"Honey, I'm home," Chief Madison said, sauntering in through the front door.

"Not open for another half hour," Sharon said.

"Want me to get a search warrant?"

Sharon straightened her sunglasses then flipped on the neon Open sign hung in the front window. "If it makes you feel better."

Madison tugged the University of Oregon football jersey creeping up over his generous belly.

"Didn't think you'd miss the Closed sign, trained observer and all." Sharon wiped the last of the bar crumbs onto the floor and reached for a beer pitcher.

Madison grabbed a handful of napkins from the dispenser and dabbed the sweat from his forehead. On another napkin, he hastily scrawled a note then stuffed it into his pocket. "Game day. Civil War. Don't you ever watch football, woman?" He scooted a bar stool back, clearing four tracks through the peanut shells littering the floor. "Oregon versus Oregon State. Where's your community spirit?"

She pulled the Budweiser tap and filled a pitcher, letting the foam spill down the side. "Isn't that like three hours from now?"

Madison reached across the bar and grabbed the remote. He pointed it at the TV and began switching through the channels. "When you gonna get a bigger set? I may have to take my business elsewhere if you can't do better than twenty-seven inches. Only a few of us got more than that," he said with a wink.

"Don't you wish," Sharon said. "Randy can you help with the banquet room before you leave?" She filled a basket with peanuts and slid it in front of the chief.

Randy walked out of the office and hurried toward the front door. "No can do. Meeting some friends at the

. . . in an hour." She watched in the mirror as he grabbed a fist full of nuts from the chief's basket and shelled one.

"Chief," Randy said.

"Randy," Madison said, continuing to flip through the channels.

Randy bit down on a peanut. "Guess I'll be going." He stood in the doorway, a black silhouette against the morning light. "Keep the door open in the back for awhile, it'll help with the smell." He nodded toward the chief. "Can't promise it'll do much about the stink up here."

Sharon rolled her eyes and smiled. A throb of pain pulsed through her cheek. She slid the wet pitcher of Bud down the bar to Madison.

Madison dug his hand into the nuts and popped one in his mouth as he cranked up the volume. He groped for the pitcher's handle, still intent on the TV, finally found it and filled his mug. He drained the mug in one long drink and filled it again. "Gonna be hot." He wiped a wet hand on his jersey and lit a cigarette.

Sharon began arranging the bottles at the far end of the bar. A peanut shell ricocheted off the bow of her sunglasses.

"Sharon, come here," Madison said.

She glanced at him through the mirror and continued arranging.

"Darlin', come here."

A small voice from sixteen years ago finished the familiar lines. *I won't hurt you. It's just between you and me. You don't ever want to tell anyone else.* She wanted to run, but walked over to Madison, unable to refuse whatever service he might demand of her.

He cupped her chin, turning her swollen cheek toward the dim light. "Kind of dark in here for sunglasses." He gently removed them. "Hit you again, didn't he."

She stood numb, unable to form the words. For a breath, she might have seen compassion in his eyes, and she felt ashamed. He'd probably blame her again, but this time, she'd tell. This time she'd follow through. Her lips parted as she willed the words to come.

As she struggled to find the words, Madison seemed to catch himself, and he recoiled from this unexpected expression of caring. His face switched from good cop to bad cop. "Well if you don't want to report it, there's nothing I can do. When you're willing to press charges, let me know. It's about time you quit covering for him. Think of your son, for Christ's sake."

Just like the rest, she thought. It's always easy for cops. Haul somebody off to jail. End of story. But it wasn't. What the cops don't understand is what it's like for a victim to wait in fear, dreading the day a prisoner got released, the day he came hunting. After months to think, Hank would return with all the more reason to finish what he'd started. They're blind to the hell their quick fixes have brought in my life already.

She pulled her face from his hand and snatched back her sunglasses. "I am thinking of my son. That's all I ever do."

As the chief parked himself on his favorite stool at the Reservation, the whine of the vacuum cleaner almost saved Terrence.

Terrence felt an urgent need to rewind as much of yesterday morning as he could. He flipped on the vacuum cleaner and shoved the rubber nozzle into the cracks in the seats. The shards of glass ticked and rattled as they were sucked into the hose. He dug in the gaps, searched beneath the floor mats, and wedged his fingers between the radio gear bolted to the console, searching for a bullet. His finger tip touched a hard object beneath the shotgun bracket between the seats. He shined his flashlight into the cracks and dug further. Bronson barked and sniffed in the seat beside him. Terrence popped the trunk and grabbed the Slim Jim. The thin strap of metal snaked beneath the bracket and popped the object free—a shotgun shell—one of his own. Satisfied he'd run the vacuum nozzle over every nook and cranny inside the car, he emptied the vacuum canister and dug through its contents hoping to find the bullet that had pierced his windshield. Wrappers, hair, bits of gravel, shards of glass, and a shoe lace were all he found.

His failure to apprehend the shooter seemed more the rule than the exception in Terrence's life. Always coming up short. The road he traveled always narrowed and twisted, always terminated in a dead end. He'd hoped the uniform would win him some respect. Flash a badge and people would notice and straighten up. That's how it was in the cop shows. Cops didn't fail. His bad luck clung to him closer than his bullet proof vest two sizes too small. The uniform seemed to shrink more each day.

He coiled the vacuum hose and sat in the front seat. Bronson sat in the seat beside and stared forward, his tongue drooping and bobbing as he panted. Terrence dug the tennis ball out of the glove box and scratched the dog's ears. Bronson stared at the ball, holding his breath. He tossed the ball out the door and Bronson looked at him. "Go get it." Bronson eyed the ball as it rolled to rest beneath the stenciled "COP" painted on the wall that reserved the space for Madison's Suburban.

The chief's space was empty as usual. Beverly waved as she shut the rear door of the police station and pulled the strap of her purse over her shoulder, seemingly satisfied she'd volunteered enough for the day. He wondered what had called her back to the police station on a Saturday morning. Terrence admired her. She could put Madison in his place even on his foulest days. For Terrence, there was just no pleasing the man. Rookie might as well have been his first name.

Madison might be eight inches shorter and two feet wider, but there was something about him Terrence respected, even admired: his unshakable sureness, his lack of concern for what others thought of him. Hard as he tried to mimic that confidence, it always felt hollow. Terrence nervously wore it like a mask, knowing at any time it might slip and show the boy who was only playing dress-up.

Madison would light him up for this latest failure. I just need another chance, he thought. Terrence ran his finger over the spider web of cracks stretching across the windshield, as the dispatcher's voice cracked over the police radio.

"Sheridan One, do you copy?"

He grabbed the mic. "This is Sheridan One. Go ahead."

"We have a report of a suspicious death. Elderly female. Ready to copy?"

"Dispatch, I'm out of service. Maintenance. Chief said county could cover until—"

"Ambulance crew's already arrived. No county units available."

"Chief been notified?"

"Negative. Can't reach him."

Maybe at the Reservation, he thought. I could swing

by and let him know.

"Ready to copy?"

Just another chance was all he needed. He pressed the transmit button. "Go ahead."

As the dispatcher gave him the deceased's address, Terrence scribbled it on his palm. He jotted the time of the call next to it.

"Copy. I'm on my way," he said. "Keep trying to reach the chief."

"Copy. Over."

Terrence opened the patrol car's back door, and Bronson jumped inside, tennis ball in his mouth. He shut the door and brushed off the back of his pants, slicing his finger on a razor of glass clinging to fabric. He cursed and sat in the driver's seat sucking the blood from the fresh cut.

Terrence drove through the business district, feeling the emptiness of the vacant buildings. He slowed as he approached the Reservation Tavern, wondering if Sharon was working. He needed to talk with her. The chief's Suburban was parked in the handicap spot out front. He could stop and notify the chief of the call, but he dreaded the thought of Madison giving him a very public ass-chewing in front of the crowd inside. He could not bear to think of Sharon watching as he submitted to such humiliation. No. This was his chance to make it right. Besides, dispatch would notify Madison soon enough. Terrence flipped on his emergency lights and headed up Bridge Street toward the Highway 18 overpass.

The patrol car slowed as it approached Edith Sherman's driveway. Her name and address were painted in leaning letters on the mailbox. A ring of faded wooden tulips circled the rotting post it was nailed to.

The sunlight shimmered off the spider web of cracks in the windshield as he started up the pitted gravel driveway. The gate that barred the driveway leaned open on one rusted hinge. The chain that lashed it closed to a rusted metal post hung cut in two. Further up the gravel drive he saw the ambulance parked in the shade of a giant oak overhanging the sagging front porch.

As he eased to a stop in front of the hundred-year-old farm house, he took mental pictures of the scene, images that might later yield critical clues. It was often the small details, easily overlooked, that made a case—at least that's how it was in the detective magazines he'd read as long as he could remember.

Andy Jaspers and Cindy Fontaine, Yamhill County Medical paramedics, met him by the front porch swing.

"It's confirmed," Cindy said.

"Laceration on her neck severed the right jugular," Andy added.

"Nothing we could do." She looked at Andy. "Died, what would you guess . . . yesterday?"

Andy nodded.

Cindy held out a thin strip of paper with a straight blue line running its length. "Here's the EKG strip. No pulse."

Terrence reached for the strip then paused. Evidence was critical and had to be handled carefully. A sharp defense attorney could turn the prosecution's case to ash by harping on sloppy police procedure. Contamination could swing a jury and set a perpetrator free. He pulled a pair of large latex gloves from his breast pocket and worked to pull them over his hands. When the left glove ripped, he abandoned the effort.

"It's just the strip," Cindy said.

He pinched the strip like it was a dead spider and

tucked it into his pocket.

Terrence pulled out his notebook and flipped to the first empty page, trying to recall the crime scene procedures he'd learned at the academy. He jotted down the crew's names and recorded the time.

"Your report?" Terrence said

"We'll write it up tonight," Andy said.

Cindy squinted into the sunshine and nodded. "The ME—"

"ME?"

"The medical examiner. He's been notified," Cindy said. "Should be here in an hour or so."

"An hour," Terrence repeated, still searching for his mental checklist of things to do at a homicide. He glanced at his windshield and Bronson looked back, panting.

Cindy spat a wad of chew into the gravel.

"Any signs of foul play?" Terrence asked.

The paramedics looked at each other then Cindy said, "Like we said. She's got a laceration—that's a cut— about three or four inches long on her neck. No other obvious signs of trauma. Appears to have bled to death. Seems pretty unusual to us."

Andy turned and stifled a laugh.

Terrence felt his face growing hotter. "Where's she at?"

Andy cleared his throat and motioned to the side of the house. "Around back that way. After you."

Terrence focused on the details as they walked past bed sheets flapping from the clothesline like ship sails in the dusty breeze. He paused to look inside the barn that leaned on rotting timbers. In the shadows he saw a dust-covered tractor, an old Buick on blocks, bales of hay, and an assortment of sharp, rusty implements: cycles, scythes, sheers, and pitchforks. They continued past an ancient apple tree surrounded by the sweet smell of fermenting apples rotting in the brown grass beneath. Its tangled branches spread over a stump scarred from years of splitting wood. Fresh cut kindling was scattered at the stump's base. They followed a trail of blood that lead to a garden bounded by a chicken-wire fence. The smell of steer manure and rotting grass hung thick in the air. Tomatoes and lettuce fought with the weeds to suck the last of the water from the soil.

Edith's body lay face down in the brown earth. Her hands clawed the dirt. An axe tilted from the ground, its head driven into the soft soil beside her. The gash on her neck was crusted with coagulated blood, and a brown puddle congealed like pudding in the dirt beneath her left cheek. Her face was turned, and her eyes stared expressionless at the back porch as if she'd forgotten something inside.

Numbness began to wash over Terrence. He'd never seen a dead body in person before and felt the urge to touch her, to feel the reality of it. He knelt close to her and shooed the flies away from eyes clouded with cataracts.

For a moment, he regretted leaving the safety of the garage where he'd worked since he was in high school. He missed the routine: changing oil, lubricating drive trains, repairing flats. Part of him wanted to return to a place where lives did not end with a question mark.

Do something, he thought. You have to do something. Andy cleared his throat, jarring Terrence back to the present. He pulled out his notebook. "Who called?"

Cindy leafed through papers clipped to her metal clipboard. "Looks like . . . anonymous."

Terrence carefully retraced his steps out of the garden and stepped back across the chicken-wire fence.

"Oh." Andy snapped his fingers then dug in his uniform pocket. He held out a business card. "Found this in the door when we arrived."

Terrence absently grabbed it, wishing again that he had pair of gloves to keep himself from being contaminated by the crime scene. He read the name and title embossed on the card's face: John Madison, Chief of Police, Sheridan Police Department.

"Fell out when we knocked on the front door," Andy said. "Guess I should have left it there. Sorry."

Cindy shook her head.

Terrence tapped the card nervously against his palm, taking in Edith. Something was wrong, terribly wrong, but the puzzle was missing too many pieces for the answer to take shape.

"If we're done here, we need to get going," Cindy said.

"What? Oh, yeah. I'll go with you."

As the three of them returned to the front of the house, Terrence wrestled with the feeling that he was responsible. He felt like he was treading water with all his gear on. The gun belt, the bullets, the badge, all that authority was pulling him under.

Andy and Cindy stood next to the ambulance. Terrence leaned against his car, its lights flashing dimly, waiting for some part of him to slip back into gear.

"Officer?" Andy said. "Terrence?"

"Yeah."

"You all right?" Cindy asked.

"Yeah, fine. Why?"

"Just asking," she said. "Need anything else?"

"No. No thanks. I'll be in touch."

Terrence watched as the ambulance backed up and started down the driveway, bouncing a slalom course through the ruts, stirring up another cloud of dust. Standing alone, he felt like a part of him had been pushed off the edge of the world with Edith.

The Civil War football game was about to start. The Reservation Tavern was overrun with Oregon State Beavers fans and Oregon Ducks supporters. The tables by the window were filled with Beavers loyalists. The Ducks supporters claimed booths along the wall. With one exception, the indifferent sat at the bar. The temperature inside rose while each faction made predictions and debated the odds of a strong-armed quarterback versus a senior defensive line.

Madison turned up the volume on the television above the bar, only encouraging the crowd to argue their cases more loudly. He took a long drag from his cigarette and chased it with the rest of his mug of beer.

The talking heads on TV yielded as the camera cut to the captains of each team and their entourages facing off midfield. The referee between them explained the intricacies of the coin toss. As the camera followed the coin's course up and down through the air, Madison exhaled a cloud of smoke. "Heads," He said. Heads it was.

The Ducks elected to receive, and the TV cut to commercial. Sharon slid a mug of beer to Daniel Ammons seated two stools to the right of the chief. She sent another skating Elmer Caldwell's direction, a bank shot that skipped off the half-empty basket of nuts in front of Madison.

The phone rang behind the dark mahogany bar.

Sharon screwed a finger into her left ear and pressed the handset to the other. "Oh, hey Doris . . . Yeah, he's here . . . I'm not his mother." She looked at Madison. "Okay, hold on." She held the phone out toward Madison. "It's for you."

Madison's eyes were glued to the TV as the beer commercial ended and the camera zoomed onto the field. He stuck out his hand waiting for Sharon to pass him the phone. She slapped it into his hand, as the kicker positioned the ball on the tee.

"Chief Madison?" Doris said, her voice laced with irritation.

His neck knotted. "Yeah, it's me." Doris had a gift. Her words were like a gristly steak marinated in gasoline. He'd gone rounds with her supervisor, demanding that she be fired. Then Doris became the supervisor.

"Chief," Doris said. "Forget that radio of yours again? Kind of hard to reach you without it."

Madison scooped a handful of nuts. "I knew you were working. You've got my undivided attention."

"Terrence is asking for you."

"That right?" Madison felt his face redden as he recalled ordering him not to leave the station. Terrence, like most new officers, was eager, too eager. One of the few young people in town who had both the interest in being a cop and a clean enough record to pass the background. At over six and a half feet tall, he could command respect. But Terrence stood in a perpetual slouch, like his skin had shrunk in the dryer. Madison wondered what Terrence had gotten into this time.

"What's he need?" Madison said.

"Got a suspicious death he'd like some help with if you can fit it into your busy schedule."

Madison tossed a nut into his mouth and bit. "I told him to park it. Didn't he tell you?"

"No other units were available. It is your jurisdiction—"

"Suspicious how?"

"Neck injuries, near decapitation. Ambulance crew's getting ready to leave."

"Okay, I'm on my way. Tell him to hold tight until I get there." Madison held the phone toward Sharon who continued to wipe mounds of peanut shells floating in puddles of beer onto the floor.

"What's it this time?" she asked. "Cows in the road? Kids smoking at the park? Music too loud?"

He rolled his eyes and shook the phone. "Wouldn't you like to know." The phone slipped from his moist fingers, bounced off the bar, and landed at her feet. "Gotta go." He grabbed a fistful of nuts, chugged down the rest of his mug of beer, and took a last look at the TV. The ball sailed high into the end zone where the Oregon receiver caught it and ran to the five yard line where he was blasted. The ball sprang loose and Oregon State recovered.

Madison walked out into the dusty October haze and climbed into his sweltering Suburban. He cranked down the window and turned the air conditioner on high, as beads of sweat ran down his forehead. He slid on his sunglasses, wondering how much damage Terrence had already done.

The morning's liquor churned in his stomach, as he rehearsed the tongue lashing he'd unleash on Terrence for disobeying orders. Traffic was picking up on the freeway below as he crossed Highway 18. His stomach lurched as the Suburban tossed and pitched up the driveway toward Edith's. He rolled under the shade beside Terrence's dust covered police car.

Terrence leaned heavily against the car, fanning through his notebook. A low rumbling growl came from Bronson in the back seat, looking through the bars covering the back windows.

Madison's gut felt like he'd swallowed a life raft that was steadily inflating. He sat a moment longer, breathing in the air conditioned breeze then rolled down his window.

Terrence walked through the settling dust and propped his arms on the top of the Suburban.

"What part of park it don't you understand?" Madison demanded.

Terrence looked down. "Dispatch said no county units were available. They couldn't reach you—"

"We'll deal with that later. What have we got?"

"Deep laceration to her neck made with a sharp instrument. Didn't see any sign of struggle though. Strange—"

"Has the medical examiner been notified?"

"Yes, sir."

"How long till he gets here?"

Terrence thumbed through his notebook, "Medical examiner was notified at 14:13 hours. Dispatch said he was delayed and would get here as soon as he could."

The dusty air drifted in through the Suburban's window. "Let's have a look. Where is she?"

"She's out back."

Madison felt his gut expanding. The dust stirred with each step as he followed Terrence around to the back. Terrence pointed out his observations along the way. Madison made a few of his own.

They stopped at the edge of the chicken-wire fence, and Terrence pointed. Edith's body lay sprawled face-down, an axe wedged in the dirt beside her head.

"Looks like the perpetrator used the axe on her. You can see the gash on her neck where she bled out." Terrence nodded toward the apple tree. "The trail of blood comes from over there. I figure she was trying to escape to the back door when she collapsed here. The perpetrator must have approached her from behind and surprised her. I didn't see any defensive wounds. May have got off some blows of her own before . . . "

Working the north end of Portland, Madison had seen his share of murder scenes. None of them like this. He looked at the axe sticking out of the earth like it had grown there with the tomatoes. Then he considered the droplets of blood, liquid breadcrumbs leading to the splitting stump. He looked up at Terrence's grimy face. "What makes you say that?"

"What?"

"'She was attacked from behind? May have gotten off some blows of her own?'"

Terrence picked up a rock then dropped it. "The position of the axe. Appears she had it in her hand when she fell. There's blood on the handle and her hands. Seems reasonable, pending further investigation of course."

The pressure in Madison's gut was boiling into his chest. "Terrence don't you have something useful you can do?"

"Thought I'd get the camera and take some pictures. Document the crime scene."

"Crime scene? You sure about that?" Not wanting to hear his answer, Madison waved him off.

Terrence started toward the front. As he neared the

corner of the house, Madison shouted, "Terrence, who called this in?"

Terrence looked at his notebook and shrugged.

"We don't know who called?"

"No, sir. Dispatch didn't say. The ambulance crew said it was anonymous."

Madison felt the ground start to tilt and grabbed the spindly wire fence to steady himself. Terrence returned with the Polaroid camera and started snapping crime scene photos.

Madison had taken this job as a working retirement — emphasis heavy on "retirement." He'd grown to hate big-city department politics that got him into such grief in Portland. In Sheridan, Madison was content to finish his career as a big fish in a little pond. The chief's badge turned the little town in a Sunday buffet of sweet rolls and gravy. He intended to keep it that way.

When the ground steadied, Madison opened his eyes and looked again at Edith's body sprawled in the dirt. He rose and brushed the dirt from his hands. "Too bad. I hear she was a decent lady. Careless with an axe though."

Terrence lowered the camera from his eye. "Careless?"

Madison waved toward her and shrugged.

"You think she killed herself by accident?"

He nodded and dabbed beads of sweat from his forehead.

"Are you sure, Chief? The blood . . . her neck . . . how could she—"

"Terrence, how many deaths have you investigated?"

"I don't . . . this one's my first, but—"

"One. And where did you receive your training in crime scene investigation?"

"The academy." Terrence smeared a dirty streak of sweat across his forehead and stared blankly.

"That's right. What, ten hours? And who's been doing this since you were still filling your diapers?"

Terrence nodded.

"Right again. Now be a good boy and help the medical examiner load her up when he gets here. I'll talk with him tomorrow. Any questions?"

"Yes, sir. I mean, no, sir."

"Good. Don't forget to write your report tonight before you leave. I'll need it by tomorrow morning. We can fix it when I get in."

"You'll have it by morning." Terrence fumbled again with his notebook and scribbled. "Oh, there was something else." He pulled a business card from the back of the notebook.

Madison's gut was doing somersaults and his bowels cramped. "It'll have to wait. I have some business to attend to. Get your report done before you go home."

Terrence slid the business card back into his notebook. "Yes, sir."

Mayor Dickerson led his entourage through the front doors into the gloom of the Reservation Tavern. Steven Ambrose, Deputy Director of the Bureau of Prisons, and Maureen Thracker, his legal adviser, strutted just behind him. Two men in suits and sunglasses followed next. Madison dabbed the sweat from his forehead as he trailed at the rear.

"Hello, Mrs. Sherman," Dickerson said.

"Mayor Dickerson," Sharon said, "room's ready. I'll be back in a minute to get your orders."

"Thank you, Mrs. Sherman." He turned to his court.

"Follow me. We will be in the General Sheridan Room."

The Tiffany lamp hanging in the center of the room cast a yellow and red sunset over the round table beneath. The walls were decorated with paintings of General Sheridan seated on a white stallion surrounded by vanquished enemies kneeling at his feet.

Dickerson sat in a plush leather chair.

Maureen Tracker's eyes flitted about the room aware and wary. Steven Ambrose pulled a wooden chair out and nudged Thracker further away from Dickerson and sat between them.

Madison sat as far away from the mayor as the round table allowed. One of the suits stood with his back to the door while the other examined the walls and ceiling vents.

"So good to see you again," Dickerson said. "I trust your flight was pleasant."

"Always nice to get out of town," Ambrose said.

Thracker looked at the laminated two-page menu.

"And your accommodations?" Dickerson said to Thracker.

"Quite a place. Survived a fire in thirteen and flood in sixty-four," she said.

"Yes, indeed. One of two buildings that did. This is the other. We are looking forward to revitalizing the downtown when this deal goes through."

"Progress," Ambrose said. "*Tempus fugit.*"

The suit by the door opened it, and Sharon walked into the room. She plucked the pen from above her ear and poised it over her order pad. "What can I get you?"

"I'll have some coffee, decaf," Thracker said.

"Martini for me," Ambrose said. "And water."

"I'll check on that. Beer for the chief?"

"Beer would be fine," Madison said. "You know the

one."

"Budweiser for the chief." Sharon said.

That will be all," Dickerson said, shooing her away.

"No refreshments for you, Mayor?"

Dickerson ignored her. "Shall we get started?"

Ambrose said, "As we discussed last time, the acquisition of the property is time-sensitive. Washington needs to show movement on this. There's some concern that funding could be in jeopardy. Midterms are coming up and revenues aren't meeting projections. Our democratic colleagues have other priorities. We need progress on the prison or we stand a chance of losing our funding." Ambrose looked at Thracker, "I'm told legal has yet to receive the papers for their review."

"That's correct," she said. "The committee's window for review is quickly closing."

"Are we making progress with her signature?" Ambrose asked.

Dickerson said, "I think we have good news on that front."

The door bumped into the suit standing guard. The sound of glass tinkling was followed by a splash.

"Shit." Sharon's voice grumbled on the other side of the door.

Ambrose waved, and the suit stepped aside and opened the door.

Sharon entered with a tray of drinks, one lying sideways, and the others standing in a puddle of beer. She set the tray on the table and passed out the wet glasses. "Chief, I'll be back with the rest of your drink. She balanced the tray with its puddle in her palm and walked over to the suit blocking her way.

Sharon stopped at the door and the suit pulled it open. "Might not want to barricade the door. I'll be in and out." The tray tipped, spilling amber liquid on his shinny black shoes.

Ambrose and Thracker exchanged smiles.

Dickerson continued, "Chief Madison can provide you with the documents. You did bring them?"

"Documents?" Madison seemed to have forgotten what the word meant.

"The contract? Mrs. Sherman?"

Madison spun his mug. "There have been . . . developments. Perhaps we could discuss them in private for a moment."

"Nonsense." The mayor looked at the inquiring eyes of his guests. "We have no secrets here. Of what developments are you speaking?"

Madison's finger drew on the moist drops running down his glass. "I'd rather . . . "

"Did you bring the papers or not?" Dickerson demanded. "It's a simple question."

"She wasn't home."

Dickerson felt his face grow hot as he glared at the chief. He turned to Thracker and Ambrose. "She signed them but gave me the wrong copies by mistake when I visited her recently. She's not as mentally sound as she once was."

"I don't need to remind you we can't proceed until we have her signature," Thracker said. "If we have doubts as to her mental capacity, that's a whole other issue. I'm beginning to have grave doubts about this arrangement."

"Ms. Thracker, I assure you there is no reason for concern. Perhaps I've overstated. Edith—Mrs. Sherman—is in full possession of her faculties. She assures me she is delighted with the sale of her property. This is simply an oversight we can easily correct. We will have signed copies before the council meeting next week."

Ambrose sucked the gin and vermouth from his olive. "Anything we need to know, Chief?"

"Nope. Everything's just great," Madison said.

The final presentation to council will go forward as planned," Dickerson said. "You'll both be in attendance, I assume?"

"Wouldn't miss it for the world," Ambrose said. "We will be happy to address any concerns that may arise." He looked at Madison again. "Chief, what's the mood?"

"The mood? Same as always. Old and cranky."

Ambrose sipped his drink. "How cranky?"

Dickerson shook his head. "The usual malcontents—"

"Armed malcontents," Madison said.

"Armed with what?" Thracker asked.

"It's all legal," Dickerson said. "Local militia, harmless. Just like to wear uniforms and play war on the weekends."

Ambrose sipped his martini. "Militia?"

Dickerson said, "A handful of boys with nothing better to do. Fancy themselves patriots fighting to defend themselves from the tyranny of government. That sort of thing. All show and no go. They won't be a problem."

"We have dealt with their type before," Thracker said.

Ambrose said, "We've had good success with such groups. We simply offer them a chance to wear a real uniform at the proposed facility."

"Good luck on the background," Madison said.

"I am sure some of them could pass it," Ambrose said. "At least we can hold out the possibility . . . "

"Wonderful," Dickerson said. "Then we're all set."

"We do have one issue to address," Thracker said.

"The will. It appears—"

"Coming through." Sharon spoke through the crack in the door.

"I thought that was amended?" Ambrose said, as Sharon squeezed through the door. "Besides, if she's signed over the property, what difference does it make?"

Thracker sat back in her chair silent, while Sharon dealt out the plates. Sharon looked over the table. "Ketchup's by the napkins. Here's the A-1. Chief, need another mug?"

"Thanks darlin'," Madison said. He tipped his mug for a drink. "Remember what I said."

"That will be quite enough," Dickerson said. "Thank you, Mrs. Sherman. Please, no more interruptions." The suit stepped back as Sharon exited, and locked the door behind her.

Thracker frowned at her plate then pushed it aside. "With all due respect, the heir certainly could object to the disposition of the property. I understand he doesn't approve of the sale."

Dickerson sliced off a strip of steak and held it dangling on his fork. "He's an addict and a cripple. I don't see why he should have any say. If you knew the grief he's caused—"

He's certain to raise the question of her mental capacity."

"Hank?" Ambrose said.

Dickerson chewed the gristly steak. "Her son. War hero gone bad. A crackpot. I can handle him."

"And his followers?" Thracker said. "The militia you called it?"

"A bunch of good-old-boys just trying to defend American values. Harmless." Dickerson said.

"How harmless are their guns?" Thracker asked.

Ambrose sawed through his charred steak. "Like I said, show them some uniforms and promise them a good paying job. In my experience, a sharp uniform and some beer money is all it takes."

"Hank's had his fill of uniforms," Madison said. "Doubt it would appeal to him much."

"Let's get back to Edith's capacity," Thracker said.

"Let Hank contest the sale if he wants," Ambrose said. "We've got her signature."

"It means nothing unless it was freely given." Thracker turned to Dickerson. "You've been visiting her for how long?"

"I've known her for thirty-some years. She was my teacher in eighth grade."

"That's not what I asked. How many times have you been to see her about *this*?"

"A few, I guess. I don't see—"

"Did you make her any promises? Offer any inducements?"

"Just my appreciation on behalf of the citizens of—"

"Are you confident she understood the terms of the contract? Was she given opportunity to—"

"I explained it to her very thoroughly. She seemed satisfied."

"She seemed satisfied?"

"She understood."

"She understood she was selling, if I can even use that term, selling her property for about a hundred dollars an acre?"

"She wanted to help the community. She viewed it as her legacy."

"If her mental state is in question, Hank will certainly contest whether her signature was freely and knowingly made. How can you be certain she knew what she was agreeing to when she signed the forms?"

"She knew," Dickerson said.

"Did she?" Thracker continued. "I understand her husband founded the Sheridan Militia. He was not exactly a strong supporter of the government. Now she's agreeing to practically give her land away to the very government he opposed? That's a difficult argument to make."

"She isn't giving it away."

"One hundred dollars an acre? Sounds like a gift to me."

Dickerson sawed on another piece of steak. "I can assure you, she was in full possession of her faculties when I spoke with her. We became very close following the death of her husband. I was a great comfort to her in her time of grief. She welcomed the opportunity to do something meaningful with her land. She thought of it as a kind of memorial to her deceased husband."

"A sentiment her son does not share," Thracker said.

"He never was any help to her. A waste. Hank would let it rot or turn it into some kind of boot camp for the militia."

Ambrose said, "Even if he is opposed, in my experience, his kind are easy enough to persuade. We simply play up his status as a decorated war hero and defender of freedom. Maybe we can offer him a position at the prison."

"Aren't you forgetting a small detail?" Madison said. "The background check. How is Hank going to get past those questions about drug use? And a physical. Can't see Hank doing too good at that either, missing fingers and all."

Ambrose smiled. "Background and physical, like the ones you passed? I said we could make the offer. If by some miracle he passes, we give him some title with no responsibility."

"Unless you can get Hank on board," Thracker said, "I must strongly advise moving to the alternative site. We just don't have the time litigation could take."

"I can handle him," Dickerson said.

"That still leaves the vote for approval," Thracker said.

"The council won't be a problem," Dickerson said. "They see the value of the prison. They've watched this town slowly crumble and want to see it revived as much as I do. Besides, I've added a little incentive."

Thracker slid her coffee cup away. "Should I even ask?"

"Mayor, we've been at this for a year and a half now," Ambrose said, "and frankly, my boss is beginning to wonder if you can get this done. There are other sites under consideration. Yours is our first choice, but . . . "

"I got you the land didn't I? I will get you the vote. And when I do, don't forget your end of the bargain."

Ambrose smiled, "You deliver and so will I."

Terrence sat in the driver's seat of his police car trying to reassemble the puzzle that exploded when Chief Madison arrived. The car's emergency lights turned in slow circles dimmed to a dull glow beneath a thick layer of dust. The red sun melted into the west hills, painting the fields crimson.

Beneath the fading dome light, Terrence thumbed through the notes he'd scrawled in his notebook since he arrived, then flipped to the back cover where the chief's business card was tucked. John Madison, Chief of Police, Sheridan Oregon. A man used to getting what he wants.

He flexed the card in his fingers. Why had the chief been to Edith's earlier? How could he be so certain her death was an accident? Terrence couldn't erase the image of her lying in the dirt, staring vacantly into some other world as the blood congealed beneath the gaping gash in her neck.

Terrence's thoughts drifted with the warm evening breeze to the one-room schoolhouse where Edith once reigned supreme. He could still feel the straight-backed wooden chair with one short leg he'd occupied until outgrowing it in fourth grade. She'd patiently helped him with his letters after school. Terms like dyslexia or attention deficit disorder were not a part of her vocabulary.

Terence believed he occupied a tender spot in her heart, and that was why she pushed him all the more. She called him Terrible Terrence, a name that was soon on the tongues of all the kids on the playground. She'd say it with a smile, and he'd drink in this rare taste of adult affection. By the sixth grade, he stood head and shoulders above her. A slight woman, she commanded respect by virtue of her skill wielding the wooden ruler. She'd painfully measured his knuckles more than once.

The medical examiner's van turned from the main road and began up the driveway. The lights of the van flashed in Terrence's rear view mirror then pulled in behind him, kicking up a fresh cloud of dust like it had just touched down on the moon. The driver's door swung open, and the ME stepped out. The glow of the sunset turned him into a bronze statue standing on bowed legs. The short man dressed in a dark suit, cowboy boots, and a bolo necktie, looked like a rodeo star who'd been thrown too many times. His hair was pulled back into a gray ponytail.

He tipped his hat. "Officer. Don't know that we've met." He reached out his hand covered with blue latex. "I'm Joseph Walksontop, Yamhill County Medical Examiner. You can call me Joseph."

Terrence seized the thick hand that squeezed like a vise. "Officer Washburn. Pleased to meet you." Bronson stood alert behind the metal bars covering the back window and bared his teeth. "You can call me Terrence."

Joseph turned to the dog and muttered something. Bronson looked at Terrence, sniffed, and laid down. "You're new aren't you?"

"No. Well, I've been here a couple years, in Sheridan. So, yeah, I guess . . . "

Joseph smiled. "The dispatcher gave me most of the details I need. Anything you want to add?"

A warm gust bent the dried grass and lifted leaves into the air. "No. Not really. I'll give my report to the chief." Terrence plucked a reed and began sucking on it. "Seems we have a slight difference on how we see things."

"Oh?" Joseph stood slightly stooped and lopsided. His brown eyes stared unblinking, reflecting the dying flame of the sunset. "How so?"

"Nothing. It's just . . . it doesn't add up."

Joseph studied him.

"I just don't see it. How could . . . " Terrence shook his head then pointed to the back of the house. "I'll show you where she's at."

"Before we go back, could you help me with the gurney?" Joseph limped to the back of the van and pulled open the doors. "My back's not what it used to be. The rest of me either."

Terrence slid the metal cart out of the back and the

legs scissored open. He pushed the gurney from behind while Joseph steered the front. As they approached the splitting stump, Terrence nodded. "The blood trail starts over there where she split the wood. Probably where the axe came from." The front wheels dropped into a rut, and the gurney nosedived, jamming the frame into Terrence's gut. Joseph raised the front and Terrence pushed. They steadied the cart and resumed their course. Terrence pointed to the garden. "There she is." They parked the gurney beside the chicken-wire fence and loosened the straps that held the black plastic body bag in place on top.

Joseph studied Edith then stepped across the fence. He stood over her body, mumbling. Terrence stepped across the fence and crouched beside him to look at the injury to her neck a last time.

"Too bad." Joseph said. "She was a nice lady."

"You knew her?"

"Most folks in Sheridan did. I knew her only by reputation."

"Oh?"

"Maybe now she can find peace."

"Must be awful to go that way," Terrence said. "So violent, savage . . . "

Joseph crouched beside Terrence. "When we look at the dead, it's often ourselves we see. What do you see when you look at her?"

"What?"

Joseph pointed at her. "Look. What do you see?"

"Edith. The cut on her neck. The blood. Mostly her eyes." Terrence brushed the flies away from them. "Her face, terrified."

Joseph looked at Terrence and cocked his head. "Terrified?"

"Wouldn't you be if someone attacked you?"

"If I was attacked." He pushed on his knees to stand. "I see relief. Peace even. The end of suffering."

"I wish I could believe that, but it just doesn't make sense. Like you said, we see what we want to see."

"Would you mind helping me load her up?"

Joseph unzipped the black body bag and laid it out beside her. "Help me lift her into the bag. I'll get the feet. You get her arms."

Terrence's feet sank into the soft soil above Edith's head. He stared down at her lifeless face. The side of her face touching the ground appeared bruised where the blood pooled when her heart stopped. He fought the urge to close her eyes and grabbed beneath her shoulders instead. Her skin was cool against his sweaty hands as he lifted. Her head slumped backward, and a gurgling sound escaped her mouth as they carefully laid her on the bag. Joseph grabbed the zipper by her feet and began to pull upward.

"She was my teacher all through grammar school," Terrence said. "Nice lady, one of the few." The contours of her body bulged up against the black bag as Joseph pulled the zipper over her face. She'd be suffocating in the heat if she was still alive. Terrence felt the urge to unzip the bag, to give her one more chance to breathe.

Joseph cinched the straps over the body bag, and they wheeled her around front and loaded the gurney into the van. Joseph started the engine and closed the rear doors. "Have the chief give me a call if he's got any questions. I'll do the forensic examination tomorrow. I would like you to join me if possible. Sometimes the officer at the scene can answer questions."

Terrence used his sleeve to wipe the sweat from his forehead, remembering the autopsy video he'd watched at the academy. He'd closed his eyes when the first cut was made. "Anything I can do to help. I'll be there."

"I'll let you know the time."

Terrence opened his notebook and thumbed to the last page. "What do you think killed her?"

Joseph pulled the handkerchief from his back pocket and wiped the sweat from his brow. "The laceration on her neck severed her jugular vein. It wouldn't take long—a minute or two—to bleed to death." He folded the handkerchief and looked up at Terrence. "If it helps, with an injury like this she probably didn't feel much pain. It would be sort of like falling asleep."

"Yeah, but the chief thinks it was her own carelessness. Do you think it was an accident?"

The van's tail lights reflected in Joseph's eyes. "Son, in my thirty years in this business I've seen things you wouldn't believe—people plowed under by their own tractors, drowned in their own bathtubs. When sharp tools are in play, anything is possible. Don't even get me started with guns."

"But it could have been something else? Maybe it wasn't an accident?"

"I can tell you what specific injury lead to a person's death. I can even give you a pretty good guess as to the time. The body tells me all I need to know." He stripped off his gloves and wiped sweaty grit from his neck. "Accident or murder? That's a question I leave to you. Sometimes, things aren't what they seem."

But sometimes they are, Terrence thought. Sometimes people don't want to face the truth. Sometimes they have things to hide.

Joseph climbed into the van. "Thanks for your help." He looked to the black hills as the last of the sun's evening glow gave way to the brightest stars. "Take care of yourself young man. I'll talk with the chief on Monday."

As the van weaved down the driveway, Terrence struggled to shake the feeling that he'd forgotten something.

Bronson barked in the back of his car and pawed at the door. Terrence opened the back door and Bronson leapt into the dust. Each pad of his paw sent up a tiny mushroom cloud. The dust clinging to his fur dulled the shine of his coat. Bronson sniffed the ground as he trotted over to the roots of the giant oak tree.

There is still so much to do, Terrence thought. Why didn't the chief see it? How could the ME believe her injuries were the result of an accident? Terrence's report could support that theory. *Let sleeping dogs lie,* Madison would say.

An accident would be so much easier. No imagining the horrifying last moments of her fight to survive. No hunt for a killer on the loose and the panic that would spread through the town like a swarm of locusts. Life could resume in the illusion of safety. Sheridan could shake its head at Edith's foolishness and dwell on the good memories she left with four generations of students.

He sympathized with the relief writing a less horrifying ending to her story could bring. He shared the desire to end her life in peace. But would it be the truth?

Bronson sniffed the oak's roots and lifted his leg. "In," Terrence said. When Bronson had finished his business, he leapt into the back seat and dug the tennis ball from the floorboard. He sat with the ball in his mouth as Terrence shut the door.

Terrence walked back to the garden for a final look at

the crime scene. There he saw the axe's wooden handle leaning into the evening air like a moonlit sundial, a slender shadow stretching across the place where Edith had lain moments ago. His heart jumped as he realized he'd almost forgotten this critical piece of evidence, the piece that might trap her killer and perhaps remove the blinders that kept people from facing the truth. He pulled the axe from the soil, feeling the smooth wood grain in his palm. The heavy steel head was caked with blood and dirt. He carried it back to his car and carefully wrapped it in a paper bag to preserve trace evidence. Maybe he'd get lucky and the blood of her attacker would be found. He laid the axe in the trunk between a box of flares and the spare tire.

The warm air swirled, caressing his face with dusty fingers. Terrence realized he was not alone. The ghosts of the departed hung in the air.

Dickerson sat simmering in his Cadillac beneath the flickering alley light, replaying the chief's drunken behavior. If Madison wanted to disgrace himself, that was his business, but his behavior among these distinguished guests was too much. Something would have to be done. His thoughts were interrupted when Madison tapped on the window. Just the man I need to talk to, he thought. He pressed the button and the tinted window slid down.

"We've got to talk," Madison said.

Dickerson's shoved the car door open against Madison's gut. "Come to tender your resignation?" He stood and adjusted his pearl-studded cufflinks. "What the hell is the matter with you?"

Madison shrugged. "What?"

"If our guests had any doubts you are a drunk, they have them no longer." Dickerson shut the car door. "I gave you a simple job, and you fail. Then you show up drunk to the meeting. You're an embarrassment. Perhaps it's time you and I parted company."

Madison's bloodshot eyes studied him. "Nothing I'd like better. Just thought you'd want to know I went to Edith's."

"Yes, I know."

"No, after. Dispatch sent me. Terrence was there already."

"Terrence?"

"The kid you hired."

"Yes, I know who Terrence is. Why was he there?"

Madison leaned against the Cadillac and lit a cigarette. "Because she's dead."

"Who's dead?"

"Edith."

"Edith Sherman?"

"The very same."

"Are you sure?"

Madison blew a jet of smoke over Dickerson's head. "Yep. Saw her myself."

Dickerson leaned against his car door. "How?"

"Looks like an accident. Cut her own neck with an axe while splitting wood."

"Jesus, when I asked you to persuade her, I didn't mean . . . and you expect me to believe she cut her own neck? With an axe?"

"Seen stranger things."

"You can't be serious. If this is another one of your—"

"This is no joke, though its irony's not lost on me." The orange ash at the end of his cigarette brightened as he drew in another breath.

"Why didn't you tell me before the meeting? If our guests had found out—"

"I tried. You were nowhere to be found. Once we got here, I didn't have a chance."

"Tell me this is another example of your twisted sense of humor."

"Don't take my word for it. Ask the ambulance crew or Terrence. I'm sure he'd be happy to fill you in. He's convinced it's murder. Rookies."

Madison pulled out a flask from his vest pocket and took a long drink.

Dickerson began sifting through the possibilities. Murder. The idea hung in the shadows. It just wasn't a word suited to Sheridan. "Are you sure?"

"Seen enough dead bodies for three lifetimes. I'm sure."

Dickerson recalled Hank's insolence when he last visited Edith yesterday. Edith seemed anxious to be rid of her drunken son. Maybe he'd returned when Dickerson left. He imagined the brutal scene. In a drunken rage Hank would have raised the axe, swung, and chopped her down.

"Hank," Dickerson said.

"What about him?"

"He was there when I visited her yesterday."

Madison squinted and held out the flask.

Dickerson reached for it and remembered his promise to swear off the bottle. Surely these were exceptional circumstances. Perhaps just this once. He took a long swallow. "When I left, Hank was there. Of that I am certain. He seemed to be in a foul mood, as usual. They must have been arguing. Edith also seemed upset. You don't suppose—"

"Hank killed her? Wouldn't put it past him. But like I

said, the way it looked—"

Dickerson's thoughts gained momentum. "Hank and Edith had a fight, he attacked her with the axe and made it look like an accident. Is that possible?"

"Not likely."

"Is it possible?"

"Well, yeah, it's possible. But—"

"He stabs her and he inherits the farm."

"Didn't stab her."

"I thought you said—"

"Cut. There's a difference." Madison drew his pocket knife, flipped open the blade, and thrust it toward the Dickerson's stomach. "That's a stab." He swept it across his chest. "That's a cut. The difference between a half-inch wound three inches deep and a three-inch wound half an inch deep." Madison began digging the dirt from beneath his thumbnail.

"Put that disgusting thing away."

"Now in Edith's case, it's not quite so clear. An axe, that's unlikely. But like I said, I've seen stranger. Saw a lady once who got run over by her own car—three times. Seems it slipped into gear as she was unlocking a gate. The wheel was cranked so it drove in a circle. Imagine lying there watching the car come at you the second and third times."

"You'd have us believe she sliced her own neck? With an axe? Not likely."

"There's plenty of blood on the handle. The head of the axe was wedged into the ground beside her."

"Any signs of struggle? I believe you call them defensive wounds."

"Nope."

"No other injuries?"

Madison shook his head and shifted the knife to his

other hand, examining the dirt under the remaining fingernails.

"Any evidence at all?"

"Other than the cut on Edith's neck and her bloody axe?"

Dickerson sipped again. "Witnesses, fingerprints, something to tie Hank—"

"Careful, Mayor. You'd be on the list."

"What is that supposed to mean?"

"You were there, too. The knife cuts both ways—or in this case, the axe."

"We all know Hank's history, his propensity for violence, his psychotic episodes. Who's next? I understand he's no friend of yours, either. We may have a killer on the loose. Hank murdered his own mother for God's sake."

"Bit of a stretch don't you think? Sure, they didn't always get along, but still, I just don't see it."

"Don't you think it would be prudent to at least bring him in for questioning? Perhaps you could conduct an actual investigation? It's about time you earned your salary."

Madison folded his knife and clipped it to his front pocket. "Does kind of take care of him fighting the sale of her property."

"Bring him in, get a confession, and solve the murder. You could be a hero by the time this is over."

"You think I came here to be a hero? It's overrated."

"What about that eager young officer of yours?"

"Terrence? Too eager. What about him?"

"You said he is convinced Edith was murdered. Did he say who might have done it?"

"Don't think he got that far. He was pretty shook up."

"You know Terrence looks up to you. He respects

your expertise and experience. Perhaps with some guidance you could help him solve this case. We could get rid of Hank, finalize the sale of the property, and make Terrence a hero. It's almost too good to be true."

"You know what they say about things that seem too good to be true."

"Come out tomorrow and we'll go over the details."

Madison took the flask, tipped it, and began to shuffle into the darkness. He turned and smiled. "You sure she was alive when you left?"

The game crowd had melted away hours ago. The Oregon State fans left complaining the refs stole the game. The Oregon faithful predicted the wide receiver who'd caught the winning pass would be a first-round draft pick. Well-lubricated regulars had drifted out the front door to their cars, too drunk to walk a straight line. The odor of sweat and beer lingered in the cigarette-smoke haze.

Musty air drifted out the back door into the night's dusty breeze. Cooler air crept in the doorway, crawling around the table legs and chairs, depositing a fresh layer of dust.

Terrence parked his cruiser and walked wearily to the chief's favorite booth in the back—Madison's other office. The dim, yellowed bulb above the table highlighted a crack that ran up the middle of the vinyl bench cushion. He spread his papers and Polaroid photos over the crumb-speckled table and began the part of police work he dreaded most.

Once he'd spent three days reporting the theft of a half-rack of Budweiser from Sheridan Grocery. The chief marked up each draft with a red pen and told him to rewrite it. Each fix met with the same fate—more red pen, more redoes. By his sixth try, it seemed the report was almost back to where he'd started. When he turned it in, Madison simply handed it to Beverly and told her to pick up where he'd left off.

An hour later, Terrence shook the cramps out of his fingers as he considered the questions a defense attorney might ask. A black-and-white Perry Mason courtroom drama unfolded in his mind.

He imagined a high-powered lawyer from way out of town scrutinizing each word of his report, yanking them out of context, and twisting them into pretzels. The witness chair would give him little comfort as all eyes of the jury fixed on him. The defense attorney, dressed in a pinstriped suit, would lean on the rail before the jurors and smile. "Officer, you wrote, and I quote, 'the deceased was lying face down in the garden,' but you also wrote, 'she was looking over her right shoulder.'" The jurors would look at him with accusing eyes as the attorney approached the witness stand, waving his thin, handwritten report for dramatic effect. "This is your report isn't it, officer?" His finger would stab the report with each word. "Well, which one is it? Was she looking down, or was she looking over her shoulder?"

Terrence returned to that section, thankful he'd used an erasable pen and rubbed away "face down." He squeezed "on her stomach" in its place. The new phrase didn't feel right as he mumbled the words. The letters were too small, too scrunched together, so he erased again.

Sharon approached with the coffee pot, and Terrence slid his empty cup toward the edge of the table. The aroma of burnt coffee drifted in the air as Sharon dribbled the bottom of the pot into his cup. "How much longer you going to be, Terrence? You know we closed twenty minutes ago."

Terrence spread his hands over the report and sighed. "It's been a long day." He looked up at her frowning face and noted the sunglasses she wore. "Kind of dark in here for sunglasses, isn't it?" Beneath the foundation covering her swollen cheek, Terrence thought he saw the faint darkening of a bruise.

She slid her sunglasses up and picked up a Polaroid. "What are you working on?"

"Can't go into the details." He snatched back the photo and placed it on the table upside down. "Paperwork." Terrence leafed through the seven pages of scrawl he'd produced so far. Too many if Edith's death was an accident. Not nearly enough if it wasn't.

Sharon set the coffee pot on the corner of a manila envelope stamped EVIDENCE. "The chief was here earlier, before the game. I spoke with the 911 operator when the call came in."

"Saw his car out front," Terrence said. "Thought maybe you'd see . . . " He took a sip of tepid coffee.

"You know how it is here," Sharon said. "Didn't think it would stay a secret for long, did you? Who knows what rumors will spread tomorrow. Hell, they're already spreading."

Terrence emptied the cup and looked at the grounds lining the bottom.

She grabbed his cup and poured in the rest of the pot. "When people don't know what's really going on, they fill in the gaps. Someone's got to tell them the truth. I figure you're the best one to do that."

"What're they saying?"

"Oh, you know, filling in the details."

Terrence glanced through the gloom, making sure

they were alone. He leaned toward her and spoke in a low whisper, "What do you think? You think it was an accident?" He fanned through the pages of his notebook, waiting.

She grabbed one of his French fries, rolled it in ketchup, and popped it into her mouth. "What matters, is what you think."

Terrence looked at Madison's business card. "I'm not so sure it was an accident."

She leaned in and stopped chewing. "Me neither."

Terrence welcomed the most reassuring words he'd heard that day. "What do you think happened?"

"You're the expert. All that training you guys go through. What do I know? Seems kind of obvious though, don't you think?" She slid into the booth beside him and put her hand on his.

Terrence relished the once familiar warmth of her hand. With her touch the room grew warmer, and he felt the kinship of two souls about to embark on a dangerous journey. "I think she was murdered."

He dipped his own fry. "How was she supposed to cut her own neck with an axe?"

"Well maybe, I don't know. Stranger things have happened." Some secret seemed to be swelling up inside her, busting to get free.

"What is it?"

"Nothing." She grabbed the Polaroids with trembling fingers and sorted through the photographs. "Who do you think did it?"

Terrence picked up the chief's business card lying next to an evidence bag. "Chief's got this one wrong. I'm telling you, something's not right."

"I'd say. He was at a meeting earlier with the mayor and his cronies."

"He was here? With your dad?"

"Yeah. Him and Ken and Barbie. Some other guys in suits. Chief wasn't looking too good. Not acting like his usual cordial self. Seemed nervous, distracted, like he was being watched."

"The chief was here with the mayor?"

"Yeah, Terrence. They had a long meeting. One of the guys practically threw me to the ground when I walked in to pass out drinks. I heard them talking about Edith and Hank. Something about her farm. When it was over, they left out the back. Cheap SOBs didn't even leave a tip." She plucked the chief's business card from Terrence's hand and read the message scribbled on back, "'Stopped by for the papers. Please call me ASAP.' Where did you get this?"

"Edith's. Paramedics said it fell out the front door when they got there." He held out his hand and she carefully placed it in his palm, holding it there with her own.

She leaned closer. "So what's his business card doing at her place the day she was murdered?"

Sharon was always so certain, so quick to let logic run its course, and willing to stand by her conclusions. He'd looked up to her since they were in grade school. Three years his senior, she didn't mind challenging her teachers—even knowing the punishment that inevitably followed. She possessed confidence, a quality he'd hoped to find in a uniform.

She punched his arm. "What if he had something to do with her murder? What if he's, you know, involved?"

"If he was, why would he leave his card?"

"I don't know. Maybe he never planned to kill her. Maybe things got out of hand. You know she wasn't exactly all there."

"No way. He wouldn't do that."

"What makes you so sure?"

He knew the question was an invitation to an argument he wouldn't win. Her confidence split him into opposing parts. One part wanted to trust his instincts, to uncover leads, to solve a heinous crime. The other wanted to withdraw into the familiar habit of surrender, hoping to earn approval by doing as he was told. He felt like a mutt—part wolf, part lap dog. Sharon was dangling red meat before the predator. The lap dog spoke. "I was with him at the crime scene for one. Chief Madison was investigating—"

"Investigating? More like covering up."

"He examined the scene and listened to me, before he said it was an accident."

"Terrence, sometimes I wonder what's going on inside that head of yours."

He sipped from his cup.

"Don't you see? He kills her then goes back out with you to cover his tracks. Let me guess, he walked all over the place, handled things, left fingerprints. Did he touch her?"

"No. He didn't. He even had me take pictures."

"Was he ever alone with her?"

"No. Well, I guess for a little while when I got the camera."

"There it is."

"There what is?"

"That accounts for anything that might tie him to the murder." After you got the camera, did anything look suspicious?"

"How do you mean?"

She punched him in the shoulder again. "The body. Had it been moved? Anything messed with?"

"Not that I could tell. She was still lying there, and the axe was right beside her. The blood was where you'd expect it from the cut in her neck."

Sharon sat back in the booth staring at the table and the papers spread across it.

Terrence felt like his foot was caught in the jaws of a trap and she was clamping them tighter. "He said it was an accident. Seemed pretty certain . . . "

Sharon picked up a Polaroid showing the gash on Edith's neck and turned the picture toward him. "How was this an accident?"

"Look, I just want to keep an open mind, consider all the possibilities."

"Seems to me like you don't." Sharon looked up startled.

Terrence turned to see Randy standing behind the booth staring at the photos on the table.

"What the . . . "

Terrence took the photo from Sharon and quickly scooped up the rest.

"I'll lock up." Sharon said. "Randy, you go home."

Randy wiped his hands and picked at a sore on his cheek. "What's this?"

"It doesn't concern you, Randy," Sharon said.

"Is that who I think it is? Isn't that Hank's—"

"Randy, you go," Sharon said. "I'll close up. See you tomorrow."

"Want some alone time?"

"I gotta get going, too," Terrence said, stuffing the papers into his briefcase.

Randy winked at the two of them. "Adios, amigos." He shook his head and walked into the office.

"Look," Terrence said, "I've already said too much. Chief's got more experience than I do. It's probably—"

"A cover-up. Don't be so naive. He's playing you."

"Why? Why would he want to kill her? Just doesn't make sense. What's his motive?"

"That's what you've got to figure out. It's called *investigating*, or didn't they teach that at the academy?"

He closed the latches on his briefcase. "I just can't believe it. The chief I mean."

"Who then?"

"I don't know. Let's just forget—"

"Forget that an old lady was murdered and the chief is trying to cover it up? You really just want to close your eyes? I thought you were better than that."

Terrence shook his head. "I've got to turn in my report."

She stood and tapped her fingernails on the coffee pot. "What's that saying written on the side of your car?"

"Emergency Call 911?"

"Hah, hah. The other one. The one you seem to have forgotten—Protect and Serve."

He took a last look at the grounds in his cup and stood.

Sharon said, "I'd suggest you ask yourself if you're cut out for this job."

Sunday

Chief Madison's arm throbbed, and his stomach churned as he drove to Mayor Dickerson's house the next morning. His eyes squinted against the morning sun boring through the fog in his skull. The twisting road up to Chateau Dickerson seemed to slither. He passed under the brick archway that marked the boundary of Dickerson's estate then through an iron gate posted No Trespassing. The Suburban began the winding climb to the tallest hill topped by the mayor's house and wine cellars. He dug through the glove box searching for the bottle of aspirin, emptied the bottle into his hand, and popped four into his mouth.

Madison set the brake as Dickerson rocked in his favorite chair on the porch of his mini-mansion. The house was everything Dickerson was not — tall, elegant, and stately. The vineyards stretched in long rows down the sweeping hills from the house for two hundred acres. Brown-skinned workers tended vines the drought would have left shriveled had Dickerson not diverted water from the city's wells to his fields. While the town rationed, he fed the hungry roots that would ensure a bumper crop of Pinot Noir and Pinot Gris. This year's harvest promised to make Chateau Dickerson a regional label.

Madison clenched his left fist, feeling the unwelcome but familiar tingling in his fingers. He closed his eyes, trying to calm the pounding in his chest and wiped the sweat from his forehead.

"Good morning, Chief." Dickerson raised his glass of lemonade then puckered as he sipped on the straw. "Margaret, would you be so kind as to bring the chief a glass of lemonade? He looks . . . parched." Dickerson tipped the rocker beside him, spilling Chester, their beloved Chihuahua, onto the porch. "Have a seat. You don't look well."

"I'm fine." Madison fell heavily into the chair.

"Perhaps if you reduced your alcohol intake to half a gallon a day?"

Margaret pushed open the screen door. "Chief Madison, nice to see you." She was a dear. Her big brown eyes peered from beneath blue tinted hair, as she stooped and offered him a sweating glass of lemonade.

"Thanks, Margaret," Madison said. "How's my favorite movie star?" He smiled as he remembered her performance as The Woman in last year's production of *Death of a Salesman.*

She blushed then glanced at Dickerson.

Madison pressed the glass to his neck trying to ignore the building pressure in his chest.

Dickerson held out his glass. "A little more."

"Anything else I can get for you, Chief?" Margaret asked.

"What?" Madison felt the throbbing growing more insistent, bringing back memories of the last time his chest had revolted in this way. He rubbed his neck and slowly rotated his head, hoping to dissolve the tension.

"Anything else?" Margaret asked again.

"No, dear. I'm fine," said Dickerson.

"Maybe you should both go inside. The heat—"

"That will be all, Margaret," Dickerson said, rattling the ice in his glass. "Could you be a dear and close the door behind you?"

She frowned and leaned closer to Madison. "Chief, are you sure?"

"Margaret, that will be all," Dickerson said.

She brushed past his outstretched arm and let the screen door slam shut.

Madison's heart thumped unsteadily as he closed his eyes and labored to take deeper breaths.

Dickerson rattled his ice and looked at his glass. "Just be glad Edith isn't here. She would certainly have a homemade remedy. Some concoction of molasses and who knows what. You should have seen what she gave me the day I visited. God rest her soul."

"Guess you won't have to worry about that anymore." Madison took another drink and slumped deeper in the chair. "You wanted to talk."

"The project is at a critical stage. I don't need to tell you what the prison would mean to this town. Tragic as it is, Hank may have handed us a gift. Once he's been brought to justice, he will have no claim to the property. With him gone, we can get on with construction, revitalize this decaying town. We can't dance around this any longer."

Madison looked at the hornets circling their nest tucked in the eves. "So you want me to ignore the evidence? Say Hank killed her?"

"I mean, we need to put this to rest. It seems he's the only real suspect in this case. I would be willing to testify to his presence at her home the day of the murder and to his state of mind. He was intoxicated and irrational."

"Like I said before, the knife cuts both ways. You were there. What if he says you killed her? It's your word against his."

"All the better. Who do you think people are more likely to believe? Me or a drunk with a history of violence? Everybody knows he's not been right ever since his discharge."

"Suppose Hank says he left first. Says you and his mother were together. Maybe he adds that you were upset with her. Points out you were after her property, and she wasn't exactly cooperating."

"Ridiculous."

"Humor me. Then he says you attacked her and left her in the garden for dead. Now you have the land you were after. The trifecta—motive, means, and opportunity. Plausible enough to plant a seed of doubt. Enough to keep him from seeing the inside of a jail cell. Probably not the kind of publicity you want, either."

"I seem to recall that you paid her a visit as well. Perhaps a jury would consider that as a more likely scenario. Your own trifecta as you call it. It would seem you have more motive than I. The building of a prison, expanding your police force, increasing your salary. Your reputation isn't exactly spotless with regard to violence. Suppose some person laid her death at your door?"

"And who would that be?"

"I wonder."

Madison's chest felt like a truck was parked on it. "If I didn't know better, I'd think you were threatening me. Not a smart thing to do to a man with my reputation."

"It's seems you've found a most unfortunate time to acquire a conscience. Or is it fear? Is Hank a little more than you can handle?"

"Please."

"We both know people just don't go around killing themselves with axes," Dickerson said. "Suggesting her death was her own doing reeks of cover up. I, for one, do not relish the idea of spending any of my days behind bars."

"Seems a little extreme," Madison said. "Gotta say though, the thought of you in prison does bring up some images."

"She was murdered, and we both know who did it."

Madison felt throbs of pain pulsing from his neck to his arm. "If this goes to trial, we'll need something called evidence."

"You will do whatever investigating is necessary. Find the evidence and fast. I'd like to have this wrapped up by the council meeting."

"We'll be lucky to have the ME's report by then. You want us to investigate a murder, we'll need assistance."

"Assistance?"

Madison's chest felt like it was catching fire. "The state's Major Crimes Team should handle it. We don't have the horsepower."

"You don't have the motivation, you mean. No. I want this handled internally. The last thing we need is a bunch of nasty headlines."

"Then you better forget murder. Stick with accidental death, like I said."

"I don't think it's too much to ask you and Officer Washburn to handle this."

"That's because you've never investigated a murder."

"Don't play me for a fool, Chief. I hired you for your

experience. Don't pretend you don't know how to investigate. If it's motivation you need —"

"Please, motivate me."

"Let's just say, you will be handsomely rewarded when this deal is closed."

"Reward or bribe? Don't forget who you're talking to."

"Advice I would offer you as well. The knife cuts both ways, remember."

Margaret stepped out with a tray of homemade zucchini bread and a fresh pitcher of lemonade. "I made a little treat."

Dickerson smiled and placed two slices on a napkin in his lap.

Margaret pivoted the tray toward the chief.

Madison waved the offering away.

"Chief, are you sure you're feeling well?" Margaret said. "You look a little pale."

"Margaret, the chief is fine. He was just about to leave. He has important business to attend to."

"Oh?" Margaret said.

"Official business." Dickerson lifted his glass. "I'll give you three days, Chief."

"Then what, the resurrection?"

The rusty car jack leaned as it held the front end of Hank's Jeep off the dirt floor of Randy's garage. Randy sat in a lawn chair in front of the Jeep, nursing a bottle of Bud. Terrence's boots splayed out from beneath the Jeep's engine.

"How's it going under there?" Randy asked. He shook his head at Terrence's size-sixteens flopping back and forth, as he shrimped around beneath the oily engine.

"Yep, it's what I thought," Terrence said. "Oil's leaking out of the head and dripping onto the manifold. Hits the exhaust pipe and burns. From the looks of it, I bet it goes through a quart of oil a tank. Also leaking antifreeze. Head gaskets are shot, I bet."

"I'm sure Hank appreciates you doing him a solid. Not sure where he went to." Randy tipped back his beer and tapped a cigarette from the pack. "Maybe he's out hunting for some two-legged animals."

Terrence's feet disappeared as he squirmed further under. "What's that supposed to mean?"

"He's got to have heard about his mom by now. If what you and Sharon were talking about is true, I'd hate to be the chief."

"How do you know what we were talking about?" The Jeep rocked on the Jack. "It's still under investigation."

Junior pushed his scooter into the garage and called inside. "What are ya doing?"

"Scram, kid," Randy said.

"Just fixing this," Terrence said.

Junior leaned his scooter against the back bumper and got down on his hands and knees. "Can I help?"

"Careful," Terrence said. "Don't get too close. The jack . . . "

Hank stood in the doorway, and Randy felt his stomach knot. Hank let out a long belch and said, "Junior, stay out of the way." He took a drink from a bottle of Jack Daniels and threw the empty out into the driveway. "Glad you didn't forget."

"Hank," Randy said. "We've been working on this all morning."

"We? I don't see any grease on your fingers." Hank

sat in the lawn chair beside Randy and pulled his cap down over his eyes. "Junior, go play. Can't you see we're working?"

"How you doing?" Randy asked.

"How am I supposed to be doing?" Hank said. He nodded at Randy's beer. "Give me one of those."

Randy got up to fish one out of the cooler as Junior peered underneath the engine.

Terrence's foot kicked in the direction of a plywood box filled with rusty tools. "Junior, see the toolbox over there? Toss me the screwdriver."

Junior dug through the box and pulled out a crescent wrench. He fiddled with the adjuster and banged it on the dirt floor.

"He said screwdriver, dumb-ass," Hank said. "You know what that is?" Hank belched again. "What's it look like? Can you fix it?"

"I . . . yeah, I can fix it, for now. Needs more work, though."

Junior dropped the wrench back into the box and pulled two screwdrivers out. "Which one?"

Terrence grunted and the Jeep rocked. "What?"

"The plus or the minus?"

"The flat one. I guess that would be the minus."

Junior dropped the other one back into the tool box and crawled under the car.

"Thanks, buddy," Terrence said. "You're a good helper."

"I guess so."

"Just takes practice. I had no idea how to fix stuff at first. Just keep fiddling and you learn how."

"Sure looks different from here," Junior said.

"Sure does. People keep the top all shiny. Most keep the inside nice, too. Underneath is a different story.

Things are never as they seem." Terrence's feet kicked and shuffled as he squirmed again. "See there? The muck coming from that hose?"

Junior's foot kicked the jack. "I guess."

Hank tipped the last of his bottle and tossed it onto the oily dirt floor. "You girls gonna talk all day? I got things to do."

Randy dug into the cooler and handed Hank another. "Man, working on cars always makes me thirsty."

"That brake line," Terrence said. "Looks like . . . "

Junior's shoulder poked out then his knee. "That what that is? What's it do?"

"Junior," Hank barked. "Leave him alone. Get your ass out of there. Can't you see we got work to do?"

Junior squirmed out from under the Jeep and frowned at Hank. He dusted off his pants and wiped a smear of oil across his cheek. He ran his fingers over the jack and grabbed the tire iron. "What's this do?"

"What?" Terrence said.

Randy nodded at Hank. "Looks like this could get interesting. You about done under there, Terrence? Might want to speed it up."

"Just checking the brakes," Terrence said. "Looks like the fronts are in pretty bad shape. These brake lines . . . "

The rusty jack swayed as Terrence grunted again.

Randy elbowed Hank and pointed to Junior who had pulled the tire iron free and was trying to shove it back in place. Hank slapped his hands together as if he was squashing a mosquito. "Kind of tight under there?"

The Jeep swayed again. "Just got to tighten the last . . . rusted pretty good."

Junior began to fiddle with the lever that kept the jack from ratcheting down.

Hank drained the last of his beer. "How much longer

is this gonna take?"

"Just about there. That should slow the leak, but you'll need to bring it into the garage to fix the pan. May have to pull the engine. Wouldn't hurt to—"

The tire iron jerked up and the Jeep dropped an inch as the jack slipped. Junior jumped back, tire iron in hand. "Get away from there," Terrence yelled.

Junior dropped the tire iron and buried his hands in his pockets. "I didn't mean to . . . "

Hank chucked his empty beer bottle, banging it off the bumper. "Get away from there. Let him finish."

"I'm sorry," Junior said. "I didn't mean to."

Terrence began to scoot out then stopped. "It's all right. Just be careful. Better do what your dad says."

Junior picked up the tire iron and slid it back into the jack.

Terrence's knees slid out. "Just got to finish with these . . ."

"Come here, boy," Hank said.

Junior stared at the ground as he shuffled slowly toward Hank and stood just out of Hank's reach. He glanced at Randy through watery eyes.

"Closer," Hank said.

Junior shuffled a little more.

"I said closer."

He inched a half step closer, still staring at the ground.

"Ain't you got something to do? Are you stupid?"

"No, sir." Junior said.

"Don't sass me, boy."

"It's okay, Hank," Terrence said. "He didn't mean to."

"I asked you a question, boy."

Tears began to slide down Junior's dirty cheeks. "Yes, sir."

"Yes, sir, what?"

"Yes, sir. I'm stupid."

"Now get out of here and leave us alone." As Junior turned to leave, Hank kicked him in the butt sending Junior sprawling into the dirt.

Junior crawled back to his feet, grabbed his scooter, and pushed it out of the garage.

The Jeep rocked hard. "He was just trying to help," Terrence said.

Randy opened the chest, fished around in the ice and pulled out the last bottle of beer. He popped the cap and tipped it up for a drink.

"Give me another one," Hank said.

Randy paused. "Looks like this is it."

Hank turned to Randy and held out his hand. Randy reluctantly gave up the bottle. "Guess you better get some more."

Randy nodded and slumped deeper into his chair. "Terrence, you must be awfully tired. What with you and Sharon talking about what happened to Mrs. Sherman."

Hank took a swallow and squinted at Randy.

Randy continued. "The pictures were pretty . . . let's just say I hope she rests in peace."

"Just about done," Terrence said. "But like I said, you'll need to get it into the shop."

"Randy, what the hell are you talking about?"

"Terrence and Sharon talking last night," Randy said, pointing at Terrence. "All cozy like, talking about what happened to your mom."

"Talking about Mom? What about her?"

Metal clanked against metal. "Ouch. Son of a—"

"You all right, Terrence?" Randy asked.

"One of the bolts stripped."

"Anything I should know about, Terrence?" Hank

said.

"Like what?"

Randy smiled. "Like maybe what happened to her."

Terrence's feet sprawled then the Jeep rocked. "Couldn't say."

"Sharon sure seemed in a hurry to get rid of me," Randy said. "Almost shoved me out the door. But I guess if she was a murdered—"

Hank glared at him. "Murdered? Who was murdered?"

An oily rag flew out from beneath the Jeep. "Randy, nobody said—"

"Sharon was sure convinced."

"Of what?" Hank said.

"That she was murdered."

Hank stood. "Who the hell was murdered?"

Randy slumped lower in his chair. "Your . . . I thought you knew."

"Randy, I swear to God, you tell me now or I'll—"

"Your mom. I thought . . . "

A wrench shot out from under the Jeep and Terrence slid out feet first. "Hank, it was probably an accident." He grabbed the rag and sat on the ground wiping his dirty hands.

Hank stood over Terrence. "Tell me what's going on."

"I can't. It's under investigation."

Hank wrapped his fist around the tire iron and slid it from the jack. "Tell me what happened."

"You shouldn't have heard this way. I thought they reached you last night. I thought that's why you were gone."

"Knew what?"

Terrence looked up at Hank. "Your mom. She's no longer with us."

"No longer with us?"

"She got cut . . . cut herself. The medical examiner said she probably didn't feel any pain."

"What are you saying?"

Terrence twisted the greasy rag. "Your mother's dead."

Hank wrapped his other fist around the tire iron. "Mom's dead?"

Terrence stood and took a step back. "That's how it looks."

"How?"

"Like I said, looks like she cut herself or . . . "

Hank slammed the tire iron into the Jeep's door. "How?"

"I'm really not supposed to say."

Randy sat up. "I heard it was an axe."

Hank turned to Randy and raised the tire iron. "An axe? She killed herself with an axe? How?"

"Don't make no sense," Randy said. "Murder's more like it."

Hank glared at Terrence. "Boy, you better start talking."

"Like I said, we're still investigating."

"We?" Hank said.

"Me and the chief."

"Figures." Randy said.

Hank turned to Randy, "Got something to say, say it."

"I'm just saying the fox guarding the hen house. He's not the most honest guy."

"What? You think he killed her?"

"Him or someone he's covering for."

Hank swung the tire iron into the jack and the Jeep ratcheted down in jerking clunks. "That son of a bitch. That's why he was out there."

"He was at her place?" Randy asked.

"When I left he was sweet talking mom. Sleaze bag. Didn't think he had it in him—"

"Hank," Terrence said, "you got to let us investigate. Don't—"

"You and the chief investigate?" He pointed the tire iron at Terrence's face, then slammed it against the Jeep's door. "You go right ahead. I'm gonna do some investigating of my own."

Terrence pulled into the parking lot behind Sharon's apartment half an hour late. It had taken longer to fix Hank's Jeep, and he'd had to work extra hard to scrub the dirt from his hands. His usual patrol car was at the glass shop waiting for a windshield to arrive from Portland. For now, he'd have to settle for the backup Chevy Caprice pushing 186,000 hard miles. In the afternoon sun the thick film on the inside of the windshield painted everything a fuzzy shade of yellow. At least it's in one piece, he thought. Without a cage in the back for his dog, Bronson got the day off.

He put the patrol car in park and pressed the bandage covering the throbbing flap of skin on his barked knuckle. The uniform was a welcome change from the oily coveralls.

He honked and waited, wondering how Hank could not have known about his mother. Could he not be reached because he was holed up in one of his caves in the hills plotting to overthrow of the government? Or maybe he knew more than he let on. Hank's shock at hearing the news seemed more rehearsed than real. There was no telling what Hank was thinking or where his "investigation" might lead. Terrence knew the clock was ticking, and the longer it ran, the more people would get hurt.

The sheet covering the window beside Sharon's front door swept aside and Sharon looked out, pointing at her watch. A minute later the front door swung open, and out she came. He drank her in as she knelt to give Junior a hug. Up on the landing, dressed in a sleeveless pink turtleneck, tight blue jeans, and high heels, she was no longer the tomboy he'd played basketball with in grade school. Though she was three years older, he'd always stood at least a head taller. At just over five feet, she was sturdier than the models on the cover of *Cosmopolitan* and would rather kick a soccer ball than pose in skimpy clothes. A bubble of confidence surrounded her, a certainty that her life would turn out the way she hoped. In Terrence's eyes, she was more than beautiful, she was alive.

Sharon slid on her sunglasses and brushed the red hair from her eyes. Her hips bent awkwardly forward as she descended the steps. He'd not seen her wearing heels since her senior prom. They made her seem vulnerable, easier to catch.

"Hey," she said as she slid into the seat beside him. "You're late. You could have called."

"I did call, about a dozen times. How come you didn't answer?"

Sharon ran her fingers over the toggle switches on the console. "I've never ridden in the front before." She laughed. "How do you keep all this stuff straight?" She turned up the volume knob on the radio then punched a switch labeled Shotgun. The metal clamp that wrapped around the grip of the shotgun clicked but the gun remained at attention between them, pointing up at the car's roof.

"Careful now," Terrence said. "Don't want any accidents." He pushed on the clamp, clicking it shut. "You promised—"

She ran her hand across the dash. "How fast can this car go?"

Terrence looked at the arching numbers on the speedometer topping out at 120. "Over a hundred."

"What's the fastest you've gone?"

"Well around here the roads—"

"I've done a 110. You must have gone faster than that."

"Well, it tops out at 120," Terrence said. "Takes special training to go that fast. Feels almost like flying."

She popped open the glove box and pulled out a box of Federal .357 ammunition. "Ever shot anybody?" She smiled. "Maybe today will be your lucky day."

He shook his head and put the box of ammo back. "You look nice today."

"Thanks." She gave him a sarcastic grin and said, "I just love a man in uniform." She pushed the presets on the radio until her favorite country station filled the air with the warbling of Randy Travis.

Terrence lowered the volume. "How are you?"

"Good." She looked serious then flashed a smile. "Well?"

"Well what?"

"Are we gonna go or just sit here all day? Come on. We got bad guys to catch."

"Forgetting something?"

She looked puzzled then dug in the crack of the seat and pulled out the seatbelt. "Let's go. She flipped on the overhead lights and siren as Terrence backed up.

"Stop. Listen, are you gonna—"

"Behave? What do you think?"

He flipped off the switches and pulled onto the street.

"Listen," Terrence said. "I've been thinking. I'm not so sure it wasn't just an accident. I mean, it does make sense." He looked at her, hoping for some sign of agreement. She was already lost in the music, her head bobbing in time. "I'll be seeing the chief when he gets back from his meeting with the mayor. I'm sure he will tell me about why he was out there."

Sharon adjusted her sunglasses and examined her neon red fingernails. "And what's he going to say?"

"I don't know. That's why I have to ask."

As the car neared the park, two kids on swings waved. Another at the top of the slide jumped for a frayed rope dangling from a rotting tree branch. A young girl straddled her bike, shouting orders to a boy who held a squirming snake by the tail.

"Terrence," Sharon said, "don't get me wrong. You're a nice guy—too nice. You're like a big puppy dog, always trying to please. Always willing to believe what you're told. Problem is you can't be that way all the time."

Terrence waived at the kids. "What am I supposed to do? Tell the chief I'm taking him in for murder? Based on what? A business card?"

"Don't be dumb. Of course not. But you can't just believe everything he tells you, either. I don't know what you see in him. As far as I'm concerned, he's a fat slob. Worse, he's a crook. Ever wonder how he got his job?"

Terrence stopped at the red light for Bridge Street. For a moment he thought he could smell smoke in the breeze. "The mayor hired him."

"See, that's what I'm talking about. Of course Dad hired him, but why? Why would anybody hire that guy?"

"His experience. He worked for more than twenty years as a police officer in Portland."

"After twenty years he was a police officer."

"That's right."

"First step," Sharon said. "Isn't that a long time without being promoted? And I hear they shoved him out the door. Corruption or police brutality. I heard he might have killed somebody."

"Who told you that?"

"My point is, he's a crook. I wouldn't put it past him to do in some defenseless old lady if it got him something."

The light turned green, and they began across the bridge. Its steel girders arched overhead, climbing then descending in riveted triangles. "What's he get from killing Edith?"

"I'm just saying don't believe everything your told."

Terrence laughed. "At the academy they said, 'Believe only half of what you see and nothing of what you hear.'"

Sharon punched his shoulder. "There it is."

Terrence backed into his favorite fishing hole to snag unsuspecting drivers with his radar gun. The Sheridan Grocery sign advertising the week's special on tomatoes and ground beef would give them cover. Tucked behind the sign, they had a good view of the traffic light, the pedestrian crossing, and two stop signs. The locals were familiar with this trap and seldom tempted fate by running a red or speeding. Only those in the grips of dementia failed to watch their driving in this stretch of downtown.

Folks from Portland would occasionally take the freeway exit, thirsty for gas. In a hurry to kick the dust of Sheridan off their feet, they'd often run the red. Terrence viewed them like a plague invading their quiet town. Keep Portland weird, he thought, but leave Sheridan alone.

Even after stopping a violator, pangs of guilt would urge him not to write a ticket. But he had a quota to make, and each ticket would bring them one step closer to buying a new police car.

Sharon grabbed the handheld radar that looked like a fat gun with a stubby musket cone and pointed it out the window. The display in the back that showed the speed of the target blinked double zeros. She pulled the tuning fork from the pouch Velcroed on top. "What's this for?"

"Hit it and hold it in front."

She struck the tuning fork against the barrel of the shotgun.

"Not against that."

"You said . . . "

He smiled as she held the humming fork. "Now hold it in front."

Sharon gave a puzzled look.

"There. In front of the cone."

She held it there, and the Speed Gun began to hum in harmony with the fork. "It says thirty."

"See the numbers on the back. That says it's calibrated. Now you know it's working right. So when you go to court—"

"Look." She pointed the Speed Gun at Jimmy Anderson riding his skateboard on the sidewalk. She tracked him in the Speed Gun's sights. "Isn't that illegal? Are you going to arrest him?"

Terrence shook his head. "I'd give him a warning if we weren't already working traffic."

"A warning? How come I never got any warnings?"

She lowered the radar and ran her hand across the black cone. "I bet you write lots of tickets with this." She pointed the radar at a pickup headed their way on Bridge Street. The Speed Gun emitted a low pitch tone that grew higher as the truck picked up speed. The display read twenty. She pulled the trigger and the display locked, blinking twenty-one. She squeezed the trigger again, and the display read double zeros.

Terrence enjoyed watching her play with her new toy. Even in high school, she was the daring one. The first to drive a car—two years before she was old enough to get a driver's license. The first to convince the kid working nights at Sheridan Grocery to sell her beer. The first to go all the way. The first to get suspended and the first to get expelled.

The Speed Gun seemed to help her focus. Maybe she felt the same sense of power he'd hoped to find in a uniform. The power to control and direct. He wondered if she'd feel the subtle fear that electrified each contact with citizens who always had something to hide.

His amusement turned to shame as he examined her swollen cheek buried beneath a heavy layer of makeup. Three red finger marks wrapped around her throat. Wispy bangs partially covered a scratch on her forehead.

"There's one," she said, squeezing the trigger when the display hit twenty-nine. "It's Jack Strower. Self-righteous SOB. Stop him!"

"Sharon, I don't think—"

The Speed Gun's tone gradually lowered as Jack's station wagon passed. "Go, Terrence. He's getting away."

"I can't just . . . you're not trained."

Sharon flipped the siren toggle and its whine filled the inside of the car. "Go! Hurry!" Then she flipped on the lights. "Look, he's slowing down. Guilty as charged!"

Terrence turned off the siren and reluctantly pulled in behind Jack's Buick.

The siren whined again as Sharon flipped it back on.

Terrence turned the siren off again as Jack's front tire climbed the curb then slid off as he rolled to a stop. "Leave the siren off. He's already pulled over. You stay here while I talk with him."

"Come on. I won't get in the way. Promise."

"No. You need—"

Sharon opened the door and stepped out, waving at Terrence to hurry up.

He rose out of the car, put on his police cap, and tipped it toward Betty who stood watching under the awning outside the beauty parlor. Jimmy Anderson kicked up his skateboard and held it frozen like somebody had hit his pause button. Two seniors gawked from the Sheridan Grocery store parking lot.

The Buick's window lowered as Sharon cut in front of Terrence, shaking her finger at Jack.

"Sharon, you need to—"

"Jack, how you doing?" Sharon said.

"Sharon. Well I, uh, I . . . "

"How come you were driving so fast?" she started in. "What's the hurry? Late for choir practice?"

Jack looked at Terrence who was pushing his way in front of Sharon. "Terrence. I mean, Officer Washburn."

"You didn't answer my question," Sharon said. "What's the hurry?"

Terrence stood in front of her. "Sharon, I'll handle this."

Sharon elbowed her way in front of Terrence. "What's the Bible say about violating the law, Jack?"

"Officer Washburn, I'm sorry." Jack's eyes ping-ponged between the two of them.

"Mr. Strower, I'll need to see your driver's license, registration, and proof of insurance."

Jack fished in the glove box and pulled out a wad of church bulletins, a New Testament, and a crossword puzzle book. He snatched a magazine wedged in the back, quickly stuffed it beneath the seat, and sat momentarily dazed. His hands shook as he flipped down the visor and fumbled to pull his registration and proof of insurance card from beneath the yellowed plastic. He handed them over to Terrence.

"License?" Terrence said.

"Oh, sorry." Jack pulled out a wallet thick enough to cause curvature of the spine from his back pocket and fished out his license. "Here you go, Officer Washburn. Lovely day, isn't it?"

"Yes, sir. I'll be right back."

"I'm still waiting," Sharon said.

Terrence grabbed Sharon's arm and walked her back to the police car. "You need to let me handle this. I mean it, Sharon."

"Handle it then." She pointed her finger in his face then lowered it. "You're going to let him off, aren't you?"

"You're not trained. Besides he was only—"

"Breaking the law."

"No. He was only going a little over the speed limit. It's called officer discretion. If he'd been going faster—"

"Or if he'd run over somebody? Killed someone, maybe? What about officer discretion then?"

"He didn't. He wouldn't."

Sharon glared back at Jack then shot the same accusing look at Terrence.

"Just stay here, please." Terrence walked back to

Jack's open window and held out his papers.

Jack took back his driver's license and registration. "I'm sorry. I was on the way to Mother's. I didn't think I was speeding." He squinted in the side mirror. "What was she—"

"Mr. Strower, she's a little, well you know."

"Is she an officer now? I mean, why's she stopping—"

"No. She's just doing a ride-along." Terrence drummed the roof of the Buick with his stiff fingers. He looked back at Sharon who was waving at rubberneckers. Jimmy dropped his skateboard and slowly let gravity pull him closer. Betty lit a cigarette.

"Mr. Strower, I'm going to let you go with a warning this time. Sorry for the inconvenience. You have a good day."

"Thank you, Terrence. I will."

Terrence walked back toward the patrol car, keeping his eyes on the Buick as Jack eased back into traffic.

Sharon slammed her door and sat shaking her head. "What was that?"

"What was what?"

"That! Letting him get away with breaking the law. Why didn't you give him a ticket?"

Terrence turned off the overhead lights and leaned against the seat as Jimmy skated away. "Sharon, he's a good person. He's no criminal."

"How do you know? Suppose I told you he's not as innocent as he seems."

"It's what the chief wants. Give the locals warnings, unless someone does something serious."

Sharon frowned. "Locals? Is that what we are? *Locals*? What's that make you? Mr. Big City?"

"You know that's not what I mean." Terrence felt the quicksand starting to sift around his feet. "Unless the citizens of Sheridan do something serious, I'm supposed to give them a warning."

"Serious? Like what?"

"You know."

Sharon grabbed the Speed Gun and pointed it at him. "No, I don't. Educate me."

Terrence looked again at her swollen cheek and swallowed the words he lacked the courage to say.

"How about robbery or murder?" Sharon's voice began to shake. "Does someone have to get killed to get help around here? Getting beat up isn't enough?" The strength seemed to drain from her arm and she let the Speed Gun fall into her lap.

"You know that's not true." Terrence put the car in gear and hit his turn signal. "I just want to help. If you need help . . . "

"What? You'll what? The chief doesn't care. Hank's your buddy. What are you going to do, wait until I end up like Edith?"

"Has Hank been—"

"Beating the shit out me? No, Terrence. Things are just great."

"You know we can't do anything if you don't report it."

"Maybe you forgot what happened the last time I tried that. Jail was real helpful."

"I'm sorry. It's just—"

"Take me home. I want to go home. I think I've seen enough of law enforcement. Let the bastards go free and lock up their victims. You should be real proud." She wiped her eyes and looked at him, mascara running down both cheeks. "Just take me home."

Terrence searched for something to say as he began to pull into the traffic lane.

"On second thought, I'll get out here." She shoved open the door, and Terrence hit the brakes. The door sprang back shut, and she slammed her palm against the window.

"I'm sorry," Terrence said. "Let me take you home."

"Leave me alone. That's how you can help."

He put his hand on her shoulder, and she flinched and slapped his hand away. "Gonna arrest me for assaulting a police officer?" She pushed open the door and stood. "Thanks for nothing."

Betty blew smoke into the dusty air and flicked the butt of her cigarette into the street. "Everything all right dear?"

Sharon stomped away from the police car, shaking with anger. Betty stood beneath the awning of the beauty parlor, her hair twisted up into a giant beehive. Her face still had a hint of the beauty that won her homecoming queen twenty-three years ago. In the interim, her body had blossomed into a plus size, the number of which, she kept strictly to herself. Betty's raspy voice spoke in puffs of smoke. "Looks like you could use a little freshening up."

"What?" Sharon asked.

Betty drew one finger down her cheek. "Your mascara, honey."

Sharon looked at her face in the beauty parlor window and wiped the smears of mascara.

Betty pulled a Kleenex from her sleeve and held out the round mirror from her compact.

In the mirror, Sharon looked like she had been crying ink. She dabbed beneath her eyes, gingerly avoiding the bruise on her cheek. "Bastard."

Uh-huh," Betty said. "What happened this time?"

Sharon slid her sunglasses back on and held out the dirty Kleenex and compact.

Betty took the compact and scowled at the Kleenex. "That's on the house."

"Oh, yeah." Sharon stuffed the used wad of tissue into her purse. "Terrence."

Betty examined her own face in the mirror then wedged a long fingernail into the gap between her front teeth. "Terrence?"

"Guess he has a different idea what protect and serves means."

Betty frowned. "Let me guess. It includes a stiff backhand now and then?"

"What? No. Not Terrence. He wouldn't."

"Hon, there's no need to cover for him. You'll just make it worse. They say they're sorry. Promise to never do it again. Maybe even beg for forgiveness. But that only lasts until the next time they need to blow off a little steam."

"Terrence didn't hit me, Betty."

"They call it battered wife's syndrome, or some such. The missus just takes it, and takes it, until the day she wakes up with a steak knife in the chest, or he's missing the family jewels."

Sharon fished a pack of Kools out of her purse and lit one. She drew in a deep breath and felt the smoke begin to calm her on the inside. "It's not Terrence."

Betty took a drag of her own. "I guess that would leave Hank."

Sharon nodded.

Betty blew a ring of smoke up toward the awning. "Men."

"Men," Sharon said.

They stood gawking in front of the beauty parlor as Terrence's cruiser swung a wide U-turn and slowly drove past.

Betty waved. "Whatever happened to you and him?"

"We got married."

"No. You and Terrence."

"That was a long time ago. I was just a kid. You know how it is."

Betty dropped her cigarette butt and ground it out with the heel of her tennis shoe. "Don't I. Come on inside. My next appointment's not for half an hour. Let's get you fixed up."

"Thanks, but I don't have any—"

Betty's plump fingers lifted Sharon's chin. "Hon, this one's on me." Her marshmellowy arm draped over Sharon's shoulder and she ushered her through the door. "Let's freshen you up a bit."

Sharon relaxed into the padded chair, staring awkwardly at her image in the mirror as Betty collected the tools of her trade. Right now Betty was the closest thing to a friend Sharon could hope for. The beauty parlor was a kind of confessional for ladies. Maybe it was time to unburden.

Betty arranged the scissors, brush, and a tube of styling gel on the work table beside the chair. "Now you just relax." Betty slid Sharon's sunglasses off and placed them beside the scissors. She snapped the drape and tucked it around Sharon's neck. The rubber band took a few hairs with it as Betty untangled it from her pony tail and began picking through the red snarls. The room tilted as Betty leaned the chair back and lowered Sharon's head over the sink.

The chair seemed to wrap its arms around Sharon as the warm water flowed over her forehead. As Betty's fingers messaged her scalp, she tried to ignore the throbbing in her cheek.

Betty held out a tangled lock of hair and examined it. "I love that red hair of yours. Can be a little wild, though." She wrung the water from her hair and raised the chair. Betty swiveled the chair facing the mirror and toweled her head. Sharon once again looked at her face in the mirror, wondering how she had aged beyond her years.

"So what happened with you and Terrence? Or should I say, Officer Washburn?"

"Strower." Sharon said. "Terrence let him off. Good-old-boy's club. He's such an ass."

Betty snipped the scissors. "Terrence or Strower?"

"Take your pick. It's just not fair. We all know what Strower did after choir practice."

Betty squirted a glob of conditioner into her palm and rubbed them together then kneaded gel into her hair. She grabbed a tissue and dabbed mascara remover on it and wiped the remaining black smudges from Sharon's cheeks.

Sharon winced. "Ouch."

"Sorry, hon. Let me guess. Private lessons?"

"What?"

"Strower. A little one-on-one choir practice with a few of the girls?

"Mostly for his benefit," Sharon said. "He's the one making all the oohs and ahhs. Maybe he should do a moaning solo in church next Sunday."

Betty snipped the scissors. "I could give him something to moan about. I thought that was just rumors. How come you never said anything?"

Sharon shut her eyes. "I tried. They'd rather think I was lying than believe he's a pervert. I stopped trying."

"But what about the others. I mean if enough girls complained . . . "

"Call the kid a liar. That's easier than thinking about rape.

"Asshole . . . " Betty pulled a tangle and snipped. The lock tumbled down the drape and clung to its edge.

"Terrence," Sharon said. "There's another piece of work."

"I think he's kind of handsome in a giant sort of way. That's a lot of man." Betty smiled. "I've sometimes wondered if he's big all over."

Sharon shook her head. "You'd be surprised."

"Try me."

Girl talk, Sharon thought. Always the same. Poison words on the lips of women. Too often Sharon had been the subject. Maybe this time she could use wagging tongues to her advantage.

"If I tell you a secret, you promise not to tell?"

Betty snipped again. Their eyes met in the mirror. "You're secret's safe with me."

"Have you heard?"

"Heard what?"

"About Edith?"

"Edith?"

"Sherman."

Betty pulled another tangle into the jaws of the scissors. "What about her?"

"You promise?"

Snip. Another curl slid down the drape, and Betty nodded.

"Edith Sherman was murdered."

Betty spun the chair and looked into Sharon's eyes. "Murdered?"

"Throat slit," Sharon said. "I saw the pictures. Her

body was dumped in the dirt."

"How?" Snip. "Who?" Snip.

"Terrence's investigating."

"Oh my God. Murdered? You sure?"

Sharon closed her eyes. "Can't get the pictures out of my mind. Her lying there, throat sliced open. Staring up like she'd been begging for help."

The scissors snipped haphazardly for a few moments. "How? I mean—"

The bell above the door tinkled, announcing Jolene Canton's arrival She perched herself in the seat two spots over. "Hello, Betty." She was all smiles as she began to leaf through a seven-month-old edition of *Cosmopolitan*.

"What's up, Jo?" Sharon said.

Jolene peered over the top of the model posed seductively on the magazine cover. "Oh, Sharon. I don't recall seeing you here before. Betty, when are you going to get some more current reading material? I believe I may have this one memorized. Do you have today's newspaper?"

Betty said, "If you want news—"

Sharon grabbed her arm and squeezed.

"I'll see what I can find. Give me a minute."

Sharon picked through the stack of dog-eared tabloids beside her chair and opened a *National Enquirer*.

Betty rolled the hairdryer over and positioned it over Sharon's head. "Now you just sit here and relax." She lowered the hood, and a warm whoosh of air whirled around her scalp. "I'll be back with you when it's dry."

Sharon raised the *National Enquirer* and pretended to read. Listening through the hum of the dryer was no more challenging than following the drunken dialog of patrons at the Reservation yakking over the noise of clacking pool balls and Jimmy Buffet's "Margaritaville." Sharon peered over the tabloid cover, pretending to be enthralled with the aliens who had abducted some poor woman and probed her mercilessly.

Betty snapped open another drape and tucked it beneath Jolene's turkey neck. Crow's feet stood at the edges of her eyes collecting bits of two-day-old makeup in their folds. Betty glanced at Sharon, smiled, and bent closer to Jolene. "Have you heard?"

"What?" Jolene's voice boomed.

"Shhh," Betty said, "Have you heard the news?"

Jolene shook her head.

"Edith Sherman was murdered!"

Jolene turned her ear to Betty and cupped behind it. "What?"

"Edith Sherman. Someone slashed her throat ear to ear and dumped her body in a shallow grave."

Jolene's jaw fell agape.

Betty glanced at Sharon and lowered her voice. "Murdered."

Jolene's hand pressed against the loose skin of her neck. "Murdered?"

"Edith Sherman, you remember her? Anyways, the cops are investigating."

"No." Jolene's eyes widened, "The cops killed Edith Sherman?"

"Not the cops." Betty scowled. "They're investigating."

"Who?"

"They don't know, at least I think they don't." Betty smiled at Sharon whose eyes darted back to the page just in time. "The killer is still on the loose."

"Oh my."

The bell above the front door tinkled again. Gloria

sashayed in as if she were walking the red carpet. She grabbed a three-month-old edition of *Newsweek* and wedged herself into the middle chair. "Morning, ladies." She flipped the magazine to the back and started paging forward.

"That poor woman," Jolene said.

Betty slid her fingers into the cuticle scissors and scooted her chair closer to Jolene. She picked her knobby middle finger to begin. "And that's not the half of it." Betty's voice lowered. "I heard she was attacked, you know, *sexually*."

Gloria dropped her magazine into her lap. "What are you two talking about?"

"Edith." Jolene said. "Haven't you heard?"

"Heard what?"

Betty and Jolene exchanged glances, then Jolene crossed herself and whispered, "Edith, God rest her soul, was murdered!"

"Murdered?" Gloria mouthed.

Betty nodded. "Throat slit ear to ear."

Jolene's hand crawled up to her throat and clutched her drape. "And abused. *Sexually*."

The three jumped as the front door thumped open. Jack Strower backed against the glass door, wrestling his mother's wheelchair over the entry. The bell tinkled again as the door bounced against the armrests of her wheelchair. Granny Strower smiled vacantly, muttering as Jack wheeled her into the room.

Jack humphed as he fought against wheels determined to roll in opposite directions. "Ladies." He nodded and parked her in the corner.

Sharon lowered the tabloid and gave Jack a death stare.

Jack appeared startled and looked away. "Be back at

the usual time, Betty?"

Betty snipped her scissors and nodded.

Jack looked at the ladies frozen like manikins in the JC Penney window display. "How we doing this fine day?"

"Haven't you heard? Edi—" Gloria began until Betty's hand corked her mouth.

Betty blinked.

"Heard? Heard what?"

"About Edith," Jolene said, before her own hand plugged her own trap.

Granny Strower began to laugh for no apparent reason. The unpleasant and undeniable odor of flatulence began to drift into their nostrils. All heads swiveled in her direction.

"Okay, then," Jack said. "Guess I'll be going." He removed his hat, tipped it to the ladies, and fanned his face as he hurried out the door.

The bell tinkled, signaling the all clear to resume their conversation.

The heat was growing beneath the dryer as Sharon turned the page of *The Enquirer* and lowered it just below eye level.

"Murdered. Throat slit ear to ear," Betty said.

"No!" Gloria said.

"Poor woman. And assaulted, you know—" Jolene added.

"*Sexually*," Betty and Jolene finished.

"Can't say I find it a complete surprise though," Gloria said.

Betty and Jolene stared aghast.

"What? We all know how he was. Him and his guns. And the boys—Hank especially. Never was the same since he got back. Running around with his goons, playing Rambo. Some war hero. No telling what he might do."

"Jolene, she was *raped*." Betty said.

"We all had our suspicions that things just weren't right up there," Gloria said. "That's all." She looked in the mirror and tugged at her temples.

"Hank?" Betty said. "You think Hank killed her?"

Gloria picked up her magazine. "I'm just saying . . . "

Betty and Jolene exchanged looks of disbelief. "Just the same we've got to take precautions," Betty said.

Jack's mother burst into another jag of laughter.

They held their breath as Betty cracked open the front door and wedged a folding chair in place to let fresh air in.

Silly women, Sharon thought. So quick to fill in the gaps, let their imaginations go wherever they might lead. Maybe this would be useful.

The three breathed in the fresh air, then Betty snipped a curling hangnail. She shook her head. "Precautions. We need to be careful. Who knows who might be next? Anyone who would kill such a sweet woman in such a vicious way, no telling who might be next."

Betty opened the top drawer on her work station and pulled out a canister of mace. "Got this in town. And if it doesn't work, I've got backup. Want to see?"

Jolene and Gloria nodded.

Betty dug behind the cotton balls and pulled out a revolver.

Gloria smiled. "What's that for?"

"What do you think?" Betty said. "Protection."

"Can I touch it?" Gloria asked.

Betty handed it to her, barrel first. Gloria ran her fingers down the steel barrel and squeezed her finger into the trigger guard. "It's heavy." She pointed the gun over Betty's shoulder and aimed in the mirror at Sharon.

"It's kind of exciting."

"Careful," Betty said. "It's loaded. Doesn't take much to make it go off."

Gloria laughed. "Just like a man."

"Let me see," Jolene said.

Betty grabbed the gun and stuffed it back under the cotton balls and closed the drawer. "I'd suggest you get one, unless you want to be next."

Terrence patrolled the quiet streets hoping to clear his head. Of course he was right. Law enforcement is not a game, something Sharon would never understand. Their argument was a painful reminder he and Sharon could never manage a truce for more than a few days. They were like gas and water—one always bursting into flame, the other unable to put it out. The wheels of the police cruiser clacked across the expansion strip that marked the boundary of the bridge.

The water below reflected the bony limbs of leaf-barren trees. Sharon's words bit hard and chewed at the raw edges of his mind. Doubt crept in and brought with it the certainty that he was a coward. As he stopped at the light, the pressure to return, to make it right overwhelmed his better judgment. He flipped on his overhead lights and pulled a U-turn, rehearsing the words he wanted to say—a jumble of contradictions. *I'm sorry. I should have given him a ticket. I should do something to help you. I'll make the beatings stop. I won't be afraid anymore.*

The car slowed as it rolled past the beauty parlor. Inside, beyond the reflection of his car in the windows, he saw Sharon sitting beneath the cone of a hairdryer while Betty talked with two other ladies. Stop and say you're sorry for being stupid. Sorry for not having the guts to do the right thing. Apologize for the cruelty of men.

His car drifted past, and a shudder rippled down his spine as he recalled a time he'd almost given in to the urge to lash out. Only the look of shock on Sharon's face had kept his fist from striking. She'd broken his heart again, and a man could only take so much. Ever since, he'd kept the door to his heart under lock and key, but the bars that kept his rage in check were getting rusty.

Terrence continued past the Reservation Tavern. Hank's Jeep was parked in front. In the shadow beneath the front wheel, a small puddle of black fluid pooled. A final lap around town would help calm his nerves and delay sitting at the report writing desk in direct line of any insults Madison might hurl his way.

The car seat pushed his holster up, digging the butt of his revolver into the gap in his vest that exposed his ribs. Body armor was a new thing, and Madison wasn't a fan. Too confining, Madison said. In the heat, the Kevlar panels made him feel like a baked potato wrapped in foil.

At the academy they'd listened to an officer who'd been shot three times but survived, thanks to his vest. The story was enough to convince Terrence body armor wasn't optional. Finding a vest his size was another matter. He could only hope a bullet or knife wouldn't find the exposed spots. The butt of his revolver did often enough to fray his shirt and rub his skin raw. Terrence shoved the pistol down and thought of how he'd come by it—and what he'd agreed to do.

Hank was his ride the day he left for the police academy in Monmouth, Oregon, two years ago. Terrence was packing inside his mom's trailer when

Hank's Jeep erupted into a coughing fit under her carport. The latches on his suitcase strained to stay closed as Terrence sandwiched eight weeks of clothes inside. He took a last look at the basketball jersey tacked to his wall and the *Sheridan Sun* news clipping taped below it showing him taking the final jumper in the state championship game. He could still feel the air leave the room as the home team bleachers let out a collective groan of disappointment when the ball rolled off the rim. He kept the yellowed clipping as a reminder of his promise to make it right. He'd hoped a different kind of uniform would give him that chance.

"Mamma. I'm going. Francine will be here in a few minutes."

His mother had sat expressionless in her recliner, wearing her pink bathrobe and leopard-skin slippers. Her vacant eyes reflected the gray glow of the TV. Monte Hall pointed his microphone toward a couple dressed as boxes of cereal, eager to make a deal. Her hand clutched the remote and turned up the volume.

Terrence bent down and kissed her forehead. A tear slid down her cheek as the TV cut to a Crest commercial. Each day she seemed to retreat further into a world beyond his reach. Is she reliving the memories of a lifetime ago? he wondered. They call it the long goodbye. Will she even know me when I get back in eight weeks?

"Love you, Mamma. I'll be back soon." He'd checked the gauge on her oxygen condenser, then the one on her backup oxygen tank. The needles were both in the green. Whether she would have the presence of mind to switch to her tank if the condenser stopped, he could only guess. Francine will be here soon, he assured himself, though she'd never been this late before.

The Jeep's horn honked a long blast. Terrence ducked out the front door and pulled it closed. He walked down the wheelchair ramp, avoiding the soft spots where the plywood was rotten beneath the outdoor carpeting.

Hank threw his hands up in a what-took-you-so-long gesture.

When Terrence reached the Jeep, pangs of guilt urged him to return, to make sure his mother would be okay. He wedged himself into the Jeep, fighting the feeling that he was betraying the only other survivor of his family.

Hank smiled behind the wheel. "Big day, my boy. The academy. Damn. Never thought I'd see the day."

Terrence glanced at the trailer door and returned the smile. "Got to admit, I'm a little surprised, too. Hope I'm up to it."

Hank laughed. "Don't take much brains to be a cop." He smiled. "Got you a little going away present."

"Present? What kind of present?"

The Jeep backed out of the carport and started toward the trailer park exit. "Look in the glove box."

Terrence popped open the glove box and saw the brown wood grain grip of a gun.

"Go ahead. Take it out."

He curled his fingers around the grip of the revolver and turned it over, admiring the silver gleam of the stainless steel frame. The ornate Smith and Wesson decal on the grips made it more than a gun. It was a part of history, a proud tradition of freedom won by those willing to fight for it. He looked down the sites at the hula girl swaying on the dash and began to squeeze the trigger.

"Careful now," Hank said. "It's loaded."

"She's a beauty. Where'd you get it?"

"Never mind where I got it."

Terrence's thumb slid the cylinder release forward and it swiveled out. Six bullets were seated there, stamped S&W .357. He pressed the ejector and dumped the silver bullets into his palm. Terrence rolled one between his fingers and examined the hollow point, a slug of lead pressed into a puckered silver steel casing. He slid the bullets back into their slots and spun the cylinder like they always did in the westerns. With a flip of the gun, the cylinder snapped shut. "A real beauty."

Hank nodded as they turned onto Washington Street. "Look in the bag in the back seat."

Terrence grabbed the bulging gym bag. "What's this?"

"Open it."

He unzipped the camouflaged bag and saw a new black gun belt and holster. The smell of leather scented the air as he held the heavy belt up and brushed his fingers over the basket-weave design. The revolver fit snugly into the stiff holster.

Hank smiled. "Happy birthday."

"Why?" was all Terrence could say.

"Can't be a cop without a gun. That's how it works. With your mom and all, I figured you could use some help."

"But I can't—"

The Jeep came to a rattling stop at the red light at Bridge Street. "Terrence, or should I say Officer Washburn, you deserve a shot." He pulled a can of Budweiser out from under the seat. "I figure you can do the militia a favor. We need someone on the inside to keep track of what they're up to. It's no mystery the chief's not our friend. Big city types just don't understand. But you, you understand what we're about. My old man always liked you." He winked and popped the tab of his beer. "You're doing us a favor. Think of this as a token of our appreciation. Just keep your eyes open, if you know what I mean."

"Thanks but can't—"

"Bullshit. You can, and you will."

A horn honked behind, and Terrence felt the butt of the revolver digging into his ribs. In his rear view mirror, he saw Jolene Canton pointing up toward the green stoplight. He shoved the gun down from the raw spot in his ribs and pushed the gas.

Sharon tossed her car keys onto the kitchen counter and collapsed into the recliner. She knew Terrence meant well. Maybe she'd been too hard on him, but more was at stake than he understood. Edith's death would soon have everybody pointing fingers. She'd have to make sure they pointed the right direction.

Her shoes dropped to the floor, and the cool air caressed her throbbing toes. How many more shifts would she endure at the Reservation? She reclined back and thought of younger days when she still entertained dreams of finding her knight in shining armor. They'd move into a luxurious house and raise obedient children. She'd sit on a big porch sipping lemonade with Mr. Charming, bound forever in an unbreakable bond of love. The dim glow of her watch read 2:34 a.m. Hank, no prince charming, would be delivering Junior soon. How easily dreams become nightmares, she thought.

She pulled off her sunglasses and massaged her temples. Her gut began to twist as she anticipated Hank's Jeep pulling up. Surely Hank had gotten the news about his mother's death. He'd likely be hunting for someone, anyone, to blame. He'd want revenge, she'd have to be careful. Her life hung by a spider's web she could not easily escape.

She flipped off the switch on the lamp beside the recliner and let the darkness envelope her. In the shadows, her life seemed unreal, and escape felt possible. The echoes of the Reservation faded as she lit a cigarette and drew the smoke into her lungs. The ash at the end of the cigarette glowed orange then faded as her eyes closed.

When Sharon woke, a long stub of ash clung to the filter of her cigarette on top the armrest. Hank stood over her, his face expressionless.

"Hank, what—"

Junior stepped between them. "I'm tired." Smudges of dirt painted his cheeks. The smell of urine clung to his dirty jeans.

"Go to your room," Hank ordered.

Junior brushed the hair out of his eyes and began to crawl up into Sharon's lap.

"Did you hear me?" Hank grabbed Junior's arm and shoved him toward his room. "Now." Junior stumbled then stomped to his room and slammed the door.

Sharon kicked the foot rest down and sat upright. "What was that for?"

Hank stared down at her blankly, detached, and propped his muddy boot on the arm of her chair.

"Time for you to leave." Sharon pulled herself out of the recliner and shoved past Hank to the front door. She pulled it open, hoping her neighbor was listening.

"Did you know?"

"Hank, I don't know what's on your mind but it's late. I'm exhausted. Can we talk about this later?" She nodded toward the door.

"Answer my question. Did you know?"

She glanced at the drawer where she kept her gun, then looked out the door, hoping she hadn't given away the weapon's hiding place. "Know what?"

"About Mom."

Sharon's heart began to pound. "What about her?"

"You knew, didn't you?"

"Rumors. Maybe I heard some talk. Can't trust rumors."

"Rumors." Hank began massaging the scars on his mangled hand.

"Yeah. At the beauty parlor. The girls were talking."

"Cut the shit. What did he say?"

"Who?"

"Who do you think?"

Sharon tried to remember if the gun was loaded.

"Randy says you and Terrence were talking at the Reservation about Mom."

"Randy. You believe anything that fool says?" She sat on the edge of the table, slid a finger into the drawer latch, and eased the drawer open a crack.

Junior's voice drifted from the hall. "Mommy, come and kiss me."

Sharon shouted, "Daddy was just leaving. Be there in a minute."

Hank stood over her, the hate filling his eyes. "Don't lie to me. You knew. I can see it. Never were a good liar. Randy says you and Terrence talked." He leaned forward, and she smelled whiskey on his breath. "You know more than you're saying."

His hand brushed her swollen cheek and he smiled. His fingers smelled of gun powder and solvent. "I just want to know what happened."

"You think Terrence knows so much, ask him."

"Already did. Got real nervous when I asked. What's

he so afraid of?"

Her finger tugged on the latch, and the drawer slid open a finger-width. "I don't know. Maybe his job. The chief. Who knows."

"Why would he be afraid of that pig?"

Sharon turned her cheek away from his hand. "He's not exactly the most honest cop there ever was. Maybe he's—"

"Mom." Junior's voice came muffled through the bedroom door.

"Just a minute." Her voice shook.

Hank's lips almost touched her cheek. "What are you saying?"

Sharon pulled away. "I got to tuck Junior in. You're a smart guy, you figure it out."

Hank cupped the back of her neck and pulled her face closer. "Oh, I will. First, I want to know what Terrence told you."

"He didn't—"

Hank grabbed a handful of hair and pulled her head back. "What did he say?"

A thousand needles stabbed into her scalp, and her eyes began to tear. Her fingers tugged at the drawer. "He was out there. He found his card. He was there before, and maybe is trying to cover it up."

"Mommy. Come and kiss me," Junior called.

"Terrence saw him?" Hank said.

"He was there with him. Told him it was an accident."

"He was with him?"

"After. Not when it happened." Her fingers groped for the gun, and a finger slid into the trigger guard.

Hank let go of her hair. His eyes continued to bore into hers. "You sure that's what he said?"

"Yes, I'm sure." Sharon held her breath as Hank

142

began to pace. She pulled her finger free of the gun then slowly slid the drawer shut. "Time for you to leave."

Hank stood in the doorway, staring into the dimly lit parking lot. He spoke into the night. "I want to know everything Terrence tells you. You'll do that for me, won't you?"

Sharon began walking to Junior's room. "Yeah. Sure."

"Looks like we got a murderer running around. I'd hate to see you or Junior be next."

Sharon's body vibrated with fear, her legs almost buckled as Hank passed through the doorway and staggered down the stairs. She ran to the door and her fingers shook as she fumbled with the door chain. The look in his eyes haunted her as she locked the door and hurried to Junior's room.

Junior's lanky body was sprawled on top of the covers. The light from the Sesame Street lamp tattooed his pale skin with green and pink. His red hair was a dirty tangle. Sharon pulled off his mud-caked socks and wet, soiled jeans, and kissed his grimy cheek. "Sleep tight. Don't let the bed bugs bite." She pulled the covers over his shivering legs and switched off the lamp.

Her toes stubbed into the foot of the kitchen table as she carried his dirty clothes to the laundry basket. She sat, messaging two toes she was convinced were broken. The tears began to flow as she stared through the dirty kitchen window at the glow of the moon. Sharon lit a cigarette, and cursed herself for not cleaning Hank's filth off Junior's skin.

The shadows deepened as a cloud drifted, blocking out the moon. That look. Hank's haunting, soulless eyes. The few remaining threads that tethered Hank to this world were fraying. When they tore apart, he would fall into a personal hell and would drag them down with him. The cloud passed and silver light highlighted a heart Junior had drawn on the dirty window. You want to know what Terrence says? I'll tell you everything you need to know.

Madison felt like he was sliding down the throat of some creature whose gut reeked of burnt coffee and beer. Below, a hulking shadow raised a long, serrated knife above his face. His eyes reflected back from the polished blade, wide with terror. Blood trickled down his neck from split lips.

The knife slashed down, sawing through his badge, and slicing through his jacket, and swept upward. The shadow's skeletal fingers, dripping in red, slashed downward again. Madison groped clumsily for the shadow's hands but grabbed the knife blade instead. Its serrated teeth drew back, chewing through skin, severing tendons, digging into bone with searing heat. He tried to scream, but only a faint whisper escaped from his throat.

Madison reached for the service weapon concealed in the shoulder holster beneath his jacket. He flipped the snap that held the gun in place and pulled the gun from the blood soaked leather. The gun barrel sank into the shadow like it was pressing into mud. He squeezed the trigger but heard only the dull thump of the hammer. The shadow slashed again, filleting the backs of his fingers.

Then Madison was lying in Edith's garden, the soft, moist soil boiling up around him, swallowing him into a grave. The smell of the rotting vegetables and maggots feasting on flesh filled his nose with suffocating sweetness. Deeper he sank into the earth as the pit rose up around him. At the lip of the hole, an axe handle overhung the opening. His bleeding fingers gripped the slick, wooden handle as it sprouted long thorns that stabbed into his torn flesh.

Edith peered down from the top of the grave, holding a shovel heaped with dirt. She frowned and shook her head, then tipped the shovel, letting the dirt fall. As the clods slapped him in the face, Madison choked and spat them from his mouth. Another shovel full thumped on his chest, and the walls of the grave began to crumble. He coughed dirt from his lungs and pleaded with Edith to stop, to give him another chance. She plunged the shovel into the earth above and held the heaping blade above his face and tipped the shovel sideways.

Then Madison was seated in a folding chair, looking up at an oak desk that rose ten feet above him. On the edge of the desk, a cassette tape recorder sat on end, the spokes of the tape inside slowly turning. Two familiar voices spoke unintelligibly above. The internal affairs sergeant behind the desk leaned forward and peered down at him. He toasted Madison from a shiny flask and tipped a drink. The shadowy, camouflaged face of a man hooded like the Grim Reaper loomed over the edge of the desk. Two fingers of his hand gripped a scythe.

Edith stepped from the shadows behind them, dressed in a black judge's robe. A hangman's noose dug into a bleeding gash in her neck. *Guilty. You're all guilty. The whole lot of you.* She raised a huge, dark, wooden gavel. *Chief, put your hands on the desk.*

Madison clenched his shackled hands together and watched in horror as Edith pulled the chains and his hands began to rise. *No. No!* he screamed as his hands slowly stretched upward. *No. Please, stop.* Pain stabbed from his wrists as the sharp-edged metal shackles tightened, opening flesh as they squeezed skin against bone.

On the desk! Edith commanded.

Madison gasped as a sulfurous fire burned in his chest. *Please, help . . .*

Edith raised the gavel higher. As it paused mid-air the handle grew, and the head narrowed into the shape of an axe blade. *If I can't have your knuckles, I'll have your neck.* Her head wilted limply to her shoulder exposing severed tendons and blood vessels that squirmed like a nest of snakes. The hooded man grabbed the noose hanging from Edith's neck and pulled her head upright. Edith's eyes glowed red and a forked tongue slithered from her mouth. *I sentence you to death.*

Madison pulled against the shackles as the hooded man lifted him and pinned his head on the desk. The axe swung in a long, sweeping arc, and the blade sliced into the soft skin of his throat, sinking deeper, severing tissues, and splintering bone. The warm air rushed from his lungs as his windpipe parted. His jaw clinched, shuttered, then fell open. Then Madison was strangely weightless, floating with eyes open, watching the room tumble.

Terrence stood beside Edith, looking down at him. *Things aren't always as they seem. No, sir.* He turned and ran to a chain link fence and leapt onto the woven steel.

Madison bolted upright from the nightmare, gasping in agony from the pain exploding in his chest. He groped in the dark for the phone beside the bed and punched the buttons for 911.

"Police, fire, or medical?" Doris's voice spoke.

"Doris? It's—"

"Is this an emergency?"

It's me. Chief Madison."

"Chief Madison?"

"I need—"

"My, aren't you up early today. To what do we owe this honor?"

A flaming arrow shot through his chest. "I think I'm having—"

"Hold on a second, Chief. Got an emergency call coming in."

"This is an—"

Waves of nausea rolled over him as the phone line cut to elevator music. The music stopped, and her voice spoke from a distance, "So what can I do for you, Chief?"

"I think I'm . . . heart . . . "

"Chief, I can't hear you. Speak up."

"Ambulance . . . heart attack."

"Chief? I can't hear you."

I've died and gone to hell. Only the flames of hell could explain the pain searing through Madison's chest as he tumbled in the darkness. Did I miss the light? I thought we got the option to return, go to the light and get a second chance.

"Chief. Chief Madison. Can you hear me?" Her voice spoke from somewhere above.

He was drowning, sinking, thrashing to gasp air as a tube slid down his throat triggering a gag against waves of fire. Voices spoke far away, a language of urgent fragments. "BP 176 over 102, pupils dilated, prophylactic—Can you hear me? Mr. Madison? Can—"

A plastic mask covered Madison's mouth and nose. His cheeks puffed as air billowed into his lungs. Another cracking punch to the sternum followed by rhythmic compressions against his chest. A voice counted, one, two, three, four, five, then another rush of air into his mouth and nose. More compressions crunching the splintered cartilage attached to his breast bone. Madison wanted to curse with each breath. *Leave me alone. Get your hands off me!* Then he slid into the black again.

Madison felt the press against his eyelid, then it raised. Her face loomed over him. The nurse scowled, gray curly hair sprouting beneath her white uniform cap. Her bushy brows were a thicket of thorns above dark eyes. "Mr. Madison, can you hear me?" She split into twins then Madison's eyelid lowered. Fingers wedged the other eyelid open and a light slid across the horizon like a comet slicing through the night sky. The light darted left then right. Some light, Madison thought. It's not supposed to hurt.

Another stab in the arm and he was falling backward, sliding down into the darkness, the fire in his chest fading as numbness spread into his arms and legs.

"Chief Madison!"

"This isn't happening," he mumbled as nausea swelled in his stomach and crawled up his throat. "Not again."

Madison felt a slow dislocation from himself as if he were peeling off wet clothing. Free of their weight, he rose and watched with detached fascination from above as the frantic ghosts below handled him like a slab of beef.

"Stay with us!" a doctor ordered.

Then Madison was sinking, being pulled down, being sucked into the limp, bloated body lying on the table.

Monday

Terrence looked out his patrol car's new windshield. Without the accumulation of nicks and the yellow film of cigarette smoke, the world looked cleaner. Even Bronson seemed to notice as he sat up in back, staring forward.

Terrence turned onto Bridge Street and saw Sharon leaning over the bridge railing looking down at the river. Bronson barked as if in recognition. Sharon turned as he pulled the car to the edge of the roadway beside her and rolled down the window. "Don't jump!"

Sharon flashed a faint smile. The sunlight painted her shape in shadows beneath her white blouse. The breeze lifted her hair and sent wisps of red curls across her sunglasses. Freckles peppered her cheeks in a mischievous way. She leaned further over the railing and spat.

Terrence pulled across the bridge, parked at the side of the road, and walked back to join her. "That's against the law you know."

"So arrest me."

"I'd normally let you go with a warning, but I know

what you think of those."

She spat again, and Terrence looked over the railing, watching it drift down and ride on the smooth green surface of the stream. "Listen, about yesterday, I may have overreacted a little." Terrence smiled and kicked a pebble over the edge of the sidewalk. "I didn't mean to be so hard on you. I was just frustrated."

"It wasn't your fault." Terrence said. "I'm sorry, too."

He stared down at the water twisting around the dry rocks, the sun sparkling off the water like a thousand twinkling stars.

Sharon said, "Remember how we used to dare each other to jump?"

"When you jumped, I thought you'd killed yourself." Terrence rubbed his stomach. "Belly flop from twenty-five feet. I don't know what you were thinking. Course, if you jumped now, you'd break your neck. There was no dare you wouldn't take. I always admired that about you."

"You didn't jump, even when all your pals were calling you chicken. I always admired that about you." She leaned her back against the railing and raised her sunglasses to face the sun. "Things were simpler then."

"You can say that again. Sometimes I wish I could go back and do things different."

"Like what?"

"You'll laugh."

"I know. A professional basketball player. You were good you know."

"I guess I was all right, but not that."

"President of the United States?"

"Yeah, right. The air force. I'd have been a pilot. One of the Blue Angels. Can't imagine anything more exciting than flying."

"And dropping bombs or shooting other planes."

"They don't do that."

"No offense, but I can't see it. The shiny planes and fancy uniforms, they're all just a cover up for the nasty things they do."

"They show what the planes can do. They fly to keep us free."

Sharon looked at him with one eye squinted shut. "Freedom."

"Freedom," he said.

"Sometimes freedom's the scariest thing I know."

Bronson barked at three boys walking too close to the car. They jumped and ran. "You boys get on now," Terrence said. "Kids."

"Kids," Sharon said. "I remember the days. Never thought things would turn out this way."

"Would you do anything different?"

Sharon laughed. "What wouldn't I do different? I'd have to go back to the third grade. She turned and looked down at the riverbed again. "My first fight with Edith. You were there. I remember you sitting in the back on the first day of school. I thought you were in my grade because you were so tall. When Edith told me to sit down and quit talking, I just had to stand up."

"I remember you said, 'I'm the boss of myself.'"

Sharon shook her head. "People have been trying to prove me wrong ever since."

"I thought you were the most beautiful girl in the whole world. Couldn't stop staring at that curly red hair of yours."

"You sure it wasn't the missing teeth?"

"I didn't care. You were a red-haired angel."

"I thought you were pretty cute, too."

"Is that why you kicked me on the playground?"

"We were kids," Sharon said. "I couldn't just say it."

"Do-overs. I wish we could still have them, sometimes."

Sharon picked up a pebble and threw it.

Terrence said. "I'm going to do something about you and Hank."

"Terrence, you're a good guy, but I can handle myself."

"But you shouldn't have to. We've . . . I've let you down. Everybody in town knows he hurts you. We should have stopped him a long time ago. It's not okay."

"What are you going to do?"

"My job. I'm going to do my job."

"What's that? Your job I mean."

"Make him stop hurting you."

"How?"

"I'll . . . "

"What can you do?" If you threaten Hank, there's no telling what he might do. Probably just make things worse, if that's possible."

"If he hurts you again, I'll arrest him. They'll put a restraining order on him. If he comes around again, he'll go to jail."

"You always were naive," Sharon said. "You think enforcing the law will make people stop hurting each other. You really think Hank cares if he goes to jail? I think he's more at home in there than out."

"At least when he's locked up he can't hurt you."

"No. But he'll have lots of time to think about how he will when he gets out."

"The restraining order—"

"Won't mean a thing if he's drunk and bent on revenge." She looked like she wondered how he could be so uncomprehending. "You able to stand guard at my place twenty-four hours a day? That's what it would take. Even then, he'd still get to us."

"I won't just stand by and let it happen again. It's about time he picked on someone his own size."

"Do you really think you're big enough?"

Terrence felt her eyes sizing him up. They betrayed a moment of hope that blew away in the breeze.

"I think so. Next time he hits you, call me first."

"Why? So you can fly your plane over and drop some bombs?"

"Just do it."

"I'm not so sure you'd like what you saw."

"Like what?"

"I've gotten in a few licks of my own. What if you had to arrest *me*?"

"Self-defense. You're allowed to protect yourself."

"Am I?"

"I'm trying to help. But you —"

"Have to help you. I've heard it before. The last time I called, I went to jail."

"It'll be different this time. Just call me before you do anything crazy."

"Crazy? Is that what it was? You want to hear what happened the night your buddy, Madison, arrested me?"

"That's in the past —"

"I think you should hear it." She gripped the railing. "Madison refused to listen. The judge sure as hell wasn't interested. It's about time somebody did."

"Sharon, you don't have to. It's water under the bridge, pardon the pun."

"Ha, ha. You need to know. It's called rape, Terrence. It's called being strangled and left for dead. It's called torture."

"You don't have to let it continue."

"Don't I?" She spat over the railing again. "Funny thing is, sometimes I think I deserve it."

"You can stop it."

"Only if someone listens. Everyone around here is deaf."

"Leave then."

"God, it's so easy for men. Pack up and leave. It's not so easy for women. You wonder why I stay?"

"I don't."

"I stay because if I don't the courts will hand Junior over to him. Imagine Junior living with him. How long do you think he'd last? If he survived, what kind of twisted life would he have? Hank's whipping boy or worse."

"I won't let it come to that. I promise."

Sharon's voice quivered. "Who do you think I am?"

"What?"

"You don't know who I've become. I'm no longer that girl in third grade. I'm a drug addict, getting old before my time. I'm gonna live and die an empty life in this town and be forgotten like the rest." Sharon covered her face and began to cry.

Terrence pulled her into his arms and held her. "You're a good mother. Don't you see how Junior loves you? You don't miss anything, except what a good person you are." He lifted her chin and looked into her eyes. "You're the only girl I ever loved. I don't care what's happened. I'll make it right for you and Junior."

Sharon looked up, searching his face. "I want that too."

"Come on, let me give you a ride home." He walked her to his police car and opened the door. Bronson wagged his tail and barked.

"No radar this time," Terrence said.

Madison felt like he was coming up for his last breath. His eyes opened, and he thought he was floating down a long hallway dotted with lights, then his head cleared a little more, and he realized he was being rolled on a gurney. The air was cold and smelled of alcohol and Lysol. Nothing good can come of such a smell, he thought. He slowly rolled his head, trying to catch his bearings. The face of the nurse came into focus. "Where am I?"

She smiled. "McMinnville General Hospital." He realized her smile was an upside down frown.

"What?"

"You're in the hospital. It appears you had a heart attack—apparently, not your first."

The ceiling pivoted ninety degrees, and the ceiling tiles took on the golden hue of the morning sun. "Your room is this way. I see you have a visitor already."

Madison rolled through the doorway, and the nurse parked him beside the bed. "Don't try to get up. We'll move you."

He had no interest in trying to move—until he saw Dickerson seated in the corner, and the first throbbings of his awakening chest began.

"Just wait here," she said, as if he could do otherwise. "We'll be back to situate you in the bed. Is there anything I can get you?"

"Don't suppose Scotch is an option?"

She rolled her eyes and slid the cloth curtain closed that shielded him from the hallway.

Dickerson folded an edition of the *Sheridan Sun* and asked, "How are you feeling?"

"How does it look?"

"Perhaps now you'll heed the doctor's advice and stop those disgusting habits before you end up in the morgue."

"If I give up those habits, I might as well be there already."

"Keep it up and you'll get your wish."

Madison's eyes went blurry and wandered in separate orbits for a moment, making Dickerson seem to do-si-do with himself. "I could use a little more of whatever they gave me for the pain." His tongue felt like a stuffed potato sprinkled with taste buds.

Dickerson turned the page. "Dodged a bullet again. How many lives do you have left?"

"Stopped counting."

"You just relax. Doctor says it'll be awhile before you get discharged. He says you're lucky to still be with us."

Madison's eyelids suddenly felt like they were anchored with bags of sand. He let them slide closed then hefted them open again. "Terrence."

"What about him?" Dickerson said.

"Stop," he drifted again then snapped back. "Tell him to stop whatever he's doing. Not another step . . . Edith." One eyelid refused to stay open and drooped down halfway.

"Now don't you worry about him. Your job right now is to get better."

Madison rolled his head toward Dickerson and saw his dual images slide further apart then merge back together. "You don't understand. He's got no idea."

"You leave him to me. I'll make sure he gets the job done."

"That's what I'm afraid of."

Dickerson scooted his chair next to Madison and

lowered his voice to a whisper. "Don't you see? With you recovering, Terrence can pursue the investigation wherever it may lead. He's a smart boy. I'm sure he will agree with us about Hank's involvement. People will expect action. The rumors are already spreading, and you wouldn't like some of them."

"Rumors? Like what?"

Dickerson's voice lowered further. "Like Edith was killed so we could seize her farm. Like you were hired as a hit man."

"Nonsense," Madison said.

"You and I know that, but they don't. People are scared. In my experience, scared people aren't the most rational. They want someone to blame, someone to lynch."

"So let me get this straight. Under your guidance, Terrence arrests Hank for his mom's murder."

"Precisely. The lad becomes a hero, and you and I are freed of any suspicion."

"We *are* innocent—at least I am," said Madison.

"We both are, but you cannot be so naive as to think the court of public opinion has any concern with the facts. No. Let Terrence arrest Hank and our worries are over."

"Only one problem," Madison said.

"What's that?"

"Arresting Hank. You really think Terrence is up for that?"

"We'll cross that bridge when we come to it. The important thing is for you to focus on recovering."

"How am I going to recover with Terrence chasing Hank and his buddies all over the countryside?"

"Unstop those ears of yours. I said I would direct the investigation."

"You? What gives you any right? I seem to recall your only experience with law enforcement was the night I locked you up."

"The boy's been to the academy," Dickerson said. He's accounted for himself well for nearly two years. I think he's ready."

The anesthesia faded further, ushering in another round of chest throbbing. The pressure behind Madison's eyes made them feel like they were about to pop free from their sockets. "I hate to break the news, but he's not. You've got to turn this over to the state. They'll know what to do."

"Do you really want them poking their noses into our business? I seem to recall some financial decisions that might not sit well with them. Their investigation is bound to unearth your sordid history with Portland. Heaven help us if they start combing through the city books."

Madison's head felt as if it was splitting. "You don't know what you're saying." The line of the heart monitor began to zigzag faster, and his blood pressure climbed.

"I've decided to reorganize the department, temporarily."

"I'm the chief. I make those decisions." The throbbing in Madison's chest felt like someone was playing the drums on his sternum with a pair of hammers.

"Not while you're recovering," Dickerson said. "I'm promoting Terrence to chief, at least until you return."

"What?" Madison croaked. "You can't—" The alarm on the heart monitor began to emit a shrill beep. Voices yelled in the hallway near the nurse's station. Footsteps turned into a small stampede as a voice called code blue over the intercom.

"I can and I will," Dickerson said, as a male nurse

swept back the curtain and pushed in the crash cart.

Terrence stared through the window in the waiting room as the first light of morning reflected off the windshield of an ambulance parked by the emergency entrance. One of the crew loaded a gurney through the ambulance's rear doors. His partner, dressed in a matching blue Yamhill County Medical jacket, slammed the doors shut. A bead of sweat slithered down Terrence's back beneath his stiff Kevlar vest. He stretched to awaken muscles that had settled into a hunched stiffness brought on by five hours of anxious waiting in a hard plastic chair.

A runny-nosed kid pushed a plastic fire truck in circles across the tile as his mother stared at the floor. Her bloodshot eyes met with Terrence's, and she glanced away as if she'd been caught in a lie. Her thin smile betrayed a hint of distrust for the big man in uniform. Her head leaned back against the wall as the TV broke from Good Morning America to commercial.

Down the hall, beyond the doors stamped DO NOT ENTER, someone yelled, then the intercom cracked "Code blue." A stampede erupted on the other side of the intensive care ward doors. "Code blue," the speaker in the hall blared again. A gruff male voice shouted, "No. You'll have to leave. Now!" Dickerson's voice protested indignantly just before the double doors flew open, and Dickerson skated across the freshly waxed floor. A burly male nurse pointed to the emergency exit doors. "Exit's that way."

Dickerson straightened his glasses and tugged his shirt sleeves. "I was just trying to—"

"Keep walking," the nurse said before noticing

Terrence. "Officer, if this man comes back, I want him arrested." He scowled at Dickerson and shoved back through the doors.

Dickerson looked at Terrence then gave a final tug on his suit-jacket collar. A red blush plumed on Dickerson's face as his fingers ran through his thinning gray comb over. "The indignities!"

"What was that about?" Terrence asked.

Dickerson sat in the chair beside Terrence. "Seems the chief's taken a turn for the worse. His temper, the drinking, and cigarettes finally caught up with him. Stubborn as a mule."

Terrence leaned back in his chair as the TV gave the morning traffic report, trying to shake the feeling that this was all a bad dream. The TV showed grainy pictures of cars crawling at caterpillar speed along the Banfield Freeway.

Dickerson leaned toward Terrence and whispered, "The chief needs better medical care than they can provide here. Between you and me, I wouldn't trust the witch doctors here to de-flea my dog. He's stabilized, for now, but it's touch and go. They plan to move him—"

"How serious is it?"

"Serious as a heart attack—literally. You know it's his second? He won't be back for awhile—if at all. Looks like he may need a transplant. Waste of a good heart if you ask me."

"A transplant?"

"Yes. But I'm afraid we've got much more serious things to worry about right now."

"A heart transplant? Doesn't get more serious than that."

"Yes, yes." Dickerson leaned closer and Terrence slumped lower. "I understand you responded to

Edith's."

"Yes, sir." Terrence watched the kid playing out some imaginary emergency in the lobby as he parked his fire truck next to a Gideon's Bible apparently fully engulfed in flames. His mom paged through a tattered magazine. Terrence shifted, feeling for the one spot he'd found in the seat that didn't bore into his behind. "Chief said it was an accident. Edith cut herself."

"Accident?" Dickerson's eyebrows raised and his eyes bulged behind the thick lenses of his glasses. "I detect a note of disagreement with that assessment?"

"He's got a lot more experience than I do."

"So you agree?"

Terrence straightened. "I . . . "

"You have doubts."

"Doubts?"

"Doubts, yes. It's written all over your face."

Terrence whispered, "It's just the way it looked. I don't see . . . let's just say more investigation's warranted."

Dickerson patted him on the knee. "I just spoke with the chief."

"Oh?"

The kid knocked over the Bible and shouted orders to imaginary firefighters to find more water. Apparently the truck had gone empty.

Dickerson leaned closer, and Terrence slouched deeper. He whispered into Terrence's ear. "The chief said it was critical for you to gather whatever evidence there may be. He agreed further investigation was necessary to solve this case, and you were just the man to do it. The chief took note of your thorough work at the scene of her tragic death. He was especially impressed with your police instincts—"

"Are we talking about the same guy?"

"I know the chief may seem overly critical of you at times, but that's because he sees your potential. That's why we chose you, Terrence. We both believe you just need a chance to prove yourself."

"He really said that?"

"And that's why I'm confident you will solve this case. With your investigative skills and my resources, we'll catch the man who murdered poor Mrs. Sherman. I'd say the list of suspects is pretty short wouldn't you?"

The TV cut to blue and red emergency lights strobing at the scene of an accident. Terrence's thoughts collided and jammed. Why Madison's newfound confidence in him? Was it the medicine? The brush with death? He'd heard of dying confessions. Maybe this was Madison's last chance to unburden his conscience.

Dickerson's voice broke into his thoughts. "Terrence, I won't presume to tell you how to do your job, but I think it's pretty clear who the killer is. Don't you?"

"Mayor Dickerson," Terrence began, "it's important not to jump to conclusions, to narrow the list of suspects too soon. Too easy to ignore the facts or force them to fit a theory. First rule of good detective work—keep an open mind."

"Very good. So who—"

"Motive, means, and opportunity. Those are key."

Dickerson nodded. "And in Edith's case who fits that bill?"

Terrence pulled out his notebook, clicked his pen, and turned to a blank page. He poised his pen above the paper.

"Think, Terrence," Dickerson said. "Who has the most to gain from Edith's death?"

Terrence saw the answer in Dickerson's eyes as plain

as day. Madison had often bragged of the big raise he'd get when the prison was built. The feds had promised lots of cash would flow into the town. That would mean a bigger office, more officers, and a fat retirement check when the time came. He wrote "Madison."

Dickerson examined the page and looked puzzled. "We need to keep this between you and me. Is that clear?"

The thoughts continued to pile up in Terrence's head. If Dickerson suspected Madison, the chief would have to be kept out of the investigation. *If I work fast enough, maybe I can wrap up the case while he recovers. An investigation kept within the department would limit the splatter from this juicy roast, but why would Madison want me to conduct an investigation that might finger him for a murder?*

"Why me, Mayor? Shouldn't the state step in? I appreciate your support, but if we're right . . . "

"We've got to keep this between us. If he finds out, there's no telling what he might do. You and he have quite a history together. He likes you, trusts you—at least as much as he's capable of trusting anyone. We all know he's unpredictable and dangerous. He has access to God knows how many guns, and it's no secret he's caught up in that uniform and all that paramilitary nonsense. Who knows what goes on in his head. If he got wind that you were investigating him, who knows what he might do. No. This has got to stay strictly between you and me."

"What about when he gets out?"

"Gets out?"

"From the hospital."

"I'll handle the chief. He's scheduled to have another surgery soon, anyway. He'll be out of commission for a while."

The crew outside crawled into their ambulance and flipped on their emergency lights and siren. The boy jumped up and ran to the window. "Look mommy!" His mother flipped the page of her magazine and closed her eyes. The ambulance pulled a hard U-turn and drove off into the dusty sunrise.

Dickerson patted Terrence's shoulder. "You look worried. Everything will be all right. I promise."

"It's just so hard to believe."

"You may think you know him, but believe me, I know him better. I'm not surprised at all. Anything you need, just ask."

"Yes, sir. I will."

"Remember. He must not get wind of the nature of this investigation. That means no talking to anyone—especially Sharon. I know how persuasive she can be."

"Well she—"

"No, Terrence. Stop right there. She can *not* know."

"But the chief—"

Dickerson smiled. "He was the chief. As of today, you bear that title. I'm promoting you to chief."

"Chief?"

"Promoting you, yes."

Terrence let the title roll around in his mind. He'd often wondered what it would feel like, though he'd entertained little hope of ever finding out. Right now it felt like climbing the first hill of a roller coaster, knowing that somewhere down the track the rails had come loose.

"This is your chance," Dickerson said. "Make us proud."

A chance to shine. He swallowed hard. "I'll do my best."

"I know you will. Don't forget, I'm behind you. The

whole town is behind you. You've got what it takes. Trust your instincts."

Terrence chuckled.

"What's so funny?"

"The chief once said, 'If I want you to have instincts, I'll issue you some.'"

Dickerson patted him on the shoulder. "People will be looking to you now. While you're in charge, you'll need to run the investigation through me. I need to approve any important decisions you make. If you have any questions, make sure you come to me—and only to me. I want no communication about this with the chief, for obvious reasons—even if he orders. Understood?"

Terrence nodded.

"Good boy. You're a born leader. Let's see how well the office of chief suits you, Chief Washburn. Make us proud and remember, any help you need, call me."

"Yes, sir."

The double doors opened and the male nurse who'd ejected Dickerson stepped wearily through and glared at them. "Why are you still here?"

Dickerson scowled at the nurse and hastened to the exit.

The nurse made a what-gives gesture to Terrence. "Officer . . . "

"Washburn. Chief Washburn."

"Whatever. You'll have to come back later. He's been sedated and will be out for a while. I think he's had about all the visitors he can handle for one day."

"Thanks for your help doctor—"

"Nurse. Nurse Johnson," he replied and pushed back through the doors.

Terrence imagined sitting behind the chief's desk, bracketed by the twin flags of Oregon and The United

States. He could feel the slick surface of the glistening mahogany. The knots in his back untangled as he imagined sinking into the plush leather of the executive chair. Chief Washburn, he thought, time to get to work.

The kid ran his fire truck in several circles until it collided with his mother's foot and flipped. "Truck's on fire! Run! It's gonna blow!"

Terrence pulled into the parking space stenciled COP. The Suburban's air conditioning cooled the interior as he listened to The Eagles on the tape cassette player. Finally a car he could almost sit in comfortably. He'd clean out the empties on the passenger's side floorboard later. Madison was a slob, no doubt about it. Time to bring some respectability to the chief's position.

He wondered how Madison was doing. How could a man staring death in the eyes continue so many bad habits? Why don't some people learn? He set the parking break and thought of his own mother, wheezing and lighting up cigarettes, breathing the air fed into her nose through clear tubes while her oxygen tank stood beside her with a sticker warning of fire hazard. And Sharon, the victim of frequent beatings and mental abuse, unwilling to cut her ties with Hank. And Junior the next in line when Hank's anger needed someone to tie to the whipping post. Why did she keep coming back when Hank brought them both such suffering?

Maybe he could change things now, get some justice for Edith, for Sharon, and for Junior. Terrence shut off the engine and sat in silence trying to think like a chief.

He took the three steps up to the back door of the police station in one stride. So many things to do, so many questions to be answered. He pushed open the door and saw Beverly seated behind the counter with the newspaper spread before her.

Terrence suddenly realized everything had changed. Beverly had often lectured him on the proper way to perform his duties. He'd taken it, allowing for the need some old folks had to feel in charge. He was the boss now, and so many things were going to change.

"Good Morning," Terrence said.

Beverly looked up from the paper and pasted on a thin smile. "Good morning to you, Chief."

Chief. The title felt like the first drink of lemonade on a blistering summer day. There it is, he thought. Her eyes drifted back to the paper, and she scribbled on the crossword puzzle.

No time like the present to set the tone of his rule. "You heard. Gonna be a busy day," he said. "Hold my calls till I can get things organized."

"Roger."

Maybe this won't be so hard, Terrence thought. Madison wasn't much of an act to follow. He made rare appearances in the office, and the phone rang little, most likely because folks knew he wouldn't answer, and their requests for return calls would go unheeded. Starting now, that would change. Time to engage—that was the word they used at the academy. In fact he'd go further. Community Oriented Policing would be his push. The job was his—at least for now—and he was going to drive it like he stole it. He wrapped his fist around the door knob to his new office and turned to Beverly.

"On second thought, don't hold my calls."

Beverly peered at him over pink readers, "Send them through. Yes, sir." She smiled and pulled a stack of mail and a manila envelope from the chief's mail slot.

He twisted, but the knob didn't budge. "Beverly, it's

locked."

She stood before him holding the stack of envelopes. "Indeed. He always keeps his office door locked." Beverly handed the stack to Terrence. "Here is your mail and your reports for the past two weeks."

He took the stack. "The key?"

She smiled and rolled her eyes.

"The key to the office. Do you know where it is?"

"The chief always keeps it with him. I don't believe there are any duplicates. You might consider using his other office," she said.

The suit jacket Terrence hadn't worn since high school graduation seemed to be slowly strangling him. Though the sleeves and pant legs were two inches too short, it was the most official looking outfit he owned for his new position.

"I'll be out," Terrence said. "Hold my calls after all."

Beverly smiled. "I think Harvey's Locksmith has a master. I can have him drop it off if you like."

"Why does he have a key? Kind of defeats the purpose doesn't it?"

"This wouldn't be the first time the key got misplaced."

"I guess that would be fine," Terrence said. "I'll be at the other office."

Beverly picked up the phone and nodded.

Terrence pulled down the block to the Reservation and parked the Suburban in the handicap spot out front, Madison's customary spot. He remembered his pledge to reform the chief's reputation and pulled around back instead. He walked through the backdoor and took the familiar booth in the corner. The dim cone of light would help him focus on his next moves. He hoped Sharon would be working, so he could impress her with the news of his temporary promotion. He opened the menu and his sleeves crawled further up his arms.

"Look what the dog drug in." Randy stood beside the booth in the shadows. "What are you all dressed up for? Is that the suit you wore at graduation?"

Terrence closed the menu and tugged at his sleeves. "The very same. I forget, what did you wear to your graduation? Oh, that's right . . . "

Randy frowned.

"I'll have some coffee—black."

"Haven't seen your buddy Madison. Usually he's here by now."

"Mayor's put me in charge for a while."

"Put you in charge? Of what?"

Terrence pulled out his leather badge holder and pointed at the gold badge. "It says Chief of Police, Sheridan Oregon. This town is my responsibility, at least until he recovers."

"Recovers? From what, a hangover?"

"I'm not authorized to say, but it's serious."

"Let me guess, heart attack?"

Terrence opened his briefcase and pulled out the stack of mail. "Like I said—"

"No Shi—"

"Randy." Sharon's voice came from the back growling with irritation. "I could use some help back here."

"Hey, look who's here," Randy yelled. "The new chief of police. All dressed up and nowhere to go."

Sharon walked out from the back rubbing her hands on a dishtowel. "What are you—"

Terrence smiled and tugged at his sleeves. "Sharon, good to see you."

Sharon grinned. "What are you all dressed up for?"

"The mayor's put me in charge."

"In charge of what?"

"That's what I said," Randy blurted out.

Sharon waved her towel toward kitchen. "You mind?"

"Not a bit," Randy said, then walked into the office.

"Mayor's appointed me chief until Madison gets back."

"So you'll be in charge of yourself?" Sharon said.

"I'll be executing all the duties of the chief's office. Now, if I could get some coffee?"

"Where's Madison?" She slid into the booth opposite him.

"Can't say. He's just—"

"Heart attack," Randy shouted.

"Heart attack?"

"Yeah, maybe." He shuffled through the mail: a manila envelope from a vacation resort, three envelopes from the assessor's office, and something that might have been from a collection agency. "Anyway, I'm in charge now. At least until he gets back."

She grabbed his badge holder and ran her finger across the metal. Chief Washburn. Sounds kind of good, doesn't it."

"Yeah, I guess." He flipped over a coffee cup and held it up. "How about some coffee for the new chief?"

"Coffee's still brewing." She leaned in and whispered. "Any more news about you know who?"

"Maybe." Terrence spun the cup. "Seems my hunch wasn't so bad after all."

Sharon slapped her hand on the table. "See! I told you!"

A pot clanked on the kitchen floor and Randy cursed.

"Mayor agrees, too," Terrence continued. "Said I was doing a good—"

"Wait, so Dad said Madison did it?"

"Not exactly. He just said I should trust my instincts."

She folded his badge holder and handed it back. "My instincts say don't trust him. What else did he say?"

Terrance could feel his feet tangling in the net she had cast. He knew the more they talked, the more confused he would get. "Sharon, I can't discuss an ongoing investigation. Let's just say, I'm keeping an open mind. It's important to follow all leads. Right now, we don't know who it was."

"The card Terrence. Why was the chief out there?"

Terrence slid his cup toward her.

She took it and shook her head.

"It's all about the evidence."

"So what's your next move?"

"The examination. The medical examiner said I could attend."

"Examination?"

"The forensic evaluation. The autopsy. Once we know the cause of death—"

"Isn't that kind of obvious?"

"See, that's what I'm talking about. You can't jump to conclusions. You have to investigate, look at all the facts."

The front door swung open and two regulars bellied up to the bar.

Sharon took Terrence's cup and scooted from the booth. "Little town like this, lots of folks will talk. I'll keep my ears open. If I hear anything, you'll be the first to know."

Tuesday

After a fitful night's sleep, Dickerson woke early, trying to convince himself Terrence would do as he was told. As long as he kept the investigation between the two of them, his plan had a chance of working, but promotions had a way of changing people. Maybe Terrence would find the courage to do a real investigation, if he even knew what that was. I'll have to keep him on a short leash to make sure he doesn't miss evidence tying Hank to the murder.

He rolled out of bed careful not to wake Margaret and dressed for a stroll through the vines flowing in uniform rows down the sloping hills from his house. The crisp morning air had a way of putting his mind at ease, if only for a short while.

The night of the council vote was a little more than a week away. A divided council had derailed the new federal correctional facility from the fast track more than once. The promise of an infusion of federal money did little to allay the fears of Sheridan's elderly citizens. Like most, they lived in the happy delusion that real criminals resided elsewhere. They also shared the not entirely unreasonable belief that someone would eventually escape from the prison, no matter how secure they built it. There could be no more delay. This time he'd get the vote he wanted. No more waffling and hand wringing. The fence sitters would get a shove.

Dickerson quietly closed the porch door and leaned on the upper deck railing surveying the rolling hills of vines. He imagined Edith lying in her tiny garden bleeding from the neck. A sad end to a life spent raising the kids of the town, he thought. She'd turned the one-room school house into home for four generations. Dickerson had spent his final three years of school under her tutelage, learning not to let his slight stature keep him from his dreams. He credited her with his rise from runt of the litter to mayor and benefactor of Sheridan.

Dickerson descended the steps from the porch to the back lawn and walked through the dewy grass into the soft soil of the vineyard. The morning fog settled over the fertile valley and drifted around the lower rows. Dickerson breathed in the cool, moisture-laden air and felt a rare moment of peace.

To his left, he heard the rustle of vines. His pesky companion this morning was a raccoon pulling at a cluster of shriveled grapes. Dickerson bent slowly to seize a rock as the raccoon stood on his hind legs tugging a branch. Dickerson's fingers searched the rough surface of the rock for a grip. He squeezed and slowly pulled back as the raccoon plucked the cluster and sniffed the air.

"Sure you want to do that?" The gravelly voice sent a ripple of electricity up Dickerson's back and clinched his gut. He froze, half-cocked, considering just where the voice had come from. A breeze stirred the grape leaves.

"What do you want?" Dickerson said, still searching.

"Might just piss him off."

Dickerson turned in the direction of the voice behind him. Hank's camouflaged pants and boots were visible beneath the vines, and the crown of his militia cap rose above a tangle of branches. "I felt one's claws and teeth once. Pretty sharp. Feisty little shit till its neck broke."

"What do you want, Hank?"

Hank's boots stepped closer. "I want to know why."

"Why what?"

"Why you did it."

"I don't know what you're talking about." Dickerson slowly backed away.

"Oh come on. You were there. Was it for the farm? The money?"

"I don't know what you think I did, but I had only your mother's best interests in mind. She—"

"She was losing it, and you took advantage of her." Hank's boots walked closer. "Taking advantage of an old lady. Don't get much lower than that."

"I never—"

"She wouldn't give you what you wanted."

"She wanted to sell the farm, for your dad, for you."

Hank laughed. "Expect me to believe that?"

"Your father's legacy, she called it. And you with enough money to make something of yourself."

"How much money? I bet you were real generous. How much?"

"The exact amount wasn't set, but it would have been fair."

"To who?"

Dickerson gripped the rock and hoped to get a clear view of Hank's head. He might have one shot.

"So why then?"

"Why what?"

"Why'd you kill her?"

"Do you really believe I killed her? Let the investigators do their job. Let's see to whom the finger points."

"The investigators. You mean Terrence and Chief Lard-Ass?"

Dickerson felt the vines shove against his back and realized he was cornered.

Hank's boots continued their steady forward march. "I'd expect them to finger whoever you said." His head came into view and he smiled. "Let me guess. You got me in your sights, right?"

"I've instructed Terrence to conduct a thorough and impartial investigation—"

"As long as he says what you want." Hank's camouflaged face melted into the vines.

"Why would I tell Terrence to investigate if I had anything to do with it?" Dickerson's trembling fingers squeezed the rock.

Hank pulled out his K-bar knife and slashed at the vines between them. "I ain't stupid, Dickie. You know Terrence will tell you whatever you want to hear. Tell you what. I got an offer."

"What could you possibly offer?" Dickerson felt for an opening in the vines behind him.

Hank stepped through a gap in the branches. "I'd suggest you hear me out before you do something stupid."

With a clear view of Hank's face, Dickerson's fingers gripped the rock tighter. He had one shot.

Hank's eyes glanced at his hand. "Miss a raccoon and he'll run off. Miss me, well, let's say, I won't be the one running. Course you'll only get as far as I let you. But like I said, maybe we can help each other out."

Dickerson hurled the rock with all his might. He watched the stone rip off several leaves, and ricochet off the post beside the raccoon. The raccoon hissed and scampered away.

"That's probably the best throw you ever made."

"What do you want?"

Hank stepped closer and looked over the hillside. "The two of us out in the middle of the dirt. Lord knows what can happen to old folks once they're out in the dirt."

"I won't stand here and be threatened."

Hank cut off a branch and sharpened its end. "Don't see as you got much choice." The skin of bark curled away as his knife ran down the branch.

The porch door creaked open and Chester pranced out, announcing his arrival with a growl and a bark. Margaret followed and stood at the railing looking over the fields.

Hank smiled at Dickerson. "She know about you and Mom?"

"There was nothing to know." He wanted to yell, to warn her, but if he did, Hank would probably take pleasure plunging the knife into his belly and leaving him for dead. Who would protect Margaret then?

Chester sniffed the air and barked again.

"Dickie?" Margaret called. "Dickie, you have a call."

Dickerson swallowed hard then called back. "Yes, dear. I'll be right there."

Hank ran the blade of his knife down the tip of the branch. "Punji sticks."

"What?"

"Heard of punji sticks?" He brushed his thumb over the tip. "In the war, the gooks dipped them in shit and buried them in the ground. Covered them with branches and twigs so they were invisible. Step on one of those and it was likely to jam up through your boot and into the underside of your foot. Hurt like hell. Wasn't crippling at first, but once infection set in, your leg would swell up. A few days was all it took. We'd spend a million bucks on a bomb to kill a dozen people in a village. They'd lay a field of punji sticks and take out a platoon for nothing."

"I suppose that's one you're making there."

"This? No. Bends too easy. Doubt it would go through your pants, let alone the sole of a shoe. This would have another use. Snake its way right into softer openings."

Dickerson felt sick as he imagined it. "So what's this deal of yours?"

Hank whittled on the sharp end of the branch and squinted. "Simple. You confess, and I'll let you both live."

"Confess? I have nothing to confess."

Hank ran his thumb over the tip of the branch and sharpened the end some more. "How about chopping down a defenseless old woman for starters."

"I told you I had nothing to do with that."

"Oh, I think you did, and for your old lady's sake, you might want to confess."

The screen door creaked open and Margaret stepped out. "Dickie, Chief Madison's waiting. He says it's urgent."

Hank's hand clapped over Dickerson's mouth. His arm clinched around his neck. His eyes watered and his throat felt like it was being crushed. The sharpened end of the branch poked into his cheek.

"Might want to think real careful about your next words. Be a shame if anything happened to her."

Dickerson's fingers clawed against Hank's arm as he

struggled to gasp for air. His eyes felt like they would burst in their sockets as he watched Margaret pick up their Chihuahua and stroke its head. He nodded and Hank let go his stranglehold, dropping Dickerson to his knees.

"Be—" he coughed and cleared his throat. "I'll be right there." He gasped and gagged again. "You leave her out of this."

"That's up to you, Dickie. I'd suggest you get to writing your confession. In fact, here's an idea. Mom's funeral. Just the place to make a confession in front of God and all those witnesses. You do that and we'll be even. If not, it's an eye for an eye."

"And if I confess, you'll not harm Margaret?"

"You confess, I won't have to."

"No . . . no you don't have the authority to do that," Dickerson's voice grew more shrill as he shouted into the phone. "The doctor's—"

Margaret opened the office door in the basement of their house and walked in carrying Chester. "Dickie, what happened? Your face . . . "

Dickerson covered the mouthpiece with his hand as Madison's voice ranted through his fingers. "Nothing dear. I tripped." His voice was hoarse, and he felt like he was swallowing gravel.

"Your neck. Are you sure?"

"No you won't. The doctor won't release you to work until—"

"Your cheek," Margaret said. "Dickie are you sure you're alright?"

"Yes, I'm fine. What? No, I'm not talking to you. Margaret, I'm on the phone. Could you give me some privacy?"

"Who were you talking to out there in the vineyard?"

Dickerson covered the mouthpiece again. "Raccoon."

"Raccoon? You were talking to a raccoon?"

"Yes, no. Sort of. Margaret, please let me finish—"

"Did it attack you? It must have had rabies. Raccoons are such filthy animals. You need to get that looked at."

"I'm fine. He didn't have rabies. He's gone." Madison's voice squawked louder through the earpiece. "Just leave it alone!" Dickerson yelled. "I'm on the phone. Let me finish then I'll explain."

Margaret grabbed the phone from his hand. "Chief Madison? Would you talk some sense into my husband?" She handed the phone back and stomped out of the room.

"My God. That woman," Dickerson said.

Margaret's feet stomped up the stairs, then the front door slammed.

"Margaret, wait!" Dickerson yelled. "Don't go out there." He dropped the phone and ran after her.

Chief Madison pushed the emergency call button for the sixth time.

"Don't make no difference."

Madison looked at the crumpled bag of flesh who'd taken the other bed in the room the day after Madison's arrival. The old coot seemed to pride himself in displaying his toothless gums at night.

Madison pushed the button again.

His roommate changed the channel to General Hospital. A nurse and doctor held each other in passionate embrace, discussing the worsening condition of her boyfriend and the travails his wife was enduring in the mental ward. The throbbing between Madison's ears had become the roar of a jet stuck in a tunnel.

"Nurse is probably smooching with some doctor," he said, pointing the remote at the television. "Patients be damned. Took me three hours to get someone once. No one came till the alarm went off. Had to resuscitate me."

"Maybe if you put those teeth to regular use."

"It's my mouth. The teeth just make it worse."

"Remind me. You're here for what again?"

"Hernia. Should have been out in a day."

Madison pressed the button and kept it pinned. Ten minutes later, a stout nurse with rolled up sleeves ripped back the curtain that offered meager privacy from the traffic in the hallway. "What is it this time?" she asked.

"Feels like a train came off the rails between my ears. I could use a little more of the good stuff."

Nurse Ratchet looked at her watch and lifted his wrist, pressing a finger hard into his soft throbbing tissue. Never had checking his pulse hurt so much. She let his wrist fall limp then scribbled a note on the patient's grease board mounted on the wall by his bed.

"Can't give you any more for another half hour."

"What good's this button then? You said to push it if I needed anything."

Her eyebrows bunched together, and her huge eyes studied him behind twin magnifying lenses. "Anything else I can get for you?"

Madison leaned toward her and lowered his voice. "How about something for the you know what?"

"Stopped up are we?"

"Stopped up. That's the worst," the hernia said. "I could use a little something myself."

"How long since your last movement?"

"Long enough I'm starting to taste chocolate."

"You're full of shit!" The hernia said, breaking into a jag of laughter that ended with him grabbing the dressing over his stitches amid tears of pain. "The stitches, feels like I broke some."

Nurse Ratchet attended to his crying roommate as the doctor entered.

The doctor grabbed the chart clipped to the end of Madison's bed and began flipping through pages. A year, two at most out of residency, Madison guessed. Mexican? He couldn't be sure. The doctor's name tag wasn't much help either. Dr. Hiljamon. What kind of name was that? His brown eyes puzzled over the pages as if he was deciphering some secret code. East Indian? Mexican? They all looked the same to Madison. He scribbled a few notes in the chart then clipped it to the bed.

"How are we doing today?"

"Don't know about you, but I've been better."

"I'm Dr. Hiljamon." He clamped two fingers around Madison's wrist and stared at his watch. "How is the pain?"

"Painful."

He pointed to a chart of smiley and frowny faces with numbers beneath each. "On a scale from one to ten, ten being the most severe pain you have ever felt, corresponding to the most frowny face, where would you say you are?"

"In the hospital."

He plucked a penlight from the pocket protector in his white lab coat and shined it in Madison's left eye, then blinded his right. "Try using the scale from one to ten."

Madison wanted out. He felt terrible and would have ranked the pain somewhere closer to twenty. "Three or four," he said, hoping to impress the doctor with his rapid recovery. "How long until I'm released?"

"That depends." Dr. Hiljamon played hopscotch on his chest with the stethoscope, all the while telling him to breathe in and out. "Let's have a look. Say ah."

Madison opened his mouth and let out a low, rumbling groan. The tongue depressor felt rough and dry as it wrestled with his tongue. It slid further back tickling his adenoids, bringing on a gag. The slivery wood quickly withdrew as the muscles of his throat started to convulse.

"Doctor wh—"

A thermometer slipped under his tongue. "Close your mouth but don't bite down."

"Um-hum."

"Chief, or would you prefer Mr. Madison?"

"You can—"

He pushed Madison's mouth shut. His focus shifted from the thermometer to Madison's eyes. "You had a heart attack. More severe than your prior one in . . . " He flipped the chart open and paged again. "In eighty-one. Serious enough to do further damage. Normally we would have placed stents in several vessels that were significantly blocked, but the blockage was too severe. You need bypass surgery. You will have to be transported to a larger hospital. We can schedule it tomorrow." He grabbed the thermometer and examined the mercury. "One hundred and one. You also seem a little shaky. Is that normal for you?"

"Just when I haven't had a drink."

"Any other symptoms—hallucinations, nausea, disorganized thoughts?"

"I'm not an alcoholic, if that's what you're getting at. I don't have the DTs."

"Would you say you consume more alcohol than most?"

"I would say you ask more questions than most. Listen, I have some business to attend to at the office. Very important business. What can we do to get me out of here sooner than later?"

"You need to understand, Chief, you had a major event. Your heart was already compromised. This heart attack could have been fatal. If you leave before your condition has been treated, your life will be at risk. I'm sure whatever is waiting for you at the office will be there when you get back."

Madison lay back against his pillows and closed his eyes. "I'm sure it will."

A thundershower during the night lubricated the streets with a slick mixture of oil and water, making the tires of Terrence's Suburban hiss. The traffic accordianed as impatient drivers jockeyed for position on Highway 18. The twenty-minute drive to the medical examiner's office would be double that this morning.

When Terrence finally arrived at the ME's office in McMinnville, he sat for thirty more minutes in the lobby, struggling to reconcile the conflicting orders he'd been given. To disobey Madison meant the end Terrence's career, but Dickerson would have his head if he didn't pursue every lead. The final choice, if it could be called a choice, Sharon had already made painfully clear. Protect and serve. Wasn't that the police motto painted on the side of both police cars? He had a duty, and he was compelled to carry it out—no matter what the cost.

Terrence looked through the observation window into the autopsy room where Joseph Walksontop stood at the stainless steel table dressed for surgery.

Edith's body lay on the shiny table in front of him. The smell of formaldehyde hung heavy in the air. A stainless steel basin at the foot of the table would collect the bits of dirt and blood that Joseph washed from her body before making the first incision. Pruning shears, hacksaws, and a bone saw hung from hooks on the wall. A rack of stainless steel serrated butcher's knives were spread in a tray beside her. Metal mixing bowls were stacked at the foot of the table ready to receive the contents of her body.

Terrence took a deep breath and donned his blue surgical gown, blue cap, blue face mask, and goggles. The blue Latex gloves resisted as he struggled to pull them over his big fingers. When he walked into the procedure room, his goggles fogged in the cool air.

The string on Terrence's gown dug into his neck, and the paper gown made a faint tearing noise as his shoulders hunched forward.

Joseph's eyes squinted behind his goggles. "Since you were the first officer on the scene, you may be able to answer questions I have during the examination. The procedure will be recorded, so make sure to speak loud enough the microphone can pick up your voice."

Terrence wiped the beads of moisture on his goggles and nodded.

"Okay, Terrence—Chief. I should warn you, some people find the examination a little disturbing, so if you start to feel lightheaded, let me know." He picked up a scalpel and poked toward a steel folding chair near the observation window. "Just take a seat there if you need to."

Terrence wiped the sweat on his forehead.

Joseph pressed the foot switch for the audio recorder

and began describing the condition of Edith's body.

The medical jargon soon left Terrence wondering what language Joseph was speaking. English was challenging enough. Medicalese was English rototilled. As Joseph's voice spoke in the background, Terrence's eyes were first drawn to Edith's face. Her skin resembled partially melted wax. Her cheeks drooped to the side where her face had rested against the dirt. Bits of soil were clotted in her mouth and dried in her hair. Her eyes stared unblinking, dry. Her neck was still caked with the crusty, dried blood that had oozed from the gash in her neck. He steadied himself against the cold steel table as the room began to tilt.

"How are you feeling?" Joseph said. "Everything okay?"

Terrence nodded.

The recorder light blinked on again, and Joseph resumed his narration. Eventually, he broke back into English. "Nothing remarkable on her skin, other than the laceration to her neck. Next I'll examine the organs and collect samples for toxicology. As I go, Chief, let me know if you have any observations that might be important. Ready?"

Terrence felt sweat dampening his paper cap, and his goggles fogged again. He wiped the clear plastic and nodded as Joseph poised the scalpel over her chest.

The knife made a large y-shaped incision from the edge of her collar bones to the breastbone. Terrence felt a wave of nausea wash over him. Next the scalpel separated the skin from the bottom of her sternum down to her pelvic bone. Terrence's chest tightened as Joseph pealed back the skin, exposing her ribs.

Joseph pulled the pruning sheers from their hook, glanced at Terrence, then took the first rib into its jaws.

185

With the first snap, Terrence flinched and felt a surge of adrenalin shoot into his stomach. Once the ribs were severed, Joseph pulled the breastplate free with a sucking slurp.

Terrence swallowed hard.

With the abdominal cavity exposed, Joseph began removing the organs. Each organ was placed in a bowl, weighed, and measured. He sectioned off samples from each and placed these in labeled jars.

When the room began to fade into a white haze, Terrence took a slow, deep breath and gripped the edge of the cold steel table. I've seen guts before, he told himself. But these were the organs of a human being.

Joseph paused the recorder and nodded at the chair behind Terrence. "Maybe you should sit, we have quite a bit more to do. No shame in taking a seat if you need to."

"No, thanks." Terrence pointed to the organ-filled bowls. "So what will you do with those?"

"We'll examine them for disease and run toxicology. Though the injuries to her neck are severe, they may not have been the cause—the sole cause—of her death. Disease is common in persons of her advanced age and may have contributed to her death."

Terrence struggled to keep from being sick as Joseph proceeded to remove the remaining organs of the torso, noting the condition of each. Though her skin was pale and gray from blood loss, the organs retained their bright color.

Edith's eyes seemed to plead, and Terrence felt the urge to apologize for this hollowing out of her body. He recalled seeing her lying in the garden, blood pooling from the gash in her neck.

"Some indication of cardiovascular disease, typical for

her age," Joseph said.

The words jarred him back.

"The left anterior descending artery is partially blocked by atherosclerotic plaque. The other organs appear unremarkable. Liver has some fatty deposits consistent with alcohol consumption. Otherwise, no indication of significant disease beyond what one would expect for a woman of her age."

Terrence glanced at her eyes and his fingers tightened on the edge of the table. "There was some concern for her mental state."

"I will examine the skull and brain in a moment. If there was a struggle, we might find hematoma or other signs of brain trauma. A skull fracture would strongly suggest a struggle. The brain's a highly complex organ that requires microscopic examination to confirm the presence of disease. The lab would have to provide that degree of analysis."

"Any sign of struggle other than her neck?"

Joseph lifted her left hand and spread her fingers. Then he examined her right. "No signs of injury, just calluses. Some debris beneath her fingernails which we will collect for possible DNA. But no defensive wounds consistent with a struggle. You know what defensive wounds are?"

"Yes, sir." Terrence recalled the graphic photos he'd seen in his crime scene investigation class at the police academy. The photos showed the remains of a female who'd tried to protect herself from a jealous, knife-wielding boyfriend. One of his classmates hurried out the door as the instructor presented a dozen slides showing deep cuts to the victim's forearms and hands.

"I don't see any on Mrs. Sherman," Joseph said.

"So she wasn't attacked?"

"We can't be certain. Perhaps she was surprised and didn't have opportunity to defend herself."

"Or maybe the killer grabbed her arms," Terrence said.

"I don't see any bruising. No marks on her arms or elsewhere consistent with being restrained."

"So it was an accident?"

"That has yet to be determined. Examination of the neck may help answer that question." Joseph placed a steel ruler next to the wounds on Edith's neck, photographed it, and noted the length of the laceration. Next, he probed the depth of the wound and carefully removed the tissues surrounding the injury.

"What's it look like?" Terrence asked.

Joseph placed the excised skin in a bowl and returned to his examination of the muscles on the front of her neck. "No damage to the cartilage. No sign of strangulation. Once I remove the neck block, we should know if she suffered spinal injury." He pulled the trachea, thyroid, and esophagus free from the base of her tongue and pushed his hand into Edith's mouth, making her head nod.

Terrence fought back a gag.

"Her neck is not broken. The cervical vertebrae feel normal."

Terrence felt a lurch in his stomach as Edith seemed to be swallowing Joseph's hand.

"Damage to the tendons. The jugular and carotid are severed." He poked his finger into the opening where the wound now gaped open. "See here? The clavicle has been compromised." He inserted forceps into the opening and pinched a white sliver of bone and held it up to the light. "A chip from her clavicle." He dropped the bone fragment into a jar of formaldehyde.

"Can you tell what kind of weapon killed her?"

"Given the injury to the bone and the jagged edges of the laceration, a heavy, edged instrument."

Terrence smeared the droplets fogging his goggles with his glove, and leaned closer. "A knife? An axe?"

"A knife would not make such a blunt opening or damage the bone to this degree. The margins of the laceration are consistent with a heavy object like the axe you recovered at the scene. We will compare the axe to the incision. Preliminarily, I would say the damage to the bone and the presentation at the margins of the incision are consistent with the blade of an axe." Joseph made a chopping motion toward Edith's neck. "A blow approximately forty-five degrees to the neck, severing the tissues and striking her clavicle, would be consistent with the injuries. I've collected bits of debris the lab can compare with trace evidence on the blade of the axe you recovered." He flipped off the recorder. "When will we have the axe for examination?"

"I'll get it to you this afternoon."

"Okay. Let's take a look at the brain." Joseph flipped on the recorder and made a u-shaped incision over the crown of her skull from ear to ear then pulled the scalp away. He draped the flap of her face forward toward her neck. The back flap was also peeled back to expose the fibrous tissues covering her skull.

Terrence felt his knees begin to buckle and leaned against the table to steady himself.

Joseph used the surgical bone saw to cut off the crown of her skull. The saw made a high pitched whine as it vaporized bone particles and blood into the air. He completed cutting the halo around Edith's skull and pulled the skull cap off. "No sign of subdural hematoma, and the dura mater is intact. Terrence?

Terrence . . . "

The room seemed to fill with a blizzard as the strength in Terrence's legs drained. He stumbled backward and fell into the chair. He closed his eyes and took several deep breaths, waiting for the nausea to pass, but the smell of formaldehyde made the air feel thick and sticky. The paper mask seemed to stop the air from entering his lungs, so he pulled it down beneath his chin and slid the foggy goggles onto his forehead.

Joseph stood, bone saw in hand, and frowned. "Better put those back on. The procedure vaporizes blood into the air."

Terrence rose on wobbly legs and headed for the door. "I think I'll go get the axe."

Wednesday

The more Terrence thought of it, the more convinced he became. The axe was the key. Fingerprints, blood smears, fibers too small for the eye to see would make or break this case. He tried to recall the condition of the axe and the marks on the handle. So much had happened since the day he arrived at the scene, the mental pictures were becoming fuzzy.

Terrence opened the file cabinet in the chief's office and pulled the thin folder with Edith's case. The evidence sheet listed the axe he'd recovered and gave the locker number where he had placed it into evidence. It showed "TW," Terrence's initials he'd written when he placed the axe into evidence. The columns to be filled out by anyone removing the evidence where blank. Terrence opened the safe in the chief's office and pulled out the key to the evidence locker. Inside the locker he found only the tracking sheet. He thought of Harvey's Locksmith and the master to his office. Did the locksmith also have one to the safe? How many other copies were in circulation unaccounted for?

Only he and Madison should have a key. Chain of

custody, it was called. But why would Madison have removed the axe without signing it out? To wipe it clean of prints? To plant it somewhere else? If Madison had really killed Edith, he would certainly destroy any evidence that might link him to the crime.

Maybe it's at his apartment, Terrence thought. The chief was a private man. Never once had he invited Terrence to visit. His suspicions grew, the more he considered this puzzle piece. If the axe was at Madison's apartment, he'd need a warrant to search for it. Search warrants required probable cause. Suspicions about extra evidence locker keys wasn't enough.

Maybe Madison would give permission to search, but how could he ask? Madison would be a fool to consent to a search if he had hidden the axe there. No. Terrence would have to employ a ruse. Maybe Madison needed something from home while he was in the hospital. He could just offer to pick it up and take a look around while he was there. If Madison refused, then what? Either way, by asking, he'd know more than he did now. Terrence wondered if a man could know too much.

Terrence pressed the get well card he'd picked up at Sheridan Grocery to the wall outside Madison's room and signed his name. It showed a man lying in a hospital bed with a puckered look on his face as a nurse examined a rectal thermometer. The caption read "Bottom's up!" He almost laughed when he entered the room and found the nurse shaking one out.

"Chief. How are you feeling?" Terrence said.

Madison sipped from a Dixie cup then grimaced. "You know what they say about the cure being worse than the disease. I'll be all right if they ever stop trying to cure me." He winked at the nurse, who might have been in her second year of nursing school, and she rolled her eyes.

She turned to Terrence and said, "We'll all be glad to see him cured!" She jumped as Madison patted her on the butt. "Is it time for another blood draw?" she said. "Maybe you'd like your temperature checked from the other end next time."

"Promises, promises." Madison said.

She checked the IV bag and winked at Terrence on her way out the door.

A shadow of fear settled over Madison's face. A brief glimpse of vulnerability.

"She's cute," Terrence said. "I'd think you'd want to stay longer." He handed Madison the card. He opened the card and laughed, the first Terrence could remember.

"You look good," Terrence said.

Madison scooped a bite of applesauce. "I feel good. Looks like I'll be shipped out of here soon." He shoveled in a mouthful and swallowed. "You knew I had a heart attack before, a few years ago?"

"I think you told me."

"Haven't been quite the same ever since. Strange how something like that can change a man."

"You just relax and get better. Is there anything you need from your place? I can drop by and pick up—"

"What I mean is, it made me a little more intense. I didn't used to be so . . . you know." He shoveled in another scoop and stared into space.

Terrence wondered what ghosts his eyes saw.

"Look. What I'm trying to say is, I may have been a little hard on you at times. I know you mean well. But this job will eat you alive if you let it. Take Edith for example—"

The knock on the door announced another arrival. The white lab coat and stethoscope tagged him as the doctor. He held out his hand to Terrence. "I'm Doctor Hiljamon," he said with half a smile.

"Chief Washburn."

Doctor Hiljamon looked at his gold chief's badge then turned to the Madison. "Your replacement?"

Madison scooped more applesauce and shook his head.

Doctor Hiljamon winked at Terrence. "Just make sure you don't end up like your predecessor. A heart attack is all but guaranteed." He flipped open the chart. "We have your latest test results back. Angiogram confirms the severity of the blockages. When was your surgery?"

"Some years ago."

"Oh?"

"When I retired from Portland."

"The angiogram shows more blockage. The blood flow to your heart muscle is approximately eighty-six percent restricted on one side and sixty-five percent on the other. Hence the pain and the other symptoms you've been experiencing."

"Maybe I should ask for my money back from the last operation."

The doctor pulled two x-ray films from the envelope wedged beneath his arm and clipped them to the light above the bed. "See those white spots? Those are the stents they inserted in your prior surgery. Stents can be effective for less severe blockage, but your disease has advanced to the point we need to take more aggressive action. Full bypass of the arteries is required. You have significant damage to your heart muscle. With the compromise to your heart, you will need to adjust your lifestyle."

"I know. No more drinking, smoking, and lose fifty pounds," Madison said.

"You've heard this before, I see. There's not much more I can say. With your advanced disease, I also can't recommend returning to your previous line of employment."

The green numbers displayed on Madison's heart rate monitor began to climb. "And if I do?"

Doctor Hiljamon slid the films back into the envelope. "You will be putting yourself and others at risk. You'll continue to have more severe episodes—chest pain, sweating, nausea, dizziness, shortness of breath. Eventually your heart muscle will be overtaxed and you will die."

Doctor Hiljamon examined the chart at the end of the bed. "We have scheduled you for surgery tomorrow. We don't have the facilities here, so you will be transported by ambulance to Portland."

Madison looked at Terrence and said, "I've got some things to clean up first."

"You don't seem to understand how serious your condition is. The next heart attack will be your last."

"Seems pretty clear to me, Chief," Terrence said.

Madison glared at him. "Everything seems clear to you."

Doctor Hiljamon picked up Terrence's get well card and smiled. "What is it with assholes?" He put the card down by a dish of prunes and walked out the door.

Terrence slid a chair beside the bed. "What are you going to do?"

"Shit."

"What?"

"As a matter of fact, that's exactly what I'm going to

do." Madison threw the sheets off his pale legs and stood on the tile floor, in his non-slip socks. He pointed at the IV stand, "You mind swinging that around?"

Terrence wheeled the silver pole that held the clear bag of fluid to Madison's side of the bed. Madison gripped the pole, wheeled it into the bathroom, and shut the door.

A teddy bear dressed in a patrolman's uniform leaned on the table by the window next to a flower arrangement. Terrence read the greeting on the card. *Get well soon, Bill and Margaret Dickerson.* Yesterday's edition of the *Sheridan Sun* sat crumpled on a chair in the corner. The headline read "Senior Citizen Brutally Murdered." The article continued, *Edith Sherman was discovered dead at her residence Saturday afternoon, the victim of a brutal axe murder. Sources say her only surviving son, Hank Sherman, was seen leaving the residence about the time of the murder. He is wanted for questioning by police. Mayor Dickerson says an investigation is underway, headed by the new chief of police, Terrence Washburn. Police could not be reached for comment.*

The toilet flushed and Madison walked out the door with a smile on his face. The IV stand banged against the door, and the tube tangled on the foot of the stand. "Could you help me with—"

Terrence grabbed the IV stand as Madison bent down to untangle the clear line, exposing his dimpled backside. He backed into the bed and hoisted himself up. Terrence pulled the covers over his legs.

"Thanks. See the headlines?"

"Yeah."

"Now the fun begins."

"What are you going to do?" Terrence asked.

"Not much I can do. You heard him."

"No. I mean, about going back to work."

"Don't see I have much choice. Timing." Madison pointed at the chair. "Take a load off."

Terrence sat.

"Maybe it's time. Retirement. Funny how folks just can't wait to pull the plug, but once it's pulled, all the electricity stops. When the lights go out, all that's left is to sit in the dark. Might as well be dead.

"This job isn't the easiest. It can get to you, start fraying you at the edges, change the way you see things." Madison picked up a slice of toast and started spreading jam on it. "This was your first death investigation. That's hard on some people. I remember my first one. I was convinced the Mafia had done a hit on this guy. Hell, I had good reason. Italian, nice home, business man. Wife found him hung in the garage between a Mercedes and a BMW. I was convinced the suicide note he'd left behind was a fake. Of course, his wife didn't want to believe he'd hung himself, either. They were in the middle of a nasty divorce. He kills himself, no life insurance. We found out he was having an affair, and his girlfriend had drained his bank account before she left for another guy. It all fit. I felt like a fool.

"It's easy to get too involved. Don't let Edith make a fool out of you. You've got to keep distance, be objective. I feel bad for her, too, but accidents happen. Sometimes in our desire to fix things, we just make them worse. You hearing what I'm saying?"

"Yes, sir."

"It's for your own good, I'm telling you. I read your report. It's generally fine, but I made a few changes. We'll work on keeping your speculations out of your reports in the future. Take the day off. Get your mind off

Edith. You don't want to end up like me." Madison smiled. "I asked for a sponge bath today. She's cute, huh?"

Terrence smiled and felt his face flushing. "Sure is."

Madison took a bite of toast.

Terrence shifted uneasily. "Is there anything you need from your apartment? I'd be happy to get—"

"You're a good kid, Terrence. Trusting and honest. So was I once. I learned the hard way some people can't be trusted. Politicians are the worst. You hearing what I'm saying?"

"Yes, sir."

Madison studied Terrence for a moment. "Dickerson's no exception. Don't be fooled. He doesn't give anything without asking for something in return. Mayor's not a cop. If he thinks he can run a murder investigation, he's fooling himself. If you let him tell you how to run it, you're a bigger fool." He took another bite and chewed. "Let me guess. He doesn't want you bothering me with the details of the investigation. Wants to run it himself. Am I right?"

"It's just, he doesn't want you worrying."

"Right. Let me give you a quick lesson about small-town politics. It's pretty simple. Don't believe anything anyone says. You know how you can tell if Dickerson's lying?"

"No, sir."

"His lips are moving. And don't let that gold chief's badge fool you. I learned a long time ago, its just there to make it easier to know who to blame."

"The medical examiner said his report will be done in a few days. He's pretty sure the axe is what killed her."

Madison chewed. "Doesn't take a medical degree to figure that out."

"The ME needs to compare the axe to the wound."

Madison began to spread jelly on another slice of toast.

"Chief," Terrence said, "the axe, where did the axe—"

"How many times do we have to go over this?" Madison pointed his butter knife at Terrence. "Let it go."

Terrence removed the chief's business card from his notebook. "I didn't get a chance to tell you. The paramedics found this at Edith's the day she was murdered." He gave the card to Madison. "I was going to ask you . . . "

Madison took the card, flipped it over, and tossed it next to his milk carton. "Terrence." He took a deep breath. "Did you hear anything I just said?"

"Yes, sir. I just thought—"

"That's the problem. You just keep thinking. You don't listen." Madison took another bite. "I didn't want it to come to this, but, as of right now, you're investigation is suspended. I don't care what Dickerson says. Stop the investigation now or you're fired. Got that?"

"Yes, sir."

"Why don't I believe you? Listen to me. If you don't stop this nonsense right now, I want your badge on my desk."

"But the mayor—"

"The mayor my ass. I'm still the real chief of police. I'm ordering you to stop this investigation as of right now. If you can't do that, I'll take your badge." He picked up his business card and flipped it off Terrence's face.

Terrence fished the card out from under the bed then slumped deeper in the chair. "And what am I supposed to say to the mayor?"

"Say whatever you want. Tell him you're still working the case. I don't care. Just don't do anything more until I'm back."

"But you heard what the doctor said."

"Worrying about what you're doing will kill me before another heart attack. As long as you pursue this foolishness, I don't have much choice."

"You sure there's nothing I can get you from home?"

"I think of anything, you'll be the first to know."

Sharon pulled back the smoke-stained sheet covering the front window and watched Dickerson park his Cadillac beside her Camry. She tamped out her cigarette and emptied the ashtray into the garbage. She grabbed the clothes strewn on the couch and floor in the living room and threw them into the closet. She collected the dirty dishes on the coffee table and deposited them with the others in the sink. She opened the cabinet door beneath the sink and tossed the beer bottles in the garbage can. The rose scented air freshener she emptied into the apartment did little to mask the odor of smoke and garbage. The doorbell rang as she pulled her hair back and wrapped a rubber band around the tangles. Through the peep hole, she saw Dickerson standing, shifting nervously from one foot to the other. She slid back the safety chain and opened in the door.

"To what do I owe this great honor?"

"Sharon. May I come in?"

She swung open the door and stepped back into the living room. "What brings you down here?"

"Your mother is concerned about you."

"Is she? What's she so concerned about?"

Dickerson's eyes roamed the room, and his face drew

into a subtle scowl. He walked over to the couch and began to sit then stopped mid-squat and straightened. "You and Junior."

She pulled on her sunglasses and lit a cigarette. "Have a seat." She sat in the recliner.

He sat on the edge of the sofa. "How are you?"

"Fine. Why?"

"You don't look fine. A little dark for sunglasses don't you think."

The bedroom door opened, and Junior ran out. "Grandpa!" Dickerson froze, and Junior wrapped his arms around his skinny neck. "Did you bring me anything?"

Dickerson patted him on the head and held his hands up like he was being robbed. "Not this time."

"Dad got me a new gun! Come here, I'll show you." Dickerson pulled back as Junior reached for his hand.

"Stop pestering Grandpa. Go play."

"I wanna show him."

"Don't make me say it again. Now go."

Junior gave Dickerson another hug then frowned at Sharon and sulked off to his room.

Dickerson sat teetering on the edge of the sofa. "He's gotten so big."

"They do that."

"Ten?" Dickerson said.

"Since June. His birthday. Thanks for the card. Maybe if you saw him once in a while."

"Ten. He's so tall. Is he . . . doing better?"

"How do you mean?"

"In school?

"Is he still in special ed? Yes, Dad. He's still slow. Not headed for college anytime soon."

"And his other handicaps?"

Sharon blew out a puff of smoke. "Just say it. I'm a bad mother. Isn't that what you want to say?"

"I'm not blaming you, though you could have been more careful. You should have thought about how your habits might affect him."

"I think about what my 'habits' cost us every time I look at him. He reminds me how much I've messed up so many things."

"We all have to live with our choices," Dickerson said.

Sharon let the smoke boil from her mouth. "We sure do. Like your choice to have me."

"Never. We have never said that. Your mother . . . we still worry about you. Our offer is still on the table. Your room is just as you left it."

"You don't want me home. Smoke in the curtains, remember?"

"You can smoke outside. No drugs, though."

Sharon remembered her old room. She'd talked them into buying her a king-sized bed. The sterile white paint and the white carpet made it feel more like a hospital ward than a bedroom. Their rules, their straitjacket of dos and don'ts, and the mind-numbing dullness of their conversation were more than she could bear. The worst was the unspoken rule to never disagree or entertain an opinion that might threaten the peace. They lived in a suffocating harmony bought at the expense of being the persons they really were. The need to conform, to comply, wrung the life out of her.

"Would you really want Hank dropping by for a visit? Might dirty the white carpet."

Dickerson shook his head. "We can only go so far. I'll never know what you saw in him." His eyes fixed on her face. "Has Hank been . . . "

Sharon pulled off her sunglasses. "What do you

think?"

"Why do you put up with that? Why do you provoke him?"

"I guess you just answered your own question. I must like it."

"Why can't you just leave?"

Sharon slid the sunglasses back on and took another drag from her cigarette. "Did you even see your grandson just now? Or were you too afraid you might catch some disease if he touched you?"

"I saw the dirt on his face, his unwashed hair. His clothes smelled of urine. He deserves better than this. You know we've always cared about him. Your mother misses him terribly." Dickerson swallowed. "We love you both."

"I'm not sure you know what love means. You also said you loved me before you kicked me out. Some kind of love."

"Maybe you've forgotten about the drugs, the stealing, the nights when we had no idea where you were."

"I was a kid." Tears began to moisten her eyes. "I was lost, confused. I needed a dad, and all I got was judgment. And Mom, she was always disappointed I wasn't the girl she wanted."

"Well, the past is the past. Now you've got Junior to think about. Maybe I can help if I knew when—"

"Sometimes you can't just bury the past. You still blame me. I get it. I'm an unfit mother. Junior's broken, and it's my fault. I admit it, okay? It's my fault. I made him that way." She wiped the tears from her cheeks.

Junior's door opened and he walked out pointing a plastic gun. "See what Daddy got me?" He held it in both hands and pointed it at Dickerson's face. "Bang.

Bang. You're dead." He smiled.

Junior swung the gun at Sharon. "Bang. Bang. You're dead. Kill all the bitches."

"Junior!" Sharon said. "Don't say that. Who taught you to say that?"

He lowered the gun, looking confused.

"Don't ever say that again. You hear me? Go to your room." She pointed at Dickerson, "You can thank Hank for that. He's been learning all kinds of great things at his father's."

"We'll it's going to stop, if you'll let me help. We have to make it stop."

"And how are we gonna do that? There's this thing called visitation. Trust me, you don't want to mess with it."

"It's got to stop," Dickerson repeated.

Sharon's hands shook as she wiped her eyes. "Careful now, you might make me think you care."

"I know I haven't always said so, but we do care. Your mother has never been the same since you left. She misses her grandson terribly. Every day she hopes you'll call."

"Phone works both ways."

"Each year she grows more frail. Her heart's broken. I see the life draining out of her."

"And what?"

He stood and glared at her. "And I won't have it. I won't have any more of it."

"What are you going to do? The law says Hank gets to see him. There's nothing I can do."

"Maybe there's nothing you can do. There's plenty I can. Maybe the law can fix what the law has broken."

204

Terrence stood by the emergency entry door at the hospital watching the Yamhill County Medical crew unload their human freight. He was no closer to finding the axe than when he'd ducked through Madison's hospital room door. Can I get you something from home? What a stupid question. Either he had probable cause to search Madison's apartment for the axe or he didn't. Maybe he should have just asked. Maybe he just didn't see the big picture, as Madison often said.

"Washburn?"

Terrence recognized the voice of the female paramedic who'd greeted him at Edith's. What was her name? He looked in the direction of the voice but didn't see her.

The rear door of the Ambulance parked under the awning slammed shut and there she stood, looking puzzled. "Whatever happened with the old lady?"

"Edith."

"That's the one." She nodded. "Was it an accident?"

"Still under investigation. I can't really talk about —"

She chuckled. "I'm sorry, I don't mean to be . . . you know."

"Like I said —"

"It's just, you seemed kind of confused when we were at her place."

The dip of chew in her lower lip gave her a pouty look. For a moment Terrence felt the urge to indulge in a chew. He read her name tag. "Cindy. We met at her house."

"Wow, look at you," Cindy said as she stepped closer, focusing on his gold chief's badge. "Andy, look here."

Andy exited the ambulance, clipboard in hand, and joined them. "Look at what?" He looked up at Terrence and said, "You're from the axe murder, right?"

Terrence felt the all too familiar sensation he was about to become the butt of another joke.

Cindy shook her head. "Andy, show a little respect. You're talking to Sheridan's chief of police."

Andy looked puzzled then leaned forward, his eyes focusing on Terrence's name tag. "Washburn, T," he said. "Terrence. That's right. Chief Washburn?" He stepped back beside Cindy, and both looked at him as if expecting some important news.

"Just visiting the chief," Terrence said.

Andy frowned. "I thought you were chief? You have two of those in Sheridan?"

"Acting, at least until he's well."

"Acting? Is that like pretend?" Cindy added.

Terrence felt the irritation begin to itch at his neck. "Mayor Dickerson appointed me until—"

"Mayor Dickerson?" Andy said.

"That explains it." Cindy spat.

"Explains what?"

"Nothing," Andy said. "Did you ever figure out what killed her?" They both broke into a jag of stifled laughter.

Terrence felt the blood rushing into his face as the anger swelled inside. He was chief, so why did he feel so embarrassed? "If you'll excuse me, some of us got work to do." Cindy and Andy broke into unbridled guffaws.

"We're sorry," Cindy said, wiping the tears from her eyes. "We didn't mean anything by it. You've got to learn to lighten up, Chief."

Andy held out his hand. "No harm meant. I have a pair of gloves if you'd rather put them on first?"

Cindy shook her head.

Terrence shook his hand and squeezed hard enough to shuffle his bones. Andy's grin melted into a grimace.

"None taken."

The chief's badge doesn't mean anything, Terrence thought. Where is the respect? He felt foolish for wearing a badge he was not prepared for. He'd gladly give it back as soon as Madison returned. For now, he'd carry the weight of the title as best he could. If the badge didn't give him the respect he deserved, he'd have to demand it.

Starting now.

Terrence opened the door to the Suburban and sat behind the wheel, trying to calm the simmering anger that burned in his gut. He'd teach them to show respect. If not for me, then at least the position. By God he'd earned it, or soon would, starting right now.

He began to back out of the parking space and heard a strange flapping of rubber. The Suburban listed to the side. Terrence got out and found the rear tire flat.

"It's only flat on the bottom," Andy yelled. He and Cindy gave each other a look and both broke into more laughter.

Terrence bit his lip and held back a clever retort he couldn't quite string together. He opened the back door of the Suburban to get the spare and there it was. The axe with its head still in the paper bag he'd used to cover it the night he retrieved it from the murder scene.

Terrence pulled into the parking spot reserved for law enforcement in front of the ME's office. The axe was in the back of the Suburban, its head wrapped in a paper bag sealed with red plastic evidence tape. How it got there was a mystery he'd have to sort out later. He was anxious to get the medical examiner's opinion on the likelihood it was the murder weapon. But even if it was, that was just the start. Axes don't kill people; people kill people.

His thoughts returned to Madison's indifference at the crime scene. He was so sure Edith's injuries were self-inflicted. Terrence hoped the ME's take on the axe blade and Edith's wounds would settle his doubts.

He shut off the engine and took a deep breath. He recalled the position of the axe, its head wedged in the dirt and the blood trail leading from the splitting stump. If she somehow injured herself splitting wood, she would have had to carry the axe to the garden where she collapsed. Why would she carry it with her?

If someone attacked her with the axe, why didn't her killer dispose of it? Would a suspect leave such an obvious piece of evidence lying next to her?

At the academy, they'd learned about staging. The criminal would rearrange the scene, position the body or put weapons in their victim's hands to mislead investigators. Most murderers lacked the knowledge necessary to pull it off and few had the nerve. Only a psychopath, someone without remorse, fearless and calculating, could successfully manipulate the evidence at a murder scene. It took a special breed of criminal comfortable with death to mop up. If Edith's death was staged, the murderer had to know what an investigator would look for. Someone experienced, a cold-blooded killer.

He was certain he'd seen a couple promising fingerprints on the axe handle. He'd taken pictures with the Polaroid, but those photos were too fuzzy to be of much value. Maybe the ME could examine the prints under the microscope, make out the fine ridges and swirls that made each fingerprint unique.

The Oregon Crime Lab could process the axe with one

of their new fangled gadgets and lift prints not even visible to the naked eye. They could plug the prints into their computer and compare them with arrest records and comparison prints from personnel at the crime scene. If they got lucky, the prints might match a criminal in the national database. Terrence thought it likely they would belong to one of Sheridan's own. The town was home to at least one man who fit the bill.

Terrence grabbed the axe and went inside. The smell of formaldehyde filled the lobby and made his stomach lurch as he thought about the autopsy he'd witnessed. He imagined himself back in the cool examination room, watching Edith's glassy eyes staring as the ME scooped out her insides. A sign by the buzzer on the counter advised him to push if he needed assistance. He pushed and waited.

An olive-skinned woman dressed in a white lab coat walked through the steel door behind the counter. She appeared dressed for surgery. Her voice came from a speaker box overhead. "Can I help you?"

Terrence spoke through a hole in the safety glass above the counter that separated them. "I have something for the medical examiner." Terrence held up the axe like he'd just won the Stanley Cup.

She slid her goggles to her forehead and looked at something on her side of the wall. "The schedule says he's not available until two o'clock."

"I have some evidence he needs to look at. It's pretty important."

She shook her head. "The schedule says he won't be available until this afternoon."

"Is there any way I can talk to him?" Terrence asked.

"Do you have an appointment?"

"I'm chief of police. Sheridan."

"Chief Sheridan?"

"No. Sheridan Police Department. I'm the chief."

"Pleased to meet you." She flipped over pages on the desk calendar. "I don't see you on the schedule."

"Terrence Washburn."

She shrugged. Her dark brown eyes examined him, unblinking below the plastic goggles.

"Listen, I know he's busy. It's just, this is a murder investigation." He read her name tag. Angela Walksontop. He saw it then, the ME's daughter. "Your dad said it was important."

"Grandfather."

"Grandfather?"

"My dad's father. The medical examiner is my grandfather."

Terrence held up the axe. "I just need to see if the blade matches the wound."

"Two o'clock."

Terrence pulled the bag off the axe's head. "See this? I need to know if it caused the wounds on the victim's neck."

She shrugged.

"Officer Washburn." The voice came from behind him. "What's going on?"

Terrence slid the bag over the axe and felt his face flush.

Joseph frowned. "I see you've met my assistant. Thanks, Angela. I'll take it from here."

Angela shook her head. "Guess he's available now." She exited through the doors the way she came.

Terrence felt his face getting warm. "I was . . . she wasn't—"

"Is that the axe from the scene?"

"Yes"

"Leave the bag over the head and don't touch anything else. Follow me." Joseph ushered him through the door, to the stainless steel table where Edith had lain. Terrence's stomach lurched again as he imagined her lying there.

The ME slid gloves over his hands then covered the examination table with butcher paper. "This will collect any traces that might flake off during my examination." He held out his hands to receive the axe.

Terrence carefully handed it over like a priest offering the host.

Joseph slid the evidence bag from the axe's head and placed it on the butcher paper. He opened the drawer beneath the table and pulled out a metal ruler. He positioned the ruler beside the axe's blade and recorded the length of the edge and noted its condition. Tiny bits of dirt flaked onto the butcher paper as he carefully turned the axe over to document the condition of the other side. Joseph pulled a pair of forceps from the drawer and nudged a tiny fleck onto the white paper.

"Terrence, you see how fragile the evidence can be. The lab will have to examine this under a microscope to determine if this is dirt or dried blood. The crime lab can also check DNA."

Terrence nodded. "The cut, could it have made it?"

Joseph swiveled a magnifying lamp over the axe's head and carefully lowered a pair of tweezers to a speck on the paper. Under the magnifying glass the tweezers looked like silver drumsticks sliding toward a curled strand of twine. They pinched the black and red twisted strand and turned it over. "See that?"

"Yeah. What is it?"

"Fiber," Joseph said. "Transfer from some man-made material. We can compare it with the gloves she was wearing. Doubtful though."

"Doubtful?"

"The gloves you retrieved from the scene. They were leather. This appears to be a synthetic material. I believe your report says the axe was wedged or driven into the ground, though your report was difficult to read—lots of erasures in that area. I would guess this transfer occurred after the axe was recovered from the scene." The tweezers turned the fiber in the magnified light. "Nylon? The weave is thicker, perhaps a strand of carpet. Your report didn't say how the axe was handled. Did it come into contact with such material?"

"I'm not sure—"

"Terrence, did the axe come into contact with other surfaces where fibers like this were present? You learned about the chain of evidence at the academy, right?"

Terrence nodded. "And Locard's Transfer Principle: 'When someone enters a crime scene, they always leave something behind. When they leave, they take something from the scene with them.'"

"Very good. So you know how critical it is to guard against contamination. An entire investigation can hinge on a single bit of trace evidence." He tweezed the fiber again. "Even a single strand of fiber." Joseph dropped the fiber into a clear evidence envelope. "We'll mark this and note the circumstances of its retrieval. It will need to go to the crime lab as well."

"Yes, I know."

"If this should go to trial, you will be called upon to testify. The defense will call into question your handling of the evidence. They will try to show negligence. Not a very pleasant experience from what I have witnessed. That's why you must be careful to document how you found the evidence and exactly what you did with it.

You must avoid any unnecessary handling or display of it. I've seen the careers of fine officers come to an unfortunate end for nothing larger than the fiber we examined beneath this lamp."

"I understand."

"Do you?" The ME studied Terrence's face. "I'll compare these measurements with my notes from the forensic examination. At this point, it would appear the wound is consistent with the axe blade." He pointed to bloody smudges on the handle. "I assume you've seen these?"

"Yes."

Joseph ran the magnifying lamp across the handle and hovered over an egg-shaped smear of red. "Smudged but still may be useful." He examined the next. "Good. This one is much better. You can see the swirls and loops. It should be suitable for comparison. And then there's the DNA."

"Next stop is the crime lab," Terrence said.

"They can test the blood to confirm its origin—if it is from the decedent, someone else, or both. The lab may find smaller fibers and other evidence as well." He folded the paper beneath the axe, wrapping it in a large envelope. "The paper will keep any trace evidence with the weapon." He sealed the envelope with tape and initialed the seams. "Terrence, you were careful in your handling of the evidence?"

"Yes, sir."

"I can't overstate this point. If your procedures were not adequate, the lab might find bits of fiber from your own clothing or even your own fingerprints."

"I was careful."

Joseph placed the envelope in a larger bag and handed it to Terrence. "I will add this examination to my report. You will want to make sure you haven't left out any details relevant to your own handling of the axe."

"Yes, sir." I read once, Doc Umentation says, 'If it's not in the report, it never happened.' That's what they taught us at the academy."

The ME pulled off his gloves. "Some officers forget they're the most important witness in a case. Everything hinges on their actions. That's why the defense will call into question your credibility at trial. They will challenge your competence. The defense will certainly look for any gaps in the chain of custody. If they find any, they will try to convince a jury you mishandled the evidence. They might even accuse you of tampering. I don't mean to unduly alarm you, Terrence, but as I said, your career could hinge on such a minute detail. If the courts find any cause to doubt your honesty, your career as a police officer could be over. In some cases, officers have been criminally charged. I don't have to tell you, life for an officer behind bars is not one you would enjoy."

Terrence leaned on the table, staring at the shining steel reflecting back his worried face. "Can you just say whether this was an accident or murder?"

"I can tell you the wounds Edith suffered are consistent with the axe we just examined. I can also conclude that the injury to her neck caused her death. I see no evidence of sexual assault. No drugs or alcohol. Unfortunately, I just don't have enough evidence to conclude whether the manner of death was homicide or accidental. For now, I'll mark the disposition 'Undetermined.'"

Thursday

Terrence pulled a stool up to the bar, hoping to talk to Sharon. Randy approached from behind and slapped a wet hand on Terrence's back. "Officer Washburn, Nice to see you."

Terrence jumped. "Randy."

"What'll it be? Coke on the rocks? Root beer?"

"Bud would be fine."

"One Budweiser coming up." Randy pulled the towel from his shoulder and wiped his soapy hands. He took a bottle from beneath the bar, slammed it on the counter, and pried off the cap. White foam erupted and spilled down the side of the bottle. He slid the bottle to Terrence, leaving a trail of foam behind, and leaned on the counter.

Terrence wiped the amber glass with a napkin, tipped it for a drink, and paused. "Sharon working?"

"Maybe."

Terrence held the bottle half-tipped, smothered in his over-sized hand, and sneered at Randy. Always a smart-ass, he thought. More than once he'd imagined picking Randy up by the shirt and shaking him like a chew toy in the jaws of a pit bull. He'd like to dunk him headfirst in the garbage can out back with the rest of the trash. Can't do it, he told himself. I'm chief now, and I have a reputation to uphold. He took a drink.

Randy stared at him with a shit-faced grin.

"What?"

"Just can't picture it," Randy said.

"Picture what?"

"You and Sharon. I mean with Hank and all. You got to know what will happen."

Terrence spun the bottle then slid it back to Randy. "Another one with a little less shaking."

Randy grabbed another bottle and dropped it on the floor. He popped the cap and watched the foam spill onto the counter top.

"Just saying, if Hank don't approve, could be trouble."

"Last I checked, they were separated." Terrence grabbed the wet bottle and guzzled the third that hadn't escaped from the bottle. "She could do better."

"I thought you were his boy."

Terrence examined the bottle label and started pealing it. "It's her choice. Far as I'm concerned, he lost his say the first time he hit her."

"Hit her? Who says he hit her. She tell you that?"

Terrence imagined reaching across the counter and grabbing him by the neck. He'd drop Randy on the floor and keep him there until he licked up every drop of beer he had spilled. "When does she work next?"

"Schedule's not up yet. Can't say."

Terrence felt his heart begin to beat faster. Remember, he thought, you got a reputation to uphold. He stood and turned to leave.

"Gonna pay for those?" Randy asked.

Terrence opened his wallet and left three dollars in the puddle on the counter. "That should cover what you didn't spill."

The vision of Edith's body lying on the steel table, peeled open, haunted Terrence as he drove to her house. The certainty that he had forgotten something gnawed at the back of his mind. At the scene, he'd allowed the sight of Edith lying dead to pry his attention away from the details that would make or break an investigation. He could almost see Edith scolding him for not paying attention.

Everything rested on the axe. The fibers, blood, and dirt clinging to its sharp edge could eliminate a suspect or tighten the noose around his neck. His gut began to churn as the haunting voice of doubt spoke louder in his head.

His fingers crept toward the switches for the lights and siren on the Suburban's dash. He wanted to be there, to assure himself he'd not made a fatal mistake. As the Suburban gained speed, Terrence again recalled the condition of the axe handle. Fingerprints. Now he had confirmation there were some. Perhaps the crime lab would find a print with the detailed ridges needed for comparison. The lab should have enough DNA to find the markers necessary to narrow the list of suspects.

First he'd eliminate the paramedics. Though they'd said they hadn't touched the murder weapon, he had to be certain. With the unaccounted for movement of the axe, Madison's would also have to be checked.

If prints were found that didn't match anyone who'd responded the day of her murder, identification might be made through comparison with arrest records.

Murderers weren't likely to appear out of the blue. Most had a long history of crime—theft, assault, robbery—before they took a life. Anyone who would murder a defenseless old woman would likely have left a trail of arrests, each one with its own set of pictures and fingerprints.

Finally, he'd compare his own, since he'd entered the axe into evidence. He cursed the damned gloves, two sizes too small, that ripped when he tried to stuff his hands in. There was a chance his own prints might show up. If they did, he'd have some explaining to do.

Forty-eight hours. Two days. That was the narrow window of time during which most murderers were caught. As time stretched out, the trail grew more stale. More time meant more distance for a fleeing suspect. Terrence pressed down further on the gas pedal, and the Suburban's engine rumbled louder.

As he crested the Highway 18 overpass, he saw a combine bouncing down the two-lane road ahead. The lumbering factory-on-wheels filled both lanes, and Terrence's speedometer slowed to fifteen miles an hour. For a moment he envied the farmer seated behind the wheel six feet up in the air. Mow the fields, bail the hay. Leave one job behind and go on to the next. Cutting long swaths of grass up and down the golden fields, no mysteries to solve, no killers to bring to justice. Just the smell of freshly cut grass and the warm fall breeze.

The combine slowed to a walk, swung to the right into a flat spot on the shoulder of the road, and began up a grassy hill. Terrence pulled wide and felt the Suburban lurch forward as its engine whined. He turned into Edith's driveway, churning up a cloud of dust, and rolled to a stop where he'd parked the day he'd been called to the murder. He shut off the engine, taking in the silence so still, he could almost hear the dust settling.

Terrence sat trying to focus, struggling with thoughts that kicked like a bull in the shoot, anxious to stomp the fool roped on its back. He sucked in a deep breath of dusty air and walked back to the garden.

The chicken-wire fence seemed shorter. The garden a pitiful patch of earth. The afternoon sun cast shadows that revealed the shoeprints pressed into the tilled soil. The position of Edith's body was painted in shadows where she'd lain in death. The wedge was still visible in the soil where he'd pulled the axe from the ground beside her. He was close, very close to what he was looking for. It was here. He felt it.

"Looking for something?" the gravelly voice asked.

Terrence spun, not sure at first where the voice had come from. Hank stood in the shadows of the barn door.

"What are you doing here?"

"I was about to ask you the same question."

"Investigating."

"That so?" Hank said.

"You never answered my question."

Hank struck a match, and his face glowed as he lit a cigarette. He shook the flame out and stepped from the shadows. He tossed the match into the dry stubble and watched as a small plume of smoke rose. "Dry out here." The smoke sparked into a small flame that began to crawl up the dry blades of grass. Hank stomped it out with his boot and walked over to the splitting stump. "Maybe you forgot this is my house." He ran his fingers over the grooves chopped into the top of the stump.

"Still haven't answered my question," Terrence said.

Hank pointed to the revolver in Terrence's holster. "Seems you forgot our deal."

"Our deal didn't include obstructing or hindering an

investigation."

Hank drew in a deep lungful of smoke. "Investigation. Is that what you're calling it?"

"I'm still waiting."

Hank looked at him curiously and sucked in another rasping breath. "Got a suspect?"

"The two usually go together."

"Some crime scene. Murder?"

"What makes you say that?" Terrence said.

"My dead mom, for starters."

Terrence pulled out his notebook and wrote the time. He slid the Miranda Warnings card from the back.

"Why are *you* investigating?" Hank said. "I thought there was some big team of guys who solved murders."

"You still haven't answered my question."

"Let me guess. Madison put you in charge."

"What if he did?"

"Probably wanted to investigate himself, but I hear he's in no shape to right now." Hank dropped the smoldering butt of his cigarette and ground it out with the heel of his boot. "I'd say you're in over your head."

"Mayor doesn't think so." Terrence knew he'd regret the words, but they were already out of the barn.

Hank hocked up a long sling of snot from his throat and spat it against the tree. The wad crawled down the bark like a slug. "Now don't that figure. The mayor wants you to solve this case. Let me guess, he's got some pretty good ideas what might have happened and who might have done it."

"I'm in charge, and I'll make sure this case gets investigated impartially and thoroughly."

"Any chance he might have mentioned my name?"

Terrence shook his head. "I'm not a liberty to discuss the investigation."

"'At liberty.' They really educated you at the academy, didn't they."

Terrence studied Hank's unblinking eyes. "I'm waiting."

Hank arched his back and flexed his fingers. "Yeah, in over your head. His little dog sniffing and pissing all over the place. You fetch the paper, too?"

"I'm looking for the truth, the facts."

"He already tell you the facts you need to know?"

"What the mayor told me is no business of yours."

"Dickerson." Hank slowly rolled his head. "So he's blaming me. Figures."

"I didn't say that."

Hank eyed him. "Look, maybe we can help each other out. I can educate you about the ways of the world, and you can catch the real murderer."

Terrence walked over to the stump and stood facing Hank. "The facts. That's what I'm after."

"The facts? How do you plan to find those?" Hank pulled the pack of cigarettes from his pocket and lit another.

"I got a job to do."

"Your job." Hank drew in a breath and let the smoke drift out of his nostrils. "Just what is your job?"

"Like I said, find the facts."

Hank began to laugh then coughed out puffs of smoke. "You really think he'll let you get that far. He wants you in charge so he can make sure who gets the blame. Just another cover up."

"Justice. She deserves that much."

"Tell me something, Terrence. You in on it?"

"What?"

"I hear you got a promotion."

"And if I did?"

"He make you chief because you promised to help?"

"That's crazy."

Hank flicked ash into the grass by Terrence's feet, and another streamer of smoke began to curl up. "Because if you were, ain't no badge big enough to hide behind."

"Sounds like a threat."

"More like a promise."

Red ashen worms began to crawl at Terrence's feet. "Care to answer a few questions?" He pulled out his Miranda Warnings card and began to read. "You have the right to—"

"I've had enough of killing. But if I have to defend what's mine, I will. They say the bigger they are, the harder they fall." Hank smiled and pulled a bottle of Jim Beam from his jacket pocket and unscrewed the cap. "I'll take the fifth." He stepped through the smoke and disappeared around the front of the house.

The yellow flame licked the air and crawled up crisp blades of grass, curling them into charred black hairs. The breeze lifted orange embers into the air and dropped them like glowing feathers, sparking new patches of flame. Terrence stomped on the burning patches. Each stomp sent more embers floating.

Hank returned to the musty basement of his mom's home four hours later. His demons came with him. If he'd chased Dickerson off the property, she would still be alive. He cursed himself for being so blind. It still seemed unlikely the little weasel was capable of such a thing. Dickerson was like the big mouth in the crowd egging on others to fight but too afraid to get his own knuckles bruised.

Killed her for what? The property? Dickerson's plans

for the prison were a poorly kept secret. He'd tried to keep Edith from sharing it. She was so gullible in her advancing years.

Hank flicked open his lighter, watched the flame dance, then snapped the lid shut. The lid flicked open again, and the flame cast a dull glow on the spider webs stringing from the basement rafters. Something shuffled in the pile of sawdust beside the old furnace.

Snap. The flame died.

He sat in silence, half expecting to hear the familiar sounds of home: radio gospel music, a television soap opera, lectures from his old man about the constitution and the right to bear arms. In the deathly stillness, all he heard was the creaking of tired wood.

The flame flicked on again. A bastard, Hank thought. That's all I ever was. The unwanted consequence of Dad's night of drinking at the Reservation. A fling Mom could never forgive him for.

Snap. The flame died.

Something scampered and dug in the sawdust. A rat? Hank flicked on the flame, and the scratching quieted. He picked up a shoe from a box beside him and bounced it off the furnace. Something scurried away, and the lighter flame went out.

Sitting in the dark now, smelling the pine scent of sawdust, he felt momentarily at peace. He looked through the cobwebs stretched across the dirty basement window. The moon painted the fields in a silvery glow. The crickets and frogs filled the cool night air with shrill cries as if warning of things to come. The steady drone of the freeway mixed with a gust of dust that scratched against the window.

The farm felt small and crippled now, like the rotten trunk of a tree decaying from the inside. They're trying to steal my house, he thought. The lighter flicked open again, and he ran the tip of the flame beneath the palm of his hand. He lowered the flame to the sawdust and watched it bend and sway, licking at the bone-dry sawdust. A puff of smoke wisped with the flame. An orange glow spread in the sawdust, flickered, and went black. Hank knew they would never let him return home. Ashes to ashes.

He walked up the creaking wooden steps into the kitchen. The moonlight expanded the space. Memories crowded for attention like puppies hungry for food. He recalled the Christmas tree standing by the mantle. The smell of Mom's freshly baked pies. His father rocking in his chair, reading a Zane Grey western. Mom grading papers and warning the boys to stop roughhousing and do their chores.

Hank walked out the kitchen door, and his feet sank into the soft soil as he walked through the garden. His mother's plants were already beginning to shrivel. In the glow of moonlight, the shadows bent long across the ground. He'd learned to track in the jungles of Vietnam, to make sense of the jumble of leaves, twigs, moss, and grass. He bent low, examining the shadows cast by the footprints. Wheel tracks led from the edge of the garden to the impression her dying body had made. He walked closer to the center. There he saw the clotted mass of blood. The sight brought back the smell of gun powder mixing with the crack of M16 rifle fire in his head. He imagined her lying there, staring up at him, wondering why he'd abandoned her. Her death was his fault, and he would make it right.

Hank walked to the barn and looked into the darkness. His lighter flame danced as he walked through the bent barn door. The smell of diesel filled the air. The five gallon gas can sat behind the tractor. He lifted it and felt the gas slosh inside as he returned to the back porch and kicked open the door. Barney barked and growled. "It's all right boy," Hank said. The hackles on Barney's back stood up as he gave a low, predatory growl. He sniffed, gave a last defiant bark, and darted into the living room where he began scratching at the front door.

Hank unscrewed the cap and poured gas on the couch cushions and over his father's recliner. He ran the trail across the living room rug, then spread a trail up the stairs and into Edith's bedroom. He soaked her bed and poured gas in her dresser drawers. He spilled a trail down the wooden steps leading into the basement and wet the sawdust. He tossed the can on the sawdust pile and climbed back up the stairs. Hank stood at the kitchen door, took a last look at the family photos hung on the living room walls, and flicked open his lighter. He tossed the lighter onto the rug and watched the flame crawl along the liquid trails.

Barney clawed at the front door and whined as smoke began to fill the house.

Hank closed his eyes against the heat as the flames grew. The heat blasted his face and signed the hair on his arms. His clothes felt sticky, and he choked as he breathed in the black smoke. Barney ran toward him whining as Hank stumbled back and slammed the door shut. Barney scratched against the door as Hank stumbled onto the back porch and into the garden. His pants were smoking, and his shirt stuck to his skin as he staggered back into the grass. He struggled to ignore the pain as he watched the flames crawl up the curtains. When the searing pain grew too great, Hank peeled off his smoldering shirt and ran into the field.

He'd never felt so alive.

A gust of wind rocked the Suburban and threw grit against the windshield as Terrence looked into the glare of oncoming traffic. On the road behind, red lights flashed on top an approaching fire truck. Its siren wailed, and the air horn blasted. The fire truck's lights shot blinding light in the rearview mirror and made the inside of Terrence's car glow. The side mirrors beamed in his eyes, turning the road ahead into a black void. Terrence pulled to the right shoulder and heard the popping of gravel as the Suburban sank down on the right side. He shut his eyes to block out the glare and slowed to a stop as the fire engine roared past in a cloud of dust. The blast of air rocked the Suburban as it passed. Another siren sounded on the freeway ahead, then another. On the hillside, a black, billowing cloud boiled up from an orange glow.

Terrence pulled the Suburban onto the roadway, flashing its own red and blue emergency lights. He added his own siren to the screaming in the night and turned toward the freeway.

As he crossed over Highway 18, Terrence saw the flames crawling up the siding and leaping from the roof of Edith's farmhouse. The house's brittle wooden skeleton glowed where the fire had eaten away the siding. The front porch collapsed, charred and smoldering, erupting in steam as a fire hose doused the embers. As he drew near the turn for Edith's driveway, the ancient oak tree in front of the house exploded, sending a shower of sparks and flaming branches raining down on the firemen.

Terrence's wheels splashed into the water washing

down the long driveway from the fire hoses above. The blast of a truck horn from behind warned him to make way. He pulled into the field and a tanker truck rumbled past.

He felt the familiar dread that he'd done something terribly wrong, something he'd have to pay for. As the ash and smoke drifted around him, Terrence retraced his meeting with Hank a few hours before. He recalled Hank carelessly tossing his cigarette into the grass. He watched firemen dousing the scorched earth where hours ago dry grass bent in the breeze. His stomach sank as he realized he might not have fully extinguished the fire that had burned at his feet.

Though the blaze was still more than a hundred feet away, the heat pressed against his face and neck. Three fire engines, dripping in their own mist, pumped water into the leaping orange and yellow flames. A fourth sprayed a fountain of water into the moist air, arcing down onto the smoldering grass and bushes surrounding the house. Firemen unrolled more hose from a truck, their jackets and helmets steaming. Others shoveled dirt on black patches where embers had drifted into the grass and caught fire. The steady buzzing of a chainsaw filled the air. The flames belched embers that filled the sky like a swarm of fireflies.

Terrence looked down the hill and saw three cars pulled to the edge of the road. Six gawkers stood in front of their headlights, pointing at the flames. The tree of spotlights on a jacked up 4x4 shone up onto the hillside.

Terrence remembered his training about arsonists. At the police academy, they learned that fire starters sometimes watched in some sick sexual excitement as the flames spread. Maybe one of the onlookers below?

An explosion erupted like thunder beneath the

burning rubble. A fireman dragging a hose fell as a blast of steam shot back at the red van that served as the command post.

Terrence drove closer to the blaze, wondering how he could help. He pulled in beside the command post van and got out in a shower of ashes floating down like black snow. Terrence held his hand over his mouth, trying not to suck in smoke and ash between his fingers. Two firemen ran past. Their faces were black with soot, and their jackets and helmets steamed.

The battalion commander sat inside the van, behind a table with half a dozen radios squawking for his attention. He held a radio to his ear and shouted orders to men standing outside the van's open back doors. When Terrence approached to offer his assistance, the BC waved him off.

Terrence stepped from behind the van and was hit with a wave of heat that sent wisps of vapor from his sooty jacket. The heat bore through his uniform and sent a trickle of sweat down his back. Wind caught the falling ash and turned the air into a gray blizzard.

Terrence stood with a sense of awe, watching the flames gnaw through the wood. The roof sagged and buckled onto the second floor, throwing another shower of orange embers into the sky. With the roof gone, the exposed floor burned so hot the men retreated. The charred walls soon collapsed onto the main floor, leaving only the blackened bricks of the fireplace standing. The cast-iron woodstove glowed red. The refrigerator, tables, and chairs in the kitchen melted and bent. The television's glass tube drooped in the intense heat. The flames ate through the main floor, and a tall tongue of flame shot upward. Then the main floor collapsed, pulling the walls with it into the basement. A whoosh of hot gas exploded against Terrence. He shielded his face with his hands, and the heat made the hairs on the back of his hands curl. He stumbled backward, afraid the heat might melt his jacket.

A fireman staggered back from the flames, flung his helmet away, ripped off his oxygen mask, and fell to the ground gasping for air. Two others grabbed his arms and dragged him back.

The ground soaked up the water and turned into a pudding that sucked off Terrence's shoe. The heat grew more intense as he pulled his shoe from the mud and slid it on over his slick sock. In the ruins of the porch, he saw the blackened skin of an animal. Its tongue protruded from its swollen mouth, coated in black soot.

Barney, Terrence thought.

As the BC stood in the mud, yelling at two captains in sooty turnout gear, time began to slow. The firemen ran in slow motion, their voices yelling out of sync. His vision began to narrow, then time stood still. A hand grabbed him from behind and tugged on his shoulder.

"You alright?"

Terrence turned. A black soot oval circled the man's face where the oxygen mask had kept out the ash. Terrence felt the cooler air and realized the flames had died down. "Yeah, I'm fine, thanks. What happened?"

"And who are you?"

Terrence read the BC's name tag, Captain Jasper Kendall. "Chief Washburn," Terrence said. "Never seen a fire like this, Captain Kendall."

Jasper shook his head. "Too many of these this year. There's not much we can do but stop it from spreading."

"Any idea what started it?"

"We won't know for sure until our investigators take a look, but between you and me, looks like arson. We found a gas can, and by the smell of the fire and burn patterns, we're pretty sure an accelerant was used." He looked at Terrence then added, "In layman's terms, the place was torched. Like I said, won't know for sure until our arson investigator takes a closer look. Too hot for that right now."

The flames continued to die down as a steady cloud of steam rose from the basement.

"Nobody inside," the BC said. "Maybe an insurance job."

Terrence motioned toward the blackened animal carcass. "What about the . . . "

Captain Kendall spat. "The dog. Didn't see him at first. Looks like he made it out the door and crawled under the porch and got stuck."

"Barney."

"What?"

"Edith's dog. Name was Barney."

"Yeah?"

"Mind if I take a look around?" Terrence said.

"Be my guest. Not much to see though. Just stay back. Could be flare ups."

Terrence tromped through the mud past the barn. Its paint peeled, and steam rose from the blackened siding on the side nearest the house. The exhaust pipe of a tractor poked through a hole in the barn's sunken roof. He slogged through to the garden. The chicken-wire fence drooped, and steam rose from the soil. A puddle had formed where Edith's body once rested.

"Looking for something?"

Terrence turned and saw a tall fireman winding a three-inch line of hose.

"Yeah. Not much left."

"With a place like this, the whole thing can go up in

minutes. By the time we got here, it was fully engulfed. I've never seen one go up so fast. Nothing we could do but keep it from spreading." The fireman looked at him puzzled and asked, "Where do I know you from? You look familiar."

"Yeah?"

"Did you go to Sheridan High School?"

"Class of eighty-one."

"The buzzer. You're the guy who missed the shot."

Terrence felt his wet clothing sapping the heat from him.

"Hey, no offense. I mean—"

"Had a call some days ago," Terrence said. "Suspicious death."

The fireman looked puzzled. "I don't follow."

"Nothing. See you around." Terrence shook gray water from his hair and started walking through the mud.

"Hey," the fireman shouted, "nice try. Almost made it."

Madison's feet kicked against the tangled bed sheets. The steady beeping of the heart rate monitor kept time with the wheezing of the hernia in the bed next to him. He drifted in a cloud of morphine as Edith shook her finger at him. *You should be ashamed of yourself. That nice boy. You're throwing him to the wolves. What did he ever do to you. His biggest mistake was wanting to be like you. Now look at you, lying there, wallowing in self-pity. I've half a mind to turn you over my knee.* Then she was holding the axe. *Time you ate your peas and carrots.* She raised the axe, slicing her neck on the way up. *Cuts both ways.* Blood began to stream from her neck, running down her blouse, puddling on the tile floor. *See what you've done. Now I'll have to change. Better call the nurse, you're gonna need one. The doctor, too.*

In his dream, Madison tried to raise his hands, but they were chained to the bed. He pressed the call button for the nurse and heard, *We're sorry but all lines are busy. Please try again later. Goodbye.* He strained against the chains, then saw Dickerson standing beside Edith shaking his head. Hank stood on the other side. *Give it to him, Momma! Give it to him good!*

Any last words, Chief? Edith said. *Dying confessions? Confession is good for the soul, they say. Too bad you don't have one. Stand back, this could get a little messy.* She smiled and the blade began to sweep downward toward his neck.

We're having fun now, Hank said.

Madison's eyes opened to Hank leaning over him, reeking of smoke and booze. "Yeah, we're having fun now."

"How did you get in here?" Madison asked as he reached for the call button.

Hank held the button. "Looking for something? I'd be happy to hunt up a nurse for you. There's a cute little thing, but she's tied up right now. Old lady down the hall ain't looking so good. I figured we'd just chat for a minute."

"You son of a bitch. When I get out of here—"

"If. If you get out of here. I understand that heart of yours is clogged up pretty good. Strange how it works. I've seen people in combat die of nothing more than a scratch. Convinced they'd been shot, they just gave up. Others, hell they were missing arms, legs, even had half their skull blown off, and still they made it." He patted Madison on the arm. "You're a fighter. I can tell. Bet someone could slip a knife into your gut, and you'd still live to brag about it."

"Everyone else around here may buy your bullshit, not me. As far as I'm concerned, you're nothing but scum."

Hank held up his maimed hand. "Some of us made sacrifices, while others got fat." He grabbed the IV tube running from the clear bag above the chief's head. "Never know what's in those bags. Don't trust 'em. I can't tell you how many times they messed up when I was getting fixed. Watch 'em, that's all. Mistakes happen, believe me."

The morphine made Madison's head swim, and the room seemed to tilt. "What do you want?"

"And that pain killer—great stuff. Packs quite a punch, don't it. Guess I don't have to tell you about the dangers of getting addicted."

Madison reached for the call button. Hank pulled it back. "Ah, ah, ah. Not so fast. I just want to talk."

"About what?"

"I think you know."

Madison glared at Hank who stared back with the cold detachment of a wolf studying his prey. "I'm not going to discuss the investigation with you."

"The investigation. That what you call it? 'Investigation?'"

"As soon as I get back—"

"Investigation sounds official, don't it. We both know better. What I hear, I'm a suspect."

"Who told you that?"

Hank filled a plastic cup with orange juice from Madison's meal tray and took a drink. "Shame to let your dinner go to waste. Mind if I help myself? Biscuits and gravy? Lot better than the stuff they served at the

VA."

"Who said you were a suspect?"

Hank scooped a spoonful of mashed potatoes and stirred them in the gravy. "Just about everybody. You must have missed the word on the street. 'Hank the mother killer.' Guess I butchered her with her own axe. Near cut her head off."

"Guessed I missed all that."

"So here I am. Arrest me. Oh, I guess you're a little under the weather. Thought you might want to know my side first."

"Your side?" Madison inched a hand closer to the call button. Down the hall came a steady buzzing mixed with shouts and hurried footsteps. "Don't let me stop you."

"Ain't you gonna read me my rights? You know, the right to remain silent, blah, blah, blah? Hell, I'll talk. You might want to write this down. Oh, sorry, I forgot. Tell you what, I'll write this all out on a piece of marble for where they plant you."

Hank scooped up another glob of mashed potatoes and shoved it into his mouth. He poked at a clump of mush on the tray. "What's this? Don't know? Probably leftovers, that's what they serve at night, some surprise with all the leftovers smushed together and smothered in gravy to hide what's underneath. He forked a mound of meat and green beans.

More footsteps rushed by in the hallway. "Nurse!" Madison shouted.

"They won't hear you, Chief. Like I said, old lady down the hall had some kind of accident." He shoveled the skewered meat into his mouth and chewed. "So the point is, the morning they say I killed Mom, guess who else showed up?" He curled open the lid of a plastic cup filled with cubes of fruit. "Ice cream. Don't they give you ice cream? Guess you got to ask."

"Just say your piece and get out of here."

"So I'm getting ready to leave after I pay Mom a visit to, you know, see how she's doing, and guess who I run into? Dickie. Little Dick. Limp Dick. Our very own Mayor Dickerson. He's all grins and sunshine. Don't seem too happy to see me, though. Has that grumpy look on his face. You know like he's tried to pinch one off but only got half way. So I try to make conversation, and he's having none of it. I get suspicious. What's he up to? Then Mom gets into the act. She's all goo-goo eyes when she sees him, so I get more suspicious. Pretty soon they're both shooing me away like a couple of kids in on some secret, only I'm starting to get concerned. Mom's not thinking straight these days, and you know how Dickie is, always working things. I decide I should listen from the back where they don't see me.

"Sure enough, he's talking about how sweet she is. Then the farm comes up. He's trying to talk her into giving it to him and the feds. Sure as shit, she's falling for it. He's pressuring her to sign something. I'm about ready to shoo him off when she says she'll have to talk with me before she can sign anything. She says Dad promised to leave the place to me, so she'd have to get my okay. That's when I leave. As I'm driving off, she's waving, and he's stomping his feet. Things are getting heated. I figure she's bigger than him, and she's holding her axe, so she can handle herself. I slow down and watch as she walks around back, the axe slung over her shoulder, and he gets into his car.

"I figure their argument's over, so I leave. Next thing I know, I'm hearing she's been killed." Hank tipped the cup of fruit and drank it. "She's been murdered. Don't it seem kind of obvious who did it?"

Madison's door banged against the chair Hank had wedged between it and the bed. "Open this door," a woman's voice ordered. "Get Tom," she yelled, "the door's blocked. Hurry."

Hank walked to the window. The hernia continued to snore. Hank slid the window up and stepped through with one leg. He nodded at the hernia snoring in bed. "I wouldn't worry about him telling. Something tells me he'll be taking a turn for the worse. Let's keep this little talk between us. I'll be in touch." Hank stepped out the window "Better think hard about your investigation." He pulled it shut as a beefy orderly shoved through the door.

Friday

With the hospital in lockdown, Madison was confined to his room. He watched through his window as an ambulance crew loaded a patient, covered with a sheet, into the back of their van. He wondered if this was the old lady Hank had spoken of. How had she died? What had Hank done? Their next stop would be the mortuary or the ME's office.

It seemed too obvious now. Dickerson was right. Hank had killed Edith and didn't mind adding others to the list.

The ambulance was scheduled to transport Madison to Portland tomorrow morning for surgery. If he made it through, he'd be out of commission for another six weeks. Time enough for Terrence to screw things up royally under Dickerson's guidance. Maybe if I leave now, Madison thought, I can corral Hank and salvage the mess Terrence is surely making. But walking out now would be playing a game of Russian roulette with only one chamber empty.

Madison wrestled with his options as the ambulance drove off. Down the hallway a vacuum cleaner whined.

The muffled conversation he'd grown accustomed to from the nurse's station was absent. This night, the lead nurse barked orders and issued commands to double-check patients.

Half an hour ago, they'd drawn more blood and given him a sedative, after scolding him for barricading the door. Why he'd lied about Hank's visit, he wasn't quite sure. Madison just believed the fewer people who knew what he was about to do, the better.

He recalled the words of the last doctor's visit. *Patients often feel anxious before heart surgery,* he'd said, and went on to describe the procedure. *We'll split the sternum and graft in blood vessels taken from your leg. That will increase blood flow to the heart. Unfortunately, you've suffered significant damage to the heart muscle, which is irreversible.*

Splitting the sternum evoked images of a medieval torture chamber in some damp dungeon. He imagined the saw cutting his breastbone in half, and clamps being applied to pull the ribcage apart, exposing his beating heart. A hooded tormentor would pull a vein from his leg, to be segmented into noodles that would be spliced into his heart. The old, clogged vessels would be left in place like macaroni, marinating in his own blood. The doctor had explained his heart would be stopped while the cutting and stitching proceeded. A machine would pump his blood while his heart was on a vacation. *Not to worry,* the doctor had said, *the heart almost always resumes beating when we're finished.*

The smell of ammonia drifted in the air mixing with some other odor. Smoke? Booze? The leftover stench Hank brought with him into the room?

Madison slid up the plastic stop on his IV bag, pinching off the flow of the clear liquid. He grabbed the IV needle stuck into the back of his hand and grimaced in anticipation of the pain. *Do it quick. That way it won't hurt as much.* The tape pulled his skin up, then peeled loose, as he tore the IV needle from his hand.

The closet door between the beds squeaked as he slowly swung it open. His shirt hung on a hanger, and his pants were neatly folded on the shelf beneath. His shoes were gone.

The unsteady, rattling snores of his roommate slowed then stopped.

Madison gathered his clothing and hurried into the bathroom. The latch clicked as the door shut. His swollen fingers fumbled to button his shirt. Two buttons were missing, and one sleeve was cut in half, a casualty of the paramedic's scissors. A stab of pain jabbed his neck then radiated down his arm as he bent to pull up his pants. The room pitched, and he steadied himself against the sink. He cinched up his belt, dug into the pockets of his pants, and cursed when the wallet and keys were not there.

He flipped off the bathroom light and waited for his eyes to adjust to the darkness. The heavy bathroom door creaked when he pushed it open and walked back to the closet. His roommate lay silent, unmoving.

His fingers skimmed across the top shelf above the hangers, but his wallet and keys were just beyond reach. Madison whispered a curse and looked again at the hernia lying silently, not breathing. The monitors above him showed an unsteady, decreasing heart rate. The visitor's chair screeched as Madison scooted it across the vinyl floor to the closet.

The lips of his roommate were turning blue.

He stepped on the chair and grabbed his keys and wallet. Madison stepped down and took another look at his silent roommate. One of his eyes stared beneath a half-open eyelid. Death comes at night in these places, Madison thought. If death was paying the hernia a visit, the alarm would sound, and a stampede of nurses would soon follow. Madison stuffed his keys and wallet into their usual pockets and pulled his hospital gown over his clothes. He stepped through the doorway and headed down the hallway as the alarm blared. The charge nurse barked more orders, and others came running.

Madison pushed open the double doors and walked out a free man.

"Where's Jimmy?" Hank asked.

The eleven members of the Sheridan Militia seated at the tables looked around the smoky room as if he might have mysteriously materialized inside. Randy walked over to the door and looked through the peep hole. "Looks like he's coming now."

"Well let's get started. Times a wastin'. What time's Mom's funeral service?"

"Two?" Randy said, taking a seat.

"I heard three," another said.

Heads nodded.

"Three sounds right," Hank said. "I want everyone in uniform."

"Class A or B?" Randy asked.

"Jackets and patches. No shorts. We didn't always see eye to eye, but she was my ma."

Billy Marshall looked confused, shaking his head.

"Billy you got something to say?"

"Just, I was wondering with everything and all, you want us packing?"

"What do you think?"

"I was just . . . okay."

Ed Sanders pulled back his jacket, exposing the butt of a gun. "Wouldn't leave home without it."

"Nothing visible," Hank said. "Got that? Keep the long guns stowed unless you're on the outside and need to use them. Inside, I want them locked and loaded. Be ready in case."

Al Johnson tipped his bottle of Jim Beam and took a long swig. He swallowed, belched, and said, "In case of what? It's a funeral for chrissake."

Hank glared at him. "And that means somebody died. In this case, murdered. Now if you're too stupid—"

The door swung open, and Jimmy staggered in dragging a heavy duffel bag. "Sorry I'm late." He shut the door. "Had some problems—" Jimmy's eyes darted about the room, and sweat trickled down his cheeks.

"Problems?" Hank said.

"I handled it."

Hank felt the urge to toss Jimmy back out the door but said, "Get everything?"

Jimmy nodded.

"Good. Al was just wondering why we might need guns today," Hank continued. "Who'd like to explain?"

His twelve confederates squirmed in their chairs. Their eyes converged on Randy, the designated loudmouth.

"Because the guy who did it is going to be at the funeral?"

"That's right." Hank pulled the gun from the holster slung beneath his arm and pointed it at the ceiling. "Blood for blood. He's mine by right. An eye for an eye."

Al took a drink from his bottle. "Right there in front of everybody?"

Hank peered down the gun's sight, zeroing in on Al's

forehead.

Al scooted his chair out of the bullet's path. "I mean, I see you got the right, but you really want to do it with the whole town watching?"

Ed said, "Why not wait till he's alone? Do it clean, no witnesses."

"Do it right there," Randy said, "so the whole town can see. Serves 'em right for electing him in the first place. Hell, they're too scared to do anything about it."

"What about the cops?" Al continued.

"What about them?" Hank said. "Chief's in the hospital. Terrence, well, Terrence is Terrence."

Randy laughed. "Chief Washburn, you mean."

"He can wear whatever badge he wants. He's still one of us. He'll do what I say."

"What if he don't?" Randy said. "He's been poking around and talking. What if he tries to step in?"

"Then we'll deal with him."

"What if he pulls his gun?"

Hank pointed his gun at Randy. "I'll take care of him."

"You sure about this?" Al said. "What if county or state's there? Murder, they're likely to get involved now."

"We'll deal with them, too," Hank said. "Anybody interferes, they'll be dealt with."

Tiny spoke up. "The feds? They been tight with the mayor. You take out the mayor and sure as shootin' they'll step in."

"Oh, yeah," Al said. "They'll send in their troops and take this town over. Just the excuse they need for martial law. Pretty soon we got a war on our hands. Don't get me wrong. I'm all for revolution, but they got tanks and helicopters."

"Let 'em come," Jimmy said. He pointed to the bag he'd drug in. "We got a few weapons of our own."

Al grunted. "Got a tank in there?"

"Enough," Hank yelled. "My God, sometimes I wonder. Al, pull your head out of your ass. The feds are already taking over. At least this way we go down fighting. Do as you're told, and you won't die a coward. Everybody's already all stirred up over Mom.

"Everyone knows law enforcement is in bed with the mayor. Dickie's pulling Madison's chain. Terrence, well, what can I say. Terrence isn't the sharpest tool in the shed. Wouldn't take much to show how the cops are covering for Dickie. When the shit hits the fan who are they going to turn to?"

"The militia?" Jimmy said.

"Bingo. Once they turn to us, we finally get the recognition we deserve. With the town behind us, we stop the feds from taking over. We put the brakes on the prison, and we get our town back. We rebuild the farm into a real clubhouse like the good old days. Something we can be proud of."

Their heads nodded.

"Start showing them who the good guys are." Hank pulled a baggie of white powder from his pocket. He scooped some into the sooty glass bowl of his pipe and lit his lighter. The powder turned brown, boiled, then the bowl filled with vapor. "We look sharp. After, we do what we gotta do." He drew a long breath of vapor and closed his eyes.

The gravestones in the pioneer cemetery leaned at angles like crooked teeth sprouting from the weeds. Mole holes dotted the dried grass, hinting at the tunnels connecting the dead. Bees flitted among dandelions flourishing in green patches where three sprinklers still worked.

The backhoe's bucket reached into the soil and crunched against another boulder. The tractor's back end lifted and bounced as the teeth clawed into the rock four feet below. "Bad place for this," the backhoe operator said. "Too many rocks."

"Can you blast them out?" Dickerson asked.

"Are you joking?" Max said. "Might wake them up."

"How much deeper?" Dickerson asked.

Max had worked this job for as long as Dickerson could remember. Old and weary, Max would likely be joining the rest of his customers before long. "Another foot, maybe two. I can measure."

"Can't you just put it in as is? Who will know?"

Max frowned into the hole, removed his Beaver's baseball cap, and wiped his brow. "Too shallow. Has to be deeper." He shut off the engine and climbed down from the backhoe. "Break time."

Dickerson walked over to the hole and peered in. "Looks deep enough to me. I've seen them dug shallower."

Max slapped him on the back. Dickerson's arms windmilled as he began a slow tilt forward, his eyes looking for the softest place to land among the jagged rocks. Max broke into laughter and grabbed Dickerson's skinny arm and pulled him back.

"Sorry, Mayor. You're such a light fella. Didn't mean to scare you."

Dickerson tugged down his shirt sleeves and dusted the brown smudge where Max's glove had gripped his arm. "I should be done in plenty of time for the funeral."

"Should be?"

They stared into the hole in silence.

Max leaned on a shovel. "The whole family but one. Guess most of us figured Hank would go first, what with the war and all."

"Something tells me he'll be joining them soon enough."

"Oh?"

Dickerson fanned his face with his hat then covered his warm scalp.

Max eyed him then spat into the hole. "I'll be sure to dig the hole deep enough."

"May she rest in peace."

Max crossed himself. "Is it true how she died?"

Dickerson squinted.

Max spat another wad of chew on the rocks. "Most folks see two options. Her boy did it in a fit of rage, or she was killed by a hired gun, a pro." He stared at the mayor.

Dickerson felt the accusation. "A professional?"

"Course that would mean somebody with enough money paid him. Not many folks around here with that kind of cash."

"Why would people say that?"

"Way it was done. Axe to the neck. Her own axe."

"Doesn't sound professional to me."

"That's what makes me think it was. A pro wouldn't make it look professional. He'd set it up to seem like an accident or sloppy, amateur work."

Dickerson shook his head. "And how do you know so much about professional killers?"

"Did a little time in Oregon State Prison years ago. Had a cellmate who liked to talk. Bragging mostly, but he had some stories to tell. He was a pro."

"My money's on Hank," Dickerson said. "He's just

the type who'd do something like this. Never been the same since he got back. He's a professional, if ever there was one. And sloppy."

Max kicked a rock into the hole. "But why? I'm sure they had their words, but she always opened her doors to him. I understand with her gone, the feds are supposed to get the farm." He squinted at Dickerson. "Might be somebody else wanted her out of the way. Somebody with plans for the place. Somebody with enough cash to hire a professional."

"And maybe Jimmy Hoffa rose from the dead and did it himself. Let's not get ridiculous."

"Or maybe someone on your side of the law."

Dickerson's throat suddenly felt dry, and he craved a drink. "Okay, I'll play your game. Who might that be?"

"Let's just say, what I hear, chief's in a bad way right now. Warming a bed in the hospital. Curious don't you think. Just after she dies, he almost does too? Makes you wonder if somebody's trying to tie up loose ends."

"Quite an imagination. Has anyone thought of aliens? Russian spies?"

"Not the Russian government I'm concerned with. It's our own."

"So Chief Madison killed Mrs. Sherman, then someone tried to kill him?"

"Sounds just crazy enough to be true."

"And according to your theory, who hired the chief?"

Max peered into the hole, leaning heavily on his shovel."Seems a couple of feds were in town the day she was found. I hear they met with you and him at the Res."

"Word does get around."

"Small town."

"Well, you can tell everyone who is so enthralled with

these rumors, we are investigating her death, and we'll have her killer in custody soon."

"Who? Who's investigating?"

"Our police force."

"No offense, but half of your police force is in the hospital, and the other half, well, let's just say he's outgunned."

"Terrence is a fine young man. More than up to the task."

Max shook his head. "That boy is tall. I'll give you that. But he's still in way over his head. Kind of looks suspicious don't you think?"

"What is that supposed to mean?"

"Almost like someone doesn't want to catch the real killer."

"Don't be ridiculous."

"Word of advice?"

Dickerson looked at him.

"Small towns have a way of sweeping things under the rug. They also have a habit of going up in flames. We've had enough fires around here, don't you think? What fire burns, water washes away."

"What is that supposed to mean?"

Max pointed to the clouds gathering in the horizon. "The rain is coming. Feel it in these old bones."

Dickerson began walking toward his Cadillac. "Two more feet. Blast it if you have to. The dead won't notice."

"You sure?" Max said.

"Beverly, where's my car?" Madison said.

"Chief Washburn is driving it, I believe." She turned the page of the *Sheridan Sun*. "What are you doing here? I thought—"

"I'm chief, remember? Seems a lot of folks are forgetting that these days."

"I thought you were going to be convalescing for awhile? The mayor said you had a heart attack and would be needing surgery."

"Guess he was wrong."

"Are you sure you're feeling well? You look—"

"Fit as a fiddle. Witch doctors at the hospital don't know a runny nose from a hemorrhoid. I've survived this long, a few more days won't matter."

"Let's hope so, otherwise your tenure as chief may be shortened significantly."

Madison opened the door to his office and turned. "Why is my door unlocked?"

"Chief Washburn—Terrence says it's his open door policy."

"Figures. From now on, it's only open for me."

"Duly noted," Beverly said.

Madison stepped through the door and pulled it shut. The office was generally as he left it, except for the picture of Sharon and Junior on his desk, where the pictures of Madison's much younger days in the Portland Police Bureau should have been. He rifled through the desk drawers and found his pictures and swapped them out. He brushed the dust off the glass and looked at himself in SWAT gear, strong and ready to take on the world. He pulled the heavy leather chair out from behind the desk and sat. The artery in his neck throbbed, and his arm ached as he shook out a nitro pill and swallowed. He unlocked the bottom drawer, pulled out his bottle of scotch, unscrewed the cap, and raised the bottle to his lips.

"Beverly," Madison shouted, "I want my car back here in five minutes."

Silence.

He marched to the door and flung it open.

Beverly stood frozen mid-reach for the door knob.

"I will not let you speak to me in that tone," she said. "I respectfully request that you address me in a more professional manner."

Madison held up his hands in surrender. He could feel the blood rushing into his face. His heart began to pound, sending throbs of fire through his chest. Beverly seemed amused by his rare moment of speechlessness.

"Fine."

"Now, if I might return to my work."

"Sure." He grabbed the Tuesday edition of the *Sheridan Sun* and read the headline "Police Cover Up Brutal Murder."

Terrence pulled the Suburban into the chief's spot and pondered Beverly's urgent phone message. *Back to the station ASAP, no questions asked.* She sounded upset, not her usual formal self. He wondered if the mayor had unearthed some juicy tidbit that might break open this stubborn case. Perhaps the crime lab had identified a print, though it was probably much too early. Or was it Madison? Maybe he'd taken a turn for the worse. Maybe Terrence's new position would be permanent.

He grabbed his duty bag and the latest notes from the investigation—a statement from Todd Beckerman who'd seen the newspaper delivery van weaving around the streets of Sheridan the day of the murder—another dead end.

When Terrence walked into the lobby, Beverly grabbed her purse and passed without saying a word. "Beverly, what—" She shook her head and hurried through the back door.

The chief's door was closed and Terrence heard heated conversation coming from the other side. Madison? He tried the doorknob, it was locked, so he listened.

"Yes, I'm back. At least until this mess gets cleaned up . . . No. No you won't. Remember our deal . . . yes. I'll be there . . . we'll see." The phone slammed and footsteps stomped to the door before Terrence could back away. The door flew open. Madison grimaced and flexed his fingers.

"You!" Madison's face was red with rage. He looked older, more frail.

"Chief?"

"And don't you forget it." He walked back to the desk and fell heavily into the chair. He motioned to the chair opposite the desk. "Sit!"

Terrence sank into the chair. "I thought you were supposed to be—"

"You think too much. What did I tell you about this investigation?"

"It was just follow up, nothing major."

"See, that's the problem. You don't know the difference."

"The mayor said—"

"And what did I say about the mayor?"

"But what was I supposed to do?"

"Exactly what I told you. Leave it alone. What part of stop investigating didn't you understand?"

"But the evidence, the axe, the autopsy results . . . I had to do something."

"When are you going to get it through that thick skull of yours? You just won't listen." Madison massaged his chest. "You leave me no choice. As of right now, you're suspended. I want your gun and badge."

"But—"

"But nothing." Madison slammed his fist on the desk. "Put them right here. Now!"

Terrence pulled the revolver from his holster and set it on the desk, then unclipped his badge and laid it beside.

"Keys, too."

Terrence fished his key ring from his pocket and slid the Suburban key off.

"And the station key."

He placed the station key on the desk.

"It's for your own good. You just don't get it."

"Yes, sir."

"Pepsi generation. All you kids just don't get it. You can't follow orders. Well it's time you learned."

"Yes, sir."

"Two weeks. If you can learn to follow orders, we'll see. If you can't, consider your law enforcement career over. Any questions?"

"What about the mayor?"

"I'll deal with him. I don't want you talking to him. I don't care what he tells you. I'm the chief. Got that?"

"Yes, sir."

"Dismissed."

Terrence rose, walked to the door, and stood in the doorway. "While you were gone, some concerns about the funeral came up. You might want to talk to the mayor."

"That is no longer your worry."

"Yes, sir."

Madison grimaced and rubbed his chest.

"I'll be attending, so if there's anything I can do to help—"

"You've helped enough."

"Are you sure you're well enough to—"

"Dismissed!"

Dickerson sat in his office across the hall from the chief's. "Just another week," he said. The phone line was silent. "I promise you we will get the vote. In fact, this unfortunate circumstance may help persuade any council members who still have reservations."

Ambrose sighed and spoke on the other end of the line. "Mayor Dickerson, this situation seems to be rapidly spiraling out of control. I'm afraid under these circumstances we will be forced to—"

"You will get your vote. I bet my life on that." Dickerson cupped the telephone's mouthpiece as if trying to funnel each whisper directly into Ambrose's ear. "Just one more week. I have her signature and, with recent events, it will be a simple matter to convince the other council members."

"There will be inquiries into her death, the circumstances. I'm sorry, but the politics of it seem to be clear. I simply can't be associated with someone under suspicion for murder."

"But the politics will be just the opposite. What better proof could we want that the prison is necessary?"

"And the investigation—"

"Is proceeding as I had hoped," Dickerson said. "The evidence is overwhelming. Her son, Hank, is the primary—the only—suspect. If all goes as I anticipate, he will attend his mother's funeral and will be taken into custody, then and there."

"And if he becomes violent?"

"All the better. His own actions will be his undoing.

Following his arrest, the vote will be a mere formality."

"Are you sure you have the resources to arrest him?"

"Yes. I have just the man."

"Chief Madison?" Ambrose said. "You'll forgive me if I remain skeptical."

"No. I have another young man in mind."

"And if he fails?"

"He won't."

"A few more weeks. That is all I can give you. If the council has not approved the facility by then, we will be forced to go with our backup site."

"That should be more than enough. The next call you receive from me will be to announce the capture of Edith's murderer and the council's approval of the project. I will do whatever it takes to make this happen."

The phone line was silent, then Ambrose said, "That's what I'm afraid of."

Terrence sat in a booth in the back behind the pool table. The only light in the room shed a cone over the green felt and rack of balls on the table. He nursed a beer in the shadows, wondering how he went from being chief of police to being suspended so quickly. For once, he was glad Sharon wasn't working. She would scold him for not listening. Hadn't she warned him about Madison? He'd been warned about trusting Dickerson as well.

Randy walked over with a mug of beer. "Drinking on duty?"

"You see a uniform?"

Randy held the mug. "Working undercover?"

"What's it look like?" Terrence grabbed the mug and felt the coffee in his stomach souring as it mixed with adrenalin.

"Looks like you lost your badge and gun."

Terrence took a drink. Randy never changed. A big mouth since grade school. Always stirring things up. "Yeah, well." Terrence washed down the words he wanted to say with another gulp.

"What's the matter? Isn't this town big enough for two chiefs? Maybe you just weren't up to it."

"Don't you have somewhere else to be?"

"Nope. I work here, remember?"

"That what you call it?"

"Could use another dishwasher if you're looking for work. If you're looking for Sharon, she won't be back till tomorrow."

"Who says I'm looking for anybody?"

"You got that pussy-whipped look on your face. If you need anything else, ask someone who cares." Randy dropped the bill on the table.

"Asshole," Terrence mumbled.

"Pig," Randy said. "Be seeing you soon."

Terrence left a five on the table and walked out the back door into the clearest day the town had seen in a month. The sun shot long streamers of color through the clouds gathering over the hills to the west. The air was filled with a static charge that raised the hair on his arms.

Terrence needed to move, so he began the two mile walk toward home. He crossed Bridge Street, wondering what to do next. As he neared the park, the rumbling of Hank's Jeep broke through the soft drone of the freeway noise in the distance. Terrence smelled the odor of burning engine oil as the Jeep pulled up beside him. Randy leaned out the driver's window, a cigarette hanging from his lower lip. Terrence walked faster and considered cutting through the park.

The Jeep's engine sputtered then raced. It lurched forward, pulling in front of Terrence then stopped as the engine choked and died. Terrence stepped around and kept walking as the starter cranked the engine over. The Jeep shot out a belch of smoke, and the engine raced again. The wheels chirped, and the Jeep lurched then idled along beside as he walked.

"Need a ride?" Randy said, his head and arms poking out the window. Hank smiled across the seat from him.

"No, thanks," Terrence said.

The Jeep rolled faster as Terrence took quick, long-legged strides.

"Terrence, you forget our deal?" Hank said.

"What deal?"

"The one we made the day I gave you your gun."

"I'm still . . . was investigating."

"What'd you find out?"

"Still under investigation. Was until . . . "

The Jeep pulled in front of Terrence and blocked his path again. "Until what?"

Randy spoke up, "Till he got fired."

"Suspended," Terrence said.

Hank said, "Suspended?"

"Ain't Chief Washburn no more," Randy said.

"That right?"

Terrence considered walking around the Jeep but decided it would just delay the inevitable. "That's right."

"Kind of suspicious don't you think?" Hank said.

Terrence shook his head.

"I mean, we both know who did it. Or maybe some folks just don't want you to solve this one."

Terrence started walking again.

"Cover up," Randy said. "Plain and simple."

"That right Terrence?" Hank said.

Terrence stepped onto the pathway that cut diagonally through the park.

The Jeep squeezed in beside him.

"Randy tells me you been talking with Sharon about your investigation," Hank said. "That true?"

Terrence kept walking.

Randy edged the Jeep closer. "I asked you a question."

Terrence thought of the bruise on Sharon's cheek, and he felt ashamed he'd not done something about it. "I don't see what business that is of yours?"

"Ooo, tough guy," Randy said.

The Jeep's rear wheels spun, slinging dirt and grass into the air. It swerved in front of Terrence and stopped. The door opened, and Hank stepped out. He stood before Terrence, looking up at him with dead eyes. Randy jumped out and stood in Hank's shadow.

"In case you forgot, you promised to tell me what he's up to. That was our deal." Hank stepped closer. "You know Sharon's playing you, right? Always playing games. So why would you want to do something so stupid?"

"Yeah. Why are you so stupid?" Randy said. "I warned you."

Terrence felt the rage beginning to build inside. If he snapped, no one would see, he thought. No. Not now. Terrence turned to walk away then felt a heavy hand slap on his shoulder, yanking him back.

Hank glared at him and tucked one hand into his militia jacket pocket. "Better watch yourself, boy. She gets into your head, you ain't never getting her out. Like it or not, I'm the only friend you got."

Terrence pealed Hank's hand off and squeezed. "Why?"

Hank's eye twitched, but he kept his grin. "Why what?"

"Why do you hit her?"

"Bitch. She tell you that?" Hank said.

"Didn't have to." Terrence said. "I can see it in your eyes."

Hank pulled his hand free and raised a fist to Terrence's face. "You really want to do that? Think you can interfere with me and my wife?"

The rush of rage began to swell. Terrence felt like a wolf, vibrating with energy, ready to leap. The muscles in his chest and arms began to quiver, and the darkness began to fall.

Hank's expression changed to one of puzzlement. "Time to face facts, Terrence. Everybody's playing you. I can see it. You can't decide to shit or go blind. Stay away from her. This is your only warning."

"Or what?"

Hank stepped closer. "Never were too bright. I guess you'll just have to wait and see."

"Wait and see," Randy said.

"We ain't done," Hank said.

"No, we're not." Terrence said.

"Stay away from her if you know what's good for you." Hank walked to the open passenger's door. "I mean it. Watch yourself." The Jeep roared to life then dug up more sod as it spun off down the park.

Terrence thought of Sharon and Junior. Hank was right, now that she was in his head, there was no way he could let her go.

The clouds rose higher into the evening sky as Terrence walked home. The electricity in the air seemed to discharge with each step.

Terrence unlocked his mom's trailer door and closed it quietly behind him. She sat in her recliner, staring at the television screen. As he stepped into the living room, her eyes wandered slowly toward him, and she blinked.

Terrence bent down and kissed her forehead. "Momma."

Her eyes stared at him vacantly, as if unable to place who this big man was, then drifted back to the TV.

Terrence sat on the couch and let the jitters diffuse. The threats were real. Hank had bragged of the terrible things he'd done in the service, and Terrence was sure he'd do them again to protect what was his. Freedom can only be bought with blood, he'd say. Hank had paid more than his fair share.

"Momma, it's starting to happen again," Terrence said. "It's getting worse. I'm not sure how much longer I can control it." His mother's eyes drifted to the ceiling, and for a moment she seemed to hear him. His own eyes followed hers, and he wondered what she saw there. "Momma?"

Was it a tear he saw welling up in the corner of her eye? Then he saw the slight drawing down at the corners of her mouth and narrowing of her eyes. Her eyes met his, and she stared, seeming to comprehend some terrible secret she could not speak.

"Momma, what is it?"

Her mouth trembled, and a faint moan escaped her lips. Terrence bent forward and reached for her hand. She withdrew, and a tear rolled down her cheek as her eyes were drawn back to the television.

Terrence flipped on the milk barn heater at his feet and laid back on the couch. "I got suspended. Maybe this isn't for me. Seems like I can't do anything right. And the spells, if they start again, I just can't risk it." He closed his eyes and let the yakking of a used car commercial crowd out his thoughts. You've got to let it go, he told himself. It's over. Accept that and move on. It's not your responsibility.

He lay on the couch, his feet dangling over the armrest, and drifted back to the Sheridan High School gym.

Edith's casket sat on the free-throw line, and an organ played "Nearer My God to Thee" in the background. The bleachers on either side were full. On the home team bleachers, Hank sat in the front row. The risers behind him were full of militia members wearing their jackets and patches. On the visitor's side sat Sharon, Madison, and Dickerson. Terrence stood at the free-throw line beside Edith's casket as the clock ticked off the final seconds of the game. Sharon yelled at Terrence to shoot the ball before it was too late.

The ball. Where's the ball, Terrence yelled back.

It's inside, Dickerson said. *Hurry.*

Terrence grabbed the casket lid and began to lift.

I wouldn't do that, Hank shouted.

Hurry, Terrence, Sharon yelled.

He strained to raise the lid that felt like it was made of concrete. Once opened, he saw Edith, lying there looking serene, her eyes wide open, holding the basketball.

Shoot, Terrence, Edith said. *You can do it, but you've got to hurry. We're all counting on you.*

Terrence grabbed for the ball, but it was slick with blood, and his fingers slid across its dimpled surface. The clock ticked down to three seconds, two seconds as his fingers slipped, unable to find a good grip to shoot.

Shoot, Edith said. *Now!*

He heaved the ball and watched it spin off a swirl of blood as it arced through the air. The organ music stopped, and the gymnasium filled with the collective gasps of both bleachers. As Terrence watched the ball falling toward the rim, the darkness fell until he could see only the ball spinning in space. It bounced off the rim once, twice, then circled the hoop, leaving a red rim of dripping blood.

No, not again, Terrence pleaded.

The ball fell off the side, and the buzzer became a shrill screech. Terrence woke to the whine of the oxygen condenser alarm. His mother gasped for air, her eyes wide with panic. The television was silent and the screen black. Only the light above the kitchen stove was still on. The circuit breaker had gone again. Terrence ran to the electrical panel and flipped the breaker. The oxygen condenser whirred to life, and the alarm fell silent.

Terrence unplugged the heater at his feet and took his mother's hand. It felt cold and brittle. Her breathing slowed, and the panic in her eyes turned to rage. "I'm sorry, Momma." He kissed her on the forehead. "I'm so stupid. I'm sorry." When she drifted off to sleep, he locked himself in his room, wondering if she felt the darkness as he did.

He peeled off his pitted shirt and pulled the empty holster from his bottom dresser drawer. The gun belt felt so light without his service weapon. He imagined pulling the gun from the holster, and in his mind's eye, raised the sights to the target taped to his wall. In his imagination, he felt the smooth pull of the trigger, then the snap of the hammer igniting the bullet. "Bang," Terrence said, looking above the imaginary sights into Hank's eyes.

Funeral

The morning of Edith's funeral, the air around Sheridan was filled with the smoke of a thousand fires. The facts of Edith's tragic death roasted on a spit dripping juicy rumors of how she'd met her end.

The Reservation filled early that morning. The pulse of the town could be measured by the conversations at the different tables. Sharon carried a tray of burgers and fries to a booth by the window, grateful the tavern would shut down long enough for her to attend the service. She listened carefully to the pockets of conversation detailing the specifics of Edith's untimely demise.

Two men she'd not seen in the Reservation before carried on a loud debate with Ed, one of her regulars. "I heard she was in her bed, doing her evening devotional when the intruder broke in and attacked."

"Was more than one. There was three, one locked the doors, one cut the phone line, and one did the act."

"No. Wasn't that simple. Two of 'em jumped her when she was in her car. Took her dog and slit his throat before her eyes then stole all her money. When she tried to run away, cut her down with an axe, like in that movie."

Sharon scooted the hamburgers and fries on the table in front of Ed, the most senior of the group, and spoke into his good ear. "Is that what happened?"

They glanced at each other like they'd just been caught with their hands in the cash drawer.

Ed winked.

She pulled the ketchup bottle from her apron and set it on the table. The bell rang back at the kitchen counter. As she walked back to fetch another order, the conversations grew more graphic.

"Man they're really stacking up out there," Randy said, sliding a plate of biscuits and gravy through the pass through.

She grabbed the plate and balanced another growing soggy under the heat lamp. "Yeah. Nothing like a funeral to bring folks together. You going?"

"Wouldn't miss it. Gonna be a good time."

She loaded the plates onto the serving tray and added two beers. "If a funeral's what you do for a good time, you got bigger problems than I thought."

"At least I'm still standing," Randy said.

"For now."

"What's that supposed to mean?" Randy's eyes were once again wandering in different directions. His face was sweaty and his hands shaking.

Sharon weaved through the tables to the booth in the corner where a group of women conspired.

"What's the world coming to?" Harriet said. "Nobody's safe. It's that darn television. It's got all the young people's heads full of violence."

"And video games," Violet said. "Shootin' monsters, stealing cars."

"Movies," Henrietta added, shaking her head. "Filled with sex."

The others looked at her. "And violence. The two seem to go together as often as not these days."

Vye said, "So it's true. She was you know . . . abused?"

"Ladies," Sharon said. "Biscuits and gravy."

Harriet raised her hand. "Thank you dear. What do you think?"

"About?"

"About . . . you know." She exchanged glances with the others. "Edith."

Sharon passed out the food. "I think we all got reason to be nervous."

They looked at her alarmed.

"Nervous?" Henrietta said.

"I'd say scared shitless, but that might be a little harsh."

Vye gasped.

A bite of Harriet's gravy-slathered biscuit slid off her fork.

Sharon tucked the tray under her arm. "Edith murdered. Killer on the loose. And Chief Madison gone. Seems kind of suspicious."

"Suspicious?" Vye said.

"I'm just saying," Sharon said. "First the murder then he suddenly disappears."

"I heard it was a heart attack, or the cancer," Vye said. "You don't think he was in on it?"

"What about Terrence? He's such a nice boy. I understand he's trying to solve it, " Harriet said.

"Chief Washburn, Harriet," Henrietta said. "Don't get me wrong. He's a good kid and all, but chief? A bit of a stretch, don't you think?"

"Mayor doesn't think so," Vye said. "Course, Dickerson hasn't had the best luck with chiefs, if you know what I mean." Henrietta elbowed her and nodded toward Sharon. "Oh, I didn't mean—"

"I heard it was her son." Vye said. She looked around the groups seated in the gloomy tavern and leaned in. "Him and his goons. Murdered his own mother."

Harriet spat a bite of biscuit into her napkin. "Salt. Too much salt. You know I can't. Blood pressure."

Sharon shook her head and grabbed the plate. "I'll get you a new one."

Harriet reached for the plate, "Give it here dear, no point in letting it go to waste."

Vye snapped her fingers. "You're saying Madison's in on it?"

Sharon shrugged. "I'm just saying, it's pretty suspicious that his business card shows up at her door the day she's murdered, and then he disappears."

Violet waved her hands. "I have a nephew who's with the Portland Police. He says Chief Madison was pushed out. Says he was fired for police brutality. He shot a man in the back. I never trusted the man. I wouldn't put it past him."

"It's always the ones you don't suspect," Harriet said.

The kitchen bell rang again. Sharon walked back to the pass through where two plates of sausage and eggs sat incubating beneath the heat lamps.

"Coffee pot's almost empty," Sharon said.

"Get to it when I can," Randy said. "Kinda busy right now."

She loaded her tray and took in bits of conversation as she made her way past the pool table in back.

" . . . Smith and Wesson. More reliable . . . "

" . . . .357 is just a .38 that hasn't been shaved off. .308, now there's stopping power . . . "

" . . . German shepherd. There's a guard dog. Or Doberman . . . "

" . . . If they're on your property, you can shoot 'em. It's in the constitution. Right to use arms . . . "

She reached the booth in the far back where three militia members sat. "Who had the sausage and eggs?"

Three hands went up.

Jimmy smiled. "You sure look nice today."

She slid his plate in front of him. "Your sausage looks a little limp today."

Billy Marshall elbowed Jimmy and said, "Short, too."

"You going to the funeral?" Jimmy asked.

"I'll be there. Looks like you three are all dressed up with nowhere to go, unless you're also attending."

Jimmy spoke up. "Oh, we'll be there all right. Hank says you got the inside track on who did it."

"I'll bet he did," Sharon said.

They looked at her like cows chewing their cuds.

"Who's got the authority to keep this hush-hush?" Sharon said.

"That son of a bitch," Jimmy said.

"Terrence says he was out there, even left a calling card," she said.

Ed swallowed. "Damn."

"Well we got a surprise for him," Billy said. There was a stomp beneath the table and Billy winced.

The others grinned.

"Give a man a shovel," Ed said.

"Dig his own grave," Jimmy added.

"What's one more," Sharon said. "Anything else you boys need?"

Jimmy smiled. "How about your phone number?"

"How about you leave a tip this time?"

The kitchen bell rang again, and Sharon headed back for another load.

" . . . I'm just saying," Al Johnson continued, "if they're on your property, you have the right, that's all."

" . . . somebody comes at me with an axe, doesn't matter where I am, I'm gonna fill them full of lead . . . "

" . . . self-defense. Second or third commandment . . . "

Al raised his bottle of beer. "I'll drink to that."

The others joined him in a toast to the constitution.

The light flashed on the answering machine on the chief's desk. Madison pushed the play button and impatiently listened to the rambling complaints about speeders in the school zone, kids drinking in the park, and an unruly dog that insisted on yapping through the night. The fourth message was in the unmistakable whine of an upset Mayor Dickerson. "I stopped by the hospital today. Guess who had checked out. Don't do anything stupid. In fact, don't do anything at all until we talk. If you're still alive, call me right away."

Madison walked into the private bathroom he'd had them build in his office and stared at his haggard looking face in the mirror. His heart pounded in irregular rhythm. He popped two more nitro pills, hoping it would pass. The hand he'd pulled the IV needle from was bruised and stiff. He leaned against the counter and stared at the dark circles under his puffy eyes, trying to ignore the floating sensation in his head.

How had it come to this? Madison marveled at how badly rookies could screw things up. If Dickerson wasn't so bent on an investigation that would tag Hank, they could have handed it over to the state patrol from the start. If they'd washed their hands of the case, the dark cloud of suspicion that now hovered over their heads would never have formed. Every step they took now only fueled the rumors that Edith's death wasn't so accidental. If this wasn't wrapped up soon, the state would come, and they'd find plenty. Some green detective eager to make headlines would start digging into his past. With the first whiff of corruption, the state would bring in a backhoe, and soon they'd be mired in a pit deeper than the quarry.

Madison wound a piece of floss around his fingers and snapped it between his back molars. We all see what we want to see—investigators included. In an election year, he and Dickerson would be some politician's proof a regime change was needed. If I'm going to be a target, he thought, I wouldn't be the only one.

A cramp crawled up Madison's neck as he pulled his shoulder holster over his head. It became a knot when he tugged the sleeve of his suit jacket over his arm. He slipped in the other arm and opened the cylinder of his revolver to confirm there were five bullets seated there. He closed the cylinder, slid it into the shoulder holster, and snapped his handcuffs into their holder beneath his other arm. This was one funeral where a man would be a fool not to be packing.

Edith Sherman stared vacantly into the neon glare in the prep room in the mortuary basement. Her face wore a heavy coating of makeup that made her look like her smile had been molded with lumpy clay. Dickerson's eyes watered as he stood beside the casket, staring into the terrible dryness of eyes that no longer blinked. He wanted to shut them, to keep them moist. It was the tears, he realized, that made them look alive.

The collar of her dress covered the sutures that closed the severed flesh of her neck. She looked as if she'd crawled into the casket in her Sunday best. Her face, though, reminded him of the slice of pie she'd offered him, the rubbery remains of fruit, once juicy and sweet, now in the grips of decay.

Dickerson's thoughts turned to her farm. The debate over the prison was sapping the life out of his weary bones. He almost envied Edith, lying in silent repose — her arthritis no longer throbbing in her hands, her cataracts no longer blurring her vision, her ears deaf to all the clamoring voices telling her what to do. He tucked back a curl of gray hair that had drooped down over her forehead. How easy it is to be dead, he thought.

As a boy, Dickerson and his best friend, Joey Anders, had explored the shiny caskets on display upstairs. Joey dared him to crawl into one, and he obliged. Once inside, he found it less comfortable than it appeared. Joey lowered the lid, and immediately the air began to grow stale and suffocating. Dickerson pushed up against the heavy lid as Joey held it shut. In the darkness, the satin sheets seemed to close in, and he thought of the dirt that would one day surround the buried casket. Dickerson yelled at Joey to open the lid, then screamed and pounded his fists against the satin cushions padding the lid. He fought back swelling panic long enough to turn over onto his hands and knees and shove the lid open. Free from the casket, he collapsed to the floor, gasping while Joey doubled over laughing. Ever since, Dickerson could only imagine the panicked eyes of the deceased, their feeble arms straining to escape as they were lowered into the ground.

Dickerson looked at Edith's photo taped to the casket lid, one from much younger days. It bore so little resemblance to the woman lying there, he pulled it free and tucked it into his pocket.

Edith's earlobes were adorned with pearl earrings. A matching necklace was draped over the collar of her blouse. "Edith, you never looked so good," he whispered and took her cold hand in his. "You'll thank me. Yes, you will. Think of it, the correctional facility employing more than a hundred of our young men. Imagine the life those jobs will breathe into our community. I wish you could see it. If you could, you would agree it was worth it. Sleep well, darling."

He bent forward, kissed her on the cheek, and dropped the lid.

Idiots. I'm surrounded by idiots, Madison thought, as he parked the Suburban behind the Church of The Nazarene. Shooting fish in a barrel, that's what it could be. God knows how many guns might be present. Doesn't take a genius to pull a trigger. If it did, he'd have nothing to worry about. Not many Einstein's in the Sheridan Militia. They'd be there, of that Madison was certain. And Hank too, the ringmaster of his own little circus.

Madison surveyed the parking lot and imagined the snarled traffic and jockeying for spots that would turn the dusty gravel into a destruction derby in an hour from then. Not nearly enough handicapped spots. Half the lot could be reserved for the disabled, and still they'd need more.

The throb in his arm started again. His heart began to thump its unsteady beat and gained momentum. He thought of the doctor's warning about the big one rolling his way, and more adrenalin shot into his chest.

He took three deep breaths and tried to think like a halfwit. How will the militia try to take control? They'd stand by the doors waiting for the service to begin. Once the doors were closed, they'd seal the place, no one in or out. Once everybody was seated inside, then what?

What did Hank want? To keep the farm.

What will Hank do when Dickerson proclaims that Edith's farm is now the property of the feds?

Just about anything.

Hank would see Dickerson standing behind the pulpit, a peacock fanning out his feathers for all to see, robbing Hank of the only thing that gave him hope.

So what will Hank do next? He'll pluck Dickerson's feathers, one by one. Pluck his feathers and wring his neck.

Madison looked inside the auditorium at the uniform rows of pews. Hard pine benches with straight backs and bare wood seats.

Edith's casket lay at the end of the center aisle. A polished wooden box with brass handles. The lid was divided in two. The upper end would be opened, exposing Edith from the waist up, half of her on display for all to view. Madison wondered how skillfully she'd been restored. He'd find out soon enough.

Behind the casket, the platform rose three steps. The lectern stood in the center, above Edith's casket, flanked by a baptistery to the left and a table for communion on the right. Further to the right, a side door allowed the officiating minister, Reverend Holland, to enter the platform. Dickerson would follow behind, relishing the spotlight.

Madison walked down the center aisle. The front two rows were draped with bows. Place cards reserved spots for the immediate family, relatives, and local dignitaries.

I'll sit on the right, Madison decided. Hank will take the left. If he makes a move, I'll be close enough to stop him. If things go south, I can get Dickerson out the side door.

His eyes were drawn to the casket as he approached. He brushed his fingers over the shiny surface and lifted a heavy brass handle. Solid, real, he thought. The door to the sanctuary opened behind him, followed by a hushed apology. Randy?

Madison turned as the door clicked shut. He let go the brass handle and patted the gun holstered under his arm. Reassured it was still there, he walked through the side door.

"He's here," Brandy, Junior's favorite sitter, shouted behind the apartment door. The door swung open and Brandy stood in short shorts and a halter top, smiling. "Hey, handsome."

Terrence felt his face blush. "Hi, Brandy. Sharon ready?"

"Just about. You look nice today."

Junior ran through the living room wearing a toy gun belt with two six-shooters and a silver sheriff's star, and squeezed past her. He drew one of the guns and pointed it at Terrence's chest. "Bang. Bang. You're dead."

Terrence grabbed his chest and dropped to one knee. "Got me." His eyes rolled up, and he leaned against the door jam, feigning the last throes of death.

Junior laughed. "Makin' bacon!"

"Junior, don't say that," Brandy scolded. She pulled him back and looked Junior in the eye. "That's not how you talk to the cops. You hear me?"

Junior's eyebrows knit together, and his lower lip pouted.

"Oh, it's all right," Terrence said. "I'm sure he didn't mean any harm." He mussed up Junior's hair. "Did you buddy?"

Junior shook his head and holstered his gun.

"Want to come in?" Brandy asked.

Junior grabbed his hand and tugged. "Let me show you what Dad got me."

"Stop pestering Officer Washburn."

"It's all right," Terrence said.

Brandy took Junior by the shoulders. "Come with me young man. Let's get your things."

Terrence walked into the living room as Sharon stepped from the bathroom, dressed in a little black dress that hugged her curves. Her red hair tumbled over bare shoulders.

"It's the only black dress I own. Do you think it might be too . . . informal?"

Terrence struggled for the words. "No, you're beautiful." He felt like they were on their way to the senior prom all over again.

"Thanks. You're sure it isn't too—"

"Trust me, it's perfect."

"Okay then," Sharon said. "Brandy, thanks for watching him. Shouldn't be too late."

Brandy smiled and pulled Junior to her side. "We'll see."

Terrence held the door. Sharon's hip brushed against him as she stepped through. Junior giggled, and Terrence felt his face blush again. He walked down the stairs behind her, distracted by the cleavage her low neckline exposed.

Terrence held open the door of his mom's Buick, and Sharon scooted in. He caught himself peeking at the short hemline creeping up her thighs.

The steering wheel pressed against his legs as Terrence wedged in behind the wheel. He felt her eyes appraising him beneath her sunglasses.

"What?" he said.

"It's just . . . you clean up nice."

"You, too." Terrence turned left into traffic.

"Hey, I'm sorry for Junior. He shouldn't have said that."

"Not the first time I've heard it. You've seen the T-shirt with the two pigs in the act dressed like police officers? 'Makin' bacon' is what it reads. Can't tell you how many oinks I've heard. Part of the job, I guess."

"I don't care. He shouldn't have. Hank's been teaching him lots of new words. He said 'bitch' the other day, 'kill all the bitches.' Can you imagine?"

"No, I can't."

Sharon tugged at the skirt inching up her thighs.

"He's getting so big," Terrence said. "Reminds me of me at that age."

Sharon sat silent then cleared her throat. "You've heard?"

"What?" Terrence asked.

"Hank will be there. Him and the rest of them."

"Kind of figured. She was his mother."

"Yeah, but people have been talking."

Terrence turned onto Bridge Street and stopped behind the traffic waiting for the light. "When aren't they?"

"Maybe this time you should listen. What if Hank does something?"

"At his mother's funeral?"

"Terrence, I wouldn't put it past him."

Terrence shrugged.

"You don't know him like I do. He's like a stick of

dynamite just looking for a match. I got a bad feeling."

The traffic began to crawl forward toward the church. "Listen, you've got nothing to worry about."

"Nothing to worry about?" Sharon said. "Maybe if I had a gun, I'd be a little less worried." She looked at Terrence. "You have yours, right?"

Terrence let the car roll into the space ahead as traffic inched forward.

"You do have it?" Sharon said.

He shook his head.

"Terrence, I can't believe you don't have a gun. What good is a badge without a gun? Might as well paint a bull's-eye on your back."

"I guess I don't have to worry about that." He slowly pulled forward. "No badge either."

"No badge? Why don't you have it?"

"Madison . . . we had a disagreement about the investigation."

"Figures. What did you expect? He doesn't want you poking around—"

"He suspended me."

Sharon sat speechless, staring at Terrence.

"No badge, no gun. That's why I'm not carrying."

"He's going to get you killed. You know that don't you?"

"I'll be alright."

"Terence, what if something happens? You going to just sit there?"

Terrence twisted the leather steering wheel cover. "You let me worry about that. Right now we need to remember a wonderful lady."

Sharon took his hand and held it in her lap. "Just promise me you won't do anything crazy."

"It's a funeral, Sharon. What can go wrong?"

Jesus hung on the cross, painted in a rainbow of light as the afternoon sun shone through the red, tan, and blue stained glass behind the pulpit. His eyes looked down upon Edith's casket from a tortured face. The crown of thorns dug into his scalp, sending drops of crystalline blood running down his brow. Mary knelt at his feet weeping, and the Apostle John comforted her. Multicolored light shone off a spider web above the crown of thorns.

Dickerson paced the platform then stood on a stool behind the pulpit. He imagined the mourners seated in the pews, reliving their memories of Edith's eighty-plus years in Sheridan. A Sunday school teacher, Women's Altar Guild member, and surrogate mother to a quarter of the citizens of Sheridan. Half of those in attendance would have been her pupils in the one-room school house.

The windows rattled as the church organ broke into "Nearer My God to Thee." Phyllis, the organist, walked too heavily on the base pedals in her later years as her hearing began to fade. Gordy warmed up his raspy vocal cords with the first verse, heavy on the vibrato.

Dickerson stood solemnly behind the pulpit, rehearsing for the service less than an hour away. He imagined the pews filled with the grieving, the organ music soothing and reverent, Edith's favorite hymn reverberating off the walls while the low base pedals thundered as if God himself was singing bass. In his imagination, the 120 seat auditorium transformed into Saint Peter's Cathedral crowded with a throng of mourners fit for the pope.

Dickerson's eyes lowered to the front pew, and he

imagined the ghosts of Edith's deceased husband, Wilbur, and Bobby, her youngest son, seated there, welcoming her to join their final rest. Dickerson would think of them as he extolled the virtues of the new prison made possible by the acquisition of Edith's farm. Wilbur would surely turn over in his grave, but the storyline would serve his purposes. Militia members who refused to believe that the sale was Wilbur's wish would bend soon enough. Those who were smart— those he could count on one hand—might even find employment there.

Hank was the last obstacle in the way of Sheridan's rebirth. Dickerson had lain the bait and would soon close the trap. He thought of the verse he'd chosen to use in his eulogy: "Unless a seed falls to the ground and dies, the plant cannot grow."

He would extol Edith's life of service and her greatest gift, the sale of her property, a tribute to her fallen husband and son. It was fitting that her casket rested at the feet of Jesus and his mother Mary. Edith would be a grieving saint who had given all she had so the town could be reborn. How fitting her death ended in a garden. Her own Gethsemane, betrayed by her own son, her Judas. The kiss delivered with an axe. Her blood shed for the lives of others. In a grand resurrection, she would rise not as an individual, but as an institution, touching the lives of thousands. The words came so easily at times such as these.

Dickerson imagined the walls of the prison, the watch towers joined by chain link fences, the uniformed men, law-abiding and clean-shaven, modern-day fishers of men. The federal money would flow like milk and honey. The schools would be renovated, and the crumbling downtown rebuilt. The revenue would ensure healthy wages for city workers and a stipend for council members. He and Madison would finally be properly compensated. Best of all, the dismal pall that dulled life in Sheridan would lift, and the flight of the town's youth would stop as they found satisfying employment.

Dickerson felt renewed as he looked up at the cross and whispered, "Thank you, Edith."

Madison returned to the sanctuary through the front doors. Margaret sat in the front pew, dabbing her nose with a handkerchief, staring at the floor. Dickerson stood behind the pulpit, apparently rehearsing some great silent oratory, arms spread wide, an incarnation of the crucified Jesus above. Madison smiled as he imagined a spike pounded through each scrawny palm.

Dickerson's head lowered, and his eyes closed. After a long pause, they opened and swept over the pews, drifted past Madison, then darted back. Dickerson gaped at the chief like he'd just seen Edith's ghost. "I thought you were scheduled for surgery today?"

"I was."

"So what are you doing here?"

"Apparently saving your ass again."

"My message. Did you get it?"

"Nope."

Margaret turned, her hand frozen, holding a tissue in front of her cheek. "Chief Madison?"

"Margaret, dear," Dickerson said, "would you mind waiting for us in the foyer?"

"You don't look well," Margaret continued. "Are you sure—"

"I'm fine," Madison said.

Dickerson stepped from behind the pulpit and descended the stairs. "Please, dear. We need to speak privately."

"I . . . we were worried," Margaret said. "Are you sure—"

"Margaret, please, a few moments."

Margaret took Madison's hand. "I'm so relieved you're here. I don't share Dickie's confidence. Do you think there might be trouble?"

Dickerson placed his hands on her shoulders and turned her toward the aisle. "Thanks, dear."

She patted Madison's hand and began up the aisle.

"Seems to be taking it pretty hard," Madison said.

"Edith meant a lot to some of us."

"I wasn't talking about Edith."

"Why does everything have to be about you?" Dickerson said.

Madison shrugged. "So is he on the guest list?"

"I assume you are referring to Hank."

"Who else?"

"I believe he is." Dickerson rubbed his neck. "In your absence, he paid me a little visit."

"What for?"

"Let's just say he had recommendations about my eulogy."

"Like?"

Dickerson sat in the pew, and Madison joined him. "A confession," Dickerson said. "Before God and these witnesses."

"So he'll be coming to hear you confess. The irony's not lost on me. And if you don't?"

"He's threatened to harm Margaret."

"What did you tell him?"

"I agreed—as long as Margaret isn't harmed."

"That should be interesting. Tell me, why'd you use an axe? Kind of messy for a guy like you."

"Don't be a fool. My message will hardly be a confession."

"Why am I not surprised? What do you have in mind?"

"Edith's generosity, always thinking of others, the hard life she has endured, honoring her last wishes."

"And let me guess. How she sold her property to the feds for the new prison. Your grand vision of the future."

"Our vision," Dickerson said. "I seem to recall it includes a generous pay increase for the police chief."

"And if they don't buy it? What then?"

"I guess we'll see." Dickerson leaned closer. "You are armed, I hope."

Madison patted his jacket. "Someone's got to be."

"You won't be alone," Dickerson said.

Madison felt the throbbing begin to work its way down his arm. "Don't tell me."

"How was I to know you would be here."

"And did Terrence tell you I suspended him?"

"Suspended him? Why?"

"Disobeying orders for starters."

"What orders would those be?"

"To stop the investigation until I returned. You can't really believe he was up to this."

Dickerson drew a long breath and frowned. "Perhaps you're the one who should be stripped of police powers. I gave you orders. Maybe I'll just reinstate him here and now."

"You don't have the authority."

"Don't I? I certainly have the authority to fire you. Are you even fit for duty? I can't imagine they gave you a clean bill of health. Perhaps you should check yourself back into the hospital."

"And leave Terrence here to deal with Hank when he doesn't hear your confession."

"You underestimate the boy. He is capable of more than you know."

Madison stood. "I've seen what he's capable of. He's no match for Hank and his band of idiots."

Dickerson grinned. "You think Hank might become violent?"

"Think? Like the sun rises in the east."

"And what then?"

"You'll be feeding Terrence to the wolves."

"Sharon says Hank and his band of merry men will be all dressed up in their silly uniforms. Apparently Hank has given instructions that his followers are to maintain proper decorum during the service."

"He doesn't know what the word means. Is he still your suspect?"

"That hasn't changed. Of course he's my suspect."

"Does he know it? That he's suspected of murdering his mother?"

"Of course he knows."

"So Hank knows you want to tag him for the murder of his mother. He also knows that murder, being the fairly serious offense it is, he could face the death penalty or maybe get lucky and do life in prison. Yet you think he's going to waltz into church and conduct himself like a model citizen. Am I missing something? I fail to see how this is such a great idea."

Dickerson stood. "The service will follow the usual format. Greetings, prayers, her favorite hymn, then there will be an opportunity for friends and family to speak. I have spoken with Reverend Holland, and I will conclude the program by offering my own thoughts. I've titled my message, 'It's her wonderful life.' I will inform the congregation of the sale of Edith's property as well. By the time I've finished, she will be practically a saint. At least a martyr."

"What about Hank?"

"What about him?"

"You think he's just going to sit back while you steal the farm?"

"Steal? We have her signature. It's what Edith wanted. I can't help it if her son doesn't see fit to honor her wishes."

"So you think he will just sit there quiet as a church mouse while you take possession of her property?"

"What choice does he have? Once I have the support of the congregation, he wouldn't dare object."

"I still don't see Hank just sitting there."

"But there's the beauty of my plan. You said it yourself. If he does object, it will be in his usual obnoxious manner. The solemn setting will surely cast him in the worst light. If he becomes disruptive, suspended or not, Terrence will place him under arrest and escort him from the building. If he resists, I believe there's a fairly large fine for resisting arrest. Heaven forbid he should assault an officer. Once Hank is in custody, the investigation for Edith's murder will proceed more quickly. I imagine he will be much more supportive of my interests once he's behind bars. Either way, the fate of Edith's property is sealed. If he interferes, he simply makes your job easier."

"Resisting arrest and assaulting an officer is a long way from murder."

"What's the worst that can happen? He is found innocent of murder? The other charges should be sufficient to persuade him. I believe that once in custody, he will be very open to a plea bargain. If he agrees not to contest the sale of the property, I will see to it that the charges are reduced. So you see, everybody wins."

"And if Hank won't take a plea?"

"Well, Chief, then he'll have his day in court."

The dust settled on the winding road that wound down the cliff sides to the militia club house. Hank's Jeep was parked out front, the engine snapping as it cooled. In the darkness inside, Hank sat in the president's chair, alone at the head of the horseshoe of tables. The whiskey scratched on its way down his throat. He tipped the bottle again and thought he heard the distant thumping of helicopter rotor blades. He paused mid-swallow listening for the crack of rifle fire and the distant screams of the fleeing. The cries of seagulls signaled a storm at the beach, rain on the way.

All he ever wanted was respect, and what had it gotten him? Crippled and homeless. He drained the bottle and tossed the empty toward the garbage can. It hit the wall and fell spinning onto the trailer floor.

Hank spread a rag on the table before him and placed a whetstone on top. He pulled his rusty K-bar from his ankle sheath and ran the tip of his thumb over the dull, seven-inch blade. Like me, he thought, breaking down, unfit, surplus—but maybe good for one more mission. He ran the cutting edge across the stone a dozen times and examined the thin edge of silver metal. It would take a lot more to get the knife's edge sharp enough to do the work that awaited it.

He slid the edge over the stone again and again, and

his mind drifted with the rhythmic scraping. He remembered running in the fields of the farm with Bobby, hunting squirrels and pheasants. Cowboys and Indians was their favorite game. Hank pretended to wear the six shooters and badge, while Bobby carried the bow and arrows. Once captured, Bobby had a gift for drawing out his agonizing death. Savages weren't supposed to die so dramatically. The prolonged throes of death were for the white man. All others were expected to drop dead without objection.

Hank flipped the knife over and fell into rhythm sharpening the other side. He'd seen death visit men of all colors. White, red, black, or yellow, men faced death on its terms. Some fought it with all their strength, full of panic. Others just submitted, seeming to welcome death's embrace. Most faced the end bewildered, feeling cheated, wondering how it could happen to them.

Death had knocked on Hank's door more than once. Some said he had a death wish. Hank disagreed. If he'd have wanted to be dead, he'd have managed it by now. There are a thousand ways to die. That was the easy part. It was figuring out how to live that vexed him. Hank held the knife up and plucked the edge with his thumb. He felt the subtle drag of the blade, tiny bites from the burrs on the razor's edge. Almost there.

He scraped again and thought of his mom digging in her garden, the tomato plants and squash growing lush and green around her. She claimed that toiling in the dirt reminded her of the miracle of life. The earth gave life and one day received all living things again. *Roots,* she said, *are the source of life. Grow them deep, boys, and you will thrive.* Bobby's roots were forever tangled in rocks. Hank's more often wore shoes and escaped to distant lands seeking adventure.

Hank lifted the knife and examined the thin, honed edge of the steel. In the sliver ribbon of reflection he could almost read the future. The battle plan was in motion. Hank versus the U.S. government, again. He knew it was a battle he could not win. They'll take the farm, and when they do, what have I got left?

Only the battle.

The flame of his lighter licked the polished edge until it glowed. He spat on the blade and watched it boil. He imagined Dickerson standing before the funeral crowd, shoveling a truck load of bullshit, hoping to pin his mom's death on him. All the blue hairs would likely buy it, and once again, justice would ride out of town into the sunset.

Justice would have to come another way.

The lighter snapped shut and Hank examined the tip of the glowing blade. He pressed his calloused thumb against the edge. The slight sizzle and smell of burning flesh cleared the fog of whisky in his mind. The burn shot needles into his head, and he fought the impulse to pull away. He drew the knife down his thumb, opening the skin. The hot metal cauterized the severed flesh, and no blood spilled. Sharp enough now, Hank thought. A killing knife.

Terrence and Sharon inched past Sheridan High School. Three cars ahead, a jacked up 4x4 stopped. The driver's tiger-striped jacket sleeve stuck out the window. Two rifles hung in the gun rack visible through the rear window. Beyond the rifles, the hulking man on the passenger's side waved his arms while the skinny one riding shotgun tipped a can of beer and turned to look behind. He said something, and all three turned to look.

"Randy and Jimmy," Terrence said. "And Tiny."

"Rambo wannabes," Sharon said. "Can they have those rifles?"

"They can as long as the rifles stay outside."

"What about handguns?"

"If they got permits." The three turned and looked back at them again. "Not likely any of them could get one, though."

"So anybody with a permit could be carrying a gun. And anyone else who figures it's worth the risk, permit or not."

Terrence felt naked without his gun, but kept his peace.

"It would be nice to have one under the circumstances," Sharon said.

"Everybody just needs to calm down," Terrence said. "This isn't the OK Corral."

"Not yet. I just can't believe you don't have your gun."

"It would only make things worse. A church full of people. Not exactly the place for a shootout."

She pointed at the 4x4 ahead. "Tell them that. What if they don't care?"

"I care. I have to care. My job is to keep the peace—or it was."

"Their job is to stir things up. What if they start something?

Traffic rolled forward. "They won't."

"How can you be so sure?" Randy stuck his head out the driver's side window and waved. Sharon flipped him the bird. "Randy, that little weasel. Just like the rest of them. A big man as long as his buddies are around to do the fighting for him."

The 4x4 pulled into the church parking lot and the line

inched forward.

Sharon looked at Terrence and poked a finger against his chest. "I thought that suit jacket looked a little tight on you. A vest but no gun. How does that make any sense?"

"Just in case," Terrence said.

"I'm surprised Madison didn't take it with everything else." She shook her head. "At least I'll know who to stand behind if the shooting starts."

"There won't be any shooting," Terrence said.

"For your sake, I hope not."

The Buick crawled forward then pulled up one car short of the volunteer directing traffic. The black hearse was parked beneath the church's side-door awning, awaiting Edith's casket. Dickerson stood on the steps of the front door, Margaret by his side, shaking hands with a procession of elderly citizens shuffling up the wheelchair ramp.

"Nice to see so many people," Terrence said. "She was a special lady."

Sharon said, "We never saw eye to eye. You didn't know her like I did."

Terrence smiled. "Mother-in-law."

"In her eyes, Hank was always right. Of course, that made me always wrong."

"I thought you said they didn't get along?"

"They had their differences, but Hank knew how to toe the line, at least with her."

"And you?"

"The only line him and I had was the one he drew in the sand and told me never to cross. We were never husband and wife. More like mutual hostages."

"Hostages can be rescued."

"Or killed."

Their car crept forward. Terrence said, "I just keep seeing her lying there, staring. Her neck . . . she touched a lot of people. That's what I'm going to remember today."

"Still, doesn't seem fair, does it? I mean we're taught to play by the rules, treat people the way we'd want to be treated, follow the Ten Commandments, and everything will work out."

"Yeah, well," Terrence said.

"I thought bad things weren't supposed to happen to good people," Sharon said.

Terrence shook his head. "She used to say, 'What doesn't kill us makes us stronger.'"

"I guess you can only get so strong."

Jack Strower walked over to Terrence's window, looking somber. Terrence rolled down his window, and Strower bent to look inside. Words seemed to fail him as his eyes wandered over Sharon's dress.

"Jack," Sharon said.

"Sharon. We'll get you parked as quick as we can. I didn't know the chief would be here, or I would have reserved another space."

"Madison's here?" Sharon said.

Strower pulled his eyes away from her black dress and looked at Terrence. "Parked next to the Mayor."

"Great." Sharon shook her head. "Maybe at least he's armed."

Strower nodded toward a gathering of militia members in the far end of the parking lot. "Let's hope it stays peaceful."

"Have you seen Hank?" Terrence asked.

"No, not yet. I'm sure he'll be here." Strower leaned closer to the window. "I assume you heard."

Terrence shook his head.

Strower glanced at the cars lined up behind them. "It seems the church received an anonymous call. A threat of sorts."

"What kind of threat?"

"Something about revolution, getting even for Mrs. Sherman's murder. They thought it was just a prank, but when they got here this morning, there was a picture spray painted on the front door. A couple stick figures. The big one was swinging an axe at the short one. Dickie was written beneath the shorter one. It looked like someone was trying the take the mayor's head off. They scrubbed it off the best they could and hung a Welcome sign over it."

"Probably just some kids," Terrence said.

Strower studied Terrence's face. "But vandalizing a church. Can you imagine?"

Chip Skarson jogged over to Strower, and they exchanged words. Strower leaned back down. "Looks like the front lot is full. We'll have to park you around the side. Chip thinks maybe we can still fit you next to the chief. I've got to say, I'm glad you made it. With that bunch and Hank, you never know."

Randy parked the 4x4 diagonally, taking up the last two parking spaces. He pushed open the driver's door, and Jimmy grabbed one of the rifles.

"No, you idiot," Randy said. "We're going inside."

Tiny stepped out the passenger's side and the truck springs rose two inches. What Tiny lacked in brains, he more than made up in muscle.

"I don't see Hank's Jeep," Jimmy said. "He was supposed to meet us."

"He'll be here," Randy said.

"And if he isn't?" Jimmy said.

"He will be. Get the bag."

Jimmy climbed into the bed of the truck and unzipped a green duffel bag stuffed with baseball bats. He dragged the bag back to the edge of the truck bed and hefted it to Tiny. Tiny grabbed it with one hand and slung it over his shoulder. The wooden butt of a revolver stuck out from Tiny's waistband. Jimmy gave Randy a better-take-a-look nod.

"Tiny," Randy said, "you got a permit for that?"

"Don't need no permit," Tiny said. "It's my constitutional right." He flexed his meaty bicep and said, "Right to bear arms."

"Keep it under cover," Randy said, "and don't do nothing stupid."

The three walked over to the farthest corner of the parking lot. "Tiny, you stay here. When the others get here, pass out the bats. Keep it quiet. Can you do that?"

Tiny looked puzzled.

"Just pass out the bats. Nothing else. Understand me? Wait for the signal."

Tiny dropped the bag and nodded.

Jimmy and Randy headed for the church's front door.

Randy and Jimmy stood in line with the elderly inching their way toward the door. "Where's he at?" Jimmy whispered.

"I look like his mother?" Randy whispered back. "He'll be here.

Randy nodded toward Tiny who was zipping a bat under his jacket. "Looks like they're about ready out here. Now we set up inside."

"Don't we get one?" Jimmy asked.

"No, stupid. Look kind of obvious carrying a bat."

"What if—"

Randy turned and glared at him. "Don't be such a pussy. Those old timers aren't going to be a problem."

"I wouldn't be so sure."

They climbed the steps to the front door and began to walk in when Chip Skarson, all six-foot-three of him, stood in their path and poked a bulletin in Randy's face. "How are you boys today?"

"What's it to—" Jimmy began.

Randy elbowed Jimmy. "Real sorry to see her go, I mean. She was . . . " He took the bulletin and began to step forward.

Chip held another out to Jimmy and stood blocking the entrance. "Jimmy I didn't catch what you said."

Jimmy grabbed the bulletin. "Sorry."

Chip held the other end as Jimmy tugged. "Sorry what?" Chip said.

"Mr. Skarson," Jimmy mumbled.

Chip stepped forward and put a hand calloused from forty years of farming on Jimmy's shoulder. "See if you can put all those words together. A complete sentence."

"Sorry, Mr. Skarson."

Chip squeezed the muscle in Jimmy's scrawny neck, and Jimmy grimaced. "You boys behave now. This is a memorial service." He straightened Jimmy's collar. "You boys can play army all you want, but not in here. Know what I mean?"

"We know our rights—" Randy mumbled.

Chip let go of Jimmy's collar and gave a disgusted grunt toward Randy. "I'd suggest you use the right to shut the hell up, right about now."

Randy opened his mouth to speak then shut it.

Chip ushered them down the center aisle as the organ

played "Stricken, Smitten, and Afflicted." Randy scoped out the room as they walked. The back pews on each side were filled with militia members in uniform, staring solemnly ahead. He elbowed Jimmy, and they exchanged smiles.

When Chip reached the front row, he stopped and turned. He extended his hand toward the left pew and said, "Your seats. Remember what I said."

Randy walked to the far end of the pew and looked back at the congregation, old faces he barely recognized from his youth when church attendance was mandatory. Time to liven things up.

Jack Strower pushed Granny Strower's wheel chair up the ramp toward the door. "Those boys, honestly," he said.

Jack parked her three groups back of the church entrance and groaned at three militia members laughing and pointing at them. Then a beefy hand grabbed one by the collar, and they went inside.

Edna Gunderson, standing in front of Jack, turned. "Why do they have to be here?"

Jack shrugged. "Friends of the family, I guess."

"Some friends. Honestly, I don't know how she put up with him and that son of hers and that bunch."

"Let's just remember who this is about." A muffled flapping came from the seat beneath Granny Strower, and Jack fought back the gag reflex the whiff of flatulence induced. He fanned his face and granny broke into a toothless smile.

"Well, look who's here." Betty's voice came from behind. "Jack, Granny."

"Such a sad day," Gloria said. "And under such

circumstances."

Jack propped his foot behind the chair's left wheel and nodded.

Jolene walked up out of breath and frowned at a three militia members leaning against a truck on the street. "What are they doing here?"

"Paying their respects, I guess," Jack said.

"My ass," Betty said. "Stirring up trouble's more like it."

"You don't think," Jolene began then seemed to have hit the dead end of a thought.

"Respect's something they don't get," Betty said. "When have they ever shown any respect?"

Gloria waved at the group. "See those uniforms? I think they're kind of cute."

"Cute? Maybe on six-year-olds," Betty said.

Jolene glanced around and said, "Did they catch him?"

The line moved a step and Jack pushed Granny forward. The girls shuffled behind them. "Her killer," Jolene said. "I haven't seen him since, you know."

Betty fanned the air in front of her face. "I guess we'll see who shows up."

The line moved again, giving Jack a clear view through the door. The organ music drifted with the stuffy air flowing out the door. Chip Skarson held out a program. "Jack. Mrs. Strower. Ladies."

Jack pushed through the door and surveyed the congregation. His eyes stopped on the back rows where he was accustomed to parking Granny. "My, it's full in here."

"Too full if you ask me," Chip said. "Could do with a few less uniforms."

"Or a few more," Jack said.

"Is he here?" Betty asked.

"There's a lot of he's in here," Chip said. "Anyone in particular?"

"Hank," Jolene said.

Chip shook his head. "I don't imagine he'll miss. We'll see."

"So he hasn't been caught?" Betty said.

Chip glanced behind them, and his eyes narrowed.

Tiny stood there and nodded, wearing a shit-eating grin.

"Tiny," Jack said.

Tiny stared ahead stone-faced.

Terrence and Sharon walked up the steps to the front door. He nodded and smiled, but all eyes seemed to drift to Sharon's hemline. Chip led them down the center aisle, and the murmuring swelled behind them. Aaron Jenkins, seven years retired, turned and smiled as his aging eyes wandered over Sharon's black dress. His wife, Wilma, shook her head and scowled at Terrence. Sharon sneered and tugged down on her dress. Terrence walked silently through the wheezes and coughs stirring the suffocating air.

With each step, Edith's casket loomed larger. Terrence had tried to erase the memory of her lying in the dirt, eyes open and unblinking, the blood pooled beneath her neck, the coolness of her skin. He wondered if seeing her at rest would help.

Chip stopped at the front row and motioned to the pew on the right. Sharon let go of Terrence's hand and looked into the casket. She crossed herself and walked to her seat.

Terrence looked down at Edith. The satin fabric

pillowed around her like a soft white cloud. Her lips, painted too red, were bent into a droopy, lopsided smile. The edge of her lip pulled upward, snagged on a dry tooth. Her overly-rosy cheeks gave her the appearance of a wax clown, her face melting in the heat. Her hands were folded in silent prayer, her fingernails painted in bright red. She preferred brown soil beneath her nails, Terrence thought. Hers were working hands, calloused and knotty from years of loving labor.

Terrence absently rubbed the scar her ruler had left over his own knuckle. She didn't look peaceful. Posed was more like it. Staged to disguise the awful truth of her violent death. Beneath the makeup, the freshly pressed Sunday dress, and the wig, was the truth. *Terrible Terrence* he could hear her say.

Chip tugged on his elbow, and Terrence followed Sharon to the end of the pew. He took her arm and sat nearest the side aisle.

The congregation sat packed like sardines in the straight-backed wooden pews. The organ's low bass rumble rattled the stained glass windows and vibrated loose floorboards. Smoke from another field fire crept inside the church with each new attendee. The haze thickened inside, catching the light in colorful streamers.

Bernardine Jefferson shuffled behind her walker, two tennis balls skidding on its back feet. Ralph Jamison refused the usher's help as he limped against an arthritic hip, grabbing the end of each pew as he made his way forward. The seniors continued to wedge themselves into what little space remained as the clanking of folding chairs being set up echoed in the back.

The low murmuring of those gathered swelled with

each arrival, and the organ music rose with it, an unheeded reminder of the occasion's solemnity. Each new mourner walked the center aisle surveying those already seated, looking for a suitable island of friends to join and enemies to avoid. Hymnals occupied empty spaces, reserving seats, only to be reluctantly picked up as bottoms scooted closer together.

The murmur of shared condolences swelled then was interrupted by greetings to the chief. Terrence looked back at Madison walking solemnly down the center aisle and considered the injustice of his position. Before him lay Edith, the victim of a vicious crime, one possibly perpetrated by the very man who had just suspended him and stripped him of his badge and gun. And now he walked down the center aisle amid the nods and well-wishes of the unsuspecting public.

The mayor had promoted Terrence and tasked him with solving the murder only to have the suspect take that away. If this is police work, I've had enough. Let the dead bury their own dead, he thought. When this is over, maybe Sharon and I will just pack up and leave this town. Shake the dust off our feet and move on.

Chip stopped in front of Edith's casket and motioned for Madison to join them. Madison looked pale and weak, the shadow of a once powerful man. Those who abuse power eventually pay the price, Terrence thought.

Madison's eyes lingered on Sharon's dress then he sat beside her. She tugged at her hem. Madison looked at Terrence and rolled his eyes.

"You look . . . better," Terrence whispered. "Are you okay?"

"I'm fine." He nodded at Sharon. "Looks like you're

doing okay yourself."

"Are you sure you're okay?"

"Isn't the first heart attack I've had. Probably won't be the last. Surgery can wait a few days till this mess gets cleaned up."

"Who's going to clean it up?" Sharon asked. "Looks like the only cop who's worth anything in this town got fired."

Madison shook his head. "Suspended. There's a difference."

"Suspended then. Whatever." She pointed at the casket. "Point is, there she lies, and now you're going to fix it? The fox guarding the hen house if you ask me."

Terrence elbowed her and they exchanged scowls.

Someone behind shushed.

Madison gave Terrence a confused look.

"Jack told us about the threats," Terrence said.

"Doesn't look like he's going to show anyway," Madison said.

"I saw a truckload of them when we were parking," Terrence said. "Didn't see him, but he'll be here."

Madison opened his suit jacket, exposing his shoulder holster and gun. "I can only hope."

The organ began playing "Amazing Grace," and the murmuring in back swelled again. Terrence looked over his shoulder at Jimmy and Randy across the aisle. Randy seemed to have sat on a hill of ants. Probably under the combined influence of meth and alcohol.

The murmuring suddenly died down, and the organ music stopped. The organist tried to begin another hymn but seemed uncertain which one. The bass pedals rumbled, and the notes came too fast before settling into

"Nearer My God to Thee." Sharon looked at the doorway and elbowed Terrence.

Chip looked somber as he walked forward with Hank staggering behind. Hank smiled with a four-day growth of beard. He wore a tiger-striped militia jacket with the president's patch sewn on the shoulder. His jacket was unzipped, exposing his T-shirt and waistband. Terrence wondered if it was intended to show he was unarmed.

Madison shook his head and sighed.

"Here comes nothing," Sharon said.

Chip glanced at Terrence as Hank stood in front of Edith's casket. Hank shook his head then glared at Terrence. His eyes shifted to Sharon, and he smiled again. Chip took Hank's sleeve and turned him to the left. Hank yanked his arm free and sat beside Randy.

The organ music lowered, drawing out the final note of the hymn, signaling the beginning of the proceedings. The side door opened, and Reverend Holland stepped onto the platform, Dickerson following behind. The reverend ceremoniously walked to the far side of the platform seemingly bowed under the weight of the large crucifix that hung from his neck.

Dickerson took two steps left of the door and stood beside his chair, holding Edith's family Bible. He focused on maintaining an expression of dignified gravity, though his stomach fluttered in anticipation of the announcement he was about to make. He held all the aces and wondered how high Hank would bid. This was the moment he would finally win.

Dickerson's eyes drifted to Hank who sat red-eyed, staring back. Let the fire kindle, Dickerson thought. Let him burn. Dickerson grinned as he looked at Terrence, his jolly green giant. This would be Terrence's chance for redemption. Perhaps it was the euphoria he felt in anticipation of his victory, but in this moment, Dickerson felt a special bond with Terrence, a young man so needing to prove himself. He was certain this time, Terrence would not miss.

He focused on Sharon next and the euphoria turned to contempt. Her skirt hiked up so high he could almost see her underwear. She looks like a hooker, he thought. Dressed for my benefit, no doubt. A daughter set on a path of self-destruction. He was sorry for his mistakes, but hadn't he suffered enough? Perhaps he deserved her torments, but the way she tormented Margaret was unforgivable.

Beside her, sat Madison. A dangerous man who'd made too many devil's bargains. Perhaps today he too would find redemption. Even in his uniform, Madison looked feeble, like he was living on borrowed time. As long as the chief breathed, the secrets they shared could not rest easily. Pale and sweating, Dickerson wondered if Madison would live to see the end of this day. Perhaps his plan would work out even better than he'd imagined.

Finally, he gazed at Edith's casket. He stroked the papers in his lap as his eyes lingered on the shiny wooden lid. He felt an unfamiliar twinge of some foreign emotion. Guilt? His eulogy would surely clear his conscience of any lingering doubts. The actors were in their places, and the stage was set. It's time to raise the curtain.

Terrence held Sharon's hand, hoping the service would remain peaceful. Without his gun, if things got out of hand, he'd have to rely on his wits–not his strong suit. He glanced at Hank and felt his stomach knot. Hank's eyes stared back like he was sizing up the vulnerabilities of an enemy on the battlefield.

The organ pounded out a last reverberating hymn, and Reverend Holland rose solemnly and stood behind the pulpit. "Dear friends, family, and honored guests. We are gathered here today to remember our dear sister, Edith Sherman. Today we celebrate the many ways her life has touched us all. Would you stand and join me in prayer?"

The pews groaned as arthritic hands pulled against them, helping the aged stand. Heads bowed, and eyes closed. Terrence glanced at Hank through one squinted eye. Hank's face was expressionless, his eyes fixed on his mother's casket.

"Our Heavenly Father," the reverend began, "we thank thee today for the abundance of thy grace, the steadfastness of thy love, and the forgiveness thou hast so generously bestowed upon these, thy children. We thank thee for Edith, thy faithful servant, who touched us in so many ways. Though her travails were many, and her sorrows abundant, she was yet an example of steadfast love to us all. We ask that thou wouldst bestow upon her only son, Hank, gathered with us today, thy overflowing mercies and turn him from the path of sin to the way of righteousness. For as the prodigal son . . . "

Terrence's eyes drifted back to Hank rocking on unsteady feet. He wondered if the reverend could feel Hank glaring at him.

Hank smiled, raised a fist to his mouth, and coughed, "Bullshit."

" . . . like a sheep gone astray, deliver him into thy loving care for thy servant's sake. Now, bestow upon this congregation thy blessings, as we celebrate the homecoming of thy servant, Edith Sherman. Amen." He raised his arms and said, "You may be seated."

The pews groaned again as elderly legs lowered the congregation into the tired wood. "Please turn in your hymnals to number 314, "Nearer My God to Thee."

The organ rumbled into verse one, and Sharon whispered into Terrence's ear, "Let's hope she's the only one who's nearer to their maker right now."

Madison scribbled on the back of his bulletin, passed it to Sharon, and pointed at Terrence. She shook her head and gave it to Terrence. Terence read the note and shook his head. "You have it," he whispered.

The organist lingered on the last note of the hymn, and Reverend Holland stood. "I would like to invite friends and family to come forward at this time to share with the congregation how Mrs. Sherman touched your lives."

Betsy Sanders was first to walk the center aisle. As she approached Edith's casket, she stopped to peer inside then stifled a sob with her handkerchief. She turned and spoke in a trembling voice. "Edith was the dearest, sweetest lady I've ever known. She never had a harsh word. Always so giving." Betsy glared at Hank. "Even when it wasn't appreciated. She deserved better than this. The scripture says God will never give us more than we can bear. She must have been one strong woman, what with her son being the way he is. A drunk and a—"

The reverend vigorously cleared his throat.

She looked into the casket again. "We will miss you Edith. I'll always cherish the memories of your kind, encouraging face. I . . . I . . . " Betsy scowled at Hank and marched back up the aisle.

"Thank you, Betsy," the reverend said. "She will be sorely missed."

Betty Randall was next to take center aisle. She also paused at the casket then reached in, to the gasps of the congregation. Her hand withdrew then began wringing with the other. "Edith was one of my regulars. Such a sweet lady. A hard worker, too—judging by the layers of dirt I had to scrape out from under her nails. And those awful calluses, but she was always cheerful, encouraging others. We all so admired her, even when her family . . . " She glared at Hank. "Even when her son abandoned her, or worse. You should be ashamed—"

"Thank you Mrs. Randall," Reverend Holland said.

Betty's tearful eyes looked up at the ceiling. "I'll never forget her." She turned to the casket and gave a little wave. "We love you Edith. We'll miss you."

Terrence's hand tightened on Sharon's as she began to fidget. He'd seen that expression in her eyes, the one that said she could no longer let an injustice go uncorrected.

"Thank you, Betty," Reverend Holland said. "Is there anyone else? If not, we will continue by singing hymn number 452, 'Rock of Ages.' If the congregation would please stand."

The organ launched into the prelude.

Sharon stood. "I have a few words." The organ music cut off mid-stanza, and she stood, tugging self-consciously at the hem of her dress. She walked over to the casket and looked inside as if waiting for Edith to tell her the words to speak.

Hank laughed. "You gonna talk or just stand there?"

Sharon glared at him then cleared her throat. She

tugged again at the hem of her dress. "Mom was quite a lady. I always admired her. In her own way, she was strong—some would say even stubborn. She always spoke her mind. I sometimes wondered how she put up with it." She glared at Hank. "With him."

More throat clearing from the reverend.

"Three men made her life a living hell."

"Thank you, Sharon," Reverend Holland said. "Now join me—"

"I'm not done, so park it," Sharon said, continuing to glare at Hank. "And you, you worthless . . . she was too good for you."

"And you," Randy said.

"Now look at her," Sharon continued, "lying there. Why?" She looked at the chief. "And you, maybe you can tell us how her throat was cut ear to ear."

"Yeah, Chief, maybe you and the mayor can fill us in," Tiny shouted from the back.

"Murder, that's what it was," Randy added.

"Quiet down. Show some respect," someone in the middle shouted.

Sharon raised her hand and pointed at Hank. "I know what it's like to live with the likes of you. Drunk and violent." Her hem crept higher up her thighs. "I'll address the elephant in the room." She pointed at the chief. "Edith may be going to the sweet by-and-by, but she got there with somebody's help. And I think we all know who did it, Chief."

Dickerson stood. "Sharon, this is hardly the place or the time."

Reverend Holland stood next. "Brothers and sisters, please! Let us remember this is the house of the Lord. We are here to honor—"

"Put a sock in it, Reverend," Hank said. His voice was

hoarse and words came out mushy. "People want to point fingers, fine. I can point a few of my own." He rose and walked to the casket and shoved Sharon away.

Terrence began to stand, but Madison grabbed his arm and pulled him down.

"I was out there the morning she was killed." Hank pointed at the mayor. "The mayor also stopped by to pay her a visit. When I left, she was standing upright and breathing. When he left, she wasn't. Dickie, maybe you can tell us what happened?"

"Yeah, Dickie. Is that a confession your holding?" Randy said.

"Ladies and Gentlemen, please," Reverend Holland said.

Dickerson raised his hands. In his right, he held an envelope.

"That your confession?" Hank said.

"If it's a confession you want, it's a confession you'll get."

Dickerson grabbed the envelope with both hands like he was holding the winning lottery ticket. "Ladies and gentlemen, let this be my confession. A confession of my greatest work on behalf of this town. In this envelope is a document that bears the signature of the generous soul we gather to remember on this tragic occasion. It is her tribute to this town. The words she has signed here represent the future, the hope for our kids, a new beginning for young families struggling to find work."

Hank stumbled backward and fell into the pew.

"As Hank said," Dickerson continued, "I was at her house the morning of her untimely departure." He slowly paced the platform, somber and searching. "Prior to that fateful day, I had come to know her for the wonderful woman she was. She and I had many conversations about the future of this town. She was deeply saddened by the lack of opportunities for our young people. She lamented the shuttering of what was once a thriving downtown and wanted to see Sheridan rise like the Phoenix from the ashes. She was truly a woman of vision."

"Amen," an elderly voice said.

"One day she approached me with an offer. After much time spent in her prayer closet, she had come to see the Lord's will. She said the Lord had visited her in a dream, and in that dream, she was reunited with her beloved son, Bobby, and her dearly departed husband. Together, they envisioned her farm fertile with opportunity for men committed to restoring order in the new correctional institution." Dickerson gestured toward Hank. "And she saw Hank sober and clean, a leader of men as he once was. She said he was wearing a new kind of uniform, one that made her proud. That was before she met her tragic end at the hand of—"

"You, you son of a bitch," Hank yelled.

"The truth will out," Dickerson shouted. "And when it does, justice will be had."

Jimmy turned to Hank and blurted out, "I thought the farm was yours? You said—"

Dickerson raised the envelope. "These documents bear witness to her generous spirit. I know she would want me to share her last wishes with you so that even while we mourn her death, we can celebrate the rebirth of this town."

"Liar," Hank said. He rose like a boxer struggling to stand after being knocked down for the third time.

Dickerson descended the steps to Edith's casket and

ran his fingers across the shiny surface then blotted a tear from his eye. His voice trembled, "Edith, we will miss you so. I don't know how we will ever repay you."

Hank took a wobbly step toward Dickerson and said, "Bull-she-it. Let me see those papers. Let me see what she wrote."

Dickerson backed up the steps to the pulpit. "In due time, you all shall see."

"That why you killed her?" Hank said. "To steal my land?"

Madison stood and said, "All right, Hank. I think we've heard enough."

Dickerson gripped the pulpit. "Please, Hank, don't dishonor your dear mother's memory. Don't make me recount the terrible events of the day—"

Hank raised his fists and turned to the congregation. "Can't you see what he's doing? Who do you think killed her?" He staggered over to the casket and grabbed the lid. "Tell 'em, Mama. Tell these people who's guilty."

"He's mad," Betty shouted.

Hank looked up from the casket. "As hell."

"Hank, sit down," Madison said. "Show a little respect."

"Respect. You're one to talk about respect. Covering up for Dickie. You're in on it too, ain't you?"

Madison took a step closer. "Sit down and shut it."

Hank dropped the lid and smiled. "In case you haven't noticed, this is still the United States of America. You can't just kill people and steal their property. I have a right to defend what's mine."

"That's right," a chorus when up from the militia members in the back of the sanctuary.

Hank began to pace in front of Edith's casket as the

murmurs of the congregation swelled and eyes began looking at the exits.

Madison pointed at Hank. "You can either calm down right now or I can arrest you for making a public disturbance. I'm sure you'd rather honor your mother by shutting your pie hole. Otherwise, I'll shut it for you."

Hank's eyes scanned the room. "And you all just sit there. Can't you see what's happening? Don't you see what these crooks are doing? They killed my mom. They're robbing me of my land. Pretty soon they'll fill this town with more jack-booted thugs to keep us all in line." He stumbled against the pew and grabbed it to steady himself. "It ain't too late. We can stop this."

"Chief," Dickerson said, "I think we've heard quite enough."

Madison threw down his bulletin. "Hank, that's enough. Let's go."

Hank clenched his fists. "Wanna dance?"

Terrence began to stand, but Sharon clamped onto his arm. "It's between them."

Madison pulled his handcuffs and began ratcheting them for effect. Hank stood watching him with a thousand-yard stare as the pews near the front began to empty. Randy stood beside Hank, his eyes darting between Hank and Madison.

"All right now, Hank, you've had your fun," Madison said. "We can do this the easy way or the hard way."

Randy nodded to the militia members standing in the back. Hank squared his shoulders. "If it's a fight you want—"

In the back a chair banged against the wall. Chip nodded, and several others stood beside him in a faceoff with militia members. Terrence turned, watching the congregation hurrying toward the exit. The organ began to play a tune more suited to All Skate at the roller rink, then fell silent as the organist hurried out with the others.

"Somebody call the cops," Jack said.

"They're already here," Gloria replied. "Looks like they're outnumbered."

"Then call the national guard," Jolene said.

Militia members pushed in through the door as the elderly hightailed out. When the last walker crossed the exit, Tiny pulled the doors shut and flipped the lock.

Terrence walked over and stood beside the chief. "Hank, Randy, no need to make this bigger than it is. This isn't the place."

"Little late for that, don't you think, Terrence?" Sharon said. She shoved between Madison and Terrence and shook a finger in Hank's face. "You heard what the chief said." She stepped up to him. "You broke the law, it's called disturbing the peace. But if you're feeling froggy, jump. I'm sure you can do better than a misdemeanor, coward."

"Sharon, sit down and let them handle it," Dickerson said.

Hank lowered into a fighting stance. "Like you handled Mom?"

"Edith was your doing, Hank, I saw." Dickerson pointed a shaking finger at Hank. "You had the axe, and poor Edith was running around back."

Madison rolled his eyes. "Remember that just now?"

Hank laughed.

"I didn't understand at the time—"

"Funny, 'cause I left before you did," Hank said.

Dickerson's voice trembled. "Arrest that man."

Madison grabbed Hank's arm and tugged. "Time to go."

Hank pulled back. "Keep your hands off me unless you want to lose 'em."

"Resisting arrest! Threatening an officer!" Sharon shouted. "Those are crimes. I know."

Madison grabbed Hank's arm and wrist and began to twist them behind his back. "You're under arrest."

Hank shoved Madison backward. "Says who?"

"And assaulting an officer," Sharon said. "Keep digging, Hank."

"More like false arrest," Randy added. "He's got rights."

Madison shoved Hank against the pew sending him sprawling onto the bench. He bent to lay hands on Hank again then jumped back as Hank pulled the knife from his ankle sheath and thrust it toward Madison's gut.

"Come on, Chief. Just you and me." Hank rose to his feet and pointed the rusty knife.

Terrence saw the shiny thin edge of the blade and thought of the scalpel that had opened up Edith. Hank's knife was six inches longer. He'd seen how a knife can fillet human flesh.

Hank smiled. "Come and get me."

Madison drew his gun. "Just like you to bring a knife to a gunfight." Madison shoved his gun into Hank's face.

"Gun fight. Hell, that thing you got ain't a gun. Six bullets won't do it. This," he twisted his knife in the air, "this will spill your guts. Think I'll let you hold them while you die."

"Big man. Just keep digging," Sharon said.

Randy shuffled backward.

Terrence pulled Sharon back.

"Guess it's your choice now," Madison said. "Swing that at me and we're talking attempted murder. Life in prison. Is that what you want?"

"You just don't get it. I got nothing left. Nothing. Might as well be dead. Go ahead, pull the trigger. You know you'd like to."

Madison circled to his left. "Drop the knife."

Hank pivoted, holding the knife between them.

"For God's sake, shoot him," Dickerson said.

"Dickie, run," Margaret shouted. "Someone call the police!"

Hank slashed toward Madison and took the first step up the platform toward the side door. Reverend Holland crossed himself, leapt down the steps, and ran into Tiny.

"Going somewhere?" Tiny said.

"This is a house of God. You have made it . . . Wrestle Mania. Let me go."

"Run, Margaret," Dickerson yelled. Margaret's legs gave out, and she dropped like a sack of wheat onto the pew.

"Looks like she's staying for the main event," Hank said as he took the two last steps, blocking Dickerson's escape.

Dickerson backed into the corner, beneath the eternal candle. Madison began up the steps, keeping his gun pointed at Hank. "Shoot him!" Dickerson's eyes grew wide and his mouth gaped.

"Stop!" Madison ordered. "This is your last warning."

"Shoot him," Sharon shouted.

Hank winked then lunged toward Dickerson. Dickerson threw up his hands and collapsed. Hank grabbed his arm and yanked him to his feet. Dickerson clamped his eyes shut and covered his face.

"Drop the knife, Hank!" Madison ordered as he

climbed the top step.

Dickerson peeked between his fingers and twisted against Hank's grip. Hank let go of his arm, grabbed him around the shoulders, and pulled Dickerson's back to his chest, a human shield. Dickerson's eyes bulged as Hank brought the K-bar knife blade up to his scrawny neck." He pressed their cheeks together. "Go ahead, Chief, let's see how good a shot you are."

Madison crept closer, the barrel of his gun bouncing between the moving heads. "So help me, Hank."

Hank smiled. "Stop right there. Dickerson's jaw flopped open as Hank pressed the blade into his Adam's apple.

Madison inched closer.

"One step closer and he'll join Mom." A trickle of blood ran down the rusty knife blade. Madison stopped. "Not as dumb as you look, Chief. Tell you what, Dickie. Why don't you tell us how Mom died? How about a dying confession?"

Dickerson's Adam's apple slid up and down, sending another seep of blood across the blade. "What's the matter? Cat got your tongue? Maybe I can jog your memory a little." The knife blade dug deeper into Dickerson's skin. Red droplets formed then slid down his neck, soaking into his white collar.

Dickerson winced and stood on his toes. "Hank, don't. I didn't . . . "

"Terrence, do something!" Sharon screamed.

Terrence felt like he was in a dream, his feet set in concrete, unable to speak. He heard the slap before he felt it. His cheek exploded with fire. Sharon's face came into focus, enraged and screaming. Her mouth moved, but her voice seemed to be coming from somewhere in the distance. He watched passive, detached, as she stepped back and pulled her hand back to slap him again. Then his face was exploding again and turning as Randy's face loomed before him, eyes wide and mocking. Sharon screamed, "Do something."

Terrence's hand raised to his cheek as his ear rang. Then Randy pulled back for a punch, and Terrence saw his fist flying in slow motion toward his face. Suddenly Randy was stumbling backward, and Sharon was mouthing something at him that he couldn't make out. The buzzing in his ear gave way to the sound of Sharon's screams. Time began to wind faster, and the darkness began to swallow the world.

"Drop the knife." The words were Madison's. Terrence turned toward the platform and Randy stepped in his way. "This is between them," Randy said.

Terrence stopped, obeying some instinct that told him to do as he was told. "Get out of my way unless you'd like to join him in jail."

"Don't shoot!" Dickerson pleaded.

Hank said, "Go ahead, Chief, take a shot. But the way your gun's shaking I'd say my chances are about fifty-fifty."

Terrence looked down at Randy. "Step aside."

Randy's mouth lit the match. "Make me."

Randy left his feet, slid across the lid of Edith's casket, and landed at the foot of the altar steps. As he struggled to his feet, Sharon's foot connected with Randy's groin, and he fell into a heap, groaning and clutching his privates.

Terrence began to climb the steps as Madison crept closer to Hank. Hank pivoted, putting Dickerson's head in front of his own.

"So tell me, Dickie," Hank said, "why'd you do it?"

"I . . . I . . . " was all Dickerson could manage.

The knife drew across the thin skin of his throat. "Can't hear you."

Madison was within arm's reach.

"I didn't—" Dickerson's hands tugged against Hank's arm. "He—chief." The words came out choked and coughing.

Hank withdrew the knife and pointed it at Madison. Dickerson clutched his throat, gagging. "Well, well. Looks like you weren't in on this alone."

Madison stepped closer. "This is the last time I'll say it. Drop the knife."

Hank held the point of the blade against Dickerson's jugular. Beneath the skin the vein pulsed with each panicked heartbeat. "A quarter inch away from death," Hank said, then threw his hands up, dropping the knife at Madison's feet.

Dickerson's hands clutched his throat and he fell to his knees, gasping for air. He suddenly seemed to realize he was free and crawled to the side door.

Hank raised his hands in the air. "You wouldn't shoot an unarmed man would you?"

"On your knees," Madison ordered, "or I'll blow your head off."

Hank slowly lowered down to one knee. "War injuries," he said. He grunted and dropped the other.

"On the ground," Madison said. "All the way."

Terrence walked up the last step, sensing something was wrong. The way Hank had complied, how quickly he'd given up. He tried to focus. Breathe, he told himself, but the darkness was closing. Fight it, you can't lose it now. Think, Terrence. Think.

Hank put one palm on the floor then followed with

the other and began to walk his hands forward.

The knife, Terrence thought. It had fallen just behind Madison's foot. "Chief!" he shouted, "the knife."

Hank lunged. With one hand he grabbed the knife, and with the other, he pulled Madison's foot.

The first explosion seemed to surprise Madison as he fell backward. The bullet passed over Hank's shoulder and shattered a candle on the altar. Madison hit the ground as the second and third bullets passed through the ceiling. Madison's handcuffs slid across the carpet.

Hank scrambled to his knees and began to slash toward Madison's arms. Madison pointed his gun at Hank's chest. Hank froze and smiled. "Do it."

"Can't say I didn't warn you." Madison squeezed off a shot that punched through Hank's jacket.

Hank grabbed his chest and fell to the ground, grimacing. "You got me," Hank said.

Madison struggled to his feet and pointed the gun at Hank's head. "Face down. Hands behind your back!"

Hank grinned and rolled over on his stomach.

Time slowed again as Terrence watched. Something's not right. It's a setup.

Blood. There's no blood. Then Terrence saw the bulges of Hanks body armor beneath his jacket. Madison dropped his knee on Hank's back and reached for his handcuffs.

"Chief, watch out."

Sharon screamed at Terrence to take control as Randy grabbed the handle of Edith's casket and pulled himself to his feet. Tiny lumbered down the aisle with a bat in his hand. Randy grabbed her from behind.

"Get your hands off me," Sharon yelled as Randy

wrapped her in a bear hug.

"I'll teach you to kick me," Randy said. He grabbed a handful of hair and yanked her head back. "Now it's time to get even." His hand slid up the hem of her dress.

"Let go of me," she said as her pointed high heel came stomping down on the top of his foot with a crunch. Randy grabbed his foot and began hopping in circles as she slapped and punched him.

He crumpled to the ground. "You crazy bitch," he groaned, one hand on his foot, the other on his privates.

Sharon pulled her foot back to kick but was lifted off the ground, her legs bicycling in the air. "Let go of me," she yelled, as Tiny tossed her around like a rag doll.

"Time you got knocked down a few pegs." He threw her over his shoulder then dropped her onto Edith's casket.

Randy struggled to his knees. "Get her good," he said. "Save some for me."

"Time you learned your place," Tiny said. His beefy hand covered her mouth, and she tried to bite. Tiny's other hand groped her as she squirmed and clawed. Sharon worked a hand free and swung a fist into Tiny's face, but it hardly seemed to register. She slugged him again in the chest, and he smiled amused. When he let go of her mouth to trap her hands, she gulped in a breath of air and screamed for Terrence as loud as she could.

With her arms trapped, Tiny leaned down to kiss her. His eyes had the distant look of someone who'd lost their senses. "You're gonna like this." His face drew nearer, and she strained to pull away.

"Show her good," Randy said. "I'm next."

I can't hold it back, Terrence thought. It's too strong. Sharon's screams broke through the darkness, and he saw Sharon squirming as Tiny groped her.

Terrence stopped fighting the rage.

He jumped from the platform and kicked Randy so hard he flew over the second row of pews and belly-flopped onto the third.

Sharon looked at Terrence with panic stricken eyes, and the rage exploded as he dove over the casket and tackled Tiny. He wrapped an arm around Tiny's neck and began to cinch down. Tiny gripped Terrence's arm and began to pry. Terrence felt his arm slipping and cranked harder, but Tiny was steadily loosening his hold. Tiny took a gasping breath and shoved Terrence's forearm into his mouth. As his teeth bit down, Terrence jammed tighter into Tiny's jaw.

"You're under arrest," Terrence said. "Stop resisting."

Tiny groaned and bit harder.

Terrence felt the pressure of Tiny's teeth begin to burn. As Tiny's jaws clamped harder, Terrence wedged his arm further into his jaws. Pulling free would tear the skin and rip the muscle beneath, Terrence remembered, but how much longer could he bear the pain burning up his arm. "Stop resisting."

Tiny's hands let go and began clawing at Terrence's face. The anger exploded again, and Terrence wrenched his arm into Tiny's jaw until he felt the jaw joint pop. Tiny's hands went limp. Terrence pulled his arm free, slid it under Tiny's chin, and clamped the sides of his thick neck in a sleeper hold. Seven seconds, that's all it took to make a man pass out. He sank in the hold and squeezed against the carotid arteries. Tiny's hands clawed again, then his body went limp. Terrence dropped Tiny to the floor and rolled him over face down.

"It's your turn now all right," Sharon said. Randy leaned over a pew coughing as Sharon swung a bat. "Piece of shit. Go ahead, take your turn."

Randy ducked. "I didn't mean it. I was trying to make him stop." She swung again and connected against his shoulder with a hollow thud, sending him to the floor.

Madison felt for his handcuffs as he straddled Hank, but the shoulder holster was empty. He grabbed Hanks left arm and began to pull it back. A wave of pain radiated down Madison's arm, and his hand went numb. The strength drained from his muscles, and his chest began to burn. "Terrence!" Madison yelled.

Hank turned over onto his back and bucked his hips upward, shooting Madison over his head. Madison's arm felt like it was on fire, and his chest like it was being ripped in two as he fell face first onto the floor. Hank's knees landed hard on his kidneys, then Madison's arms were being pulled back. "Terrence!"

The smell of whiskey and piss filled the air. Hank's voice spoke in Madison's ear. "He's kind of busy right now." Madison struggled to breathe against what felt like a vise clamping tighter in his chest.

The blade of the knife slid into view. "You don't look so good, Chief. Gonna look a lot worse in a minute." The knife tip pressed against his cheek and slowly began to burrow in.

"Ter—" Madison's scalp felt like it was being ripped from his skull, and his head snapped back.

"Ever seen someone get scalped?"

Madison groaned.

"I always preferred ears. Had a whole necklace of

them once in Nam. They say the scalp don't feel much pain. Let's find out." The knife rose, and he felt its edge pressing against his forehead. Blood began to flow into his eyes.

The platform was enveloped in a dark fog. Terrence strained to make out the shapes of the men struggling on the platform. Slowly, he forced the fog to dissipate and saw Hank begin to slice Madison's forehead. "Stop and I won't kill you," Terrence shouted.

Hank raised the knife then looked at Terrence. "What'd you say?"

"Drop it."

Hank looked puzzled. "You'll kill me? With what?"

"It's over, Hank."

Hank dropped a knee onto Madison's gut, then smiled. "Where's your gun, boy?"

"I said, drop it."

Hank grabbed the gun from Madison's limp hand and stood. Madison rolled onto his back, the blood running down the side of his face, clutching his chest. Hank pointed the gun at Terrence. "You can thank the chief for leaving me a couple bullets."

"Drop it," Terrence said, "before it's too late."

"Too late happened the day Mom was murdered."

"Drop the gun."

"Or what?"

Terrence didn't answer.

"You'll kill me? I'm the one with the gun."

"Hank, no." Sharon's voice spoke from far off. It seemed to echo against a growing roar like some great waterfall. A burning mist sprayed against Terrence's face. The darkness tumbled down and he fell. It's just a dream, that's all this is, Terrence thought. Then he felt like he'd been punched in the chest. When his eyes opened, the world was on its side.

Hank jammed the muzzle of the gun against his temple. Voices yelled in the distance. Sharon screamed. Hank's gravelly voice mocked. The pressure grew, threatening to crack his skull. The knife dangled in Hank's hand.

Terrence grabbed the knife blade as Hank pulled back. The razor edge of the steel began to draw across his palm, and he squeezed harder. Terrence thought of the defensive wounds he'd seen at the academy and wondered at his own lack of pain. Blood seeped between his clenched fingers as he clamped down even tighter. His other hand grabbed the gun's muzzle and twisted it upward. Another flash blinded him and robbed him of hearing. The hot spray of gas from the muzzle burned against his face. Then the darkness fell.

Sharon's third swing of the bat connected with a heavy thunk against Tiny's skull. He slumped back on the floor as an explosion ripped through the air.

Terrence and Hank were locked in a dance, each holding the same gun and knife. Terrence rose to his knees as Hank struggled to free his weapons. Then they were kneeling. Terrence curled the muzzle of the gun back toward Hank's face as he gripped the knife blade in his bloody palm.

"Finish it." Hank said. "Do it now, or you'll wish you had."

Terrence ripped the gun back and Hank's trigger finger snapped. He grabbed Hank's hair and slammed his face to the floor.

"It won't end here," Hank said. "You know it'll never end."

Terrence dropped a knee onto Hank's back still holding the knife blade with his bleeding fist. "Your cuffs, Chief."

Madison grimaced, crawled over to the cuffs and slid them to Terrence.

Hank tightened his fist on the knife handle as Terrence squeezed the blade. "This is your last chance."

Terrence dropped his knee on Hank's arm and began to twist.

"Drop the knife," Terrence ordered.

Hank growled as Terrence continued to twist. Hank's growl became a scream, then the bone snapped, and the knife fell free. Terrence kicked it out of Hank's reach.

Terrence grabbed the handcuffs and cinched them tightly around Hanks broken wrist. "Give me your other arm, he ordered."

Hank stiffened.

Terrence twisted the handcuff against Hank's broken wrist. Hank screamed and pulled his other arm out and offered it to Terrence.

Hank rolled to his side and looked up with pleading eyes. "Finish it."

"It is finished," Terrence said.

The wailing of sirens swelled on Highway 18. When they took the ramp onto Bridge Street, it sounded like the end of the world had arrived. The first car to roar up the ramp toward the church belonged to the Yamhill County Sheriff's Office. Two others screamed up the ramp behind him. Then the floodgates opened, and officers from surrounding jurisdictions poured in. Three from Oregon State Patrol, one from McMinnville PD, another from the US Marshall's office. Further in the distance, the Portland Police Bureau's SWAT armored vehicle rumbled their direction. As their sirens screamed nearer, most of the Sheridan Militia saw the wisdom of beating a hasty retreat—at least those who still could.

Randy and Jimmy limped back to their truck, badly bruised, with Tiny staggering behind. Bruised and beaten, Randy regretted ever crossing Sharon. She had swung for the fences more times then he wished to remember, each time connecting with a part of him that would be tender for a month.

Tiny had made the foolish mistake of coming to in the middle of the fight. Sharon viewed this as an opportunity to get more batting practice on his thick skull. Though she had more than enough to charge the two of them with assault, she preferred street justice. In her book, she'd evened the score. They were eager to agree.

Margaret fawned over Dickerson as the paramedics applied bandages to his heroic looking, though superficial, neck wounds. In her eyes he was the man of the hour. Dickerson agreed.

Terrence stood over Madison lying on a gurney as a paramedic wrapped bandages around his scalp. Madison looked up at him, smiled, and raised his hand. Terrence reached his own bandaged hand forward then drew back and offered the other. They shook and Madison closed his eyes.

"He'll be at Emanuel," Cindy said. She nodded to Andy, and they rolled him up the center aisle.

Outside, someone shouted, "I know my rights." Chip shouted back, "You got the right to get your stupid ass kicked." Car doors slammed, and the shouting stopped.

Sharon lifted Terrence's bandaged hand. The blood was slowly spreading across the cloth. You need to get that sewn up."

Terrence nodded. "They're taking me to the same hospital as the chief. Are you okay?"

Sharon tugged at the ripped hem of her dress. Her nylons were torn, and one heel was missing. "Don't I look nice."

"You look beautiful to me."

"What will happen now?" Sharon said. "With Hank, I mean."

"They'll hold him in McMinnville, then they'll take him to Portland."

"Will they keep him?"

"My guess is he'll be charged with attempted murder and assault on police officers, for starters. It'll be his third strike. He won't be out again anytime soon."

"But he will get out?"

Terrence took her hand. "He won't, and even if he did, I'd be here to protect you and Junior."

"In case you missed it, I'm pretty good at protecting myself. Ask Randy and Tiny."

"With Hank gone, I don't think you'll have to worry about them anymore."

"Strike down the shepherd and the sheep scatter," Sharon said.

Andy approached. "We need to get you to the hospital."

"Okay, I'll be right there," Terrence said.

Sharon looked up into his eyes. "You were . . . I don't know how to describe it."

"Just doing my job."

"Terrence, you're a hero. What you did was amazing."

Terrence shook his head. "To be honest, I don't really remember much."

"Trust me, you were amazing. You are my real-life hero."

Terrence felt the flush of warmth spread over his body and kissed her forehead.

"Time to go," Andy said.

Terrence opened his eyes and saw the wheelchair parked in front of him. "I don't need that."

"It's policy."

"Sit," Sharon said. "Enjoy the ride. We'll see you there."

Terrence sat, and Andy wheeled him up the center aisle. Andy said, "Some fight, from the looks of it."

"I guess so."

"Well, you're in good hands now. They'll fix you up as good as new." Andy stopped pushing and said, "Washburn. Class of eighty-one, Sheridan High."

Terrence nodded.

"You almost made it."

Terrence felt a twinge of guilt.

"Well, you made it this time," Andy said.

When they reached the doors, Terrence took in the sanctuary once more. He looked again at Edith's casket. "Rest in peace," Terrence said. "Maybe now we can all rest in peace."

Conclusion

Emanuel Hospital was an oasis hidden in the maze of streets that twisted through Portland. Madison's bed was tucked in the corner of the last room at the end of a long, white corridor. Terrence suspected Madison's reputation had preceded him. Terrence's boots echoed off the tile as he heard the sound of familiar voices drift from the room. He felt self-conscious as he entered, carrying a small bouquet of flowers in a plastic vase.

Madison sat in bed propped up against four pillows, dipping his spoon into a cup of applesauce. Mayor Dickerson occupied a chair beside him, leafing through the Oregonian. Margaret watered the potted plants on the table at the foot of his bed. Terrence stopped at the door, feeling out of place.

"Well, don't just stand there," Dickerson said, "come in." Dickerson wore his usual black suit. The white bandage wrapped around his neck gave him the appearance of a priest.

Terrence felt the urge to confess.

"They're lovely," Margaret said. She stood tiptoed and kissed him on the cheek. "Our hero." She took the flowers and added them to the arrangements under the window.

Madison shook his head and shoveled in another scoop of applesauce.

"I'm so glad you're okay," Margaret said. "Who would have thought?" A tear welled in her eye. "My Dickie. Where would he be without you?"

"Where indeed?" Dickerson said. "Terrence, how are you holding up?"

"A little sore, I guess, but okay."

Madison swallowed the last bite of his applesauce. "We'll talk about your tactics later. Whatever gets the job done." He winked.

"Tactics?" Dickerson said. "Call it what you want, he saved your worthless hide. And without a gun. Sometimes, Chief, I don't know what you're thinking."

"Goes both ways," Madison said.

"Boys, boys," Margaret said. "You can talk work later." She brushed her hand down Terrence's sleeve, "Ignore them. But honestly, what you did . . . "

"Can't say I remember much. Last I recall, the gun went off, and I thought . . . I thought Sharon had been hit. Then I just sort of . . . well, I can't really remember."

"Fog of war. It happens," Madison said. "Adrenalin kicks in, and sometimes you just shift into some other gear. Hard to understand unless you've been there. Don't be surprised if people give you a wide berth for awhile. What you did wasn't exactly standard operating procedure."

"Nonsense," Dickerson said. "Hero, that's what you are. There's no denying it. Chief, isn't there some kind of medal for that—valor, bravery, purple heart, or something?"

Terrence smiled. "I don't need any—"

"The next council meeting," Dickerson said. "A

ceremony to recognize your heroism."

Madison laughed. "Yeah, and maybe Hank could speak a few words."

Margaret laughed. "He could pin the medal on."

"I'm not sure he'll have the use of his arm that soon," Madison said.

Terrence felt his face flushing. "No. I don't need a ceremony."

"Sharon," Margaret said. "She could—"

"My ears are burning." Sharon stepped through the doorway, Junior at her side. "I could what?"

The room fell into an awkward silence. Junior's eyes grew wide as he looked at the machines mounted to the wall above Madison's head.

Terrence knelt. "Hey, buddy." Junior gave Terrence a hug then walked to the chief's bed and began fiddling with the tubes running from his arms and chest.

"Careful now," Sharon said. "Don't want to unplug him, yet."

Junior looked at the chief wide-eyed. "Does it hurt?"

"All over." Madison said. "Won't be long and I'll be just like new."

"You ever shoot anybody?" Junior asked.

"Stop pestering him," Sharon said.

"Tried like hell—oops, heck—for all the good it did. It appears as long as I've got Terrence around, I won't need to."

Junior grabbed Terrence's hand. "Momma says you're a real-life hero."

"I was just doing my job, I guess. Anyone would have done the same."

"Mom says Daddy did something very bad and is going away. How long will he be gone?"

"Margaret took Junior by the shoulders. "Your daddy

was a troubled man. He's going somewhere he can't hurt anyone else."

"It's called prison, Mom. He knows already."

Junior grabbed a napkin on the edge of Madison's tray and began wadding it into a ball.

Margaret scowled. "Maybe now we can put Edith's passing behind us. He can't hurt anyone ever again."

Madison held up his juice cup and said, "I'll drink to that."

Dickerson nodded. "We're going to honor Terrence at the next council meeting. Sharon, if you'd like to say some words that would be nice. Your mother can help with your wardrobe."

"Don't worry, the black dress is beyond hope." She glanced at Madison then back at Dickerson. "So you really think Hank did it?"

"Who else?" Dickerson said. "I'm sure now that he's been arrested, he'll be more inclined to confess."

"Terrence," Madison said, "what are you smiling about?"

"It just feels like I've been holding my breath ever since I took that call. Seeing Mrs. Sherman lying there. Feels like I can finally breathe."

Sharon put her arm around his waist. "Me, too."

Junior tossed the waded napkin toward the wastebasket. It banked off the wall then hit the rim. As it began to fall off the side, Terrence reached out and tipped the napkin ball up and in.

The ambulance was in no hurry. No siren for the prisoner handcuffed to the gurney in back. He'd stopped asking for painkillers. The Yamhill County Deputy guarding him in the back of ambulance had little interest in easing Hank's pain.

Payback's a bitch, Hank thought.

The pain throbbed through Hank's hand, and the broken bones in his arm screamed when he tried to move.

He struggled to piece together what had happened, but saw only brightly colored glass, Terrence's big fist wrapped around his knife blade, and his other bending the muzzle of the gun back toward his face. Mostly, he saw the possessed look in Terrence's eyes.

He'd underestimated the boy.

Rage makes a man do impossible things, Hank thought. Rage looked foreign in Terrence's eyes. How many years had he bottled it up to let it bust loose in that moment?

Hank was no stranger to rage. Even now he could feel it seeping into his chest. Soon, it would take over like a foreign invader, gutting out his soul and replacing it with the need to kill or mutilate.

The ambulance would drop him off in McMinnville for a few days R&R while they sorted out Hank's final destination. McMinnville isn't so bad, Hank thought. He'd done time there before. The guards knew him by name. The other inmates gave him the respect he deserved. Maybe I'll just plead guilty this time. Maybe jail is where I belong, a place where the injustices of the outside world don't intrude. Maybe I should forget about the farm and move on.

Hank thought of the fondness he once felt for Terrence. Hank prized courage and skill in combat. Terrence had shown both. Maybe someday he'd congratulate his protégé on winning a fair fight. As much as Terrence might try to deny it, they were brothers, born of the conviction that justice should prevail. Maybe someday Terrence would see how bent the truth becomes in the hands of corrupt men.

The ambulance pulled up to the sally port at the back of the McMinnville jail. The rolling metal door cranked up, and they pulled inside. Two guards stood waiting with a straight jacket and a heavy steel chair ready to wrap him up and lock him down. He'd been in the chair before. With a broken arm, they'd have their fun. He wouldn't give them the satisfaction of screaming, no matter how they wrenched the broken bones into the jacket, or how tight they clamped on the shackles.

The paramedics wheeled Hank to Charlie, a big guard with a mean disposition. He looked Hank over then told the crew it would be best if they headed out. They chose to comply. When the door rolled closed behind the ambulance, Charlie took hold of Hank's broken arm and gave it a twist.

Hank woke up in the medical unit, two beds in a cinder block room with a drain in the floor. A nurse entered and emptied a syringe into his arm and left without speaking. The waves of pain slowly ebbed, and a kaleidoscope of memories crashed and splintered in their place: his mother shaking her head, Sharon pleading for him to leave, Terrence's eyes filled with rage, Hank's spine on fire, searching for his missing fingers, the eyes of the young Vietnamese girl resigned to death.

In his fitful sleep, Hank realized he would never find peace. Not in this life. Maybe he could find it in the next. Then the images melted into a clear light. Justice. To make the men who had killed his mother and robbed him of his home pay for their evil. Madison, Dickerson, and Terrence. Only their death would buy him peace.

He slept dreamlessly.

Terrence returned to the dusty rocks at the bottom of the Yamhill River. A white scum covered the rocks and roots of the cottonwoods reaching for water below. His hand throbbed from the stitches on his palm. He thought of Sharon and Junior as his foot slid on the dried clay, and he fell to a knee. He grabbed a root and slowly lowered himself down onto a boulder poking up out of the shallow ripples.

The shadow of the bridge crisscrossed over the rocks and painted green triangles in the pools of water. He knelt, his eyes shielded in the shadow of a beam. The cool water felt soothing against his skin as he swirled the water with his fingers.

A log truck lumbered across the bridge, its loud muffler belching out twin plumes of smoke. Terrence thought of the shots that had shaken him only days ago, and the fruitless chase of the man who had fired them. He thought of Hank, his mentor. How they'd ended up on opposite sides of the fence remained a mystery. There was just something in some men that craved the edge, walking the thin line that separates hero and villain.

How many years had Terrence spent trying to prove himself, all the while hiding behind the mask of stupidity, hoping people wouldn't expect too much? Terrible Terrence was the name Edith had given him. She smiled when she said the nickname, but in her eyes, he saw the truth of it. Inside him there was something terrible, something he'd struggled to keep locked inside.

The triangle shadows faded as clouds massed on the horizon. They boiled up from the coast fifty miles west, drifting, billowing mountains of water erupting into the sky. Beneath them, dark streaks of gray rain slanted down to the hills below. The golden glow of the sun lit their tops like molten lava flowing from a volcano.

Bronson, standing guard in his police car above, barked. A crack in the distance made Terrence's heart pound as he froze, waiting for the splash of bullets. Another crack of thunder echoed, and Bronson barked again.

Terrence picked up a flat, dusty rock and felt the sandpapery surface, worn smooth from thousands of years of grinding against others. Once fractured and jagged, now worn round in the churning of time. He threw it against the metal feet of the bridge. The steel rang as the rock broke into pieces and splashed into the water below, jagged once again.

Terrence rose on aching knees and looked again at the clouds in the west. The hot, dusty air was taking on the invisible thickness of water gathering, preparing to transform the earth from dust to mud. Winter hibernation would soon overtake the town.

Was this business done? Had Edith found rest, or would her ghost haunt Terrence until justice was assured? Terrence felt a dreaded certainty in his bones. Men such as Hank were not so easily silenced. If he could, he would return to right the humiliation he'd suffered.

Beverly sat at her desk working yesterday's *Sheridan Sun* crossword puzzle when the lobby door opened and a dripping postman walked through. She looked up, still considering ten across. He pulled down the hood of his rain jacket and looked at her through foggy, dropleted glasses. "Funny how we prayed for rain for so long, and already I'm tired of it."

Beverly was too preoccupied with the missing word to pay him much heed.

He sorted through his bulging mailbag, dug out the pieces marked for the Sheridan Police Department, and slid a stack of ads and envelopes across the counter.

"Thanks, Ernie," Beverly said as she gathered the mail. He pulled his hood back on and stepped back out into the rain. She leafed through the stack of familiar return addresses: the Chamber of Commerce, the Elks Lodge, and a special edition of the *Sheridan Sun*. She stripped the rubber band off the newspaper and examined the cover. A photo of Chief Madison frowning in his hospital bed, Terrence standing beside him, grinning sheepishly, and Dickerson smiling ear to ear. The caption beneath read "Long Arm of the Law Saves Chief and Mayor." Further down the page, a photo of Hank in military uniform sat above an article detailing Hank's fall from war hero to felon-wanted-for-murder.

How the mighty have fallen, Beverly thought. She folded the paper and dug deeper into the stack. A manila envelope from the Medical Examiner's office was stamped CONFIDENTIAL.

Beverly left the newspaper on the counter and slid the other pieces of mail into the chief's slot, curious what secrets the ME had sent their way. She returned to her puzzle, wiped her hand again across the page and looked again at ten across. Seven letters: reprisal, retribution, avenge.

Sneak Peek

Sheridan

Hunting Ground

"Attempted murder, three counts." Benjamin Solomon, Hank's court appointed attorney, sat on the other side of the stainless steel table in the gray cinderblock holding cell. The police reports and the prosecutor's plea deal were spread across the table between them.

The chain looped through an eye-bolt in the concrete floor tugged against the shackles that bound Hank's ankles and wrists as he leaned forward in the metal chair. He pinched the indictment calling for life without parole, between his thumb and index finger, the only fingers left on that hand. "What chance have I got with them trying to pin Mom's murder on me."

"That's part of the deal. They won't charge you with murder if you plead guilty to the other charges."

Hank shoved the papers back, and the steel cuff bit into his broken wrist. "If they change their minds?"

Solomon leaned forward and peeked over readers that magnified the puffy bags under his bloodshot eyes. "If you take the deal now, they won't. If you don't, they'll put the attempted murder charges back in and maybe throw in some others on principle."

Hank leaned back. "How long?"

Solomon leafed through the thick folder containing Hank's criminal record. "Normally we would point to your military service, play up your sacrifice to your country, but the dishonorable discharge and assault against two police officers and a public official . . . With your record, the possibility of parole in maybe thirty years."

Solomon dug into his leather briefcase on the floor beside him and pulled out an envelope. "This is an addendum to the plea agreement. It's an unusual offer. A generous one. As your attorney—"

"You ain't my attorney. You're one of them. We both

333

know it. The prison guard standing outside the room peered in through the window in the steel door.

"Given your status as a war hero and the possibility we could make a case for post traumatic stress disorder, they're willing to make a trade of sorts."

"What kind of trade?"

Solomon slid more papers across the table. "Sign there and you'll be a free man before you know it."

"In thirty years? I won't see twenty."

"This form releases all interest in the farm. It appears there is some urgency to get it signed. By signing this, you are saying you won't contest the sale of the farm. In exchange, they won't press the more serious charges, and you could be out in as little as fifteen years. If you don't, they are prepared to ask for the death penalty."

The metal chains scraped across the tabletop as Hank slid his hands forward to grab the envelope. "If I don't sign, I keep the farm?"

"Only for a while. You might delay the sale, but the courts are not likely to find in favor of a convicted felon. If you are convicted—a likely outcome in my opinion—there will be no one to contest the sale. You will die in jail for nothing."

"The prosecutor has offered to reduce the charges to first-degree assault against the mayor and two counts of third-degree assault against the officers."

"All for my signature?"

"Yes. And, as I said, with good behavior, you would be eligible for parole in as few as fifteen years. Frankly, I can't believe they would make such a generous offer."

Hank flipped through the pages. "Mumbo jumbo. What's it say?"

"It addresses ownership of your mother's farm. Apparently, she sold it to the Bureau of Prisons before she was . . . just prior to her death. As her sole heir, you could contest the sale. By signing this document, you are releasing all interest in the property."

"Thought you said I couldn't fight it?"

"It's a formality. There is some concern that you might argue she was not fully aware of the nature of her actions at the time of the sale."

"She was senile. Old timer's disease."

"Did you witness any behavior that would suggest she was not in full possession of her faculties?"

"Crazy as a bat, you mean?"

"If you could attest to that, the legal proceedings could tie up the sale for some time. They would prefer to expedite the sale. Litigation could delay the construction for months or longer. Though I have to say, if you were the only witness to her mental state, let's just say, your case wouldn't be very strong."

"So let me get this straight. I sign their paper, they take my land, and no life in prison. They cut my sentence in half?"

"Under the circumstances, I was able to negotiate quite a deal."

The chains scraped again as Hank scratched his three day growth of beard. "Devil's bargain. And you?"

"What?"

"What do you get if I sign?"

"Nothing. Why would I? Frankly, I've never seen a deal like this. Under your circumstances, you'd be a fool not to take it."

Hank's eyes fixed on the plump, tender skin beneath Solomon's chin that wiggled as he talked.

"It's a really good deal. The best deal of your life." Solomon laid his pen next to the papers and sat back like he'd just laid down four aces. "I advise you to sign."

Hank lunged forward, took the pen, scrawled two words on the signature line above his name, and shoved the papers back across the table. "How's that."

Solomon frowned and gathered the papers together. "This is the only time they'll make this offer. You sure you want to risk life in prison?"

Hank snapped the pen in two and spilled its guts onto the table. "Wouldn't be the first time."

Solomon stuffed the papers into his briefcase. "They said you wouldn't take it. I thought you were a more reasonable man. The offer is good until close of business today. Let me know if you change your mind."

Hank smiled. "My mind's pretty well made up. But maybe you'll be hearing from me down the road."

Solomon buttoned his suit jacket, walked to the door and motioned to the guard frowning through the window. The door's hinges groaned as it swung open.

"Close of business today," Solomon repeated.

Hank smiled. "Hold your breath."

The guard pulled the door shut, and metal grated on metal as he slid the lock closed.

Solomon exchanged glances with the guard and shook his head. "Serves him right." The guard shrugged and the two headed down the corridor.

Hank pinched the pen's spring in his mangled fingers and popped it into his mouth.

ABOUT THE AUTHOR

James Rogers retired as a police lieutenant in the State of Washington after twenty-five years. He is a Licensed Mental Health Counselor and holds two master's degrees. James enjoys traveling with his wife.

Made in the USA
San Bernardino, CA
11 June 2017